Map of
RILEY
NORTH CAROLINA
Matthews County

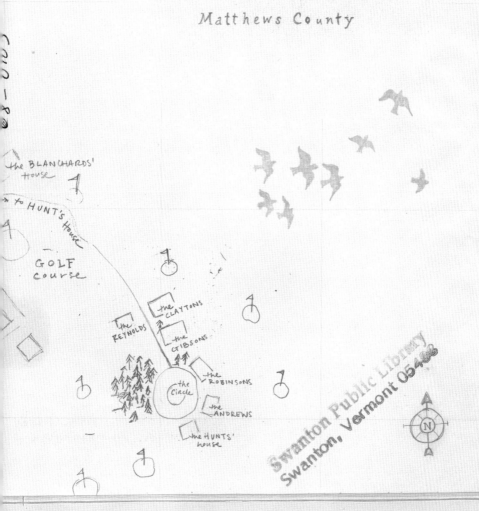

railroad tracks

the BLANCHARDS' House

to HUNT'S House

GOLF course

the CLAYTONS

the REYNOLDS

the GIBSONS

the ROBINSONS

the Circle

the ANDREWS

the HUNTS' house

N

ONE FELL SWOOP

A Novel in Stories

BY

VIRGINIA BOYD

THOMAS NELSON
Since 1798

NASHVILLE DALLAS MEXICO CITY RIO DE JANEIRO BEIJING

Published in Nashville, TN, by Thomas Nelson. Thomas Nelson is a trademark of Thomas Nelson, Inc.

Thomas Nelson, Inc. titles may be purchased in bulk for educational, business, fund-raising, or sales promotional use. For information, please e-mail SpecialMarkets@ThomasNelson.com.

Publisher's Note: This novel is a work of fiction. Names, characters, places, and incidents are either products of the author's imagination or used fictitiously. All characters are fictional, and any similarity to people living or dead is purely coincidental.

Library of Congress Cataloging in Publication Data

Boyd, Virginia, 1965-
   One fell swoop / by Virginia Boyd.
     p. cm.
   ISBN-13: 978-1-59554-399-8
   ISBN-10: 1-59554-399-6
    1. Husbands—Crimes against—Fiction. 2. Murder—Fiction. 3. Suicide—Fiction.
4. Adultery—Fiction. 5. Life change events—Fiction. 6. Communities—Fiction. I. Title.
PS3602.O9335O54 2007
813'.6—dc22   2007032037

Printed in the United States of America

07 08 09 10 11 QW 5 4 3 2 1

FOR CECIL, SALLY, BETSY, AND ED

Then said Almitra, "Speak to us of Love."

And he raised his head and looked upon the people, and there fell a stillness upon them. And with a great voice he said:

When love beckons to you, follow him,
Though his ways are hard and steep.
And when his wings enfold you yield to him,
Though the sword hidden among his pinions may wound you.
And when he speaks to you believe in him,
Though his voice may shatter your dreams as the north wind lays waste the garden.

—Kahlil Gibran, *The Prophet*

CONTENTS

FALLING

My grandmother shot my grandfather dead and then herself, this much I know. It seems no matter how hard I chase after the rest, I can't quite catch hold. Someday when I grow up, I'm going to study the ancient Egyptians. I want to learn how to put together pictures from the past with only odds and ends to go on—puzzle pieces of paintings and oddly written messages that have crumbled away until all that's left are faint trails of dots and dashes only a blind person could see. But for now, as far as I can tell I got just two things from Grandma Clayton—the same color spooky blue eyes and a big snow globe. It sits with my old teddy bear on the chest next to my bed. At night, the hall light falls across the room and makes the globe glow. It's so pretty; I love to look at it as I'm going to sleep.

There's a whole town there inside the glass, little houses and stores, trees, grass, roads, and a couple of cars—all covered in piles of sparkly white as if they'd been drizzled with icing. I pretend it's Riley, the town where my dad grew up, where Grandma shot Granddaddy, and where I've never gotten to go. I pretend that if I hold real quiet and still and barely breathe, the whole town will come to life right before my eyes. I'll be able to look down from above and watch the lights come on in the windows and fill up the dark porches and street corners. The cars will start rolling down the roads and people will appear, moving around and going about their business. I'll be able to see everything. And I'll hear stuff, too—the wind through the trees, music playing on a radio, honking and doors slamming, and voices, all kinds of voices, telling me everything I ever wanted to know.

I close my eyes and picture myself dropping through the top of the glass dome and floating down gently in a swirling flurry of downy feather flakes. An easy landing in a cloud of snow sends up fluttery puffs of confetti that twinkle and glitter in the light. I have to stop for a minute because I can't believe I'm really there. I have the same feeling you get when you wake up one morning and look outside to see everything covered in white, as if the whole world is magic.

At first all I hear is the muffled silence of snow. But then there are birds twittering, the distant sound of the wind, and people laughing and calling to each other somewhere just out of my sight. I think I even hear my name—"Ash-ley"—echo through the trees. So I head off down the road. I believe I'll find them just up around the bend. I wonder what all these people will have to say, if they still remember and if they ever knew what really happened. I try my best to imagine what kinds of stories they'll be, what kinds of things about my grandparents their memories will hold.

Tell me, I'll say. Tell me how it happened. And, please, tell me why.

IN THE END

Mitchell MacKenzie sat fully upright, still dressed in yesterday's clothes, as he listened to an early morning chorus of bird song coming from his own backyard. He hadn't slept a wink. His eyes were dry and itchy and his breath so rank with stale nicotine it made him half-sick to smell it. Despite his condition, Mitch felt nothing but glory as he greeted the new day. It was great to be alive, especially on this particular Sunday in August, a day bound to become historic if Mitch's buddy Randy Fox did indeed follow through on his promise to confess all before God and country in the First United Methodist Church.

The prospect of bearing witness to such an event had lifted Mitch's spirits beyond belief. In fact, for the first time since he could remember, Mitch felt full to overflowing with marvel and wonder at the strange and mysterious workings of his very own existence. He and his world—and all the half-crazy fools living in it—were amazing. There was no way this life could get any better.

He opened his mouth and exhaled a lungful of air and willfully breathed it in through his nose. Putrid, yes, but powerful too. Such was the stuff of real human beings and the fantastically capricious world they occupied. This all tickled him to no end. For it was this cockamamie coexistence that had placed him, a thirty-eight-year-old admittedly not-so-perfect husband and father, happy as a lark last Friday afternoon sneaking a quickie in a motel on the outskirts of town, while not ten miles away Michael Clayton faced a firing squad in his own damn living room. *She-it.* There was no rhyme or reason. Two different men commit the same crime. One dies and the other goes on home to eat a spaghetti supper and feign interest in the details of his wife's boring day. But take it as you will, it was also this very same existence that had allowed Mitch to sit in this same spot on his back porch just last night and listen to Randy explain how he was going to come clean, in church no less, turn himself in as a habitual cheater.

The whole town was in an uproar over the Clayton murder/suicide. It had shaken them all up. These were their contemporaries. Everybody had known them, or so they had thought. It was not as if Mitch had been best friends with Michael, but they had played golf together a number of times, shared a few laughs, that kind of thing. There was also the Claytons' young son—Mike Jr.—who made it a crying shame. Mitch hated to think of his own kids growing up without their mama and daddy. It was a lot to take in and he hadn't had a chance yet really to decide what to make of it.

But now Randy, Randy appeared to have made up his mind all right. Poor boy seemed to have taken it all to heart—at least that's how some might describe his reaction. Others, well, they might just call it twisted. Mitch wasn't sure that in the sober light of day Randy wouldn't change his view. Randy was not known for his dependable nature. Yet, going through with it was also the kind of thing Mitch wouldn't put past him either. It was this unbearable tension between halfway wanting to egg Randy on and, at the same time, dreading the very thought of watching one of his own cohorts roast in public hell for committing a mutual crime, that had Mitch so riled up.

Conflicted, that was it. Mitch was so conflicted he didn't know which end was up. Throw into the mix an occasional twinge of something in the realm of guilt or remorse, and it was no wonder Mitch hadn't caught a lick of sleep.

It reminded him of the sleepless hours he spent as a tortured kid on Christmas Eve, obsessively reviewing his and his brother and sister's recent behavior. Part of him secretly yearned to see one of the worst disasters his child's mind could imagine—one of them left with a stocking filled with nothing but lumps of coal—while another part of him wished just as fervently for continued good luck, yet another graceful reprieve. But in the end, these dueling emotions only made his final enjoyment that much sweeter.

That's right. And he wasn't about to miss out on one of those rare moments today, wasn't going to miss it for the world. After all, Mitch had a plan. And hope. He had all kinds of that too.

Mitchell MacKenzie wasn't the only person in town who felt ambivalent about what the day would hold. The Reverend C.B. Cooper had been vacillating for weeks about the state of his own existence, his job, his purpose for being, and his rapidly dwindling inspiration to call others to worship. This Sunday's sermon was especially troubling, however—not because of C.B.'s own spiritual burnout or even because of the dime-sized canker sore on the back of his tongue that rubbed against his molars every time he spoke—this wasn't just one of your run-of-the-mill kinds of things. Two prominent Riley citizens—he thanked God they weren't members of his own congregation—had died, one on Friday and the other early last night. Mr. and Mrs. Michael Clayton. He had been the best accountant in town, and she, a quiet, respectable housewife until finally snapping Friday afternoon after catching him conjoined in an entirely inappropriate manner with his secretary splayed across the large oak desk in his inner office. Later that evening as Mr. Clayton, worn out no doubt from a taxing day at work, sipped spirits in his easy chair, the unassuming Mrs. Clayton took a turn and sent her husband to meet his maker with the aid of a Colt .45. C.B. wondered if it was her desire to be present for this particular reunion between husband and Host that inspired her to smite her own temple with the same weapon afterwards. Or maybe she felt culpable . . . or repentant. Or maybe she just didn't give a damn. C.B. couldn't decide.

He, himself, was at a complete loss. He knew the entire town had been talking about the bizarre deaths of this couple ever since the first gunshot was heard echoing across the golf course. This is what people in a small Southern town do when life, death, and anything in-between happens— they proceed to make a casserole, don the appropriate attire, and get to talking all about it as soon as possible. This was a town where Storytelling was placed right up there in the Holy Trinity along with Good Food and Good Manners. So if tragedy struck and you were a community leader, you best be able to come up with one hell of a story, and it better offer some comfort and maybe an answer or two along the way.

First, he had considered something straightforward, an old-fashioned Bible-thumping lecture about the dangers of breaking any of the Ten Commandments. After all, it was true, they weren't named the Ten Suggestions for a reason. *Thou shalt not kill* was an obvious choice to begin with, but then things got a little sticky with *Thou shalt not commit adultery* and *Thou shalt not covet thy neighbor's wife*. He didn't want any-one to make the dangerous assumption that Regina's hand had somehow been guided by a vengeful God—that wasn't C.B.'s style. So, he decided to forego dire warnings of hell and damnation for a less judgmental and more forgiving tack.

For a while, he dallied with the idea of using Psalm 23: *Yea though I* walk through the valley of the shadow of death, I fear no evil; for thou art with me. . . . He would paint a picture of a flock of sheep mindlessly chewing clover when the wolf's shadow, unseen and ominous, crossed their path. But no, too predictable and slightly insulting. He'd refer to a flock of birds instead, caught in mid-flight, the wind rushing through the steady beat of their many feathered wings when the shadow of a great dark hawk unexpectedly dims their vision. But before he had this metaphor completely worked out in his mind, his thoughts had flown to his own nagging doubts as well as those of his congregation. For just where, exactly, was He when stuff like this went on? Why *did* He stand back and watch as the wolf closed in for his kill and the hawk swooped in for his supper?

This train of thought led C.B. to push aside the idea of comfort in the face of death for an even better idea—the power of hope for resur-rection—the acceptance of pain, death, and loss as necessary trials that must be endured in order for rebirth and true joy to take their place. Everybody had to pay their spiritual dues, ante up more or less. C.B. got a little excited about this concept, thought he was finally making some headway. Next, he decided he would turn to Lazarus and *Jesus wept*—the shortest and therefore most memorable Bible verse of all. He would set the scene describing Jesus' approach to the barren rock that loomed in his path and surrounded Lazarus's body in a dark, dusty, and seemingly impenetrable embrace. He would linger on those mourning Lazarus's death, those prostrate with fear and grief whose misery moved Jesus to tears. "Even though He knew He would raise Lazarus up and bring him back to life, He also knew that it would forever be man's lot to face the night before the dawn—to go down into darkness and death before ris-ing up to meet the light of new life," C.B. would say. Then he could assure his congregation that God did indeed know what He was doing and this was all a part of His grand plan.

While Rev. Cooper had been diligently burning the midnight oil on Saturday night, Mitch had been busy contemplating the same situation from an entirely different perspective. It had been late, well after supper-time, the kids long gone to bed. Anne was watching TV in the den when he stepped out to smoke a quick cigarette on the back porch and heard quiet steps crunch up the gravel drive and then a light knock on the screened porch door. It was Randy, four sheets to the wind. Mitch didn't think he'd ever seen Randy that drunk.

"Saw your light," Randy managed to slur between obviously numb lips. "Mind if I come in? Got something on my mind, but it's got to stay between you and me. Least until tomorrow."

"Sure," Mitch said. "Come on, have a seat."

After he collapsed in an oversized rocker and generously offered Mitch a slug of the rotgut he was carrying wrapped in a brown paper bag, Randy got straight to the point. "Mitch," he said, "Mitch, tell you what, I got myself in a bit of a pickle here. Though I believe I've figured a way to get myself out. But I'm also thinking it might be a good idea to run it by somebody else first."

"What's the problem?" Mitch offered.

"Well, of course it's on account of this business here with Michael. You know, he wasn't really such a bad guy, now was he?"

"Naw, I don't reckon he was," said Mitch. "Honestly though, I can't say I knew him all that well . . ."

"But what's to know, right?" Randy interrupted. "I mean he worked, he provided for his family and he had a five handicap. So he got a little nooky on the side—not all that many people knew it. But now right here, this is where we get to my situation—to me and mine."

Randy took another fortifying swig that leaked out the corner of his mouth and ran down the side of his neck. Then he lost his train of thought for a minute. His gaze focused on something in the far off distance until he swatted at the side of his own face, which seemed to bring him back around. "It's Debra I'm worried about. You think she'd do somethinglikethattome?"

"Like Regina did to Michael?"

"Yeah," Randy sighed. "Like that."

"Well buddy, you've hardly been discreet," Mitch felt obliged to point out. "You've built a reputation on telling about your conquests—how Lorna Everette refused to take off her high heels and garter belt, the way Nadine Ellis always called you cowboy and begged you to tie her hands to the bedpost, and that thing Dena Potter had for chocolate pudding and making you paint her toenails afterwards—I mean, who hadn't you told?"

"I know, I know, that's what I'm saying," Randy said as he rubbed his hand over his face.

"Well then, she's bound to know."

"You think?" Randy looked at Mitch from between his big-knuckled fingers.

"You know her better than I do, Randy. Come on, think yourself, man." Mitch tapped out a fresh cigarette. "Has she ever said anything?"

"Naw, she hadn't." Randy appeared fairly confident in ruling that one out.

"How about given you any kind of 'look'?"

"What do you mean, 'look'?" Randy said in a startled voice.

"You know, like she's suspicious. Or wants to blow your freaking brains out or something like that."

"Naw . . . nooooo . . . she hasn't . . . well . . . if she *has* I hadn't known it . . . But you see here, that's my whole problem. You know how women are. They look one way and say one thing and you think well fine, okay.

But the whole time she may be thinking, you do this again, damn it, and I'm gonna kick your ass. You think Michael knew what he was in for? You think he had any idea how hard she was going to take it?"

"That, my friend, we'll never know," Mitch answered between deep drags on his cigarette. "Of course, he was caught directly," Mitch added as possible consolation. "Clearly, Regina knew exactly what was going on."

"But caught is caught," Randy said in a broken voice as if he were about to sob. "Besides, there were two things my daddy always warned me never to underestimate—the power of fresh bait and a woman's imagination."

Randy reached for his bottle again and tipped it upwards as if in homage to some greater force. When he gestured toward Mitch before putting the cap back on, Mitch said "what the hell" and took a swig of his own. The liquor torched a trail down Mitch's insides and burned its way up the back of his nose.

"That does it then," Randy said while screwing the cap back on. "I don't have a choice, not much a one—I'magonnahavetodo what I'magonnahavetodo." Mitch thought Randy was slipping into nonsense which wasn't all that surprising considering his condition. Randy sort of sang the "todo" parts as if he were starting to enjoy himself. But then he stopped playing around and directed his bloodshot gaze right at Mitch's eyes. He took a deep breath that lifted his chest and straightened his posture a bit and said very clearly, "I am going to confess."

"What do you mean, *confess*?"

"Tell it. Tell all that Big Randy and Little Randy have been up to in our spare time."

"Are you kidding me?" Mitch chuckled and shook his head. "Tell it to Debra? Have you lost your ever-loving mind?"

"To Debra and the church." Randy nodded as he rolled in his lips and clamped them tightly together.

"Son of a bitch," Mitch said. He laughed outright, a belly laugh that brought real tears to his eyes and made his side ache. He could just see it all. Picturing the whole scene made him laugh even harder. It was too good. When he finally started slowing down and had a chance to catch his breath he said, "Slick, you must be drunk. All you need to do is sleep it off. That's what you need to do—sleep off this strange fit that has come over you."

"I told you, I've been thinking about this all day. You don't know what I've been going through. I can't sleep. Not in my own bed, not even after a few nightcaps and a handful of Excedrin PMs. Every time she shifts in her sleep, rolls over or gets up to go to the bathroom, my heart pounds so loud it sounds like somebody's beating a drum upside my head. You know a lot of women shoot their husbands in bed. It's not all that uncommon. You might be surprised. I read a case one time about this woman who shot her husband with the gun he kept under his pillow, just reached under there and blew a hole through his head."

"You don't keep a gun under your pillow, do you?"

"No sir, but I've had it. I'm through spending all my time worrying over what she's lying there thinking, wondering if she's busy dreaming about what I've been doing and how she's finally going to make me pay, do me in just like Regina did Michael. If I'm going down, I'm going down fighting. I'm going to tell it all tomorrow, in church, before she gets a chance to off me in my sleep. If I say it all in front of the church, then I'm saved, you see. And Debra will believe she's been the one that saved me. She'll have to forgive me. Isn't that what every woman really wants—to save some man who would be good if only she could get him straightened out?"

"You can't be serious." Mitch tried to sound reasonable as he stubbed out the end of his cigarette.

"Serious as a heart attack."

"Now, Randy." Mitch adopted a tone of voice his own father had often used on him. "Son, this is big. I mean real big. People just don't go around telling these kinds of things this way. Who knows what all this could bring about. For instance, how do you know for sure if Debra's going to react the way you say she will?"

"I have accepted and come to terms with the fact that I don't know diddly about my own wife." Randy leaned to his left side and took his wallet out of his back pocket. From the billfold section he pulled out a crumpled piece of paper and waved it in front of Mitch. "See here, I told you I have put some thought into this. I made a list. Here's all the things I am certain about Debra." He peered down at the torn scrap of notebook paper he held in his hand. Mitch could see the faint blue lines evenly dividing the ragged white space that glowed strangely in the dark.

It wasn't long though before Randy gave up on trying to read his own writing. He began to recite from memory instead as he counted each item off on his fingers, "I know she always fixes meat loaf and canned pears for supper on Tuesday night. Shaves a little pile of orange cheddar on top of each pear, don't ask me why. I know she hates it when I forget and leave up the toilet seat. I know she used to love the Beatles and still refuses to let the kids play any of her old albums. 'They'll scratch 'em,' that's what she always says. I also know that she's kept every single card that me and the boys have ever given her in the right-hand drawer of her dressing table, and that she never wears perfume but always smells like baby powder after she's had a bath. Five things. That's it," he nodded to himself. "That's all I know. The rest is a mystery."

"That's not much," Mitch agreed. "I get your point."

"Finally." Randy got up to leave. But before he could make his exit he had to stop and wrestle his wallet back into its proper place in his pants pocket. Mitch stood by the screened door watching him struggle. Eventually Randy appeared satisfied that everything was back where it belonged. He stopped once again before he went out the door and clamped Mitch's shoulder in a bone-crunching squeeze. "I want to live," Randy said between clenched teeth. "So help me, God."

Then he dropped his hand and started laughing a little as if what he had said was just a joke. "So does Little Randy. All this business has been mighty hard on the little feller. Scared the little son of a gun half to death is what. Yes sir-ree-bob. Scared the piss right out of him. Don't feel much like taking any more fishing trips these days. Can't say I blame him. Not up for one of those big adventures, if you know what I mean . . . guy's got too much weighing on his mind . . . just might have to lie low for a while . . ."

Randy disappeared quickly in the darkness but Mitch listened to his laughter stagger through the night air until the stumble and lurch of his progress grew faint, reminding Mitch of all the times he'd gotten so drunk all he'd wanted was to be able to pass out and be left alone.

Ernestine Lambert couldn't help but feel a little lonesome as she put the final touches on the flower arrangement she'd placed carefully on top of the sanctuary altar. Apparently, she was an early bird this morning. The church was big and empty. But also, she did miss her parents—both of them, God rest their souls—still, to this very day. She had been planning this arrangement for much of the past year and, she had to say, it was a beautiful and fitting tribute to her beloved parents. It was too bad they weren't here to fully witness the heights Ernestine had achieved in their names. All she could hope for was that they actually were looking down from above and could see it all—the flowers and her in her new blue dress bought just for the occasion. Maybe they could even read the bulletin announcing: *The flowers for this week were given in dedication to the memory of Mr. and Mrs. Carlton C. Lambert on the anniversary of their wedding. The couple's constant faith and abiding love for one another continues to blossom in the heart of their only daughter, Ernestine May, and to serve as inspiration to us all.*

Ernestine had already climbed the steps to the balcony just so she could see what the flowers looked like from a more heavenly perspective. The triangular shape she chose for this year's arrangement blurred slightly in the distance, but Ernestine had faith that in the afterlife all vision was twenty-twenty. But then she got worried that one side looked fuller than the other so she went back down to the altar to double-check from up close. She plucked a few of the spiky purple things from the left and stuck them in on the right. "Status" was what she thought they were called. They had been one of Mother's favorites.

This year she had opted for structure and dependability. She was glad she had told them to go light on the chrysanthemums. She couldn't help a smile of pleasure as she bent over to satisfy herself that there was plenty of moisture in the bottom of the gold plastic vase and caught the scent of a fat pink carnation that sat right beneath her nose. Not much got past Ernestine—she noticed a small wrinkle in the altar cloth which she smoothed with her hand before she took a few steps back to survey everything once again. Convinced that it was all in place, she pulled out her camera to take a few precisely framed photographs for her scrapbook.

She closed her eyes and tried to hold on to this image. Picture perfect. But even with her eyes closed, it started to fade. Ernestine frowned in concentration and felt the first small doubt start to creep in along the edge of her awareness, as if a furry little mouse had begun nervously nibbling into the back corner of a wedge of Swiss cheese. As the thought of the Claytons ate its way ever so gently into Ernestine's mind, it occurred to her that the untimely and gruesome displays they had made of their own deaths might cast a pall on all her plans, that all her painstaking efforts might be for nothing.

As he slipped into a seat on the very back pew, Mitch couldn't help but notice the flowers on the altar, though he wasn't *exactly* appreciative of Miss Lambert's floral tour de force. To him, it looked heinous, like some florist's idea of a bad joke or worst nightmare come true. Take your pick. Maybe the Methodist God liked big and gaudy. Mitch wouldn't know; he was Presbyterian. He smiled and nodded to the young couple sitting beside him. He was glad he didn't know them because it saved him from having to make up an excuse for being there. The church he belonged to was quiet and pretty and situated in a little clearing on the edge of town, kind of out-of-the-way. It was plenty respectable, but often overlooked. Mitch's wife, Anne, and their three kids were over there worshipping right now. Anne thought Mitch was off playing golf in a foursome with Jeff Hunt and a couple of other guys. Mitch realized the irony in lying to his wife to go to church to watch another man confess his sins, but Randy had sworn him to secrecy last night and Mitch didn't want to go back on his word.

The church was plenty full, that was for sure. A lot of folks looking for comfort, Mitch guessed. But he had his doubts about whether or not they'd come to the right place, because already he was having to constantly shift his weight on the unyielding wooden bench. He wondered why a church of such affluence hadn't bothered to spring for some cushions. He, himself, didn't see any harm in being comfortable and saved at the same time, since deep down everybody knew the spirit might be willing but the flesh was weak. And speaking of weakened flesh, damned if right off, Mitch didn't spot Randy, his wife, and children all sitting in a row way up towards the front. Well, hell.

Leastways he'd shown up. Mitch took this to be a promising sign. He wiped his hands on his trousers, leaned back in his seat, and stretched his legs out in front of him. Time to get this show on the road. Bring on the preacher. Mitch still couldn't get over all that he was willing to go through just to be here—lying outright to Anne, missing golf on a beautiful day, putting on his church duds and all. But it was going to be worth it. He could feel it deep down in his bones.

And, somehow, that feeling managed to last. Long after his butt cheeks went numb, Mitch continued to endure—the tedious sermon, the warbling hymns, the endless prayers—all with the stoic patience of Job and the steadfast faith of a saint. They just wore you down in church, wore you down until you didn't have any fight left. But not this time. Mitch's hope refused to waver and the feeling that Randy was going to do, at least *something*, kept on building. Just as Reverend Cooper began to wind down, Mitch glanced at the program in the church bulletin and saw that an *altar call* came next. Ah-ha.

It was a curious practice for a church such as this, a place of worship for respectable bankers and lawyers, people who carried clean, pressed handkerchiefs and brushed their teeth every night before going to bed. Pillars of the community didn't holler and jump around and fall out. It just wasn't done. Mitch was willing to bet that over the years only a faint trickle of self-conscious citizens had been moved enough to walk down to the front with eyes downcast for a few moments in silent prayer on bended knee. Only a precious few, who had taken the minister up on his offer to rededicate their lives to Jesus as quietly and with as much dignity as they could muster. Hold on now, might as well go on ahead and throw in at least a couple of overzealous teenagers. Let's not forget them. Kids. You can always count on some of them to be quick to grab a moment in the spotlight no matter who it embarrasses.

Whether or not it had ever actually saved any souls, the altar call would be the perfect time for Randy to step up and make an offering the good folks of the First United Methodist Church wouldn't soon forget. So when Reverend Cooper made the call, urging his brethren to give their lives over to God the Almighty, and Randy's head bobbed right up, Mitch nearly called out, "Praise the Lord!"

But it only got better. As Randy made his way down to the front, Mitch felt an incredible surge of excitement gathering in his own loins. And when Randy did not even slow down at the kneeling pads, when he stepped over the rail that separated the padded cushions from the altar steps and marched past the disconcerted Reverend and on up the steps to the pulpit, Mitch heard his own pulse roar in his ears. And then, when Randy actually leaned over and said, *"I've sinned and fallen short of the Lord and I've done it with other women,"* Mitch felt something comparable to his most thrilling and satisfying sexual experience ever. True ecstasy ran like wildfire all over his body. He wanted to yell, "Yes! Oh yes!" to stand up and shake his arms above his head, and, most of all, to fall over in a sublime oblivion so strong it knocked him right off his penny-loafered feet.

But then Randy practically ruined it. He just had to start meandering along the Road to Redemption. The more he hemmed and hawed and mixed his metaphors, the more Mitch could see getting Randy down the Path to Righteousness was going to be a lengthy process. Evidently, the way was tricky and steep and somehow involved fishing.

Yep, fishing. Seemed Randy, that wily old goat, was taking a few additional liberties—this time with one of the well-known symbols of Christianity. If push came to shove, Mitch guessed there really was no telling just how far a man would go to get where he thought he needed to be . . .

"And so I sat out there holding my lucky fishing pole, my mind made up. The whole world around me fell away—the heat of the afternoon sun, the

*sound of the crickets and frogs croaking along the banks. I wasn't study-
ing anything but that bobber floating gently in the water before me. All I
could think about was wondering just what might come along and take a
shine to the bait I was dangling out there on the other end of my line. I was
so full of anticipation I could scarcely breathe. And just then for a second,
I started to see how I was, how I really was, how completely deaf, dumb,
and blind I was to anything else in my life. That was when I said to myself,
'Is this what I've come to? Is this all there is for me? A lifetime of never
being satisfied?'"*

*Randy paused for a moment to let his words sink in. He had already
worked himself up into quite a sweat, so he took the opportunity to wipe his
forehead and neck with his handkerchief. The combined heat of his own mor-
tification and the collective stare of the congregation made Randy feel as if he
had been locked in a furnace. Confessing was hard work. Randy licked the
salt from his lips and got back to it, "Whenever I reach still waters will I
always feel the temptation to cast into them yet again and again, forever hoping—longing even—for a fresh, exciting, new catch? Will I always fret over
the one that got away or the one I didn't even know was down there raven-
ous with hunger for any tidbit I might throw its way?"*

"Mama . . . Mama . . . What is Mr. Fox talking about?"

Bonnie Hunt looked down and met the inquisitive gaze of her youngest
daughter. This would have to be one of the times she decided to let Suzanne
come to "big church" instead of staying in the Sunday school playroom and
helping with the younger kids. Suzanne held one of the tiny dolls she had
brought in her little "big girl" pocketbook so that the doll, a Kiddle sporting bright purple hair and reeking as if she'd just stepped from a bath of
synthetic perfume, stood on top of Bonnie's right hand. Suzanne and her

older sister Jackie had argued about the Kiddles in the car on the way in. Jackie told Suzanne she was getting too old to play with dolls in church. But Suzanne said she didn't care what Jackie said. Why was it any of her beeswax, anyway? It was better than laying her head in her mother's lap and sucking her thumb the way Tommy Jones always did, and he was her same age.

Suzanne's doll jumped up and down impatiently on Bonnie's hand. But before Bonnie had a chance to formulate a suitable answer, her twelve-year-old, Jackie, who was sitting by Bonnie's left side, leaned over her mother's lap toward her sister and said, "Don't worry. I'll explain everything to you later." Then Jackie smiled up at Bonnie so they could both acknowledge her wisdom and helpfulness before she straightened back up in her seat.

Bonnie didn't know whether to laugh or cry. She remained stubbornly insistent on trying to keep them babies just a little while longer. They were growing like weeds, their legs long and skinny, their little girl tummies shrinking smaller and smaller every day. She had pulled Suzanne's hair back into a ponytail and tied a big white bow around the rubber band this morning before breakfast. Now, baby fine tendrils that had escaped her efforts curled around the fragile bones of Suzanne's neck. Looking at them made Bonnie's throat ache. She was struck by the ridiculousness of it all.

Today they would have been better off out on the golf course with their brother and father. Here she was trying to expose her children to a little religion, to bring them up as churchgoers just as her own parents had done for her, and this is what she got. Bonnie cast her eyes upwards, past Randy's head and over and beyond the seated choir on whose faces ranged a mixture of shock and confusion that reflected her own. Her elevated gaze came to rest on the painful image of Christ's crucifixion that hung high above in stained-glass glory. *Please*, she silently beseeched, *help*.

"There was no help for me, no help at all. What it was, I had finally realized, was that I had gotten stuck in the Tar Baby of sin," Randy announced. "Yes, Lord, it's true. From the tips of my toes all the way up to the top of my head, I was stuck fast in the ways of sin and evil. The devil was using the beguiling arms of a woman to hold me tight. His tricks had me believing I was dipping into a pot of golden honey, but it was really the black, sticky tar of sin in disguise." Randy punctuated his statement by dropping his head as if overcome by such a shameful admission.

It wasn't just his head and toes that got dipped in the sticky stuff, thought Lorna Everette from her seat two pews behind Randy's wife Debra. Lorna couldn't help but notice that Debra was in dire need of a trip to the beauty parlor. Her hairdo was mashed flat in the back as if she had slept on it and not even bothered to comb it out this morning. Lorna felt just about two seconds of pity for Debra before she started to recall exactly what kind of lover Debra's husband had been.

One of his outstanding features was his wide mouth with lips so full they were noticeable. Some said their fullness indicated his sensual nature, while others pointed to them as a sign of weakness. Lorna had discovered that both parties were right. Randy knew exactly how to use those lips and use them he did. They rubbed, massaged, and caressed their way across just about every quivering inch of her body. But when they weren't busy touching all the right places, they flapped nonstop. Just as his testimony was indicating, Randy frequently suffered from what Lorna's mother called "diarrhea of the mouth." It really got on her nerves. It was so distracting.

She'd had to tell him to shut up all the time, and once she'd even resorted to wadding up one of his own stinky nylon socks and sticking it in between his lips. And they always claimed women were the chatty ones.

As he lifted his head, Randy drew in a deep breath which he blew out shakily across his lips before lifting his right index finger for emphasis. "You see, folks, Brother Fox was not always a low-down dirty dog in the manger. I used to be just a regular good old boy, just like you and you," Randy said, as he pointed to several uneasy-looking males seated in the congregation before him. "It was despite my good intentions that she-wolf, the Mistress of Evil, crept up on me inch by ever-loving inch, day by day, until my heart was plumb eaten to the core with the tarry blackness of sin and despair. You good folks can imagine my horror and surprise when I found I had cast my lot with the devil and my pole was fishing in the raging waters of hell. But my sweet wife, sweet Debra Jean, loyal motherhood personified, she did not have one thing to do with this whole mess. That was all my doing, mine alone. And that's the honest truth. I swear."

Mitch didn't have any trouble finding room in his heart for a little sympathy for Debra. Poor Debra. In trying to gauge her response, Mitch had only the general effect of her posture to go by. The inward slope of her rounded shoulders combined with the forced stiffness of her spine gave her an overall air of eroding determination. Mitch couldn't believe Randy dared say her name right out like that. Though if he was going to come out with it all, he might as well come all the way out. It wasn't like everybody didn't already know who she was. Mitch had to hand it to Randy, *this time* damned if he hadn't stuck to his word.

"So there I was caught tight in the grip of sin that was sucking the life out of me and mine. It was right about this time my bobber dropped clean out of sight and I felt a tug on my line like I hadn't never felt before." Randy appeared to be completely taken in by his own story. He had thrown himself wholeheartedly into the reenactment, furiously reeling in an invisible fishing line with his head and shoulders bent way over backward as if he were trying to resist an unseen but powerful force.

"I started turning that reel just as fast as my hand could go. I thought to myself, what have we here? I could feel the adrenaline setting fire to my veins. I was raring to go!"

Debra wanted to suggest exactly where he could go. She felt everyone's eyes on her. Hot, probing eyes. It was like being stung by bees or stabbed with a handful of daggers. Randy was so full of it, she didn't know what to do. She knew what she'd *like* to do. She'd like to tar and feather the hell out of him is what.

She also knew that Randy was afraid. The yellow-bellied lily-livered good-for-nothing pathetic excuse of a man. He was plumb *scairt* out of his mind. That was exactly what this crazy act was all about. Randy was actually afraid she might do the same thing to him that Regina Clayton had done to her two-timing husband, Michael.

Debra was many things, but she was not a ninny. She refused to look to either her left or right. She was not going to start wondering if any of the women sitting around her had slept with her husband. Debra was not going to play that game.

She didn't have the time or energy. She and Randy had four boys. Four, with not one single girl among them. Her hands were plenty full. There was also her sick mother living next door and her volunteer work with the hospital auxiliary and bridge club every other week and garden club once a month and lots of church functions. She hardly had any time for herself anymore. She hadn't even gotten through last month's Harlequin romance before the new one for this month had arrived. She couldn't take care of everybody.

Quite honestly, sex had never been one of Debra's priorities. If Randy would have just kept his damned mouth shut she could have been saved from all this. He owed her that at least. She had never asked for much and was outraged that her own husband knew so little about her, that he would actually think she might kill him in a fit of jealousy. If she ever did kill him, it would be for being so stupid. She hoped this was not a genetic trait he had passed along to their boys. She would be really furious if she found out she was raising a pack of idiots.

"I wasn't a complete ignoramus, I knew it had to be big. The Old Man and the Sea has always been my favorite book—next to the Bible of course. I can remember my daddy reading that story to me over and over again when I was just a little feller. There was a time when it was all I dreamt about. Every day, I'd walk down to Old Man Nelson's pond and sit a spell. I'd lose all track of time thinking about what all might be floating down under there—the adventure of a lifetime. So you see, folks, I had been ready for this moment all my life. I couldn't wait to see it come bursting out of the water, to get my hands on it, feel it flopping and squirming in my grasp and know it was mine.

"I was reeling like mad, when I started imagining that maybe I could hear this little voice—the noise was so small, it sounded like a mosquito or maybe

a gnat even, or something like that just barely buzzing. It was the darndest thing. I could have sworn it was saying, 'cutbait, cutbait, cutbait,' just like that over and over again. And then I thought, what? What is going on around here? Where is that dag-on voice coming from? What does it care?"

Dawn Davenport didn't have a care in the world for whatever it was that Randy Fox was going on and on about up there at the pulpit. She was getting married and not at some far off distant time in the future. The wedding was next Saturday. All three hundred engraved invitations had been hand addressed in Dawn's best calligraphy and mailed out two months ago. Everyone who mattered in the least was coming. They would all be there as "little Dawnie" became Mrs. John Wesley Williams and finally got to experience the biggest day of her life. Dawn couldn't be bothered by Mr. Fox; she was the star attraction of an extravaganza that had been completely planned and orchestrated in her honor—hers and John Wesley's that is.

Dawn leaned back in her seat and squinted her eyes. She tried to envision what it would all look like on her Big Day. She saw lots of flowers and ribbons and candlelight, the wedding party all lined up in perfect descending order around the base of the altar. And all eyes were on her. She was coming down the aisle on her daddy's arm. Magically, her feet were moving in that awkward processional half step as if they were born for it. She felt the incredible warmth of everyone's admiration and good wishes washing all over her. But then Dawn realized: this was it. After this One Perfect Moment, there was no turning back. She wanted to stop, to linger in this place she'd finally reached, to bask in the glory, but she couldn't. This made her stomach squeeze and clutch. She was afraid she was going to be sick.

Dawn tried to take a deep, relaxing breath. She could close her eyes and read the coming week's schedule printed neatly on the backs of her eyelids. So much to do and to get through before Saturday, the red-letter day. She imagined it flashing there on the page of her planner, a stoplight in the middle of a busy intersection. She tried to think of the glow of the red light as a beacon, a light at the end of the tunnel. But somehow she kept thinking of warning signals and sirens. The words "Danger! Danger! Danger!" kept intruding into her thoughts and making her feel queasy.

It was just a case of pre-wedding nerves, she kept reminding herself. Even though she was terribly excited, naturally she was also a bit upset by the most recent turn of events. Though she was trying not to make too much out of it. Her mother said Dawn always read way too much into every little situation. So when Dawn expressed her uneasiness about getting married so close to the Claytons' horrible deaths, her mother had looked up from her Sunday morning sweet roll exasperated and said, "Honey, every little thing is not about you. Now that you've graduated from college and are about to get married it's time you realized. The whole universe is not concerned with you and your wedding."

"But it happened right here in Riley, Mama, right down the street. That is hardly the entire universe," Dawn said to defend herself. "And I'm not overreacting. I'm just wondering aloud if maybe this is some kind of ill omen. After all it wasn't just a random shooting. It was a couple we knew. It was love gone terribly and tragically wrong and about as far from romantic as you can possibly get. And I—"

"Aaaant," her mother said to stop her just like she had always done when Dawn was little and she caught her doing something she wasn't supposed to. "End of story," she said. "Let it rest."

But Dawn was afraid it wasn't that simple and it made her feel even worse that her mother cut her off like that. While she was fighting it, she couldn't help but feel that she had been led astray. *The 1977 Bridal*

Almanac had certainly let her down. She had been very careful to consult it before setting the date with John Wesley. It had promised ideal conditions for her sign—Aquarius—during the entire month of August. But somebody must have misread the signals. How could it be lucky to get married so close to such a disturbing example of a disastrous marriage? Dawn also worried people would think she was callous for going ahead with the wedding. But you couldn't just snap your fingers and change it, surely they could understand that. Reservations had been made—the church, the flowers, the caterers, the guests, the honeymoon—they all had to be scheduled way ahead of time. It was like waking up to realize you were on a train that was racing down a hill without any brakes. There was no way to just get off. You were on it for the ride.

Somehow Dawn's father must have had some kind of inkling about the weight of her rapidly accumulating fears as she sat in front of her breakfast hardly daring to breathe, much less eat. He lowered the Sunday paper he was reading and said, "Come on now, champ. You want to call the whole thing off, it's fine by me. There's always other fish in the sea." She knew he was trying to cheer her up. But really, what did he know?

"I knew I had to have this fish," Randy exhorted from the pulpit. "I couldn't take my eyes off the gigantic ripple that was circling my line. Every muscle in my body was trembling with the effort, but I kept on reeling. I kept thinking of a huge trophy fish, how impressive she'd look mounted in a big arch just like she was leaping out of the water and right over my living room mantel. And what a story! I knew I'd have a heck of a time telling all about how I came to catch it. Cut bait? I'd have to be a chump to cut bait—an idiot even. It's not every day Opportunity comes knocking at my door. So, I flung it wide open and yelled, 'Come on in!'

"I reeled until my shoulders and arms ached. I reeled until my hand went numb and I was afraid I might lose my grip. But then, I reeled some more. Sweat poured into my eyes, but I didn't dare close them for fear I'd miss it when she broke through. I had my heart set on seeing the sight of my lifetime, of something so great and mighty flying up from the water and into the air. I was stuck mind, body, and soul, couldn't a turned loose if I'd wanted to. At that point it was impossible to say which one of us had caught the other. Then just as I thought I might be making some headway, right as the ripples grew so large they circled my entire boat, that monster gave an extra powerful pull, jerked me clear over the side and into the water!"

Maybe Randy had gone a little overboard with this whole story thing, Mitch thought. In fact, in the end when all was said and done, maybe they all had. Maybe they had all gotten a little too carried away with talking out of school, chasing tail and then telling about it. Problem was, it was a lot of fun. And of course they hadn't meant anything by it—just a bunch of good old boys finding a way to pass the time, keep themselves amused. But maybe now in the sober light of day, Mitch could see that somebody had been bound to get hurt.

He remembered the time a group of them had been out on the pool patio up at the club. It was some kind of dinner dance and a few of them had slipped out for a smoke when their wives went to freshen up in the ladies' room. Michael Clayton had been there among them, Mitch remembered that too. But it was Randy who had been telling them all some kind of wild story—it might have been one about Lorna Everette. Whoever it featured, it was outrageous, you could bet on that. They had all still been laughing as they flicked their cigarette stubs over the fence and turned to go back. That was when Mitch noticed Regina Clayton, standing off under a big oak by the putting green. When the embers from her own burning cigarette briefly lit her face, Mitch could tell she had been watching them and listening. Maybe they should have known better. Still . . .

As discreetly as possible, Mitch checked out the crowd. He didn't think he saw any of the other guys he and Randy drank and played golf with. They could be hiding out in the balcony, but Mitch doubted it. All he could see was the backs of everybody's heads. He saw Bonnie Hunt and the girls, but no Jeff. He couldn't help but take a second glance at Debra. She was sitting completely still and rigid in her seat, not moving one muscle. On the other hand, Lorna Everette, sitting right behind Debra, seemed plenty relaxed. She was leaned back with her husband Richard's arm draped around her shoulders, her head tilted slightly, her eyes might even be closed. Mitch wasn't sure, but it was possible she had actually dozed off.

Meanwhile that dried-up old maid Ernestine Lambert looked as if she'd never get another moment's peace. Furiously flipping her bulletin back and forth at about eighty miles an hour, she caught his eye. Miss Lambert was gulping as if she couldn't get any air; she looked like she was about to lose it. She kept taking glances back over her shoulder at the rest of the congregation. Her eyebrows climbed up her forehead as if she were saying, "Did y'all just hear that?! Did you?! Well I never!" Fair to bursting is what you'd call old Ernestine. Somebody was going to get an earful when she got out of there. Mitch could hear her right now. And, really, was that any different from Mitch and his buddies sharing a couple of jokes and a tall tale or two? What was the fun in kissing and *not* telling? In fact, what was the fun in much of anything if you didn't get to share it with somebody? They might as well all be a bunch of robots.

No, no . . . Mitch refused to take on the blame for what happened to Michael. And he had warned Randy. That was about all he could do. That, and congratulate himself for sacrificing a round of Sunday golf for being here for this. He wouldn't have missed it for anything and couldn't wait to tell everybody. Besides, he figured he might even have time to fit in at least nine holes this afternoon after the service, depending on just how far Randy aimed to take this whole thing . . .

"Once I fell in, couldn't see a thing," Randy continued after stopping briefly to take a sip of water from the glass Reverend Cooper kept stowed away beneath the big Bible on a shelf inside the pulpit. "The water was dark and murky, and so thick falling into it was like diving in a tar pit. Both my hands were still wrapped around my rod and my arms were pulled up even with my head. Clearly, things were not going in a positive direction. I went down, down, down, deeper and deeper, until there wasn't any sign at all of even filtered light. Whatever it was on the other end of the line had decided to show who was boss and had left me holding the short end of the stick.

"For the first time, I started to think about letting go. I started thinking about my family—my wife, my boys, my mama, my daddy, all my brothers and sisters, aunts, uncles, the works—all the people who had loved and cared for me all my life. What if I lost every single one of them because I couldn't see fit to let go of this thing? That was when I realized the voice was coming from inside my own head. It got louder and louder. It had changed its tune and was dying to be heard. My heart filled up with the song of life, of love and the true spirit of thanksgiving. I was wasting my time chasing after something I couldn't even see. I was too busy worrying over what I didn't have to stop and appreciate what was already in my pocket. Then I realized if I died down at the bottom of Old Man Nelson's fishing pond I might stay stuck in the gunk and never be seen again. I started to wonder about what everybody would think if I just disappeared. Would they believe the worst?

Would they think I had gone off to find the one that got away and forgotten all about them? Just imagining all this made me turn loose of that rod and start scrambling to get out of there.

"I had to kick and claw with everything I had. And let me tell you, it was a struggle. I couldn't find which way was up. My lungs were about to burst and my heart leapt in my chest as if it were trying to reach the surface of the water all by itself. But right when I thought I couldn't last one second longer, I reached clear, sparkling water and then, Pop!, my head broke right on through to fresh air and sunshine. I rose up through the water brand spanking new and improved, felt just like a baby greeting the world for the very first time. I was washed of the sin that had clung to me and my life, and God had given me a powerful new hunger and a raging thirst—to share my story and to spread the word of the Gospel. 'I'm a tell it, I'm a tell it,' I called out at the top of my lungs. With each gasp of air, I sang louder, loud as I could, to the birds, to the trees, to the cattails, frogs, crickets, grass, to even the wide blue sky. I cried out, 'I'm a tell it. Yes, Lord, I'm a tell it because I have to. Even if it kills me, I'm a tell it. Just find me a body who'll listen—I'm a tell it— yes, Lord, God Almighty, I'm a tell it all!'"

Randy Fox's impassioned words inspired quite a flurry of "telling it" immediately following the dramatic close of the Sunday service. As the congregation spilled out the front doors, it re-collected in small clusters and knots of conversation perched on the steep steps and scattered across the sidewalk in front of the church. Disbelief, disgust, and delight intermingled during the exchange, often in the response of a single individual. "Well, I never . . ." "Can you imagine?" "Such a display, it's too bad he's too big for his Mama to tan his hide . . ." "What a fool, an idiot!" "Can't remember a better time in a house of worship . . ." "I had a time keeping a straight face in there, it was almost torture." "Can't wait to get a hold of so-and-so and tell him what all he missed today." It took longer than usual for the crowd to clear, for the very last family to load up the car and head for home, the children clutching brightly colored pictures of Jesus they had scribbled over during Sunday school and the parents left holding an entirely different but equally garish image of their own.

The traditional unwinding of Sunday afternoon did nothing to get in the way of the spread of Randy's story. Tongues wagged while Sunday dinners were served, eaten and digested. Ernestine Lambert sat alone at her dining room table eating a late lunch. She tried not to look at the now slightly disheveled arrangement she had carried home from the church and placed on the center of the table. She was mumbling the Lord's Prayer between bites of cold fried chicken and tomato aspic. As it had become clearer and clearer during the service that Randy Fox was, indeed, going to tell it all, it had also become quite painfully clear to Ernestine that it was true what they say: People are never what they seem. This troubled her deeply. She felt stunned and mortified, but *excited* at the same time.

Ernestine scooted the Queen Anne dining chair closer to the white crocheted tablecloth. She blotted the corners of her mouth with one of her mother's fine linen napkins and tried her very best to block out Randy's words and to think instead of the triangular shape of the arrangement and the Holy Trinity it signified. But no matter how hard she worked at thinking good thoughts, the words *in flagrant day lick toe* kept trying to insert themselves between lines of prayer. Unbidden, this phrase rose up from her ancient past—high school Latin lessons with dashing Mr. Greenly. Ernestine couldn't remember what it meant but she knew it was something indecent. Try as she might, she could not banish these words from her mind, nor the image of tall, lanky Mr. Fox bent over in an embrace with a woman who wore only a lacy white slip with one strap hanging off her fleshy pink shoulder. Much to her dismay, Ernestine discovered she was sweating. She could not even remember the last time this had happened.

Ernestine hadn't bothered to turn on the lights in the dining room, but could feel the palpable weight of her parents' presence bearing down on her all the same. Usually she took comfort in their framed portraits which hung at each end of the table above the seats they had routinely occupied during their lifetimes. But today, their painted expressions accused and demanded. Ernestine found no enjoyment in her meal. Her head was killing her, felt like she was wearing a bathing cap that was two sizes too small. And her stomach balked at each mouthful. She just wanted to get lunch over with, change into her seersucker housecoat, and lie down for a nap.

Later, as afternoon turned into evening, the Hunt family sat down for an early Sunday night supper. It was one of Suzanne's favorite meals— BLTs and baby Cokes in the little green bottles. She was excited because she had a story of her own to share with her brother and daddy. So she jumped right in . . . telling about how she had gone to big church that day and had heard Mr. Fox's amazing adventure about going fishing with the devil.

"Well now, that sounds interesting," said her father.

"Really, Daddy, it was about getting *caught*," Jackie said with raised eyebrows.

"Uh-uh, was not," said Suzanne. Just because she was older, Jackie thought she knew everything.

"Whaaaaat?" Jeff said.

"Hanky panky," Jackie added and then had to work hard to hold her lips steady, to keep from giggling.

"Hanky panky?" asked Suzanne. "Is that like the Hokey-Pokey?"

Hayden began to sing, "Let's do the Hokey-Pokey" in a silly voice until both he and Jackie fell into a fit of laughter so hard and uncontrollable that it sent a stream of Coke shooting out Hayden's nose and he had to be excused from the table.

Suzanne looked down at her dinner plate and at the purple-headed Violet who lay on the placemat where her napkin had been. Suzanne didn't have to watch to see that Jackie loved knowing something she didn't. But Jackie didn't know *everything*. Jackie didn't know that the Kiddles had found the spare key to Jackie's diary and decided to keep it for themselves. So there'd be no more secrets just as soon as they found out where it was Jackie hid the diary. So there. Then they'd just see who it was who knew everything.

All hell had broken loose over at the MacKenzie household. The entire family was busy running around like a pack of chickens with their heads cut off. Mitch had gone straight home from church and come clean with his wife about where he'd been that morning. Then he got Anne to agree to hostess an impromptu cookout for thirty or so of his best friends and neighbors. As she agreed, she had looked at Mitch with eyes so full of her typical, benign trust, that Mitch felt another guilty squeeze on his conscience. Was it for what he'd done to her? Or was it for planning to celebrate with another round of storytelling while Michael Clayton was fixing to be buried six feet under? Mitch had already considered the possibility of giving up fooling around—and he just might. But there was no way he was going to give up on telling stories, absolutely no way. Impossible. That would be asking entirely too much.

As things turned out, Mitch couldn't remember the last time he'd had so much fun. He flipped burgers and mixed drinks well into the evening. It felt like a holiday. Even though people had to go to work the next morning, they stayed late reveling in the deliciousness of it all and letting their children run wild and eat too many sweets. Again and again, the party paused in their conversation to lift their glasses in a toast to "Randy the Fox—from hen house to dog house, a bona fide son-of-a-gun—Praise the Lord!" Which was followed by lots of hearty laughter and "Amens!"

Mixed together, the voices coming from the gathering on Mitch's lawn sounded a lot like a backyard full of singing birds. From the symphony of sound, it was possible to pick out the songs bent on seducing and those full of warning as well as the ones sung purely for the singer's pleasure of hearing his own voice. This singing never seemed to stop. Even after the last hot dog was snatched off the patio table by the family dog, the last brownie finally disappeared, and the very last paper plate was crammed into the trash bag, the telling continued. It was in this way that the story of the Claytons became intertwined with the story of Randy Fox and then with the next teller of the tale, and the next, and the next . . . Thus, it was borne aloft on the gathering force of its own telling.

The people of Riley kept on talking until the story grew into something that had a life all its own. And then it sprouted wings and their collective breath lifted and blew until it took flight, soaring high in the air. Someone might fancy that so much telling and so many voices would produce a cacophony that would shake and rattle the clouds with the sharp, startling report of a thunderclap. But when the winged tale finally reached the heavens, the sound of its song was as light as the whispery stroke of a feather against bare skin. For as it had flown, it had dwindled to the barest of exhalations that only brushed against the silence—a sound grown as soft and downy as the shush of water washing across shore or, maybe, the muted, distant cry of a dove calling in the twilight.

NOAH RIDDLE

a retiree, who lives on the outskirts of town

August 1977

I know no one is ever going to believe it, but God spoke to me, Noah Riddle of Riley, North Carolina, just last Friday while I was sitting in a ditch off Highway 54. Now don't get all nervous and shifty-eyed. I'm not some kind of religious nut. I've never had so much as a knee buckle in church and the only signs I make a habit of looking for are the kind that say "Stop" or "Railroad Crossing" or "Fertilizer— $5—10 lbs." I have been known to look for the Golden Arches, but in all my seventy-seven years on this here earth I ain't never chased a damn rainbow. The only burning shrubbery I've ever come across burnt right down to the ground with just a quick snap, crackle, pop, and not so much as a whisper or a fine "howdy do."

It all got started with the kids wanting to go for a ride in the motor home. We knew we wanted to go out to eat but that was all anybody could decide on.

"Mow-ta-home, mow-ta-home, mow-ta-home!" Our granddaughter, Jaynelle, was stomping through the kitchen and the living room in her red cowboy boots and her pink ballerina outfit. She had got a hold of our youngest daughter Noelle's old twirling baton and was raising one end of it up and down over her head like she was leading the high school band in the Fourth of July parade.

"Stop that, Jaynelle! Those boots are scuffing up Mama's floor," Noelle said. She was holding that little bitty rag mop dog of hers under one arm where Jaynelle couldn't step on him. Noelle always wants to rule the roost. Whenever she scolds somebody her head moves back and forth just like a chicken.

"You're not my mama," Jaynelle said. "You can't tell me what to do."

"Excuse me? I believe this here is my mama's kitchen, so I can too," Noelle said.

"Cannot." Jaynelle started to pout.

"I can't believe Jay hasn't taught this girl better," Noelle said. "This is a fine example of why he had to come on home so somebody could teach this wild child some manners."

"I don't want to listen to this," said my wife Belle. "This is *my* kitchen. So I am the one who gets to say what goes. And right now, I say both of you need to hush." Belle was leaning back against the counter cabinets. She had one arm wrapped around her waist and the elbow of the other propped against it while she tried to talk on the phone to our oldest boy, Eb, and his wife, Felicia. Long pieces of hair had somehow gotten loose from the smooth bun she always wears pinned at the back of her neck. Her brow was furrowed and her eyes looked weak and tired without any hint of their old sparkle.

I knew I shouldn't let her take on too much. Belle has always been the one who handled the children and kept everything going. Before cancer, she did all kinds of things at the same time and never batted an eye. She could fix supper, help a couple of the grandkids with their schoolwork, and listen to Noelle's daily woes about not being able to find a man who was willing to put up with her, without seeming the least put out or undone. But nowadays just getting up in the morning was a chore. Each new day marked another lengthy battle for Belle just to rise to the occasion brought on by each little bit of that day's living. I wanted my old Belle back. But frankly, I was even more afraid of losing what there was left of her.

"Noelle, you stirring up trouble again?" Jay laughed as he came through the door from the back hallway. His hair was wet and he was still tucking in a clean shirt. "When are you going to grow up, baby sister?"

"You don't know what you're talking about," Noelle said.

"All I ask is that you be sure and let me know the day so I can mark it on my calendar. Go ahead, give us all something to look forward to."

A flush rose in Noelle's face. "Seems to me that you and your daughter would be better off if you spent more time worrying about her upbringing than mine. Dr. Spock says—"

"You've already done more than your fair share of spreading the gospel of that man's word. I suggest you reread the Good Book and think about trying it on yourself rather than that pathetic little excuse for a dog and other people's children." Jay came up behind Noelle and gave her a big bear hug.

Pookums, Noelle's dog, squeaked out a "Yip!" I swear. I'm still not sure she don't have to wind that thing up every night.

"Let go Jay! You're crushing us. Pookums could get hurt with all this silly roughhousing. Now I'm not in the mood for this foolishness."

"What's wrong, you on the rag or something?"

"Why would she be on a rag, Daddy?" Jaynelle had quit her yelling and was paying close attention to him and his sister.

"Children, children, I can't hear a thing Eb is saying." Belle looked hard at Jay over the top of her reading glasses. "Now do y'all want to go to the Chicken Shack for dinner, or what?"

"Mama, that grease is no good for you. It does nothing but clog up your arteries. You know that," Noelle said.

"I don't care where we go," Jay said. "Whatever suits you, Mama, suits me too."

"Mow-ta-home!" shrieked Jaynelle as she thrust the baton up over her head for added measure.

"Pop, what about you?" Belle moved from where she was leaning against the kitchen cabinet and stretched the phone cord until she could get a good, clear look at me across the room where I was waiting it all out in my favorite easy chair by the TV.

"Wherever you want to go, Sugarbelle," I said. The whole thing was giving me a headache. "I thought we was going somewhere nice, somewhere you could sit down at a table and have somebody wait on you for a change. You're supposed to relax, honey. That's all I want."

Belle just looked at me for a minute and then sighed heavy and put the phone back up to her ear. "Eb, doesn't Felicia want to go somewhere nice?"

"How about Bethel's Diner?" Jay called out. "You can't get the motor home parked in the Chicken Shack lot anyway. The diner's got a big old lot. I'm sure Shelly and Dale's kids want to ride in the motor home too."

"Did you hear that Eb? What about Bethel's?" Belle said. ". . . I think the food's good. On Friday nights they've got the chicken and dumpling dinner plate special for $5.99 . . . It is kind of pricey . . . But if we get there early enough they'll still have some banana pudding and that's one of your Daddy's favorites . . . Okay then. Y'all call Leroy and Gladys and I'll call Shelly and Dale . . . No, Noelle's already over here. All right. Tell them we'll be by in about twenty minutes."

It was going on 6 o'clock before we got everybody loaded in. All our children and our children's children live right here on Riddle Road. Jay did live in Greensboro for awhile. But when Tina left him, Belle told him to come on home. I thought that was the last thing we needed with Belle being sick and all. But Belle, she said, "I might be an old bird but I don't ever want to sit in an empty nest. You know how sweet a bird sings in the springtime? Well, that's how my heart feels when I'm surrounded by my babies. That's when I know God's love."

I didn't know about God's love, but I sure felt surrounded by something in that motor home.

"I wish you'd let me drive," Jay said.

"Ain't that just like a young'un?" I said to Belle, who was in the front seat beside me. "They're just so worried about taking over now, ain't they?" I turned in my seat so I could look at Jay head on. "Don't let these gray hairs fool you, son. I reckon I can still drive my own vehicle. I'll be sure and let you know when I need me a chauffeur. You can be the first one in line for that job when the time comes, but until then, you'll just have to sit on down back there with the rest of them. And don't ask me exactly what day it'll be—I'm not up for making those kinds of predictions."

The motor home was what you'd call full up. Jaynelle sat on the divider between me and Belle. She always liked to ride there so she could see everything. And Jay stood right behind me. The way he watched over my shoulder you'd have thought he was the one who'd taught me to drive. Our other two sons, Eb and Leroy, sat in the built-in seats around the dinette table with their wives Felicia and Gladys. Noelle and Pookums were squeezed in there too. Noelle insists on taking Pookums everywhere with her. Carries him in her pocketbook. But every time he rides in a car, Noelle straps him in an old baby car seat. So there was Pookums strapped in and jammed between Noelle and Felicia.

"You know you've got a problem, don't you?" I heard Felicia ask Noelle.

"I don't know what I've done to you people today," Noelle huffed.

"Is there a sign on my back that says Kick Me, Please Kick Me? Has somebody made this Be Mean to Noelle Day, or what? I would just really like to know what the hell is wrong with y'all."

There were teenagers sprawled in a tangle on the lower bunk bed. Leroy's youngest boy, Chavis, grumbled, "I can't believe we're riding to dinner in this thing. We're gonna look like a pack of clowns at the circus when we get out at Bethel's. Why can't we split up and ride in cars and trucks like everybody else?"

Eb's oldest daughter, Shelly, and her husband, Dale, sat on folding chairs in the middle of the floor, their two little ones right there with them. Christy stood between her daddy's legs and the baby, who won't answer to nothing but ChooChoo ever since Shelly took him down to the train station, was crawling around their feet yelling, "Woooo, wooooooo!" That's all that ever comes out of that child's mouth. For him, life is just one long train ride.

It was a mighty fine day for driving. After we got off the dirt road and headed down Highway 54, it was all smooth sailing. We bought the motor home a few years ago. It was Belle's idea. She called it our retirement home and said she wanted it so we could go on down to Atlantic Beach now and then and take a break, just the two of us. We did have some good times before Belle got sick. We fished and crabbed, took long walks on the beach, and ate some good seafood. We even went to the carnival.

I found myself wishing it was just me and Belle headed down to the ocean for a spell of peace and quiet. The way the motor home dipped and rose as it floated down the road made me hungry for the sound of the surf and the feel of a salty breeze.

I had just driven past Ike and Abe's farm when Jaynelle pressed her little hand on my arm. "Look Noddy—a big hawk!" she cried.

"Hawk? Where's there a hawk?" Belle asked as both of us twisted our necks trying to look up out of the top of the windshield.

"Up there." Jaynelle pointed out the windshield with her silver baton. "It was big! Did you see it?"

All I saw was a flash of darkness—a turkey buzzard, most likely. "Sorry I missed it," I said. As my eyes traveled back down to the road, a ball of light bounced off that damn baton and right into them. I swear, I was so blinded by the glare I couldn't see that ambulance coming. One minute it was nowhere in sight, the next it was right up on us.

Maybe my reflexes aren't what they used to be. The screech of the siren kept getting louder and louder and made me feel like we were being pulled toward it somehow, as if we'd been set on a collision course. So I swerved off the edge of the road trying to get out of the way. And then with a loud *whoosh!* the ambulance was gone. It was going so fast it seemed like it brought a huge wave of speed with it that sucked us in and then spat us back out.

Before I realized it, we were ploughing through a river of tall grass and weeds and headed straight for the ditch. I pulled hard on the wheel to get her up out of there, only I guess I don't know my strength because we ended up all the way across the road and headed for the ditch on the opposite side. Everybody screamed and yelled like they were on one of those crazy rides at the beach. One way or the other, I managed to grab hold of that wheel with both hands and to stand with all my weight balanced on the brake pedal. It took a while, but everything finally came to a grinding, bumpy halt.

We hadn't wrecked exactly, but the left wheels were stuck way down in the ditch and left us hanging there sideways. You could hear the ambulance siren echoing in the distance, but nobody in the motor home said a word. For just that one time, all the Riddles were silent. It was kind of peaceful. Looking out the windshield, everything seemed pretty normal. The road was empty. The tall trees all stood straight and still on either side. I even caught glimpse of a little blue butterfly as it flitted through a clump of clover not too far from the left front tire. I don't remember when it was, but those black sun spots did finally disappear and my vision cleared. I could hear bees buzzing and caught a whiff of fresh cow manure.

As long as you looked out everything appeared okay. It was when you looked at the windshield framing and the dashboard that you could see things were definitely off kilter. Imagine a crooked picture frame, but the picture inside appears to be still hanging just as straight as ever. I found myself marveling at how strange it was and holding my breath hoping we wouldn't lean over any further to the left. Just as I was about to break the silence and make the suggestion that everybody throw their weight to the right, gravity made up its mind about exactly where that motor home was going to go. It's pointless to argue with a force of nature, but all the children picked back up with screaming even louder than before. As if that would have stopped us from falling. The motor home just kept on tilting further and further to the left until it keeled all the way over on its side. The children were dumped in a wiggling heap like a litter of brand-new puppies yelping and squealing for their mama's tit. At some point during the ride, Jay must of grabbed Jaynelle off the console. Behind me I heard him say, "We're all right. Everybody's all right. Nobody's hurt."

And I could hear Felicia and Noelle over everybody else. "Let go of him!" Noelle hollered. "You are going to break the seat. It's not meant to hold up a grown woman."

"I can't," Felicia whimpered. "I'll fall."

"It's not far. The rest of us did and we could stand it. I'm telling you, let go! The seat's already coming loose. You're gonna fall anyway."

Pookums started to whine.

"I'll get you," Eb said. "Honey, I won't let you fall."

"Dammit!" yelled Felicia. And then I heard a loud thump. "He peed on me! The little rat pissed all over me!"

"What did you expect?" Noelle said. "I told you to let go. Now, hand him over. My poor wittle baby, you wuz scared wuzn't you punkin? S'okay, mama's got you now."

Then Felicia kept calling the Lord's name in vain until I heard another voice say, "Somebody shut her up." Which was promptly followed by the sound of a hard slap.

"You're welcome," Noelle said.

All while this was going on, I was fit to be tied, thinking I'd done in Belle's heart for sure. My own was racing to beat the band. But when I looked up at Belle who was still strapped in by her seat belt, she turned her head and looked right at me and smiled. Then she started to chuckle.

"I can't get it back right, Belle," I said.

"You did the best you could. I was watching," she said.

"The light got in my eyes. I couldn't see."

"I know. Nobody's blaming you. You can't always control everything that crosses your path—only the Lord can do that. It's okay." She reached out and took my right hand. Her grip was hard and strong. "If we can ever get this thing back upright, let's you and me take a ride to the beach. No more trips to Bethel's," Belle said. "They're too dangerous."

Other than Felicia's feelings, nobody was hurt. Jay unhooked Belle's seat belt and helped her out. He opened Belle's door and climbed out first. Then he stood outside pulling and Leroy and I pushed from the inside until we got every one of them out. I was last.

The motor home looked like a beached whale, lying there with its underbelly exposed on the edge of Honey Greer's front yard. All I could think was "Damnation!" Felicia did have a mighty red cheek and a big wet stain down the front of her dress. She blubbered into a crumpled tissue, while Eb kicked one of the tires. "I'll get somebody to pull us out of here, Daddy," he said. He went off muttering under his breath as he and Felicia headed toward the house.

My legs were kinda shaky, so I eased myself down in the grass. Hell, to tell you the truth, at that point I was none too sure about my own ticker. It felt like I had choked down a restless bird and it was beating its wings against my chest trying to get back out. For a while there I thought the next time I saw an ambulance it would be from the inside. If Belle was right and the Lord was in charge, I wondered what kind of unexpected thing He was going to throw our way next. I was getting too old for these kinds of shenanigans. It seemed to me He might could ease up a little and give an old man a break. But I didn't want to upset Belle, so I figured I could just sit and wait for a spell, try to ride it out.

Honey is a beekeeper. Now that her husband, who was a dairy farmer, passed away, she gets by with selling jars of her famous Clover-Sweet Authentic Honey—Pure Gold Sweetener. Ollie Lee left Honey with a yard full of painted cement and plastic animals scattered all across the grass. I had a perfect view from where I sat. Honey's yard was a long, green slope that started at the ditch and ran down into a valley where the house sat. I've noticed it all before, it's hard not to. Sometimes when you're riding by, the motion tricks your eye and for a second it looks like a real pig or chicken or dog has gotten in among all the artificial ones and started to move around.

Honey's got what you'd call a menagerie. There were life-size horses and deer, chickens and roosters, a whole flock of sheep, dogs of all kinds, cats, turtles, frogs, pigs and piglets, a baby elephant, two pink flamingos, a stork, sea horses holding up a birdbath, a flock of wild geese and, on either side of the front porch steps, two black-and-white spotted cows.

All along the white picket fence Ollie Lee had set up a row of painted whirligigs. He loved to dip his brush in some bright color. There were red birds and blue birds, gray and white seagulls, farmers hoeing grass so green it made your teeth ache, Dutch girls with yellow hair holding pink tulips, golfers teeing-off in orange and brown plaid pants, and couples dancing in purple and lime-colored outfits. I must say, I admire a man who's not afraid to show his artistic side.

I felt the heat of the sun shining down on the top of my head and when I took deep breaths I could catch whiffs of cool, green kudzu that blanketed the woods on the edge of the Greers' property. It's got that hard-to-catch smell, like Belle's perfume. The bird caught in my chest had slowed the beat of its wings. I could still feel the grip of Belle's hand in mine. Sitting there high up like that and looking down on everything reminded me of getting stuck with Belle on top of the Ferris wheel. She always held my hand then too.

Children had spilled out all over that yard. Honey was standing on the porch trying to see what all the commotion was about. Felicia walked straight on up to her. I could tell Felicia was still crying, though I'm not sure if it was over the wreck or being slapped by Noelle. Honey put her arm around Felicia and took her and Eb inside the house.

Chavis sat on the step, his head hung low. ChooChoo tried to giddyap on the back of a mama pig. Two of the other teenagers were scrambling to get up on the elephant, while one of the girls leaned back against the elephant's trunk with one of her arms lifted high above her head in a showgirl pose. Pookums growled and yipped at a big collie that had paint peeling off its side. Noelle said, "It's not real, baby. Don't be afraid. Mama's not going to let that dog get you!"

Surveying the scene was like looking down from the top of the Ferris wheel on all that carnival craziness at the beach. And it gave me the same kind of prickly uneasiness that something might go wrong. That there'd be some kind of mechanical failure I couldn't do anything about. That our seat would come loose and we'd start to fall and there'd be nothing to stop us or catch us in time. I found myself searching for a patch of ocean along the horizon and straining to hear just a little of its ebb and flow. But instead, that's when I heard Him. Just as clear as if He had called out my name and said, "Noah, Noah, here I am. Hey, listen up boy, I got something to tell you." I knew it just as sure as if I'd heard His voice rumbling from the clouds or been scorched by the heat of His powerful breath.

It struck me as odd. Now Belle, she's real faithful. She says God speaks to her all the time, in strange and mysterious ways. But me, I ain't never heard anything from Him before this. I'm mostly a quiet man, done nothing but farm the land all my life. From dawn until dusk I've been doing nothing except listening with no TV or radio to interfere. So if He'd had a mind to speak up, I would have heard Him even if it was just a soft word passing through the trees like a light breeze ruffling the edges of an evening.

But He waited to speak to me there on the edge of Honey and Ollie Lee's yard. That's when I realized He had brushed us with the wings of death. That was the wind circling the ambulance that knocked us off the highway. His voice had ridden the end of that wave and echoed in my ear along with the siren's sad song.

"Son, this here is the end of your rainbow," He said.

God had spared us. It was as if He had opened his fist and we were cradled there in the hollow of His big old hand. One of the kids brought me a walking stick with one end shaped just like a snake's head. It was heavy, but I wasn't ready to trust it or the strength of my own legs.

Just then, I saw Jay and Jaynelle playing in a clear grassy patch by the fence. The whirligigs were turning and twisting and flashing bits of moving color all around their heads. Jay was holding Jaynelle by her underarms and was turning around and around until her feet flew out from under her. And Belle was standing right there watching them. She had one hand over her heart and the other wrapped around her waist and her head was tilted back and she was laughing. It was the same laugh she always does as our seat drops from the top of the Ferris wheel to the bottom and then starts its climb again. I hadn't heard that laugh in a long time. Jaynelle was laughing too. The sound of their voices gurgled up like a spring. It trickled and gushed through the air like water rushing through the creek bed after a spring storm. It lifted up and floated high above our heads until that siren quit ringing in my ears.

And I said, "But who will believe me? Who will I say I heard talking here in this ditch on the side of Highway 54?"

"I am who I am," He said. "I am the God of your fathers. I am the God of your children and your children's children. I am the God of Honey Greer and of Willie Wilkes who was driving the ambulance that ran you off the road. And I am the God of the woman lying in that ambulance flying down the highway to meet her death."

WHITNEY ELLIOT VAUGHN

a young mother, who works downtown
at the department store makeup counter

If I were a bird, I'd fly right out of this town. Not without my baby. I'd probably have to carry her suspended from my beak the way the stork does in the pictures you see. But instead of bringing her to somebody, I'd be taking her and me right out a here and on over toward somewhere over the RAINBOW—maybe New York City or Hollywood. I might even stop in Chapel Hill for just a while to rest my wings and see for myself what a real college town is like. I'd love to have that feeling of being FREE and able to just flap your wings and take on off. And I would. Believe me. Before anybody could catch me, I'd be gone.

Because this old town and everybody in it is a worn-out 45, just looping around the record player playing the same old scratched-up song too many times to count. And here I am, former homecoming queen and head cheerleader Whitney Elliot Vaughn, struggling with a brand-new baby and living in disgrace at my parents' house while my supposed heart's desire is rotting in jail for who knows how long. Who would have ever expected to find ME sitting BEHIND the makeup counter of the only department store in the whole damn place wondering what awful thing is going to happen next. A fall from grace may feel like forever, but it took me only two short years after high school.

All this has aged me, I am sure. I mean, it's a miracle I can get up in the morning, much less feed the baby and get myself all fixed up for working right in the public eye, promoting BEAUTY and everything. I don't want to get that hard look women in their thirties have. After all, I only just turned twenty. So I'm using gobs of our top-of-the-line moisturizer. It's called Youth Dew. I put it on religiously every night and practice relaxing my frown lines and breathing deeply. I may be down, but whatever you do, you'd better not count ME out.

I tell myself, "Whitney Kay Elliot, you are not going to let a tumble with bad luck ruin you. Your youth, your beauty, your popularity, it's all still there. Weren't you first voted homecoming queen your JUNIOR year of high school? At seventeen, you had already made history. You are not about to stop with two little rhinestone crowns and a pile of stringy old pompoms. You are destined . . . You are destined . . . You are destined . . ." I don't say what for because I haven't decided yet and I don't want to limit my options.

However, it is significant that I call myself Whitney Kay ELLIOT, because in my mind I have already gotten rid of Reggie and his old stinking last name. I am shaking him off just like a bad case of acne and returning to my former glory. I can feel it. I can still do a running walkover and two back flips in a row rounded out nicely with a steady two-foot landing AND fit EASILY into my old cheerleading uniform—a perfect size six, thank you very much. I've been working hard at it too. I've ignored all the looks I get everywhere I go. I know what they say:

"Can you believe WHITNEY'S already got a BAY BEE?!"

"I heard her husband's in JAIL."

"I heard they caught him in a stolen vehicle with ANOTHER WOMAN and five grams of COCAINE."

"Wonder what MISS HOMECOMING QUEEN OF AMERICA is going to do now that she's living back home raising a CRIMINAL'S CHILD?"

"I bet she's already got STRETCH MARKS."

"EWWWWW!"

Just like Scarlet, I have fallen on some hard times and I am struggling to face them with DIGNITY and GRACE. I wear waterproof mascara all the time so no one will know if I'm overcome with sorrow and have to have a little cry when nobody's looking. And I practice my cheer-leader smile on everybody. It's the perfect crowd smile, works just as good in the grocery store as it did on the ball field. But then, SOME-BODY bought the only fall outfit in this whole store I wanted. It's hard to find something cute in a size six. They hardly ever stock sizes that small because most of the women around here are too BIG and FAT. And I hardly ever get a chance to go anywhere to shop in real stores anymore. So, once again, I was stuck having to make the best of a bad situation.

It was a two-piece pant and poncho outfit in hot pink. The pon-cho had long fringe with bright orange mixed in with the pink. And the sides came up real high so even though your chest was covered up everybody could get glimpses of your hips and waist which were played up by the low sexy cut of the pants. Those pants fit perfect too.

Damn. ANOTHER lost opportunity. It makes me so mad. I had tucked it back behind the twelves hoping people would think we were sold out of the six. I couldn't buy it until my next paycheck. Mama and Daddy won't give me things the way they used to. All they seem to care about is buying things for the baby. And then SOMEBODY—it could only be a couple of people and I have my SUSPISCIONS—came in here during my lunch hour last Friday and bought it right out from under my nose.

And then, on the same day, Regina Clayton had to go and kill her husband AND HERSELF all over a little infidelity. You'd think nothing like that had ever happened before in the entire universe. The whole town's been in an uproar ever since. Then Randy Fox had to top things off by going to church Sunday and telling his WIFE and the ENTIRE METHODIST CONGREGATION that he had been bumping all kinds of women behind Debra's back for years. Two people are dead. One fool thinks he's saved. And now everybody else has gone nuts. All everybody does is go around getting in some kind of little cluster and talking under their breaths about WHAT HAPPENED. What a SHAME it is and how SINFUL sleeping around is when it gets OUT OF HAND. As if they haven't all been doing it for years.

This is upsetting. I wouldn't be surprised if this is exactly how the witch hunts got started. This is why I want out of this damn hick town. I've read *The Scarlet Letter* CliffsNotes, and I have no intention of being anybody's Hester. Now that my cheering days are over, I am through wearing any kind of letter on my chest.

I have no intention of having one stamped on my brain either. So thank you NOT very much, Regina Clayton, for leaving us with some kind of big heavy guilt trip we've all got to live with now and forever. How's a girl supposed to get along? Huh? Tell me that.

I'm trying to get some kind of consolation out of the arrival of the NEW FALL COLORS. If you think about it, MAKEUP IS EVERYTHING. It's refinement. It's art. It's beauty and youth and hope and promise. These little bottles and tubes may look like bits of plastic vanity. But all your potential may be held up in one of these, just floating along beside bees' egg goo or crushed iridescent crystals or maybe even just plain talcum—they do still use it, you know. That's why I'm studying makeup. IT is what REALLY separates us from the ANIMALS. All it takes is understanding proper application and, of course, a certain flair for what goes and what doesn't.

Perfectly Pink, Really Red, Passion Fruit, Orange Blossom, Burnished

Copper, and Crimson Glory. Their names remind me of my mother's roses. They're scented too. I love to open up a perfect new tip in each color and line them up on the counter. They remind me of rosebuds in crystal vases sitting there untouched and perfect, just waiting for the caress of pale, bare lips. I think of them as my artist's palette because that's what I really am—an artist. I have spent YEARS reading *Seventeen* and *Glamour* from cover to cover and memorizing all their PROFESSIONAL advice. Not only do I know how to apply shadow according to your eyes' shape and how close together they are, but I also know all about contouring to get that sunken-cheek look, the seven secrets to applying perfect mascara every time, and how to create CLEAVAGE with BLUSHER—if you need that kind of help.

Mostly too I share my KNOWLEDGE and my artist's SKILL with those who give me a CHANCE. Everybody knows I have had years of practice with looking good under pressure and getting in the spotlight and staying there. Who else has ever won Homecoming Queen or been head cheerleader two years in a row? It's unheard of. Naturally there are some who are hesitant to ask for advice. But for those who do, I am generous and I pay attention to their own individual style. You may have never thought about this, but most women favor whatever look was popular when they were teenagers. That's how I know Myra Thornberg with her old lady up-do will like thick, creamy Perfectly Pink. Janine Saunders and Bonnie Hunt with their teased-helmet flips will both go for Really Red. And Lois Honeycutt, who's been weird ever since she came back from that Northern all-girls college, will bypass the lipsticks all together. She wears only a hint of plain Vaseline. Instead, she'll demand a new supply of Blackest Night liquid eyeliner and mascara which she coats on real thick and dramatic. I have to say, it does go with her fringed pixie cut, if you like that sorta thing.

So far, the only thing I have held back from my loyal customers has been Rosy Dawn. And I'm sorry, but I've got to have a signature look or I'll lose my edge. It's practically a requirement for success. I like to wear my hair fluffed in a cloud around my shoulders. Reggie used to always talk about how it's so fine it feels like a baby's, but it does hold curl pretty good with just a little spray. And I always play up my eyes. In eleventh grade Gordon Hayes told me I had eyes just like Elizabeth Taylor's—only brown—and I've taken special care with them ever since. I favor the shiny, wet look for my lips. Rosy Dawn is a colored gloss really, and with lip liner #623, Dusky Rose, it is the perfect combination of brown and pinkie red tones for my coloring. Every time I check my makeup in the counter mirror, I am pleased with the results. Rosy Dawn holds true even under florescent light, which is more than I can say for any man I've ever met. That is why, when other women ask me about this color, I say it's been DISCONTINUED. Sorry girls, but that is the advantage to being an INSIDER in this business.

Oh great, just great. This is just what I need today. To have to see Mary Lloyd Fitchew. I'm smiling though. I'll just give her a little parade wave and she'll probably head toward the back where the maternity department is. Everybody knows she's pregnant even if she's not showing yet. Oh, no. She's headed straight for me. I wonder if she knows about me and Clarke. She couldn't. He would never tell. And I KNOW nobody saw us . . .

"Good morning, Mary Lloyd."

"Well, hello yourself, Whitney. How is the makeup department?" Mary Lloyd laughs as if she's just made a clever joke. Then she flips one side of her hair back by tossing her head as she eases herself up on the makeover stool. Mary Lloyd graduated from Riley High the same year I did. She was runner-up everything. She is right pretty. "Patrician" is what they call her features. She does have a perfect oval face and long brown hair. It's thick and has lots of body and was made for that Jacqueline Smith cut. If you have to pick a Charlie's Angels look, I'd pick hers too. Mary Lloyd probably hasn't forgiven me for all the things I won and she didn't. But SOMEBODY has to win. And, besides, isn't she married to Clarke, the handsome golf pro? Some people are NEVER satisfied.

Mary Lloyd picks up each tube of lipstick and holds it to the light. "This Really Red is just too, too—don't you think Whitney?"

"It is a bit dark for me."

"What about that color you have on? I like that one."

"Well, let me look in this new shipment. I don't think I've seen any of it. Oh, yeah, it had slipped my mind but I think it's been discontinued."

"Shoot. I can never find what I'm looking for," Mary Lloyd says. She scowls at poor Passion Fruit and has completely destroyed my nice, neat little row of just-opened lipsticks.

"Try some of these glosses. I think what you need is a more updated product. You know the wet look is in. Maybe a gloss will give you a whole new contemporary attitude."

"I don't like having to stick my finger in it to put it on. It gets all icky. I think they smell funny too. Tell me," Mary Lloyd says, scooting closer to the counter, "What kind of makeup did Regina Clayton use?"

"I guess it's no big secret . . . she wore a light foundation of Stay True Beige, followed by a dusting of loose powder to dull the shine and just a stain of Cardinal Red on her lips."

And that was it. I don't tell Mary Lloyd that I had always tried to get Regina Clayton to do something with her eyes. They were such a striking blue. To be such a light color they really had incredible impact. To look at them always made me think of our Eucalyptus Breeze Astringent Wash, so fresh and cool like a patch of mountain-top sky poured straight into a bottle. Though she didn't seem to care, said she didn't want to bother with eye shadow and mascara. And she did have such dark eyebrows and lashes I guess she could get away with it.

"I always thought she looked sorta like Katharine Hepburn. You know, classy," Mary Lloyd says. She has stopped fidgeting with the gloss pot lids and seems to be looking at me real careful. "Clarke is taking the whole thing real bad. Of course, he's played in a foursome with Michael now and then and he had been teaching Regina private lessons for the past year. He said she was probably the best female golfer in all of Riley—all of Matthews County even. He can't believe something like this has happened. But I'm not so surprised."

"Well, I am." I can feel the prickle of sweat breaking out along my back and under my arms. The coolness from the air conditioning gives me a little chill. *Relax, honey*. Remember, you are DESTINED . . . I toss MY head and give Mary Lloyd one of my wide-eyed, impish grins. "Lighten up, Mary Lloyd. Everybody doesn't have to get all desperate over a little romp in the hay. It was just sex he was having. That's all. What ever happened to the Age of Aquarius, free love, and all that good stuff?"

"It's different when you've been married. You ought to be able to get that, Whitney."

"You sound so uptight and conventional, just like our parents."

"I don't care." Her lips tighten and she raises her eyebrows. "When you're committed to someone and you have their children and then some hussy comes along and ruins everything, I can see how you might be driven to extremes. I just might myself. You know, just like a mother bird will attack anything that threatens her nest."

"Oh, Mary Lloyd." I force a little laugh and roll my eyes. "You sound so territorial. Don't get your feathers all ruffled. Let's leave the pissing contests to the men and concentrate our little old minds on our plumage. Now, how about this new color—Passion Fruit?"

"It's too pink. I am thinking about purchasing a tube of Cardinal Red. But I'm going to Chapel Hill and look at the mall first, before I decide. That reminds me. Did I tell you Clarke and I saw Brett while we were in Chapel Hill last time? He looked so cute, just like 'Joe College.' Said he was having a great time at Carolina. I came in here last Friday to tell you about it, but you had gone to lunch."

"Oh, really?"

"Yeah, I was looking for a new outfit, a quick pick-me-up, though there's certainly not much to choose from around here, is there? Anyway, he did say to tell you hello. I always thought it was such a shame y'all broke up after he went off to school." Mary Lloyd is smiling now and tossing her hair back-and-forth and side-to-side like she's in some kind of shampoo commercial. "Well, just thought you'd want to know. I'd better get going. Got to meet Clarke for lunch at the club." She slides off the stool and smoothes what there is of her short skirt. "Catch you later," she says with a lilt in her voice and spins on her heel sending her hair fanning out behind her.

She marches on out with her head held high as if she had been drinking a glass of starch while she was sitting here. I didn't tell her she has a smear of lipstick stuck to her front teeth. Just let Clarke take a look at that. If she thinks to check in a mirror before she meets him, she won't know if it got on there while she was here or after. It was JUST A KISS. That's all. How am I supposed to maintain my reputation as a FEMME FATAL if there's no one to practice on? All the good ones are already taken or off at school.

I am sure Brett is busy dating all kinds of pretty blonde Carolina girls. Girls who don't have babies and stretch marks and ex-husbands. Though give them time—they'll probably end up with them. But some-how I HAVE to get Brett back. I HAVE to haunt his dreams and all his memories. When he dances with another girl, I want him to think of my body. When he hugs her, my perfume. When he kisses her, my lips. I want him to wonder who's been kissing ME, touching me, WANTING ME. When he comes back to town knowing Reggie is out of the way, he's got to see me the way I was—a perfect red rose—lush and mysterious and powerful and graced with the sweetest scent of heaven. He's got to see that there's lots of others who are FIGHTING to brave the thorns of my life, just hoping I'll pick them to be the one to carry me away.

Mary Lloyd doesn't have anything to worry about. Clarke is sexy. But he is not the ONE for me. I just need to borrow him a little bit. Maybe that's all Cindy Worthington wanted with Michael Clayton. When I watch my little Ellie sleeping in her crib at night in my old pink and purple bedroom, I know my baby needs a father. She lays there surrounded by pictures of me in my prime all over the walls. Prom pictures, parade pictures, newspaper clippings, me in my uniform cheering, me with the rest of the squad, me waving from the back of Brett's convertible. My favorite one is of me getting crowned the first time. I am so happy and Brett is too. We're both in the picture. I'm looking at the camera and Brett is looking at me as if he'd just won a PRIZE.

You are destined . . . I tell that to Ellie too. And I am going to get both of us something worth having. We are going to get somewhere if I have to SPROUT WINGS AND FLY to Chapel Hill or even off into the unknown searching for our patch of mountain air where we can soar into quenching BLUE SKIES forever. Every girl needs her daddy and every woman needs a man. Being without one is just like going out without your makeup. Without a smooth base, the contour of blush, the accent of highlighting, the definition of eyeliner and mascara, and the enhancement of eye shadow and lipstick, your face loses everything. You could be anybody and no one would notice. Sometimes you have to just do what you can. You might have to make a dress out of old curtains, or move back home, or find a little bottle of MAGIC to make your heart grow YOUNG. But there's always something.

Maybe that's what Regina Clayton forgot—that tomorrow is ALWAYS another day. Or maybe she just underestimated the potential for POWER that was waiting right there on top of her dressing table—right at her very own fingertips—all along. You know, she did have that SCAR. It ran in a faint pink line from right below her nose down to the top of her lip. But EVERYBODY'S got scars. That's part of the BEAUTY of makeup. It's made for covering up life's little blemishes. Bumps, blotches, wrinkles, even age spots—makeup provides the perfect camouflage for them all. You can walk all around in the broad daylight and no one will be the wiser. No one will have any idea of what all is up under there. That's not to say that it doesn't take some application skill and general know-how, but I've found that most are trainable. It's more about DESIRE than it is NATURAL TALENT.

Of course, Regina Clayton wouldn't be the first woman in America who has failed to figure out the REAL SECRET to makeup, even though it says it all plain as day each time we call it by name: MAKE UP. Just a dab of this and a carefully blended dab of that and soon you can find yourself MAKING UP for all your LOST YESTERDAYS and MAKING UP whatever you want to be for ALL your TOMORROWS.

TROY MATTHEWS

husband of Delma, a local hairdresser

1979

My wife, Delma—she gets something in her head and there is no way she's gonna see fit to let it alone. Now me, I believe most things can't bear up under that kind of pressure. Sure, I think on things a little. But when I find myself bogging down, I try to just take a step back and let things ride for a while—try not to worry too much. Take for instance all this snake business Delma's got herself hung up on. Now this is clearly a case of not seeing the forest for the trees.

When Delma first told me she wanted to subscribe to the daily news-paper, sent every day all the way from Raleigh, I was right proud. Most folks are happy catching what kind of news they can in the little old Matthews County paper. But not my Delma. She said, "There's more going on out there than we know, and I aim to find out what it is." And I thought, *Well I'll be, I married me a smart little cookie, now didn't I.*

Delma has always been curious and likes to study up on things, so I was not taken totally by surprise. She's told me all about how impor-tant it is to support your spouse in their efforts to grow and improve, and I thought that was the case here. So, I said, "Sweet cakes, you read all the papers you want." I had no idea where all this would lead. I thought from time-to-time she might mention some of what she'd read, things that had especially caught her notice. We've only been married for five years, but we've known each other forever. Eventually you start to run out of things to say. So I said to myself, *Well good, Delma's gonna find us some new things to talk about. We're gonna have ourselves some real dinner conversation.*

But within the first week or so of getting that new paper, I came home to find her poring over a story about this family's pet python. It had been left alone with their eight-year-old boy—an obvious mistake. Seems somebody had forgotten to feed the snake that week and it got loose and started looking around. The first thing it took a shine to was the child's leg, which it wrapped its jaws around and wouldn't let go of. By the time the parents got home, the hungry python had worked its way up to the boy's kneecap and the child was understandably fit to be tied. As luck would have it, the snake was thinking to swallow all of the boy before he got to work on actually digesting him. So once they managed to pry his leg out of there, the boy was pretty much okay. But after Delma read that article, she sure wasn't. She kept talking about it all night long. And the next day. And the day after that. Until finally, at dinner on the third evening, I put down my fork and said, "Not again, Delma. This is hardly a fit topic for talk at the dinner table. After a long day's work a man needs to be able to enjoy a good meal—not be tortured while he tries to choke it down."

Right then, I knew I had made some kind of mistake. Delma pursed her lips together and wouldn't say another word. She just gave me this horribly mean look. It was the same kind of look her mama used to give me when I'd come to their front door to pick Delma up for a date. Delma's mama would open the door and then just stand there and give me a good hard going over with her eyes, as if she were struggling to make up her mind whether to invite me in or bite my head off. I'd never seen that look on Delma's face before, but her features seemed to clamp down on it and now I see that look all the time.

The hungry python and the boy story was about two years ago. The time is doubly marked in my mind because it was right after the Clayton incident—a rather spectacular situation that involved this couple that used to live here in town. They lived in the high-rent section over at the country club. Seems he had made himself a little habit of stepping out on her now and then. Now there is nothing unusual in this part of the story. But this woman, Regina Clayton was her name, walked right in on her husband and his hot-to-trot secretary. Her name was Cindy something or other. The two of them was letting it all hang out right around lunchtime at his place of business. He was an account-ant. Some say they were doing it on top of his desk, going at it as if they didn't have a care in the world. Just as happy as they pleased, with her ass pressed into a pile of receipts from the last week's sale at the stockyard.

Now this is the sort of tidbit that makes a story worth telling in a small town like Riley. Hearing about it, you get a little picture in your head. Folks around here like that kind of thing. But then Mrs. Clayton went and got real violent on us. Delma used to see Regina Clayton a lot at the beauty parlor where Delma works. Delma says Mrs. Clayton was a real lady—and pretty too. Not in the usual way, Delma says, since she kept her hair dark and refused to tan. I say there was more different about her than that. With the way she went on home and found a gun and loaded it and just sat there in her kitchen, waiting. I wonder what it takes to make a woman raise a gun to her husband while he sits in his easy chair? She shot him first in the gonads and then the chest before she went on and blew his brains out and her own. One. Two. Three. And then yourself. Now, *that*, that is what made all the difference.

Usually not much happens in Riley. But this topped anything we'd ever known. For a while it felt like we really lived somewhere—if you know what I mean. And I guess we can't get over the surprise of that feeling and maybe the sadness of it passing.

So it was right after their deaths that Delma started in with her newspaper clipping collection and her suspicions. Somehow these two stories—the Clayton one and the one about that pet python—got themselves wrapped around Delma's mind and just wouldn't let go. I don't know if you'd say they swallowed her or she swallowed them, but neither story nor Delma has turned a loose. Our lives have been on a steady decline ever since. Now Delma's got this whole collection of snake story clippings, and when she's not at work, she spends all her time looking for new ones. Some wives clip coupons. Delma clips snake disasters.

I reckon she figures she don't need coupons, since she's just about quit cooking. She never used to worry about her weight. Right before all this, we had even started talking about trying to have a baby. But now, Delma gives Troy Jr. and Little Delma no mention at all. She's too busy with finding new ways to starve herself. And she's managed to find the time to study up on all the words you can use to describe two-timing. At night when we're supposed to be sleeping she leans over and whispers these words in my ear: *screwing on the sly . . . sleeping around . . . straying . . . playing her for a fool . . . adultery . . . unfaithful . . . untrue . . . in-fi-del-i-ty . . . affair . . . open marriage . . . free love . . . cuckoldry . . . intrigue . . . liaison . . . Don Juan . . .* It's her way of testing me. I can feel her staring at me in the dark. She's always watching for any signs of a guilty conscience, especially when she thinks my guard is down.

Tonight when I came home from work I found her sitting at the kitchen table studying the newspaper with her mama's mean look plastered all over her face. "Hey, dumplin. What's for dinner?" I asked. In my mind, I was conjuring up a plate of black-eyed peas, greens, and some of Delma's melt-in-your-mouth biscuits. Or maybe pot roast with tender baby carrots or fried chicken and blueberry cobbler.

"Hey yourself," Delma answered without bothering to look up.

Sniff! Sniff! Sniff! I made a big show of breathing in through my nose. I had just about set my mouth on the idea of Salisbury steak and creamy mashed potatoes. "What is it that smells so good? Is it you, sugar? Or my dinner?" I walked over and bent down to nuzzle at the back of her neck. But the smell coming off her head like to brought me to my knees. We're talking serious stink. Rotten eggs and then some. "Woo-eee!" I said. "Is there something burning, sweetmeat?"

"Can't you see I'm busy?" She raised a hand to check her hair but kept her eyes pinned to the paper. "Every night it's the same thing. You come in hollering about food and manhandling me. I'm surprised you don't pound on your chest when you first walk in the door. Can't you see I might have something else on my mind besides filling your stomach?"

I took a step back and looked hard at Delma's head. There were new lumpy curls all over it. It looked like she had just taken the curlers out and hadn't bothered to brush it or anything. And she had done something to the color because there were these strips of bleached white mixed in with her natural brown. The overall effect was almost as startling as the smell. "Is that a new hairstyle you're fixing, honey?"

"As a matter of fact, it is," Delma said. "A new permanent and frosted streaks. But it's this here article that's what is really on my mind." Suddenly she turned toward me and shoved the clipping in my face. I had to pull back a little more to make out what was in the picture. It was a man standing by a kiddie pool. His left foot and lower leg were so swollen they looked huge compared to the rest of him.

"Guess what got him, Troy."

"Looks snake bit, Delma."

"And do you want to know where the snake got him, Troy?"

"Looks like in the foot, Delma."

"Smarty-pants. That's not what I mean and you know it. Right in his own backyard is where it happened."

"Well," I said and pulled out a chair and took a seat at the table. "Is that right?" There were two empty white plates and an ashtray. One of the plates sat in front of me and the other across the table in front of Delma. That was it. There was no other sign of supper anywhere. Nothing bubbling on the stove. The oven light wasn't even on. And the lazy Susan that sits on the center of the table was completely empty. No pickle relish. No vinegar. Not even a crumb. My stomach rumbled as I reached for a cigarette. "As they say, what is this world coming to?"

"His children were swimming in that pool," Delma said. She stopped then for a minute to narrow her eyes. After making sure I was paying attention, she went on. "See. It's the kind with waves painted across the bottom—and little half moons and fish. I saw them on sale at the grocery store just yesterday." She picked the article back up to take another look.

"Mosquitoes," I said.

"What?"

"Those things breed mosquitoes. Didn't he know that?"

Delma let out a big sigh. "Maybe they dump all the water out each time. That is hardly the point. Who cares about itching when there's a copperhead on the loose?"

I shrugged my shoulders, took another drag on my cigarette. It's hard to get comfortable in those chairs. It had been a long day. I was tired.

She let the clipping slip through her fingers. It floated down and settled by her plate. She is a big woman, but her hands are so small they could be a child's. "I bet the pain was terrible. I bet he'd never felt anything like it," she said. "Just look at that foot. It's the size of a water-melon. I wonder did he think he was going to die? What does anybody think at a time like that? Troy. Troy? Are you listening to me?"

"Yeah. I'm listening, honeybun. I'm just thinking is all." I said this real careful so Delma wouldn't take it wrong. You'd have thought it was me she was mad at.

"Well, you ought to be. Because there is a lesson to be learned here, Mr. Troy Matthews. Mr. It'll-Never-Happen-to-Me Matthews."

"Now, Delma," I said, "don't get yourself all worked up. Please, honey."

"Do you think this man was looking for trouble?"

"No," I said. "He probably wasn't."

"That's right. That's what I've been trying to tell you." She smacked her hand down on the table. "These things never really happen. Isn't that what you're all the time saying? Once in a blue moon. That's what you say." Delma got up and took the article over to the refrigerator. She started looking for a place to stick it. The refrigerator's surface was covered almost entirely in black and white. All those stories could not have come from the Raleigh and Matthews County papers. But if there is anything I know about Delma, it's that she does have her ways. Yes sir, the woman has her ways. She has pieced together a patchwork of snake stories that wrap around both side panels as well as the front. When you look at our refrigerator you don't see Frigidaire or a list of "Things to Do Today." You can't even hardly see any of its real color, which just so happens to be harvest gold. Sometimes I get dizzy just trying to find the handle to pull open the door. It's all part of her get-skinny plan, Delma says. She doesn't want to be tempted. She doesn't want to want to open that door. Instead, she spends her time circling round and round it—like the refrigerator is some kind of fresh juicy meat that she can hardly wait to tear into.

"Do you remember this one Troy? It's the one where that big boa constrictor got in a dog pen and swallowed a whole litter of puppies."

"It was seven of them, wasn't it?"

"Yeah. But they saved three," she said. "I can't believe anybody had the nerve to pick that big old nasty snake up and wring those puppies out from its insides."

"It took two people to do it?"

"That's right," she said, "a couple. Could you see us doing something like that? I wonder did they argue about it? Did he yell at her to hold her end up higher or to squeeze harder than she thought she could? Or did they have that superhuman power that's supposed to come to you in a time of crisis, the kind of adrenaline that lets one person lift the whole end of a car? What about you, Troy? What do you think? Have you ever stopped to consider what you'd be willing to do to save something you loved?"

"It don't have to be that hard, if you don't spend so much time thinking about it," I said. "Marriage is a partnership—right? You just do your part. That's what it's all about. I do my job at Riley Dog Food and you do yours mornings at the beauty shop and evenings right here in our kitchen. And then every once in a while I take you out so you don't have to cook. You know how it is. You scratch mine and I'll scratch yours. And nobody's left with an itch unscratched."

"Once in a blue moon is how often you take me out to dinner," Delma said. "And just how often is it that a blue moon strikes? Often enough to send you to the hospital, that's what." She was sitting across from me again and had found her cigarettes. She had pulled the ashtray over toward her so I had to stretch to reach it. Both our packs of smokes were lying by our plates. Me, I'm a Lucky Strike kind of man— plain, simple, and straight to the point—no filters to get in the way. What you see is what you get. But Delma, she's just started buying a new brand. Eve, they're called. The package was covered with all these weird vines and flowers. Sometimes, I do have to wonder where Delma gets her ideas.

"It's the same thing with lightning," I said. "You can't spend your whole life worrying just because you know one or two people has gotten hit."

Delma huffed and flipped her right hand over her shoulder in the direction of the refrigerator. "Would you call that one or two people?"

"No, but those stories have come from all over," I said. "It looks real concentrated the way you have them there. But they're not all happening in the same place. To look at that refrigerator you'd think the world was being run over with snakes. But when was the last time you actually saw a real one for yourself?"

"That's the kind of hogwash people are all the time saying to make themselves feel better," Delma said. "Like they're safe walking barefoot in the grass on a hot summer's day. Go ahead. I know what everybody thinks. Delma is an odd bird. Delma takes these things too hard. Delma worries too much. Delma can't help it. Her mama keeps plastic covers on all her living room furniture and Delma's Aunt Lula won't ever leave the house."

"You do have some strange family, Delma. That is a fact. But, sweet biscuit, that's not your fault," I said. "Besides I knew all about that from the get-go, now didn't I? And look, I married you anyway." I tried to give her one of my best grins. But she wasn't buying it. "Would you mind pushing that ashtray a tad over my way, sugar britches?"

"This here ought to settle things," Delma said. I could tell she was nowhere near the end of her point. She was going to squeeze every little bit she could get out of this one. "This man was doing nothing but playing in ankle-deep water with his two little babies," she continued. "He just happened to look over at his house and notice a pot of geraniums set out there on the back deck. Then he said to himself, 'Hey now. Those flowers is drying slam out. I best get some water.' And was he looking for trouble when he lifted his hairy toes out of the lukewarm pool and set off across the grass?"

"No," I said. "I know our backyard is safe. I've walked barefoot in our grass many a time. In fact, now that this strange thing has happened right in our county, I bet it's even safer for us to do that. What's the chances of that happening again in this area? I bet that water felt real good. I bet it made him feel like a young'un himself. Simple pleasures are always best. Maybe we should get us one of those kiddie pools. Sunday afternoons we could fill 'er up and sit in it together. Just the two of us enjoying the privacy of our own backyard. What do you say? That's an idea now isn't it?"

"I think you're crazy," said Delma. Then she just sat there for a minute shaking her head back and forth with her eyes closed. When she stopped, she opened her eyes right into mine and said, "You must think I'm crazy too. Do you imagine this man was wondering to himself, 'How about that next blue moon? Isn't one due to show up any day now?' as he made his way toward the house?"

"Nah," I said. "He was probably enjoying the way grass tickles under your feet. He was probably thinking what a good job he had done setting out that seed last fall."

"Don't you see that's exactly the kind of opportunity that snake was looking for?" Delma stabbed at the air in front of her with her index finger. "A snake in the grass is hoping that somebody won't be expecting it. That's when it most wants to strike. Being unprepared doesn't protect you from anything. Ask Regina Clayton. Ask Michael Clayton. Oh yeah, that's right, you can't. They're dead. Well, how about Lucy Macrae? She's suffered pain and humiliation, but she's still alive. No, better yet, ask Bernadette, the new Mrs. Woody Macrae, the woman who stole Lucy's husband right out from under her. There are snakes everywhere! Of that I have no doubt. Just because you can't see it doesn't mean a thing. That man couldn't tell the moon had turned blue. It was broad daylight. But he could feel the prick of those fangs just the same. Then he knew, but by then the damage was done."

"Well it is lucky the snake bit him and not his children," I said, trying to remind Delma of the bright side. "He'll get over that snake bite. He looked plenty strong to me."

"But who knows what it's done to his insides?" Delma's hands shook as she fumbled with her cigarette pack. After a couple of tries with the lighter she looked at me and asked, "Want to flick my Bic?" Then she laughed once, "Ha!" like she didn't really mean it.

"Just what is a blue moon anyway?" I said in an attempt to ward her curiosity off in a different direction. "It doesn't really turn blue, does it?"

"I think it has something to do with a ring around it," Delma said. "But I'm not really sure."

"Well I hate to bring up a sore subject, but I am starving. What's for dinner?"

"Grapefruit," Delma said. "Half of one, with a dab of cottage cheese and little bit of lettuce. If you're really lucky, I'll throw in a slice or two of pineapple."

"I got to have more than that for supper. Lifting bags of dog food all day long takes a lot out of a man. Some of those bags weigh forty pounds and the forklift can't do it all. I lost count of the number of trucks we loaded today."

"It's what I'm having." Delma reached out and gave the empty lazy Susan a hard spin.

"You can't stop feeding me, Delma."

"It won't hurt you to fend for yourself now and then. I can't be around food all the time and stick to this diet."

"I liked you the way you were, sugar pie." Which was the truth. I have always been attracted to big women and good cooks.

She tilted her head back and looked at me out of the bottom of her eyes, "That's what they all say."

"But I mean it," I said. "After all, have I ever lied to you? Ever since we first started being sweethearts in fifth grade, have I ever lied?"

"How would I know if you had?" Delma said. "How could I tell if you were lying through your teeth right now for instance?"

For a minute, I felt my ears getting hot, like I really was guilty of something. Which was downright ridiculous seeing's all I was asking for was a little food on my plate. "Baby cakes, haven't I always said 'more of everything' about you and your cooking?"

"I know what you've said, Troy. But how do I know what you honestly believe? It's the wife that's always the last to know, but I'm sure she's been listening to whatever has been coming out of her husband's mouth the whole time."

For a minute there she really had me stumped. So, in my thinking, I tried to take a little step back. While I was doing that, I also took a good long look at the woman I had thought I had known for almost my whole life. The woman I had promised to love and honor and cherish until death do us part.

I must say, Delma was not looking too good to me right then. There was the hair for starters. But then there was also her skin. It was starting to sag. She had lost the fullness of flesh that I loved. What was I going to do with a wife who thought she was living inside a country-western song and I was the man who done her wrong? For the first time that evening, Delma let the room fill with silence. We sat there looking across the table at each other for a long time. The room got still and dark. I could hear the clock ticking over the stove. I found myself wondering what was in the cupboard. What I might be able to scrape together to eat before I went on to bed.

I was still wondering when I realized the moon had risen in the window behind me. It must have been full because the light was so bright, but I wasn't sure because I thought we'd already had a full moon that month. It was reflected in Delma's empty white plate and shone across her face as if somebody was holding a flashlight right at her head and nothing else. Her eyes looked like two wet pebbles. The light hit on the silver streaks in her hair, while the dark parts merged with the shadows. I stared for so long, I started to imagine I could see those lumps moving, shifting, sliding—ever so slow. I imagined that each snake caught inside Delma's head had gotten hungry and had started looking for food, burrowing its way through her scalp. That Delma's hair was really a nest of snakes coiled all over and waiting. I wondered what it was that Michael Clayton saw the last time he looked at his wife. Did he stop to think she was still a good-looking woman? Was he hungry and wondering what she had fixed for dinner?

I knew all this thinking was getting out of hand. I needed to stop. I needed to just do my part like I had said. So I broke the silence with the only thing I could think to say, "Peaches, maybe you should stop reading the paper for awhile."

"Nobody likes the blue jay either," Delma said in a quiet voice. "People are all the time complaining that they're too loud. Obnoxious. They don't ever get any credit for the way they warn the other birds and help scare off snakes from their nests. Nobody ever thinks how hard it can be to be brave when it doesn't even make you look good."

I thought maybe I saw a tear trickle down Delma's left cheek, but I wasn't sure. I realized I had finally lost my appetite. It was as if I had swallowed a chunk of liquid cement and it was starting to set up inside my body—my whole body, not just my stomach. I tried to relax but with each breath I felt myself growing heavier, stony and stiff, like my veins were full of something hard and permanent. My legs, my stomach, my chest, my arms, my shoulders, my neck, and even my jaw—they all felt as if they had been cut from one big piece of rock. I was amazed I could still blink. All I had wanted was Salisbury steak and mashed potatoes. As I sat there in my chair doubting I'd ever be able to move again, I knew that, while Delma wasn't right tonight, one night she will be. One night she'll be able to say, "See, I told you."

PEARL NEWBY

*a widow, who frequently visits the country-club
neighborhood where the Claytons lived*

1980

Nobody really noticed until I put lights on them at Christmas, but I
planted them in the front yard right after Regina Clayton went crazy that
August killing herself and her husband to boot. My husband, Bobby, had
just passed a few months before. I found him one morning keeled over
in the vegetable patch he kept out back. That was three long years ago.
Gone in an instant is what the doctor said. A stroke. One minute he
had been tending tender green shoots of lettuce and peppers and the
next laying there sprawled out with his eyes turned blank and staring
toward heaven.

At the time, it seemed like death and dying was everywhere. I felt
knocked down, puny and weak, and just plain old. Not sixty-five but
maybe ninety or a hundred. I couldn't help but feel myself withering
up in a world where God could take from you so quick, without a
warning of any kind. And where an upright church-going woman could
destroy any chance at happiness for her and her family—gone too in
an instant—with their young son only thirteen. Every day I woke up
thinking about how everything that was alive was actually dying at the

75

same time. I can see now that I had seized hold of that half-empty cup and just couldn't seem to let go. I was trying to though, which is why I decided to check out the "Grand Opening Sale" for the brand-new Woolworth's which moved into the movie theater's old spot in the shopping center at the A&P. I was back in the home furnishings section working on cheering myself up when they caught my fancy. They beckoned to me from one of the back aisles—two large artificial trees. "Hello, Pearl Newby," they said. "We are for you."

Ficus was what was written on the ticket. But I didn't care what their name was. I was so carried away with all those pretty pointy green leaves and all those possibilities that went off in my head like so many lights turning on, I was practically blinded by my own inspiration. My yard had presented a real dilemma to me ever since Bobby died. He came from a farming family and loved any excuse to get his hands dirty. The chicken factory was where he made his living. But out in our yard in an old pair of dungarees, planting, weeding, and watering— that was where he really came alive. I loved to watch his thick fingers sprinkle seeds and handle fragile young seedlings with the delicacy of a soft breath of wind.

I myself never had much of a green thumb and grew suspicious that anything I buried under dirt would never be seen again. But not Bobby. Bobby had faith. He trusted and it worked. Not only did all his seeds sprout, they grew big and strong right before my eyes, despite my secret misgivings. We'd always had tons of vegetables in season and our front yard was the envy of the neighborhood.

It wasn't a fancy yard, mind you, but the way it looked said that everything was extra-healthy and well cared for and had been that way for a long time. Even though my son, Eugene, and my grandson, Bobby Eugene Jr., kept up with mowing the grass and clipping the bushes, it only took a couple of weeks before the yard started to look like an old widow woman who was still going through the motions but had lost all her spunk. I let the garden go to weeds. And then lightning struck the huge oak that used to sit to one side of the lot and shaded practically the whole front yard. Of course it died too and I had to deal with the mess of getting it all cleaned up. In some of the upper branches, they found a nest where a family of robins had set up house-keeping every year for as long as I could remember. It took them two days to dig up that stump. Amazed by how long that tree had lived, Bobby Eugene counted the rings and kept on about how old it had been. I was mostly impressed by how quickly it died.

So there I was. A recent retiree, who after forty years of putting her time in at Reynolds Furniture Factory had been looking forward to enjoying her Golden Years. But instead I was saddled with death and destruction everywhere. And before I could even catch my breath, my next-door neighbor Thelma started pestering me with what was I fixing to do with that yard of mine? Everybody knows that besides playing Bingo, going to church regular, and taking care of grandbabies, retirees are supposed to have real nice yards. I took to standing on the sidewalk across the street and staring at my front yard. I thought maybe a little distance would help me get a better perspective.

It was neat and clean. Two little postage stamps of grass split evenly by the walk leading up to the front porch. But mostly I kept seeing what was not there. The missing oak that used to have a tire swing hanging from one of the lower branches. The kids loved to play on that thing. I thought it had added a nice, homey touch. That old tree was so big everybody commented on it. But after it was gone, I just couldn't work up any enthusiasm to plant another. A new one wouldn't look like much of anything. It would be years before it was big enough to make a statement, and I was getting old. I didn't have all that time to wait.

Meanwhile, Thelma had already installed an elaborate cement

fountain in front of her picture window. She bought it from some man on the way to the beach. It liked to tore out the bottom of my car trunk it was so heavy. But I have to admit, it was a real novelty the way she got it hooked up so water ran out of the cherub's mouth all summer long. She put in lots of impatiens and begonias around the base of the fountain and in front of the shrubs that lined the foundation of the house, so it did have a certain air about it. Of course, some of the neighbors made jokes about hope springing eternal and wondered if this was supposed to be some kind of sign for Benny Reece, the man Thelma had her eye on at the time. However, I pointed out that how could Thelma's fountain stand for eternal hope when she had to shut it off every winter on account of the cold weather which would make it freeze up and burst? Which was, of course, a drawback to Thelma's whole yard scheme because during the winter months, when you need cheering up the most, it looked all dried up and sad.

Mary Jane's winter solution was to drape little white lights on the latticed arbor that arched over the front gate to her white picket fence. You might have noticed—she still lives right down the street at the corner. It looked like fairyland all winter long. And in the spring and summer when her roses are climbing and blooming their heads off everywhere, it is pure-T-perfection. But also a lot of trouble. Fertilizing, pruning, mulching, and mixing up all that spray. Some people have suggested Mary Jane's husband, Harvey, might have gotten his cancer from inhaling all that poison she had him douse those roses with—every ten days all blooming season long for years and years. But Mary Jane said they don't know what they're talking about because Harvey got cancer in his prostate not his lungs. And besides, that spray barely kept the Japanese beetles away, so it could hardly hurt a big man who certainly didn't try to eat the leaves. Mary Jane took on spraying the roses herself and acted real casual while she did it in front of the neighbors, didn't even wear one of those special masks. I knew she was trying to prove her point, but I've smelled that spray and I thought she was foolish. It may not kill you, but just a whiff left a terrible taste in your mouth so I couldn't help but wonder what it did to the rest of you.

You know, retired or not, everybody's yard says something about them, and I've spent a lot of time thinking about Regina Clayton's yard and what it said about her. I always thought it was kind of strange, but the new owners have left it just the way it was. Mostly there were just some skinny pine trees, prickly green shrubbery, and lots of pine straw. It wasn't much to look at even though she did have those shrunken trees growing in pots along the walk. A row of dwarves, pruned to stunt their growth so they became gnarled, twisted-looking minia-tures. Still, the overall effect of Regina Clayton's yard was quiet and woodsy. If you were to go Sunday riding in her neighborhood, her yard would probably just pass by as a blur of green in the corner of your eye. The house was real modern, built low to the ground, without any windows showing in the front. Instead, there was a tall brick wall that hugged one side of the house and wrapped around it like a secret, hid-ing the entrance from the street.

It was the Reynolds' yard I always wanted to see. They lived right across the street from the Claytons. Jerry Reynolds was the owner of Reynolds Furniture and my old boss. From what I've heard, he and his wife, Pat, came from money. I must admit I get real tickled seeing how the other half really lives. So I always turn my head to look at their yard even after we've circled the cul-de-sac and are riding back by because there might be something there I missed the first time. Besides just taking it all in and enjoying it, you never know what kind of tips you might pick up.

In fact, it was the crape myrtles that line the Reynolds' brick walk that provided the inspiration for my own little trees. One Sunday, Thelma and I were out riding around after church. I was feeling kind of blue, and Thelma was doing her best to perk me up. Just as we were passing Regina Clayton's old house—which still to this very day never fails to remind me of what she did in there to herself and her husband, and what made her do it, and what's going to happen to that poor boy of theirs—I turned my head real quick to look at the Reynolds' house and *bingo*! Those crape myrtles just jumped out at me. That, I thought, was exactly what I needed—some smallish decorative trees.

Only when I saw the artificial ones at Woolworth's several days later, my mind immediately recognized their vast superiority. Crape myrtles had to be pruned and looked just like a handful of sticks in the winter. I wanted fresh green all year long without the prickles of fir or holly. And that was exactly what I got. I did have to compromise some because they were so expensive—$29.99 each, marked down from $39.99. At that price, I could only afford two. Which meant I couldn't exactly line my front walk with them. But I knew they were worth the money because they were such high quality. The thin greyish trunks were really sturdy. And the leaves, so many of them, all made out of a durable weather-proof fabric and colored in two tones—a vivid bright green accented with a cheerful light yellow green. I was sure the shading cost extra, but it made them so natural looking it was worth every penny. So I decided to go with quality rather than quantity. This was something that I thought Bobby would have approved of.

To get the maximum impact from these fine trees, I had them planted smack-dab in the centers of my two postage stamps. I have always admired the symmetry of formal gardens. And to highlight the geometrical nature of my planting, I put round mounds of those smooth white, moon-glow pebbles around the base of the trees and in narrow strips along the edges of the walk. So far, no one has copied my eye-catching display. But I'm willing to bet that one Sunday in the not-too-distant future, Thelma and I will ride by some variation of my yard in a distant neighborhood.

My son Eugene planted the trees for me since the ground was too hard for me to shovel. He is a sweet boy and often reminds me of his daddy. I kept him company while he dug and couldn't resist looking for Bobby in the movement of Eugene's strong hands. Only Eugene's hands don't have the same light grace his daddy's did, which made me even more aware of what was missing in the front yard. The earth Eugene uncovered was solid red clay, the kind that stuck to your shoes and got tracked all over the house. It was the color of old blood—red turning to dark, blackish brown. This had me seeing the two holes Eugene dug as two small graves, and I started to question everything all over again. In fact I was so distracted I ended up letting Eugene plant them a little deeper than I had intended. So they turned out a tad on the short side.

But it was for the best, because I could reach all the branches real easy for my seasonal changes. Like I said, at Christmas I put lights in them—those big, old fashioned ones in lots of colors. Some smart aleck claimed it looked like two UFOs hovering in the dark over my yard as if aliens were trying to peek in my front windows. But I liked them. I thought they were festive and I'll probably keep putting them up each year until I get tired of the way they look. They reminded me of two big beautiful Christmas tree ornaments. And at nighttime, I imagined they were floating in the air, suspended on the invisible thread of my good faith alone.

In March, I moved all the limbs so they looked as if they were blowing in the wind. And in June, I scrunched all those branches down into tight balls and attached plastic roses to them with bread bag twisties. You couldn't see the twisties from the road, so it looked like the trees suddenly burst into showy pink and rose red blooms—without so much as one drop of spray now. Another plus that came with artificial was that nothing faded or withered. So those roses stayed perky all summer long whether it rained or not. Sometimes I snuck out early in the morning and rearranged them as if new blooms had popped out overnight. With my stay-fresh flowers I didn't have to redecorate until I was ready for Halloween. That was when I pulled the branches back out and hung scary ghosts from them. Eugene brought me bales of hay that we set out under the trees with pumpkins and bunches of Mexican corn. There was even a painted wooden witch down by the mailbox. She really added some drama to the scene. I found her on another trip to the beach with Thelma. Thelma has tried her best to convince me that painted yard art is tacky. But I think she could be a mite jealous because that cement fountain is too heavy to move around, so she's stuck with just one seasonal theme.

Anyway, I can't believe how much joy and satisfaction those trees have brought me. And I will never forget the first time I decorated for Easter. I was hanging dozens and dozens of bright plastic eggs all over the branches. So I walked over and stood on the sidewalk across the street to get the full effect. New grass had grown to cover the place where the old oak had stood and a row of Bobby's daffodils had popped up and bloomed in front of the shrubbery without any assistance from me at all. I found myself humming, *Christ the Lord is risen today* . . .

I was just about to decide that things didn't look so bad, when a robin lit on one of the top branches of the ficus on the left. A gentle breeze was rocking the eggs. So when my eyes teared up in the bright light, crystals of pink, green, yellow, orange, purple, and robin's egg blue danced across the grass and into the sun—making me want to sing out to the whole neighborhood, *al-le-lu-ia!*

JACKIE HUNT

twelve-year-old daughter of Bonnie and Jeff Hunt,
who lives down the street from the Claytons' house

I met tragedy for the first time in Dee Dee Blanchard's backyard. My name's Jacqueline Holloway Hunt, but I'm asking all my friends to just call me Jack. Dee Dee calls me Jackie—that's my old nickname.

"Jackie," she said. "Would you like to come to my house tomorrow?"

Suddenly, my life was looking up. "Sure," I said. And that was it. Open Sesame. Somehow I had figured out the password without even realizing it. Right away, I had that sort of icky excited but nervous feeling. I was relieved because I was beginning to wonder. Dee Dee had already asked Kelly, Beth, and Renee. So I was starting to feel left out.

I was afraid of becoming a loser. That can happen really quick around here. I've seen it and it isn't pretty. You go along thinking you're all right but all along people are rolling their eyes at the things you do and say and snickering behind your back. It's terrible and it can happen to anybody—even someone without big zits or greasy hair. And me, I'm not even a teenager yet. I don't want to have already blown it before I even get to any of the good stuff.

Dee Dee is already very popular. She's real little and something about her makes everyone want to stand around and watch her. She's so little, she said, because she was born premature and almost died. There's nothing really wrong with her now, she just hasn't caught up with everybody else. Somehow I think her popularity is connected to her littleness. When I say *little*, I really mean it. I'm tall for my age and people used to tease me about my baby fat. I feel like the Jolly Green Giant next to Dee Dee, who is fragile like a bird with little bony arms and legs and a long skinny blonde ponytail. I want to be little like that so the older kids will pick me up and swing me around, and I can laugh a little tinkling laugh and turn my head back so my long skinny ponytail touches my little round bottom.

But instead, I'm stuck with baby fat weighing me down and what is commonly referred to as a "bowl" cut. My hair is dirty blonde, which really means not all that blonde but kind of dingy brown. I try not to think about it. Mama says that what is important is to try your best to do the most with what you've got. Whatever that means. She just wears bright red lipstick all the time and teases her hair up real high. Somehow I don't think that would work for me.

So I am just one of the regular kids in this neighborhood. There's nothing all that special about me, except when it comes to playing four square because almost nobody can beat me. Dee Dee, on the other hand, is like chocolate pudding. She just isn't around all that much. The Blanchards live in a pink brick house that is right here at the Riley Country Club. Their house is the one almost at the top of the big hill. It's next to the clubhouse, which sits up there at the very tip-top. One time when I asked Mama what kind of house the Blanchards' is, she twisted her lips and raised her eyebrows and had to think for a minute before she said, "Well, I guess it's French Provincial. If I *had* to say."

I am interested in all things French on account of being named for Jacqueline Boo-V-A Kennedy, who's now just Jackie O. Mama always says "Jacqueline" with her teeth kind of clenched. Sometimes I wonder if she named me that just so she'd have an excuse to talk like Aunt Lindon who lives in Winston-Salem, is married to a lawyer—Uncle David—and paints her poodle's toenails to match her own.

Dee Dee's daddy is a lawyer too. And the Blanchards have their own swimming pool, fenced in so you can't see it from the street. I guess that's why Dee Dee hardly ever goes to the pool at the clubhouse. Now that I know what Dee Dee's pool looks like—small, square, deep-deep blue, and perfectly smooth and still like a big cube of blueberry Jell-O—sometimes I picture myself lying on my back on a big red raft and staring up at the sun in the center of the Blanchards' backyard.

But while you wouldn't have any nasty boys bombing you from the edge of the pool and trying to knock you off your raft (which they wouldn't even allow you to bring to the club pool), it would be lonely too, I think. And what if you started to drown and Mrs. Blanchard was inside vacuuming? There wouldn't be anybody to save you. Because they might have a pool, but they don't have any lifeguards.

I wasn't sure about going to Dee Dee's. I didn't know what I would have to say to somebody who was so little and cute. I was afraid there would be a lot of those awkward pauses in the conversation. She made me feel so big and slow—almost retarded. But one day Beth and I were out riding our bikes and a few kids were skateboarding on the Blanchards' wide white cement driveway. Dee Dee and her older brother were out there. So we stopped and Dee Dee just came up to me and asked me over.

Dee Dee only asked one girl to visit at a time, which did make you feel special but also meant you had to go alone. My mama wasn't really friends with Dee Dee's mama so that added to the strangeness. Even though I was only going just up the street, it felt like more. I was kind of dreading the whole thing.

After I got back from swimming lessons that day of the visit, I put on my white T-shirt with the navy blue bands around the sleeves and neck. "Camp Cheerio" it said in a matching blue arch across the front left corner. I remember because it was new then and now it has a red juice stain right down the front. But at the time it was sparkly white—not a spot on it. I put on a pair of short culottes. Mama said they're French too. They look like a skirt but have a split in between so they were really shorts. This pair was navy with red ladybugs all over it. My little sister Suzanne has them now. They were hand-me-downs from Cousin Betty, but they had hardly been worn when I got them so nobody could tell at the time.

I didn't even think about shoes. It wasn't until the black pavement started burning my feet as I walked to Dee Dee's that I remembered. But nobody wears shoes in the summer—only grownups—unless you're going to church or junior garden club meetings.

I was already in front of Mrs. Witherspoon's house, which was two doors down the street from ours, when I stopped to check my heels. They weren't that dirty since they'd been soaking in chlorine all morning. So I walked on. Past the Taylors' and the Greens', and Mr. and Mrs. Wright's big white mansion with the black iron boy holding a ring in the front yard. I didn't feel any different when I got to the bend in the road where the Reynolds and the Claytons lived because it was a month or so before Mrs. Clayton did her killing and changed our neighborhood into a totally different place. Back then, all I had to worry about was what I was going to say at Dee Dee's. I felt right at home walking along on my own street with all the tall skinny pines that surround all the houses and line the road and look so big and strong and rubbery and weak all at the same time. I knew all the neighbors' names—the adults, the children, and all the pets. I could even predict exactly what each family would give out for treats at Halloween.

I had no idea of what was in store. I thought tragedy was when somebody loved somebody who didn't love them back on Mama's soap opera, *As the World Turns,* or when our big black tom cat Beau got hit by a car and had to be put to sleep. I didn't know anything. I was just minding my own business. I stopped after I passed the Gibsons', whose television blew up last summer during a big thunderstorm, and waited for a foursome to tee off. There are golf rules you must *abide by* when you live around a golf course. Daddy keeps drilling them into our heads. He also insists on reminding us that *you never know where the ball is going to go.* While I waited, I thought about that big ball of fire that rolled into the Gibsons' living room. That must have been quite a surprise. Who would have ever thought something like that could happen right here?

I got to Dee Dee's right on time, which was good because I was trying to be on my best behavior. But then I had a small dilemma in their front yard when I realized I didn't know which door I should knock on. I usually go to the side door or the back door at all my friends' houses. But I didn't know how formal this visit was supposed to be.

I hesitated. Where was Dee Dee? Wasn't she looking out, expecting me and all? What if I had the wrong day? What if I had the wrong day and ended up at the wrong door? What if Dee Dee's older brother, Rich, was snickering behind one of the curtains, watching me become a loser right in the middle of their wide white driveway?

I had to make a move. The rough cement scratched the bottom of my feet as I headed toward the garage. The front door was just too far away and the pinky white steps were built up all high and mighty like you were going to make some kind of grand entrance. I just couldn't take that. Something like, "Avon calling," was bound to slip out of my mouth and then Mrs. Blanchard would think I was really strange.

All it took was a little knock on the back door and Mrs. Blanchard opened right up. "Well hello, Jackie," she said. I didn't even bother telling her about my new nickname I was so grateful.

"Hi, Mrs. Blanchard," I said. "Is Dee Dee here?"

"She sure is. Come on in."

I noticed right away that their house smelled funny. All houses have their own smell when you first walk in, though most of the time after that first whiff you don't notice it again until you go out and come back in. But the Blanchards' smelled real funny and I kept on noticing. It smelled musty. Musty, and maybe like *mothballs*—something my mama never uses.

"Dee Dee, honey, your company is here," called Mrs. Blanchard. I checked her out real quick while I stood there on the beige linoleum floor in the kitchen with my nose full of the Blanchards' weird house smell. Mrs. Blanchard was wearing a beige polyester pantsuit. She was pretty tall, bigger than my mama. And her hair was real long. It was curled and teased and poufed up in the front without any clips to hold it back. Strands of black peeked in and out from under clumps of frosted blonde. She came back from the kitchen doorway which led to the rest of the house and looked down at me and offered me the barest hint of a smile. I smiled back. And then I smiled some more, just kept on smiling.

At long last, little Dee Dee appeared and saved me from having to make any more conversation with her mother. "Hey," we both said, quick and kind of nervous.

"Now y'all go play, Dee Dee. Why don't you take Jackie and show her your room?" Mrs. Blanchard suggested as she filled a tall smoke-colored glass with ice from the automatic dispenser they had on the outside of their refrigerator door.

"Come on." Dee Dee turned back through the kitchen door and led me with her ponytail into their living room. It was so big and dark it felt like a cave. The white shag carpeting tickled my toes. They had a monster-sized television that was turned on to *The Big Valley,* one of my favorite shows. Right in front of the TV was a huge off-white sectional sofa. "Contemporary" was what Mama would call it. Everything in there looked store-bought. I wondered didn't Dee Dee's grandma have anything to pass down to Dee Dee's mama? Was everything they had brand-new?

Dee Dee walked over to the sliding glass doors and pointed out to their backyard. "There's the pool," she said. I walked over and took a look. I tried to act like I was only a little interested. But I nearly gasped when I saw how pretty it was. The water was so still and blue, it made me think of a big shiny sapphire. Just imagine living every single day with that right outside your back door.

Bright waves of light dazzled my eyes as we walked on past the TV and down the dark hall that led to Dee Dee's room. "This is my room," said Dee Dee, as she looked at me.

"Oh, wow," I said. "This is really nice."

"Pink is my favorite color." Dee Dee came to stand beside me so she could look at her room from my perspective. "My bed is new," she said and walked over and sat right down among all those ruffled pink and white pillows and stuffed animals.

"I've always wanted a canopy," I said. I did want a canopy, but I hated pink. I was thinking I couldn't stand sleeping in a pinky pink room with ruffles all over the place—at the windows, on the canopy, on the pillows, on the bedspread, on the dust ruffle, on the chair in the corner, all around the dressing table skirt. Couldn't stand it, especially with that funky smell filling up my head every time I took a breath. Pink, pink, pink and stink, stink, stink. Pink flowers were everywhere and they weren't even roses but some other kind of flower I didn't recognize. Probably one of those kinds somebody had made up.

"That's my old dollhouse," she said, pointing one of her little pink fingers toward the corner of the room.

"Oh," I said. "I have a dollhouse too. Of course, I don't play in mine anymore either." I walked over and peeked through the windows. Molded Father and Mother dolls leaned stiffly across the kitchen table, propped up by each other's forehead.

Dee Dee slid off the bed and walked over to her dressing table. "I have lots of lipsticks," she said. "Would you like to try one? My big sister Candace lets me have ones she gets tired of. Here," she said as she slipped off the top of a gold tube and twisted its bottom until a shocking pink tip poked out.

"You first," I said as I inched toward her.

Dee Dee turned to the dressing table mirror and expertly smudged a dark little pink bow over her pale little pink lips. She turned back and smiled. Her white teeth gleamed strangely in her pale face. When I got up close to her I realized she had lots of tiny freckles scattered all over. I took the tube from her and looked in the mirror and tried to act like I knew what I was doing. The lipstick smeared and went on thicker than I expected. I had a ragged edge all along my bottom lip. I didn't look like myself. My lips were gross—huge and thick. My eyes shrunk into two beady dots that almost disappeared and my forehead seemed to grow even larger. Mama had already cut my bangs so short they looked like they had shrunk in the wash. Whenever she did this she would say, "My what beautiful eyebrows you have." But my brother Hayden always laughed and called me "Teepee Head."

I looked at Dee Dee and wiggled my eyebrows. She giggled and handed me a tissue. And then I giggled too. Wiping at my lips, I said, "So where are your Barbies?"

Dee Dee looked at me blankly. "I don't have any," she said.

That stumped me. Everybody had Barbies. What did Dee Dee do?

She suddenly perked up. "I haven't shown you my closet yet," she said. "It's lined with cedar."

"Oh," I said.

She walked over and opened a little pink door and flipped on a light. "Look," she said, "I have lots of storage space. And everything is perfectly safe. My daddy had all our closets lined with cedar. My sister and my brother have them too. Moths can't get in your closets if they're lined with cedar."

"Oh," I said again and looked at the rows and rows of little Dee Dee outfits. Then I looked back at Dee Dee waiting for her next moment of inspiration. The walk-in closet did offer a break from the Blanchards' house smell. It smelled clean and fresh, like the pine-scented cleaner my Mama mopped the floor with. I was tempted to give up and stay in the closet, but I also wanted to somehow hurry up this visit so I could go on back to my house and play Barbies with Suzanne. And fill my head up with our house's smell—which actually didn't smell like anything to me, just normal air. That's the thing about house smells—you can't ever smell your own.

Dee Dee showed me a couple of her new outfits by holding them up to herself like my mama does when she's thinking about buying something at the Belk's store downtown. But soon she got tired of that, too, and we went into the living room and watched TV for a while. *Mayberry* was on, which was not one of my favorites. I would much rather watch *Bewitched* or *The Addams Family* any day. So I was more interested in the Blanchards' sofa than I was the show. It was big and soft and felt like you were sitting on a marshmallow. Our sofa at home was covered in shiny smooth cotton with these bouquets of flowers and ivy trailing all over it. "Chintz" was what Mama called it and she gritted her teeth a little when she said that too.

Mrs. Blanchard brought us some Pepsi in two of those tall smoky glasses. I was scared to death I was going to spill something on that off-white sofa. I started seeing it happen so many times in my head I had to put my drink down on their big glass coffee table. I swear, everything in that room looked like it might break or get stained real easy. I was a little disappointed too because I had hoped for a chance to try out their ice dispenser. Nobody else I knew had one yet. It was a little cubbyhole cut into the outside of the refrigerator. You just set your glass on the shelf and pressed it against something and it filled your glass right up. The ice was different, too—round with a hole in the middle. I got my tongue stuck in one of them while we were watching TV and just had to let it melt off. By then I had a chill. Their house was awfully cold in the first place, with all that air conditioning. It felt like the grocery store. And having that ice cube pressed up against the roof of my mouth for so long had cooled off my insides too.

I started to stare out the sliding glass door and to think how warm it looked outside, and Dee Dee finally got the message. "Want to go look at the pool?" she asked and set her glass down in a wet ring on the table.

"Sure." I shrugged my shoulders a little so it would look like I didn't care too much, like I wasn't really asking for anything.

Dee Dee walked over and slid the door open by leaning her whole weight on it. She opened it just a crack. I could barely squeeze through. "Look out for Prince," she said while I was busy trying to get the door closed behind me.

I turned just in time to see a very large Doberman charging towards us. "He won't hurt you," Dee Dee said. Prince came to an abrupt stop and sank to his haunches inches from my feet. Then he began a deep rumbling growl that was sort of under his breath but not really. "Prince is a sweetheart," Dee Dee claimed as she draped her fragile little self all over his broad back and wrapped her twiggy arms around his thick black neck. "Just don't move too quickly," she said as she got off Prince and headed over toward the pool.

I froze. I couldn't decide if Prince wanted to kill me or if he'd be content just to keep me from moving off that spot. He stared. And I stared back. I used my staring-contest stare. I could always outlast Suzanne. But there was no question who would win this one. Looking into Prince's eyes I got the spooky feeling that he was really thinking about something—making some kind of plan or sizing me up. I kept telling myself over and over not to be nervous because dogs could smell fear and it would make them bite you. I also started to get really upset with all the other girls who had already had their visit at Dee Dee's. No one had even mentioned Prince. You would have thought they might have said something. Suddenly Prince turned and trotted off toward some bushes along the back fence.

Dee Dee was waiting by the edge of the pool. "This is our pool," she said. "And that over there is my brother's basketball goal. And that's my old swing set and jungle gym."

I couldn't concentrate. The entire time I spent in the Blanchards' backyard, the hair on the back of my neck prickled and stood up. I felt like one of those animals being stalked on *Wild Kingdom*. I tried to keep Prince in the corner of my eye at all times and mentally rehearsed throwing my elbow around my neck to protect my jugular. That's what Daddy always said to do if a dog tried to attack you. If they really wanted to hurt you they'd go for your throat.

"Let's put our feet in," Dee Dee said. We sat down on the edge. Our feet made small ripples on the water's surface and then everything was still again. The pressure of the visit was starting to get to me. Sweat trickled down my back. Between worrying about what to say and how not to make any moves that might appear to be too sudden, I was worn out. I was trying to figure out how soon I could politely say I had to go home for supper when Dee Dee spilled the beans.

"I know a secret," she announced. "My mother had a miscarriage." The tip of her ponytail brushed the wings of her shoulder blades as she turned to look at me. "The baby slipped right out while she was going to the bathroom and there was nothing she could do but flush it away and never see it again. The baby would have come before me. It would have been after Candy and Rich. I'd still be the youngest," she said and looked at me with a question. She blinked but kept looking.

Sweat trickled down my back. The pool pump hummed. The air conditioner clicked on. I had to break her pale blue gaze and stare down at the deeper blue water. I was searching for some kind of answer when I realized I had lost sight of Prince. Trying to look casual, I started searching over my shoulder.

"How big was it?" I asked while wrenching my neck in the opposite direction.

"Tiny," Dee Dee said. "It didn't get stuck."

"Oh." I turned back around and realized Prince was quietly watching me from across the pool. Our eyes met, and I slid mine back to the surface of the water. I tried to picture what had happened to the Blanchard baby. We had flushed my brother Hayden's dead goldfish down the toilet one time. Suzanne had cried and said she was sure that fish wanted a burial. "No, honey," Mama said. "Fish love water. It's where they're born to be."

But who would put a baby out to sea in toilet water? Mrs. Blanchard must have been really sick at the time not to save her dead baby from the sewer. In fourth grade we visited the water treatment plant, and it was not a nice place. How awful. No wonder Dee Dee was so little. Probably stole her appetite just to think about it. And her mama, she probably couldn't get her mind off the child she flushed away. Wonder where Mr. Blanchard was when this happened? Somehow Mrs. Blanchard must have been left all alone. While he had been off interpreting the law for one of his important clients, he had lost one of his own children right here at home. That was sad. And I felt bad but I really didn't know what I could say. After all, I was just a kid.

"I better go home now." I pulled my feet from the water. They were shriveled and pink.

"Okay," said Dee Dee. She led me over to the gate at the end of their driveway and cracked it so I could squeeze through. Prince came up behind her and bumped her legs.

When I was safe on the other side, I turned back to look in Dee Dee's eyes through the chain link. "Thanks for having me over," I said as the metal lock clanked into place.

"Sure," she said. "See you later."

The warm pavement felt good to my feet as I walked home. They dried off and weren't so shriveled by the time I got to the bend where the Claytons and the Reynolds and the Gibsons lived. I didn't know then that about a month later Mrs. Clayton would kill herself and Mr. Clayton because Mr. Clayton had been unfaithful. My mind was full of blood spreading like a dark red storm cloud in a white toilet bowl with a tiny pink tadpole baby in the center. I don't remember even looking at the Claytons' house as I walked by.

I was so happy when I finally got back home. I felt like I had been on a really long trip, like I had been gone for days and days. When I came in the back door, I found Mama in the kitchen fixing supper. She was humming beach music and smiling. "Hey J-bird," she said.

"Come dance with your mama." She grabbed my hands and started to shuffle her feet the way she'd taught me to do when you wanted to shag. She started to sing, "With this ring, I promise I'll always love you, always love you." We danced around and around the kitchen floor. She pulled me in toward her and then pushed me back out and spun me around. Again and again, I looked into her eyes to see if there was anything I had been missing. But all I ever saw was my own reflection shining back down on me.

I've never told Mama about Mrs. Blanchard's lost baby. I don't know what she'd say. Sometimes I find myself watching her. Mama looks and acts the same as she always has. She still says "Jacqueline" with her teeth kind of clenched and cuts my bangs too short. And sometimes she still likes to get me to dance with her in the kitchen before supper. But the truth is you can never really be too sure of your mama and what kind of secrets she has. She might flush your brother or sister down the toilet without letting anybody ever see them, or she might be real sad and mad at your daddy and kill him and herself without ever giving anybody else so much as even a chance to stop her.

BUCKY MACRAE

a friend of Mike Jr.

Hunting season, 1977

This past summer, Mike Clayton and I both turned thirteen and lost our daddies. Mike's birthday was in late June and mine in mid-August. August 17. By the time my mama shot a picture of me sitting at the dinner table blowing out a blaze of candles on my favorite kind of snowy white coconut four-layer cake, Mike's mama had pulled the trigger of a Colt .45 and blown the life right outta her and Mike's daddy. Mike lost his daddy to a bullet. I lost mine to a hairdresser with big knockers named Bernadette and her two children, Sissy and Junior. Sissy and Junior are what are known as bastards 'cause nobody knows who their real daddy is. But now it doesn't matter—they've got mine.

All spring and summer, Mike and I had been looking forward to hunting season. Every time we passed each other in the school cafeteria or on the baseball field, Mike would pretend to shoulder an invisible gun, taking aim at the air above our heads. "This is the year, Bucky," he'd say, "Boom!Boom!*Boom!*" Then we'd grin at each other and high five so hard it stung the palm of my hand.

Back then both of us were certain our future was out there waiting for us in the woods in some forgotten corner of Mr. Roosevelt Padgett's

97

land. Though the way things have turned out, I don't imagine Mike's got much interest in squeezing any kind of triggers this fall. He's moved to Charlotte to live with one of his aunts. Last time I saw him was at the funeral. His eyes were open, but when you looked inside you could tell the real Mike was so fast asleep there's no telling when he'd ever wake back up. So I guess you could say when it comes to me and Mike, I am the lucky one. I might not live with my daddy anymore, but he is still around. And he swore to me that nothing was gonna change our plans, that we'd go hunting—father and son—just like he promised.

I'm alone in the woods and there's birds everywhere. Looking for food in the leaves. Hopping around. Squawking, twittering, and chirruping. There's so many, I think, "Where's my gun?" And then I hear this shot boom out in the distance. And all at once the birds lift off the ground and out of the tree branches and the air fills with flapping wings and a big cloud of dust. I want to run, but I can't see where to go. So I crouch down, put my arms over my head. I can't hardly breathe. The sky fills up, a dark feathery thunderhead with shrill cries that peal out across the land and echo deep down inside my chest, the aftershocks rippling out till they numb my fingers and lips.

It's just a dream. I know. I woke up this morning in the same old bed and the same old room I've had ever since I can remember. It's like me and this room are old buddies, laying here together waiting for this day to get started my whole life. And now it's finally here.

Mr. Padgett, the man who owns the land we hunt on, says he can see change coming. A sure sign, he says, is a flock of migrating birds, especially the ones that travel in those huge black vs strung out across the sky. Mr. Padgett's theory is that it all has to do with aerodynamics. He says all those shifting vs and flapping wings are nature's way of sucking the heat right out of the atmosphere. Cool air moves into its place. And, according to Mr. Padgett, change always rides in a pocket of cool air. He says he's seen it, a purple shadow edging fluffy white clouds.

"You mean cumulus?" I once asked.

"Do I mean what?" Mr. Padgett stopped short and gave me a sharp look.

"Well there are all types. You know, there's the skinny, wispy kind that look like unspun cotton candy. And then you've got your dark gray storm kind. They teach you their names in school. The ones that look like big balls of cotton stuck together are called cumulus."

"Cumulus," Mr. Padgett spat, his voice running out from between his lips in a long brown stream of tobacco juice. "Is that right?" He hitched his trousers and looked at me kind of tough. "Suit yourself. You can believe me or figure I'm full of it. Don't make no difference. Can't change change."

I'm not sure what all to think about what Mr. Padgett says, but today I do feel like I'm standing on the edge of *something*. I'm gonna carry that gun in my own two hands and walk next to my father into the woods and come out on the other side. The suspense is killing me. All it takes is the death of one fat bird caught in mid-flight with one true shot aimed from the heart, and I'll be a changed man.

Of course, to most folks, I probably won't look any different. I'll still be kinda small for my age with a big gap between my front teeth and a scar above my left eyebrow where Alton Davies hit me during a stick sword fight in kindergarten. But inside is what counts. Everybody knows that.

While I can smell the bacon my mama's cooking and make out the flannel shirt and jeans and new pair of boots waiting in the early morning shadows on the chair by my dresser, I burrow back under the covers. It feels like Christmas morning. Now that the waiting is almost over, I kind of want to draw it out. When I close my eyes, inside my head I can see earth, a smooth blue ball suspended in space and time, magically floating right where it belongs, right between Venus and Mars just like Ms. Pennington's model of the solar system showed in third grade.

For my older sister, Charlene, turning thirteen was all about getting her ears pierced. I remember her coming home after she had it done. Her ear lobes were so red and swollen from a distance you couldn't even see those little gold balls she wanted so bad. Though something about Charlene's face did look brand new. You'd have thought she had won a million dollars or finally figured out how to trick some boy into falling in love. She acted like she had proof she was special, and soon after that she started wearing pantyhose and talking on the phone all the time and rolling her eyes at everything I say. So the way I figure it, after today, it's just a matter of time before I take up shaving. I plan to use Old Spice. I already have almost half a bottle. I found it in the medicine cabinet after my father moved out. His loss. My gain. That's how I look at it.

I will admit, first time I saw Bernadette she did make a big impression. I had to go into Ida May's Beauty Shop to ask Mama if it would be all right for me to ride my bike over to Alton Davies'. We wanted to camp out in the woods behind his house. I was walking down that long row of pink chairs when I spotted my mama's head suspended between two of the biggest, pointiest hooters I've ever seen in real life. Bernadette was shampooing Mama's hair and something about the angle from where I stood made it look like the back of Mama's head was cradled in the cushioned valley of Bernadette's breasts.

Did you know people get lost in the Grand Canyon all the time— for days—even with a map? I was definitely losing my way in the dark, secret crack that ran down the front of Bernadette's uniform. She had a bunch of the top buttons undone which made it easy for me to see why explorers are so thrilled by the prospect of navigating uncharted territory. I was descending into darkness unknown, think- ing of the fault that runs through California and causes all those earth- quakes. I could feel Bernadette's long spiked nails dig into my scalp. I thought of planets colliding and the earth began to tremble beneath my feet. If I hadn't been so distracted, I might have wondered more about the way her fingers hesitated for just a second over Mama's scalp when somebody asked about Daddy moving out.

"How you and Woody getting along these days?" Annette Dawson is known for sticking her nose where it doesn't belong. She was sit- ting up straight while Ida May pulled sprigs of her hair through what looked like a tight rubber cap. If you ask me, women are strange. The things they think up to do to themselves.

Anyway, I did notice Bernadette's hands stilled as if they suddenly didn't know what to do and something passed over her face that reminded me of a lock clicking into place. Bernadette was new at Ida May's, so she hadn't known who we were any better than we had known her. But she recovered quickly, wrapping a towel around Mama's hair and easing up the tilt of her chair.

"I don't know." Mama's voice was tired. She shrugged her shoul- ders. "I guess we'll just have to wait and see."

"Life sure is complicated," Annette sighed as she moistened her finger with her tongue and flipped through the pages of a magazine. "I ought to be an expert on the subject after all I've been through."

About that time Bernadette's two kids came in from the back. Junior had dried snot under his nose. He was chewing a pack of nabs with his mouth open while Sissy was trying to see how many burps she could get out of one bottle of Coke.

"What you looking at?" Junior asked. Globs of orange cracker were wedged in between his teeth.

"Don't know and don't care," I said like I might have to kick his butt if he asked me another stupid question. 'Course I had no idea at the time, no idea whatsoever. But those stiff red-tipped fingers pointed just like her boobs, little daggers held at my mama's wet head. They should have told me something.

My English teacher is always talking to us about crazy things like foreshadowing and symbolism. Stuff I don't get half the time, even though Mama says I've got the sensitive soul of a poet. Just like her baby brother Homer Lee who wanted to be a great author but killed himself with drugs instead. Daddy hates it when Mama says things like that. I never told him but she only thinks that because she found out I liked that Robert Frost poem, the one with those lines in it about the woods being dark and deep and having miles to go before I sleep. I don't have the heart to tell Mama I like it because it makes me think about hunting. But I didn't think it really mattered 'cause Mama and Daddy hardly ever acted mad at each other. Mama is a good cook and real pretty. You can cut her smothered pork chops with a fork, they're so tender. And she has real blond hair and looks good in blue jeans. However on the down side, she is average-breasted. Daddy used to tease her about that.

"I married your mama for her fine derriere," he'd announce, like we'd all been wondering. He'd leer at her butt when he said it. "I'm an ass-man, and your mama here has the sweetest one I ever encountered."

Her face would turn pink. She'd say, "Don't talk like that in front of the children." But Daddy would growl and come up behind her if she was washing dishes and grab her rear end.

"Woody!" she'd shriek. Then they'd both laugh and anybody could tell they were happy.

Me, I still hadn't figured out what's so great about asses. I mean, you can't ignore a woman's breasts. They're right there.

That day in the beauty shop, Charlene came up behind me and stopped me from gawking at Bernadette's by pinching my elbow. Charlene could probably use her right hand as a pair of pliers if she wanted.

"Quit staring," she hissed in my ear. "You look like an idiot."

"Mind your own business," I said. "Can I help it if I've led a sheltered life?"

"It's rude, Bucky. Tacky and rude."

"She don't care. If she did, she wouldn't be wearing her uniform like that." I nodded toward the twin globes that shone from the deep v of her pink polyester blouse. They made me think of the moon's pale glow. I could feel the force of their pull, like they had a gravity all their own.

The next time I saw them they were all bunched up and peeking out from the dress she wore to marry my father. By then, I refused to be swayed. When I took a step back, I could see how cheap Bernadette was. Ratty-looking bleached hair. Those fake nails painted hot pink digging into my daddy's arm. Her white dress clung so tight you could see the outline of her panties.

Once I actually asked him, "What is it you see in Bernadette? What's so great about her and her kids?"

"They need me," he said. "Try to understand."

I wanted to say, *What kind of lame excuse is that? What's needing got to do with anything?* But, instead, I hit him with, "I thought you were an ass-man. That's what you always said."

"A fine pair of knockers. Now that can be a good thing too," Daddy said.

"Well I wish you'd make up your mind."

"It's all the same, Bucky, so long as you get a good handful." Daddy's face was red and I could tell he didn't want to talk about it any more. I figured what the hell, right? So I just let it go.

When Daddy pulls into the drive, I call out, "He's here! See ya later!" and run out to meet him.

I've just pulled the door to and Daddy's backing the car when Junior screams "Boo!" and springs over the back of the front seat. Bernadette's brat laughs like an evil clown with his arms thrown over his head as if he's some wonderful surprise—like a sexy chick all dolled up in feathers and sequins who's just popped out of some big phony cake.

I look at Daddy. "What the hell is he doing here?"

"Watch your language, boy," Daddy keeps his eyes on the road.

"Well?" I can feel Junior watching from the back seat.

"Junior's got to learn to hunt too. You started walking with me long before you were Junior's age."

"How come I thought it was going to be just us, just you and me today."

"What difference does it make? Junior's not going to hurt anything. We've all got to start somewhere, Bucky." Daddy suddenly cuts his eyes in my direction, like there's something in me he wants to pin down. But

I glance away, take my turn staring out the window. I don't want to even look at Junior. He's such a twerp.

The parking lot at Bethel's Diner is full. There's lots of beat-up trucks. Their usually empty gun racks are loaded and waiting. All the trucks and cars are covered with a fine layer of grime that glistens under the early morning frost. My boots are stiff and clumsy as I make my way across the uneven gravel and the smell of frying ham coming from the diner turns my stomach.

When we sit down, Junior slides in on my side of the booth. Good, I think, at least I won't have to see his face while I eat. But he has trouble settling down. He's wiggling all over the place. The springs in the seat cushions are shot, so your butt sinks and it feels like you're dropping down a hole beneath the table. Finally, Junior figures out he can sit on his legs to get his chin above his plate. He keeps looking back and forth at Daddy and me as if we should offer our congratulations. When the waitress comes to take our order, Daddy nods toward the thick white cup at my place and she fills it with coffee.

I try to act like I know what I'm doing as I add milk and sugar. I glance over at the other tables to see if anyone's looking at us. I wonder what they see when they look at our table. Do they think, *There's Woody Macrae and his two boys?* Or, *Well what do you know, there's Woody taking that little bastard he married into out hunting with him and his real son. Ain't that nice.*

The weird part is that Junior acts like he's the one who has eaten breakfast with my dad most every day of his life. He asks if he can tear the packets of sugar for Daddy's coffee and pour it in. He offers my dad a piece of his bacon, grinning as if they share some kind of special secret when he takes it. The coffee tastes rich going down, but leaves a sharp aftertaste. My pancakes are heavy and grow cold before I can finish them, and I feel myself becoming Pluto as I drift off in the distance, far far away from the force of the sun's fiery light.

On our way out, we walk up behind two old geezers, Hope Newell and Avery Eastwood, who are sitting at the counter by the cash register. They are hunched like a pair of buzzards, leaning so far over their coffee their necks have disappeared. I know they're swapping stories just like they do most every afternoon at the corner drugstore.

"Bitch had a nose on her alright. Pointed for all she was worth. Tail stiff as a board."

"Well I reckon she knew a bird that'd flown the coop when she saw one."

"Yes, sir, you got that right. Randy Fox is one lucky son-of-a-gun we didn't mistake the flash of his white behind and shoot his ass."

"Too busy getting some."

"Hell, we fired a shot up in the air just for kicks. That got his attention. Took off high-stepping through the bushes with his pants wrapped around his ankles."

"Now I'd say that's a definite instance of getting caught with your pants down—a fine example, if you know what I mean."

"It was a sight to see."

Their chuckles follow us out the door. My face is hot when I look up at my dad. But it seems he hasn't heard. He jingles the keys in his pocket and whistles a little tune.

I've been getting a lot of blank looks from Daddy lately. It's gotten to the point where I've almost come out and said, "Hello. Earth to

Daddy. Anybody home?" It is weird to look into the eyes of somebody you think you know pretty well and he's looking back as if he's never seen you before. Like he's a zombie or a robot—a fake somebody's trying to pawn off on you.

Daddy first had that look on the Saturday morning he and Mama announced they were splitting up. They sat me and Charlene down at the kitchen table and spilled the beans over breakfast—Pop-Tarts and Frosted Flakes. Said they couldn't get along any more. They had tried. It had nothing to do with me and Charlene. They would always love us, but for some reason they couldn't seem to remember how to love each other. No one was to blame was what they said.

But Charlene heard different. She came into my room after school one day to tell me what she had found out from her girlfriend, Gina Matthews. Seems Gina had heard her mama and another one of my mama's friends, Lorraine Sutton, talking about it when they thought Gina was busy watching TV. Ms. Sutton was torn up by a guilty conscience. Evidently, she had the misfortune of seeing Daddy's car parked by Bernadette's trailer late one night. Ms. Sutton and Ms. Matthews racked their brains but could not come up with a good reason for my daddy's car to be there. Yes, Ms. Sutton was sure, nobody else in town had a two-door Ford LTD with a dark body and a white top. Besides, when her headlights shone on the LTD she even saw a baseball glove and bat through the rear window. That was the final nail in the coffin, they agreed. Neither one could figure out what to do.

One thought our mama wouldn't want to know. The other insisted she would. Neither one wanted to be the bearer of that kind of bad news. But eventually Ms. Sutton decided she was going to disguise her voice and make an anonymous phone call to my mama.

Ms. Matthews said Ms. Sutton had some kind of nerve. But Ms. Sutton said she didn't care if our mom did end up recognizing her voice. "I can't sleep at night," Ms. Sutton said. "I can't even look myself in the eye in the mirror. I know what I'd want my friend to do. Doesn't loyalty mean anything any more?"

"So," Charlene said, "that's how it happened. I mean, I guess it is. It's as much as we'll probably ever know." Charlene laid there on my bed staring up at the planet mobile that I keep by the window over my desk. She hardly ever hangs out in my room anymore. It felt a little like old times. I noticed she wasn't wearing those gold ball earrings. That day she had on big hoops, thin gold wires that laid against each cheek. Before she got up she said, "I didn't know Jupiter was that color. Is it really? Who gets to decide these kinds of things?"

Daddy had that same empty look again when he told us he and Bernadette and the two mutants were moving into a house in the new section of Homewood Acres. We live in the older section on the edge closest to town. When they decided to add a new street onto Homewood Acres on the far side, I used to go over there on my bike to check it out. On the way, if you pedaled hard at the top of the big hill by the Foxes' house, you could coast all the way down to the end of the new street. I loved that feeling of being almost airborne, as if there was hardly anything holding me down.

But after Daddy moved out I lost interest in riding by that way. So I didn't see the houses going up. I guess I was busy with Pony League practice and games and all. When Daddy announced he and his new family were moving out of Bernadette's trailer and onto this new street it was just another in a long line of surprises. I hardly took any notice. I had better things to do than run over there to see which house it was. Besides, knowing can put you in a bad position. I thought a lot about Ms. Sutton's predicament and what she said about loyalty. Divorce is more complicated than you would think. It suited me fine that I could truthfully say I hadn't seen it yet when people asked, "So how do you like your daddy's new place?"

But after Daddy and Bernadette got moved in and settled, Daddy invited me over for dinner. Said the house was a split-level and that he'd cook hamburgers out on the grill. I didn't want to go though. Didn't want to eat his damn burgers. But Mama said I needed to. She said it was part of adjusting and that she knew it would be hard. "But it will get easier," she said. "Eventually."

I decided to ride my bike. That way Mama didn't have to drop me off and she didn't have to see Daddy when he came to pick me up. Mostly, I wanted to make sure nobody would be checking for my reaction the first time I saw the new house. Riding down that hill on the way over wasn't as much fun as it used to be. I guess I wasn't much in the mood to enjoy that held-by-a-thread feeling. Then when I got down to the new street, I realized I had forgotten the number. Who ever heard of having to know the number to find your dad's house, right? I thought it would be easy. I'd just look for the split-level and his car out front and that would be it. But there were two split-levels, side by side, 612 and 614. I couldn't see the cars 'cause they were inside the garages. I knew going there wasn't a good idea.

I could smell meat cooking on a grill but I couldn't tell which direction it was coming from and I didn't see any smoke floating up either. Then I noticed that the front door to the house on the left was open. The screened door was closed but the door behind it had been pushed back, as if somebody was expecting someone to drop by—like maybe their son for dinner. So I thought that must be it. I parked my bike and walked up the sidewalk to the door and knocked. No one answered. I could hear people talking and laughing toward the back of the house. I knocked again but still no answer. By this time I was running late. I hated to get them all up from the table. I was afraid it would turn my showing up into a big production, so I decided to let myself in and act like I came over there all the time. I walked on through the house toward the sound of the voices. None of the furniture looked familiar, but then I had never been inside Bernadette's house. I didn't know what it was supposed to look like. I was practicing acting at ease when I walked straight into the kitchen and called out, "Hey everybody, I made it." It took me about half a second to realize I had the wrong house. I made my apologies as quick as I could. The lady there was real understanding. She laughed a little and said, "Well, you're welcome to stay. We've got plenty."

By the time I got out of there my ears were burning and the smoke or something in their kitchen was making my eyes sting. I got my butt over to the other house quick as I could. The last thing I needed was somebody seeing me leaving the neighbors' or walking through their yard like some kind of doofus. I didn't know how I'd explain. But I didn't have to. They never noticed. I walked around back and found Daddy flipping burgers on the grill. "Hey, partner! What took you so long?" he said and smiled as if he was really glad to see me. Then I was the one wearing the blank face. That time I felt it from the inside.

We are trudging through the woods. That other side is nowhere in sight. The woods are bigger than I remember and the gun weighs a lot more than I thought it would. I've never in my life been so tired. I feel like an old man. All I want to do is lie down and go to sleep. My stomach churns and my mouth is filled with the burnt, bitter taste of coffee.

But all of a sudden, the dogs are on point, flushing the quail, a ruffled burst of startled effort before us. Something rises up with them in my own chest as I lift the gun. My dad stands in front of me and I aim just over his shoulder at a pitiful straggler, can't keep up with the rest. As I pull the trigger, that thing rising in my chest explodes in my head. I flinch and jerk the gun. The shot goes off, missing everything. The entire world swings crazily from side to side and Daddy turns around in surprise. For a minute, he doesn't seem to recognize me. And I stare back and wonder.

"What were you doing?" he asks. "There must have been a half-dozen right above you."

I glance at Mr. Padgett, but his eyes are fixed on one of the clouds overhead, as if he is too busy looking for pockets of cool air to be bothered with hunting. Dad walks over and puts his arm around my shoulder. I hope he can't feel my legs shake.

"Rushed it, I guess." I try not to buckle under the burden of his arm. "Don't worry, I won't miss next time," I say. "I'll make sure I get off a clean shot."

I'm alone in the woods again and there's birds everywhere just like before. Only this time when the shot booms out and all the birds lift off, I decide to run. But then I realize I've got no legs, no real ones anyway. They're scrawny sticks with ugly claws for feet. Damned if I'm not a bird. And I'm clueless about flying. The dogs' barking is getting louder. So I stretch my wings and try to flap them as best I can, willing myself up off the ground.

But it's as if I'm moving in slow motion through liquid air. My wings ache where they join at my shoulder. Then just as I'm about to give up, I start to get the hang of it. I think, Mama's right, it does get easier. But they're almost here. I feel that familiar pull as I begin to rise. Then all at once, when I least expect it, it snaps. And I am free and floating high above the trees. Way down there, I see Junior and Mike with my daddy. The women from the beauty shop are there, too, waving at the sky and yelling, "There he is! Get him! Shoot! Shoot!" My daddy has a gun in his hand, but it's a small handgun, a Colt .45. He points in my direction and I hear another shot ring out. Plunging into its echo, I feel a rush of air whisper through my wings. Cradled by coolness, I'm falling through space and time. I don't know whether it's toward heaven or earth, but the feeling of weightlessness makes my heart soar.

CASEY HART

a writer for the local newspaper, who is in the midst of a divorce

Acacia Anne Hart and Charles Owen Davis III, both Riley natives, were married June 1 at two o'clock in the afternoon at the First United Methodist Church in Riley. Not even the sun could outshine the joy evident on the young couple's faces as Reverend C.B. Cooper officiated their eternal union before a crowd of at least three hundred family members and friends. The host of well-wishers included the bride's uncle, Mayor Lonnie Hart, and several University of North Carolina all-conference football players, former teammates of the groom.

The bride was a vision in her mother's antique Brussels lace dress with a demure but charming sweetheart neckline . . .

—excerpted clipping from a 1969 issue of The Matthews County News

There is nothing like a good long run for getting in touch with the very beat of your own heart. Ba . . . bum, bum. Ba . . . bum, bum. Ba . . . bum, bum. At first, you may find your breath snagged in an uneven ragged struggle. But if you concentrate—breathe in real slow and then

out; in, out, out; in, out, out—you'll find your breath will soon ease into the same even, natural rhythm of your heart. See what I mean? Think of the rise and fall of the ocean's waves. Your body is just a big conch shell waiting for an ear to listen to the tide that constantly roars and echoes inside.

When I'm particularly distracted, I try to concentrate on my breathing. It helps me relax and focus only on running. There's just me and the path under my feet. There aren't any children playing over by the sandbox and swing set. There aren't any people walking on this same path. No one is riding by in their car—headed for the store, picking up kids, or going home for supper. No one has noticed that the newly divorced Casey Hart is out here running. No one is here to see the flab in my thighs jiggle and the effort it takes for me to put one foot in front of the other.

Did you know your entire blood supply—about five quarts—is pumped through your body every minute? In a single day of your life, whether it's a good day or a bad day, whether you're happy or sad, whether you don't even think of your heart at all or whether you can't think of anything but the pain of it breaking—your heart pumps nearly two thousand gallons of blood. If a person lives to be about seventy, her heart will have pumped somewhere around fifty-one million gallons of blood and beaten two-and-one-half billion times. Think about that. It's awfully easy to miss the miracle that lives right under your very own nose. Whooshes of blood entering first one chamber and then the next. In and out, and round and round. Just like a spinning bottle, you never know when it'll stop or just what direction it may point you in, as it steadily beats its way through every moment and every step of your life.

I went back to running after Charlie and I separated and I've been out here almost every afternoon ever since. My mother asks me,

"What do you think you're doing? Haven't you been through enough? I thought you were finished with running?" This from a woman who has never sweated in her life. She perspires, but only a little. She's never had sweat run down her forehead in big hot heavy drips that stung her eyes. She's never been able to wring out her underwear after a particularly strenuous workout. She's at home right now, perfectly comfortable in her air-conditioned kitchen, fixing some kind of light supper for Daddy, no doubt.

She just doesn't get it. There is nothing else quite like transcending the sluggish pull of gravity, the irritating aches and pains, and finding yourself really running—almost in mid-flight. Within that moment when all effort disappears—along with the stitch in your side, the tightness in your calves, the pain in your lungs—you are no longer weak and puny and out of shape. You're nothing but pure energy and motion. And you feel like you could keep on running forever.

My old track coach used to call it "hitting your stride." I haven't been able to run like that in ages. Today I'd settle for just a little rush of endorphins. Just a little natural mood elevation if you know what I mean. Since sex has dropped by the wayside, is that really too much to ask? It is a doubtful but persistent hope that has me out here running the trail around Oval Park five or six times a week. That, and the inexplicable need to *go* somewhere, to *do* something.

Running in Oval Park is a lot like swimming the periphery of a fish bowl, especially in the heat and humidity of an August afternoon. The trees in the park are mostly hardwoods—big old oaks, poplars, and maples. Their branches form a lacy umbrella over the bowl-shaped park. On a hazy day like today everything shimmers even in the shade. The trees, the grass, the see-saw, the metal jungle gym—they all look as if they are about to dissolve, as if with just one blink of my eye the entire park could evaporate and leave me here to realize it was all just a figment of my imagination.

On paper, the neighborhoods that surround this park would form the outline of a misshapen four-leaf clover. But if you drew in the road around the park it would look more like a child's picture of a flower. You know, the standard kind. The round circle in the middle would be the park. And each of the four petals attached to it would be the house-lined streets. The top two petals are larger and the houses are bigger and more substantial. One of those streets is Evergreen Drive, where I used to live with Charlie. My parents live on the other, Dogwood. The bottom two sections are shorter. One has small starter homes for just-married couples and retirees. The other is where I live now in a section of apologetic-looking duplexes that make a feeble attempt to hide the second door.

One thing about living in a small town is that there is a certain kind of self-awareness that comes with always having to face how others perceive you. I'm not so self-involved that I can't take a step back and see the irony in what I'm doing. I mean, here I am running virtually in place. I've just made it three-quarters of the way around the park. I'm facing a total of four loops. That makes it a three-mile trip that leads me back to the exact point where I started, all so I can feel like I've gotten away from my troubles.

I'm already sweating heavily. The blue sky, the late afternoon sun, the weighty old trees, even the air—they're all pressing down so hard I can barely breathe. There's an excruciating cramp in the toes of my left foot that refuses to go away. And my mother's comments are starting to sound like good common sense. But sometimes it's best not to dwell on the ironic. Sometimes you really do have to rely on your instincts. And mine say, "Run until you feel good. Just run, run, run.

And don't even think of stopping because you haven't gotten any-where close to there yet."

So both me and my heart keep on pumping—not like the high-school track star I used to be, but more like the thirty-year-old daughter of an ex-marine that I am today. The pace is a slow, steady shuffle—somewhere between a trot and a march—that is ideal for surviving grueling tests of endurance and bearing heavy loads over long stretches of unknown distance. It's not pretty, but nobody's handing out style points either.

I'm also thinking of this as part of my efforts to reclaim Casey Hart. Mrs. Charles O. Davis III is dead. That cute couple, Casey and Charlie, exist no more. Their two-story brick colonial home on Evergreen Drive has been cleared out and sold to another family. I have spent eight years becoming somebody else's better half, only to wake up one morning in a strange new apartment facing the unslept-in side of a double bed. No matter how many times I rearrange the clothes in my closet, with its neat, evenly spaced row of hangers, it still looks half-empty and waiting.

I have been busy making all kinds of decisions, like: How will I live on my newspaper salary? What will I do with the wedding ring quilt Aunt Rose made for us? And a real tough one, Should I torch the wed-ding album or simply cut Charlie's head out of each of the pictures?

While all my friends are busy planning nurseries, collecting pink and blue knitted booties and silver rattles, and complaining about breast-feeding and stretch marks, I seem to have regressed and have become preoccupied with looking for the old me. Bits and pieces of yourself slough off over time just like invisible flakes of dead skin. You don't even notice what you've dropped by the wayside, until you need the part of you you've left behind. So I'm looking high and low for the old Casey Hart. I keep thinking if I search hard enough, I might actually run into her somewhere downtown or at the swimming pool or maybe even on this very path. The light brown hair streaked with blonde, the perfectly round dark mole that dots the skin above the left corner of her mouth, and the knees that crack and pop as she warms up with a series of deep knee bends. All those things will be the same. But there was a jauntiness in her step and a confidence in her hazel eyes that make her seem part of someone else's existence.

In a way, I guess you could say I'm trying to run back in time. Some might say this sounds a little nutty. But if I can get rid of the dimply fat that has fallen from the bottom of my ass to the tops of my thighs, I don't think any woman in her right mind will try to argue with me. Besides, sometimes I do my best writing while I run.

On top of everything else, I've been assigned Regina Clayton's obituary. Not a happy task for anybody. At least at a normal newspaper it would be fairly cut and dried. But not at *The Matthews County News*, a small-town weekly that exists in the Twilight Zone of the newspaper industry. If I had taken the journalism degree I earned in Chapel Hill and gone to work for the Raleigh *News and Observer* or maybe even the Atlanta *Constitution* or *The Washington Post* (could this be where the real Casey Hart is living?), I wouldn't be stuck right now in this nebulous region located somewhere between hell and the Bermuda Triangle.

But no . . . I had to follow my heart and marry Charlie Davis. Charles Owen Davis III, the man destined to complete the Davis, Davis and Davis sign outside his granddaddy's law office. When Granddaddy Davis built it next to the Riley post office more than forty years ago, he went on ahead and put three Davises up there—even though Charlie's dad was unmarried and still in law school at the time. When people tease Granddaddy Davis about this, he just laughs and says, "Well it worked, now didn't it?" But that kind of thing doesn't work for everybody. After all, I have a house full of stuff marked with Charlie's monogram—dozens of sheets and towels, and piles of silverware, crystal bowls, and decanters. I think of all the things I've had and have yet to change back to Casey Hart—checkbook, driver's license, passport, address, stationery, calling cards—the list goes on and on.

So it was love that landed me a job working for a paper that defies every rule of professional journalism I was ever taught. "All the news that's fit to print," that's a newspaper motto you've heard before, right? Or maybe, "Old news is no news." Does that one strike a chord? Well how about, "We do more than report the news. We tell what *really* happened." Ever heard of that one? Me neither. But my editor Dick Alberts has that posted on a sign that hangs on the wall behind his desk. His wife cross-stitched it for him.

"Fact is, folks in this town don't read the paper for the news," Alberts says. "A man can't fart at the dinner table without the entire neighborhood finding it out, discussing it, mulling it over, and passing on what they've decided about it, before the guy's even had a chance to swallow the last bite of food on his plate. We're a weekly, for heaven's sake. We have to make yesterday's events *mean* something."

"And how, pray tell, am I supposed to find meaning in the death of a forty-something-year-old woman who shot and killed her husband and herself because she found him having sex with his secretary?" I asked when I got my assignment.

"Think of this paper as a mirror in black and white," he said. "People want to see themselves and each other in a way that makes sense of their lives."

"Yes?" I asked. "I mean come on, even a minister is going to have a hard time coming up with something appropriate to say."

"That's your job." Alberts shrugged and turned away, leaving me to contemplate the curving comma of his bent shoulders. "If you can't figure it out, you're in the wrong business."

I often get the same iffy stomach when I start out at the beginning of a long run as I do when I have to write a difficult article. It reminds me a little of wedding-day jitters. Writing, marriage, and long-distance running are really not that different. They are all about facing a blank, white page and scrounging up the courage to take the next step, to strike out on an unmarked trail, and to believe you will be able to handle whatever happens along the way. But right now, I'm afraid I'll never be able to reach that easy, natural rhythm. I won't be able to get a good, clean start or have the satisfaction of crossing the finish line. I'll have to quit. Again. "Getting divorced, quitting, they're really the same too," whispers that voice inside my head. I try to drown it out, to smother it by mentally replaying a song from the radio—Billy Preston singing "Will it Go Round in Circles"—until the sound of my own breathing can take over.

I have finished the first loop and am nearing the playground for the second time. The cramp in my foot is gone, but my knees are having a hard time lifting the weight of my feet. I can remember when there was nothing to endure about running, when it was associated only with euphoric flights across the wide-open expanse of a sandy beach or through the ticklish spray of a sprinkler in the backyard.

Little Ellie's shrieks remind me as I watch her stagger drunkenly toward her mama over by the swing set. Whitney calls, "Come to Mama, baby girl! Come to Mama!" She sits on the wooden edge of the sandbox. A candy apple-red bucket is tossed by her feet and a big yellow plastic shovel and a lime green sifter lie half-buried in the sand behind her. I think of all the times Miss Homecoming's picture has graced the cover of *The Matthews County News*. If you sorted through a file of those clippings, you would never predict the recent developments in Whitney's real life. It's hard to believe the cheerleader who roused such admiration is the same girl who ran off, married a sleazy drug addict, and had a baby all before she turned twenty. The story those pictures tell is that of a fairy tale princess, even down to the sparkly tiara and the handsome prince by her side.

It's funny just what is told in the paper, what milestones we choose to celebrate. *Not even the sun could outshine the joy evident on the young couple's faces* . . . I guess it wouldn't do to have divorce announcements.

On June 2, the family and friends of Acacia Anne Hart and Charles Owen Davis III gathered to celebrate the abrupt end of their eternal union. The mood was somber yet polite. The couple shook hands and promised to remain friends. The ex-bride wore a wrinkled khaki suit and kept checking her watch and murmuring something about a deadline . . .

As I move past Whitney and Ellie, I can't help but feel there's a lot more than eight years that separates my age from Whitney's. Maybe it's in the way Whitney holds her pale white shoulders left bare by a hot pink halter top, or delicately points her painted toenails in the sand, but somehow I am convinced she still loves fiercely, with the slightly violent voluptuousness and breathtaking beauty of a thorny rose.

It won't be all that long before Ellie will be running from little boys instead of toward her mama's arms. We all learn early. Then it's only a few years later that we try not to get caught running *after* them. It's a vicious cycle, a cyclical song that *ain't got no moral* if you ask me.

My father introduced me to running. Right here, right in this neighborhood and in this park. When we were just little things, Daddy would take us running at night after supper. As the youngest, I had the shortest legs and the hardest time keeping up. It was never long before I'd get a stitch in my side and I'd start begging to stop. Daddy would tell me to hold on just a little bit longer. He'd say, "See that big tree, when we get there we'll take a breather."

Often Daddy sang, probably to keep me from complaining. We did always end up laughing at his impersonation of a drill sergeant and our own exaggerated efforts to mimic him: "Here we go. *Here we go.* Up the hill. *Up the hill.* Down the hill. *Down the hill.* Over the hill. *Over the hill.* Around the hill. *Around the hill.* Through the hill. *Through the hill.* One, two, three, four. *One, two, three, four.*"

That's how I remember those nights running with my dad. Learning to laugh while a sword of pain pierced my side and my lungs ached in my throat. Riding the swell of my father's and sister's steady steps and the strength of their assurances as I strove to reach that ever elusive target, waiting out there somewhere in the dimly lit distance.

Here we go. Up the hill. Down the hill . . . I have hit the series of steep inclines on the far side of the trail, four knee-grinding mounds that must be conquered as you make your way back up to the top. I don't look up. I try to keep my eyes focused only on the very next step. I can feel the strain of the incline on my back and thighs. Just one step and then another. The sandy orange pebbles slip and slide under my feet.

The first time Charlie and I ran together, he made fun of me for not racing down these hills. I was so happy when he suggested we go for that run. It was a crisp fall afternoon, sunny but not hot, the kind of day that makes you want not only to run, but to leap through the air. Charlie and I were both wearing shorts and sweatshirts. I loved to look at Charlie's legs. They were long and muscular with just enough dark hair sprinkled over them to make them feel different and manly when I wrapped my legs around his. This is what marriage is supposed to be, I thought, having someone to run *with* for the rest of your life. He wants to be with me. He's picked me to run by his side.

"You look like an old lady," Charlie said. "It's harder to go that slow down a hill than it is just to let gravity have its way. You could use the momentum to get half way up the next one."

"I'm conserving," I said. "I'm resting and relaxing my breathing so I'll be ready for the next climb."

"That's your problem, you always have to be in control."

"Not always," I said in a sexy whisper.

Charlie's shoulders stiffened. "Oh yeah you do," he grunted before sprinting on past.

Immediately I felt a rush of panic and doubt. What did he mean by that? After that I became self-conscious, preoccupied by the possibility I was doing something all wrong. Maybe I should have worried less about sexual compatibility and more about running compatibility. Charlie was a sprinter. As a high-school running back, he became known as "the fastest white boy around" and broke the football team's record for the number of yards he carried the ball. At 6'1" and 180 lbs, he was really too small to play college ball, but too fast not to. So again he broke records, this time as a punt returner. He made it look effortless. Just when you thought someone was going to catch him, he'd kick it up another notch and leave them hugging empty air. Watching Charlie run like that was magic, but trying to run with him was another story. The harder and harder I tried to match my stride and pace to Charlie's, the worse I ran. Eventually, we quit trying to run together and played tennis occasionally with some friends instead.

On my third time around the trail, I pass two walkers. Bonnie Hunt and Janine Saunders are striding with stiff, energetic steps along the long flat part of the path. The smiles they flash in my direction are grimaces.

Their days of starring roles in the unfolding saga presented by *The Matthews County News* are over. Now it's their children who are featured, along with announcements of their husbands' promotions and political debates. Their coverage is relegated to the Women's Page, buried toward the back and facing the classifieds. Occasionally they appear in a group photo taken during a fund-raiser or a garden club affair. The same smiles shine in smudged unison across the page. "Look at us," they say. "We are happy. See us in the paper doing good deeds? See our husbands and our children? It's all right here. We are living the good life."

Those pictures never say, "Help. My husband is a nasty drunk, and I am afraid I won't be able to support myself and my children if I leave him. All I've ever done outside the house is volunteer work and he doesn't even really like that. If dinner is late he clenches his fists and yells, 'Charity begins at home!' frightening the children and making me scorch the rolls." When Bruce Saunders was pictured with his son's Little League team, the caption read, *Bruce Saunders loves introducing young boys to the spirit of healthy competition. "The Bobwhites are going to know how to really hit the ball this year," said the team's enthusiastic coach.* His right hand was cupping the back of the head of a small boy, his son, who stood beside him—a picture-perfect pose of loving masculinity. But if you look carefully, the anxiousness that hovers around the boy's mouth and eyes tells a very different story about being caught in that hand's heavy caress.

It's not like Charlie beat me or ran around on me or anything like that. It would almost make it easier. Then I'd have some kind of real reason for why things didn't work out. I'd have something to point to and say, "That's it. That's what did it. That's why we're not married anymore."

Being able to locate those key turning points in your life helps keep you on track. I'll never forget the day I first found my running legs. It was late winter or early spring. It had been months since my father and sister and I had gone on one of our runs together. It was one of those unusually balmy February or March days that gives you hope that real spring is on the way. Daddy came home early from work whistling. At the foot of the banister, he called out, "Anybody feel like a run with their old man?" The light that afternoon was a pale, golden wash, bathing the barren landscape in the gentle promise of its sunlit glow. I was so excited to think winter was nearly over, so busy looking for crocus and daffodil buds, I didn't notice that I wasn't out of breath or getting a stitch in my side. I just ran. It was easy.

I had grown several inches that year. I was fourteen, all legs and pent-up energy. And near the end of the run when I could see the place where we always stopped right in front of our house, I found myself easily cruising past them. I got to catch my breath while I waited for them on the front steps. When they finally got there, their faces wore the same looks of surprise I would see again when I announced my decision to major in journalism and my engagement to Charlie. My dad's astonishment was laced with happiness and maybe a touch of sadness too. He put his arm around me and said, "You left your daddy in the dust, Tiger." My sister acted more startled than surprised. She was miffed, really, the way older sisters get when you dare to do something without checking with them first. The next spring I started running cross-country, and then track the next fall.

Years of my life were spent according to the seasons of running. I loved to train, but I never liked to compete. The last time I raced was on a cross-country course. The teams were so small they started the boys and girls at the same time. And as I came in toward the finish, gasping for breath and trying to pull on past the girl who had been riding my heels for the last mile, I started to catch up to the last guy. The crowd went wild. They urged me on, yelling, "Pass him! Pass him!"

It really surprised me. I had never seen such enthusiastic cheering at a cross-country race.

Immediately every vein in that boy's body popped out and his head swiveled so he could see me over his shoulder. This is a big no-no. The coaches always drill into your head that you are *never* supposed to look back. Fear, panic, exhaustion made him tighten up. He ran as if he had been hobbled. For a moment, I considered making a real effort to beat him. I bet I could have—dug deeper, run faster. But I felt sorry for him. I hesitated to push him because he looked like he didn't have anything left. My own heart was beating just as strong and steady and sure as ever, but at the same time it told me I just didn't have it in me to be the girl who crushed his. So I crossed the finish line a respectable distance behind him and congratulated myself on beating the girl who was still somewhere behind me. Then when I casually glanced in the boy's direction to see if he was okay, the smile he threw at me took my breath away. It was full of bravado, a flash of cocky triumph. After that, I just didn't want to compete anymore. When I told my father, he seemed to understand. He said he'd always be proud of me, that I'd have the rest of my life to practice what I'd learned.

I remember my relief as I enter the shady section of the trail that winds through the shelter of a small patch of uncleared woods. I'm almost done. Whitney and Ellie left two loops ago. I don't see Bonnie Hunt and Janine Saunders anymore either. This is my last time around. Ms. Leola Wallace and Ms. Maude Ayers are resting on a wooden bench. They have the slightly bloated, comfortable-looking bodies of older women. Everything about them seems to say they're in no big hurry. There's time enough to marry, raise your children, and even to bury your husband. So you might as well stop and enjoy a cool patch of shade now and then.

"You're running awfully fast, Casey Hart!" Ms. Wallace cries with a wave of a paper fan that flutters from her right hand. A light breeze carries the sound of their contented chuckles. I want to stop and ask Ms. Wallace how she got back to feeling good after her husband Norwood's fatal heart attack. He was only fifty-three, hadn't even reached retirement yet. It happened right after I had written up a feature on what a great cook Ms. Wallace is. I cringe when I think that I actually started the piece with, *Everyone knows the way to a man's heart is his stomach, and Leola Wallace is no exception . . .* The photograph was of Leola and Norwood standing before a huge spread of food that covered the kitchen counter. Norwood was really hamming it up with a wide, toothy smile as he leaned toward Leola, who was raising a forkful of food dramatically toward his mouth. The caption read, *Norwood Wallace says his wife's food is to die for!* Now people around town are saying, "Leola Wallace, the woman who proved you can actually kill a man with kindness." And there's been plenty of raised eyebrows and clucking about Harvey Holland, who has been seen recently entering and exiting Leola's kitchen at least three nights a week. "Hope he's got a strong ticker," they say. But isn't that just always the case?

My mother is famous for insisting, "The key to a happy marriage is learning how to fill him up without weighing him down." She says this as if it is one of the only facts she knows about life and one of the only real pieces of wisdom she has to offer. Right before Charlie and I got married, Mama gave me a recipe box filled with recipes she had copied by hand on cards that say *From the kitchen of Mrs. Thomas Emery Hart . . .* lasagna; quiche Lorraine; hamburger stroganoff; layered Jell-O salad with cream cheese, strawberries, and nuts; chess pie; squash casserole—it was chock full of directions for fixing more than you could imagine.

I scoffed when she gave them to me, acted like I wasn't interested in learning to cook. But I was and I did. Night after night, I studied those cards, read and reread those directions and followed each recipe exactly right down to the last quarter-of-a-teaspoonful of the ingredients. When they said, "sift before mixing," I did. When they said, "fold carefully," I did. Even when they said, "grease pan first and then flour lightly," I did that too. I would set the table with monogrammed place mats and linen napkins. I'd have fresh flowers in the monogrammed crystal bowl placed in the center of the table. I'd have candles. I always had candles.

But none of these things made Charlie come home for dinner on time. He kept getting home later and later instead. At first he was always apologetic. He'd call me "honey" and say he was sorry . . . time had gotten away from him . . . he had a big case coming up . . . he'd do better next time. But after awhile, he dropped the excuses, the quick kisses and lopsided grins. He acted sullen and angry as if each night I was intentionally setting him up to fail, as if it were all my fault that he couldn't manage to get home before nine or ten o'clock. There were times when I thought I was too busy trying to arrange a happy marriage to actually have one.

If you're not careful, you do end up focusing all your attention on making an effort and waiting to see if it's appreciated—stepping forward and then stepping back. With each step we took, we ended up with more disappointment. Each small failure fed the space between us until one day the space had grown so large our hearts couldn't make up the distance. It's those everyday misses that eat away at you, that grind at the edges of your heart until all you've got left is a hard little lump, a dried-up pit about the size of a bullet.

As I make my way around the final bend, I get an idea for how to write Regina Clayton's obit. This time, I won't have to quit. I might have to go around in a lot of circles, but I just might surprise myself. Maybe I'll fly high up in the sky too? I used to think the words were,

We'll go round in circles. *We'll* fly high . . . I was singing at the top of my lungs one time when Charlie overheard me.

"What are you singing?" he asked. "It's *will it,* not we will. *We* will go round in circles makes absolutely no sense."

But it does. Charlie used to think it was cute the way I always got the words to songs mixed up. He'd tease me, yet I could tell he thought it was endearing. But then like so many other things, it started to get on his nerves and he'd act pissed off by my predictability. Finally he went from frustration to accusation, "You've changed, Casey. You're not the same person I married. I don't know you anymore." *We* will go round in circles—it might not be what the authors intended but it makes perfect sense to me.

All at once, that old, easy feeling of heated motion hits me as I head down the final stretch. It's as if I've breathed in the sun and it grows from inside my chest and radiates outward, filling my whole body with the warmth and power of inhaled light. A rising tide pulses from every pore in my skin. Awash in fluid energy, I am easily propelled beyond what I know. Loose and powerful, my lengthened stride carries me back toward that shadowy shape on the horizon, that place where I long to be. And I find myself thinking, *I could get used to this* . . .

RILEY—Mrs. Regina Marshall Clayton died Saturday at the University of North Carolina Memorial Hospital. She succumbed after a long battle with an undiagnosed disease of the heart. Her husband, Michael Clayton, fell victim to the same cruel illness less than twenty-four hours prior to the deceased. Regina Clayton's struggle has set an example for the entire community that few will forget in their lifetime as they mourn her shared loss . . .

SUZANNE HUNT

Jackie's little sister

You can get jinxed in all kinds of ways. Like if an all black cat—it has to be one without any white on it—crosses your path and you don't start drawing x's with your finger in the air in front of you right away, you can get jinxed and nobody knows for sure what will happen. I'm only almost ten, so I'm not a bad luck expert yet, but I am learning. I already know about breaking mirrors—that's seven years' bad luck. And I know about spilling salt and walking under ladders. You can save yourself from the salt thing if you take a pinch of what you've spilt and throw it over your shoulder. But once you've walked under that ladder, there's no going back. The tricky thing about luck is that it's sort of like your shadow; even when you can't see it, it's still there. It follows you around wherever you go.

Another kind of jinx is not so scary. It's when two people say the same thing at the same time and one hollers, "Jinx!" My big sister Jackie is all the time doing this to me. When you've been jinxed like this you can't say a word until somebody who's not jinxed says your name—"Suzanne!" And then you can talk again. This can be kinda bad if you like to talk a lot, but it doesn't really bother me too much.

Now that Mama understands about this kind of jinxing, all you have to do is walk up to her and pull on her sleeve and move your lips without any sound coming out and she'll save you. She'll smile and smooth your hair and say, "Why, Suzanne, honey, did Jack the Cat get your tongue again?"

Lately I've been thinking about the dangerous kind of jinxing that cracks in the sidewalk can lead to. 'Cause they can hurt your mama. Everybody knows "Step on a crack and you'll break your mother's back." I'm just surprised they don't take it more seriously. I don't want anything bad to happen to my mama, and I sure don't want to be the reason for it either. Have you ever looked up close at a patch of cement? Chances are, there are bad luck lines running all over it. Most people don't bother with getting down there to take a really good look. It's the same with grass. People walk over it all the time, too, without any idea of what they're stepping on. But try it the next time you're not in a hurry to get somewhere. Lie down on your stomach and wait a few minutes. At first you'll hardly see anything but green grass and dirt. But don't stop looking, because in a few seconds you'll notice that just one blade of grass is shaking. And soon a teeny tiny red ant will appear out of nowhere. And then you'll see another ant just like the first one. But it's wrestling with a dead bug. And then, you might see a shiny black beetle crawling out from under part of an old leaf and one of those neat little inchworms measuring the length of a stick. Before you know it, all kinds of things are happening right there in front of you in that little bit of grass and dirt. It's amazing what you can see if you just take a look.

This holds true for cement too. Once I really got to thinking what "Step on a crack and you'll break your mama's back" meant, I got worried. Of course, I know that it does not happen every time because I have stepped on a lot of cracks before I knew any better and my mother's back has not been broken. I also know that most people are going out and putting their feet down all over the place and not all their mothers' backs are getting broken either. But it could happen. One day your mama's back could up and break and then how would you feel? What if just that day you had skipped down the sidewalk in your favorite pair of Keds with the smiley faces drawn on the toes, thinking how happy you were and taking for granted that all those cracks that your feet were hitting time and time again didn't mean a thing?

At first, you might think all you have to do is avoid the big thick cracks that divide sections of cement into squares. But, if you're curious and take the time to look up close, you'll see that there are actually hundreds and hundreds of cracks in just one square of a sidewalk. There are short ones and long ones, wide ones and skinny ones, ones that are just getting started and others that have been cracking for a real long time. All together, they look like the crooked and curved lines on a road map, only without the different colors to help you find your way. It's just too much. I've quit walking on sidewalks. The grass is safer. It's easier to watch out for dog-doo than it is to worry about stepping into bad luck.

It's simple to get dog-doo off your shoe—just turn on the spigot and hose it off. But I don't know about a jinx. I've been trying and trying to figure this out 'cause I've noticed that the corner of our front yard has become a magnet for disaster. It's up around the mailbox that is the most dangerous, and I'm wondering if I did anything to get it that way or what I could do to get it back the way it was before all the bad things got started.

It hit me just a few weeks ago that there might really be something going on here. I was hunting fool's gold in the driveway with Angie. It was late in the afternoon and we didn't have anything else better to do. I had just found a nugget of gold as big as a baby tooth and was showing it to Angie when these strange noises echoed over our heads. They sounded weird—like big firecrackers that had been shut up in a closet. I wondered if I had really heard something or if it had just been my imagination, so I asked Angie, "Did you hear that?"

"Yeah," she said.

"What do you think it was?"

"Mmm . . . mmm," she said. Angie is not very curious. She went back to rolling pieces of gravel around looking for more fool's gold. Her family's driveway is smooth cement. It is good for roller-skating, but there's no hidden treasure in it.

I'll never forget the time we came home from the grocery store and found Angie looking for gold in our driveway without me. I bet she found a really big piece that day, but I could never get her to tell. If she did, I think she ought to give it to me since I hadn't invited her over. But Mama said, "Don't be selfish."

I was thinking again how Angie looked that day when we caught her. Guilt had been written all over her face. She knew she was being sneaky. I squeezed my new baby-tooth piece in one hand while I started looking again myself. My hands were covered with dust and smelled chalky. "I'm about tired of looking today," I said. "My knees hurt." Just then, my daddy came running from around the side of the house.

He looked straight at me and said, "Y'all stay right there," in a voice I knew meant business. Then he ran by us and on up the road without saying anything else. I noticed he was carrying a garden trowel in one of his hands. I wondered what the emergency was and what he was fixing to do with that trowel. But it was too late to ask, so I just sat there.

I looked over at Angie's house. She lives right next door and the Robinsons live on the other side. Our three houses are at the end of the street. They are lined up and face the road. There's a circle of cement and grass that the road goes around in front of our yards—we call it *the circle*. You know, we'll say, "I'll meet you at *the circle*." But it's really shaped like a teardrop. Sometimes we sit out there at night and throw things at the bats that dive down at us from around the streetlight.

Nobody came out of Angie's house . . . and I knew the Robinsons were at the beach on vacation so I didn't bother looking over there. Cracker Jack and Buster were lying in the shade of a dogwood. They are our two cocker spaniels. Cracker Jack is mine. He has patches of brown-and-white all over. So does Buster, who belongs to my brother Hayden. Cracker Jack and Buster didn't act like anything was happening either. They just laid there. I had about decided to go in and ask my mama where Daddy went, when Angie said, "Oh *look*! This one has gold sprinkles all over its side!"

"Let's see," I said. Angie held it up to my eyes, but she didn't hand it over so I could hold it myself. "Oh, yeah," I said. "It is hard to believe it's not really worth something."

"I know. It sure is shiny," Angie said. She was smiling real big. I was trying real hard to be generous, but I couldn't help myself from imagining that rock getting so hot from the sun that it burnt her hand. But she didn't drop it. I looked again at the baby-tooth cube I had found earlier. I held it up so it could catch the sunlight, too, but it wouldn't sparkle like Angie's. That was when I started to hear the cry of sirens in the distance. They got louder and louder until I knew they had turned into the entrance of the Riley Country Club, which is the neighborhood where we live. Cracker Jack and Buster heard them too. They sat up and started howling. The sirens got so loud it hurt my ears, too, and I started to think there had been a mistake and they were coming to get us. But instead, they stopped somewhere right up the street, just around the bend in the road where the Reynolds and the Claytons have always lived. By this time, even Angie was curious. We were dying to find out what had happened. But we couldn't see any of it from our end of the street. We were trying to decide whether or not to run up there when my mama came outside. I could tell right away that she already knew what was going on.

"Is your mother home, Angie?" Mama asked.

"What's going on?" I asked. "We heard a bunch of sirens."

"Something terrible has happened," Mama said, "just terrible." I could tell she was upset. Her eyebrows were bunched up in a big frown and her voice was kinda shaky. Mrs. Andrews, Angie's mama, came out from their garage and ran over toward us. I'd never seen Mrs. Andrews run before.

"Did you hear, Bonnie?" she called as she cut across the middle of their front yard. "I just got off the phone with Pat Reynolds. It's awful. I can't believe it."

"Me either," Mama said.

"Well tell us," I said. "We want to know."

Mama looked at Mrs. Andrews first . . . and Mrs. Andrews gave her a little nod before Mama drew in a deep breath and said, "Mr. and Mrs. Clayton have both been shot."

"Shot!" Angie said.

"Who shot them?" I asked. "Are they going to be all right?"

"I don't know," Mama said. "Teenie told me two ambulances came and took them away."

"That's what Pat said too," Mrs. Andrews added. "This is just so awful. I can't believe something like this has happened here." Mama took out her cigarettes and started smoking one right after the other. She dropped the butts in the grass like she didn't even care about littering. She and Mrs. Andrews kept talking. They'd look up the street and then back at each other. Their voices became hush-hush. They said the same things over and over again. Things like, "such a tragedy," "can't believe it," and "who knows?" After awhile Mrs. Witherspoon joined them. She's kind of old and lives on the other side of the Andrews. Her husband is dead and she doesn't have any children, just a Chihuahua named Frisco.

Mrs. Witherspoon said, "Well I just got the news . . . Michael Clayton is dead."

"Oh my gosh," Mama said. "What about Regina?"

"They've taken her to Chapel Hill," said Mrs. Witherspoon.

"Does anybody know where Mike Jr. is?" Mrs. Andrews asked.

"That poor boy." Mrs. Witherspoon dabbed at her eyes with a ball of Kleenex. "Just imagine what this is going to do to him," she added.

That got me to thinking about Mike. I didn't really know him or his parents. I saw them sometimes at parties and things at the country club or while they were playing golf on number 6 and 7 which run right up against the edge of our backyard. Mike didn't have any brothers or sisters. He was the only kid living at the Claytons'. He's my brother's age, but they've never been good friends or anything. Still, I did feel sorry for him. I wondered who was going to fix his supper that night and if he'd be scared sleeping in a big, dark house all by himself.

Later, Hayden came down the street on his bike. He had been up at the swimming pool. His towel was wrapped around his neck and his hair stood up in wet clumps on the top of his head. He came to a screeching halt on the asphalt in front of us. "Careful now, Hayden," Mama said.

"Daddy said to tell you he'd be home in a little while," Hayden answered. "They've got everything taped off around the Claytons' house. Police are all over the place."

"Any idea who did it?" Mrs. Andrews asked.

"Somebody told Jenkins up at the Pro Shop that it was Mrs. Clayton," said Hayden. "But I don't believe them. Why would she do a thing like that?"

Mama, Mrs. Andrews, and Mrs. Witherspoon were all silent. They looked like they had forgotten where they were and what they were talking about. "Go get out of your wet suit," Mama finally said. "Supper will be ready before long."

After Hayden went inside, Mrs. Witherspoon said, "This just keeps getting worse."

"It's a tragedy whether she lives or dies," Mama said.

"Just imagine," said Mrs. Andrews. "Just imagine."

Mama fed us hot dogs for supper and sent us out to play. A bunch of adults—Angie's parents, Mr. and Mrs. Reynolds (they always tell us to call them Jerry and Pat), Carl and Teenie Green, and Mr. and Mrs. Brantley—came over and started drinking liquor at our kitchen table. Before we went out I heard Pat Reynolds say, "Who could blame her? If it is true, I don't think a jury in this entire district would find her guilty."

"Not if it's half women," said Teenie Green, who is my mama's best friend. She tickled my back with her fingernails and then gave me a pop on my bottom. "Little pitchers!" she said and turned up her drink.

My sister Jackie and I had to go outside after that. We played swing the statue on the golf course with Angie and her little brother, Clarke. Tommy and Sandy played too. Their parents are Mr. and Mrs. Brantley and they live in a blue house right across the golf course from us and the Andrewses. Hayden wouldn't play. He's fourteen and says he's too old even though he's real strong and can grab your arm and swing you real good so you end up in a different pose every time. Hayden is the oldest. Jackie is twelve. And like I said, I'm ten—I will be soon anyway. At least Jackie will still play with me even if Hayden won't.

Tommy said little Mike was going to have to go to the orphanage. "He is not," said Jackie.

"He is if his mama dies," Tommy said. "That's what happens to kids who don't have anybody to take care of them."

"It'll be just like in *The Little Princess*," said Sandy. "The other kids will hate him, and all he'll have to eat will be cold porridge. They make you wear rags, too, and clean out fireplaces every day."

We stayed out on the golf course until it got dark and the grass turned cool and wet. I slipped and got a big grass stain on my shorts, and Tommy laughed 'cause he was the one who had swung me. They had to go home after dark, so Jackie and I caught fireflies in our yard until bedtime. We put them in a big Mason jar with little breathing holes punched in the lid and set it on the table between our two beds. Their lights winked on and off and made me think of the way Angie's piece of fool's gold shone in the sun.

I was having a hard time going to sleep. I felt strange—sort of out of breath and nervous. I wasn't really sad, but I was kind of scared, I guess—not for Mike but for me. I don't know why. I knew my parents were right there. But I had this creepy lost-and-little feeling, like I had just eaten some of the mushrooms that made Alice shrink until she was too small and the world was way, way too big.

Most of the adults had gone home, but Carl and Teenie were still there. They had moved from the kitchen table out to our back porch. The windows in my room were open, so I could hear some of what they were saying as their voices floated up into the night air. I got up and went to the window that is directly over the back porch. I could feel a little breeze blowing, so I leaned over and rested my arms and chin on the sill. Mama was saying something about Mrs. Clayton. "I can't help but think that things might have turned out differently if she'd had somebody to talk to," Mama said.

Then Teenie asked, "Who are her friends? Who did they really hang out with?"

"Nobody," said Carl. "He was always a sloppy drunk." I heard somebody strike a match and inhale on a cigarette.

"Nothing kills a party faster than a man who can't hold his liquor," Daddy said. "Especially if he starts putting the moves on your wife." Right above my head, a moth began to beat its wings softly against the screen.

"Evidently there were some ladies who liked him," Teenie said.

"They weren't ladies," said Mama. "She must have been so alone. She didn't have anybody to confide in. Just one friend might have made all the difference. For the past several weeks, I saw her walking in the early mornings and late evenings along the edge of the golf course. She looked like she had something on her mind, something that was really troubling her. I wanted to say something to her, but I was afraid she'd think I was just being nosy. But what if I had? What if I had asked her and she had been able to tell somebody all about it?"

"You can't blame yourself darling." Daddy's voice sounded like a strong, warm hug in the dark. "Regina Clayton is not the first woman to have an unfaithful husband. It was her misfortune and his. But it's just plain bad luck that things have turned out the way they have."

I listened to the pine trees that surround our yard as they moved gently in the breeze. The sound they made was a sighing whisper and I wondered what they might be trying to say. I went back to bed, but I kept thinking about what Daddy had said about bad luck and that made me remember some of the other bad things that have happened in that corner of our front yard.

The first thing I thought of was Hayden's bicycle accident a couple of years ago. He was riding my old green bike with the banana seat and he drove it real hard and fast off the edge of the pavement and into the pothole in the driveway. Hayden is like that. He likes to test everything—see if he can do whatever he wants.

But the handlebars twisted just as he was standing up tall in the seat to avoid feeling the bump. One of the handles was missing its cover and it tore right into Hayden's side. It was awful. He screamed and screamed, and there was a big bloody hole in his side. I just stood there not knowing what to do. All that blood made me dizzy, but I looked at it anyway.

It was a good thing Mama and Mrs. Andrews came and took care of him. They brought an old bathroom towel and had him hold it against his side. And then they drove off to the emergency room and left me there in the yard, all by myself. I couldn't think at all. All I could do was stand there and feel the whole world rushing into my head. I cried until they got back from the hospital and I could tell he was going to be all right.

Right in that same area is also where I had a bad roller-skating accident. I was trying to get my skates to follow the curve of the road when right by our mailbox my left skate hit a piece of gravel and jerked to a stop and sent the rest of me flying over the top of my feet. My knees got scraped up real bad and so did both my hands and my whole left arm. I still have a scar on the palm of my left hand. I didn't have to have stitches like Hayden, but sometimes real bad scrapes seem to take even longer to heal.

Another time Angie and I didn't have an accident; we just got in lots of trouble. We were bored and standing at the end of our driveway trying to come up with something fun to do. We weren't in the mood to hunt for fool's gold or play Barbies. It was too cold for swimming and Angie's bike had a flat tire.

"Be creative" is what Mama is always saying when we tell her there's nothing to do. And I guess that's sorta what me and Angie did. We had been watching this educational show on TV. It's called *The Electric Company*. Anyway, there's this part on the show where these two people's heads are on there real big. They look at each other and sound out words, and the parts that they say come rolling out of their mouths until the whole word is hanging there on the screen between their lips. Then they say the word one last time together in case you haven't figured it out. Like the man's head will say "buh" and a *b* will come rolling out of his lips and hang there waiting for the woman to say something. And then the woman's lips will open and she'll say "ad" and the *a* and *d* will come out together and sit right there next to the *b*. And together the man and woman will say "bad"—for those dummies who don't realize that "buh" and "ad" together make "bad."

I have watched this show many times and after a while the rhythm of it does stick in your head, until soon you are thinking about all your words that "wh" "ay"—"way." So while Angie and I were talking, it suddenly popped in my head that we could say bad words by splitting them up. I explained it to her and she thought it was funny too. I'd say "sh" and she'd say "it" real fast and then we'd just laugh and laugh.

But we got carried away and were soon yelling "du" "am" and "hu" "ell" at the top of our lungs. Since we weren't saying the whole words by ourselves, we didn't think we could get into trouble. But my mama finally heard us from inside the house and when she came out she was mad as fire. Angie got sent straight home and when she got there her mama already knew about it and popped her real hard on the backs of her legs with a fly swatter.

My mama didn't spank me. But she did jerk my arm so hard it pinched the skin and I had to spend the rest of the day in my room looking up good words in the dictionary. Later, when I got to come out of my room, I asked Mama, "What exactly are good words?" She said, "Any words other than the ones you were saying." And by the way she said it, I could tell she was still upset. But I realized that looking up all those good words in the dictionary must not have done a thing to lift the jinx on that corner. That night, after the Claytons got shot, when I was lying in bed thinking about all the bad luck that had happened and was waiting to happen right there in the corner of our yard, I decided I had to do something about it. I made up a list in my head. This list includes: 1. Beg God every night for forgiveness of all sins and for protection. 2. Look for first star every night and wish for good luck on it. 3. Cross your fingers every time you say a lie and it won't count. 4. Don't step on any cracks. 5. Don't walk under any ladders and don't even pick up a mirror. Of course, if I had spilt any salt since then I would have thrown some of it over my shoulder, and I always do the x's if a black cat crosses my path. I also avoid the number 13. I actually avoid all odd numbers. If I'm jumping rope I only stop on an even number of jumps. And if I accidentally mess up, I don't quit until I have jumped some more so I can stop on an even number.

I have been doing all of this for weeks since the Claytons died. Yes, Mrs. Clayton ended up dying too. And she did turn out to be the one who did the shooting. But then this afternoon when I came home from school and found our old dead tomcat, Beau, dug up and lying in our front yard in a patch of sun halfway between the mailbox and the house, I knew my efforts had been wasted. It took me a minute to realize what I was seeing, but when I did I knew that whatever I've done so far, I haven't made up for it yet.

We think Beau got hit by a car. We found him in the front yard late last spring. He was panting real hard and had a messed up leg. That leg never would heal. Beau had been so big and brave that he chased the neighbor's dogs out of our yard, but he couldn't beat this. He just laid around and got sicker and sicker. I never heard him purr again. Finally he got so he wouldn't even lift his head when you rubbed it. Dr. Earley, our veterinarian, said gangrene had set in Beau's hurt leg. It had gotten in there and grown so fast that even if Dr. Earley cut off Beau's leg it wouldn't stop it from spreading all over.

We cried for days and prayed for a miracle. But in the end Beau had to be put to sleep. He came home in a big cardboard box and Daddy buried him right by the birdbath at the edge of the garden. I sat out there while he dug the hole. The ground was deep red clay that stuck together in rusty clumps and refused to crumble. I sat there and watched Daddy sweat and dig. We didn't say anything. I wondered what would happen if I opened the box, but I was too scared to do it. I was actually afraid of what was in there, even though I knew it was just Beau. But I got the creeps wondering about how after you die you're not inside your body anymore so if your body's not you then what is it? What takes your place inside there?

It was scary and sad, but I just sat there and let my thoughts rub against my feelings like your tongue worries the hole that's left by a missing tooth. Daddy put a big rock at the head of Beau's grave and Jackie came outside so we could say the Lord's Prayer and sing, "Now the Day is Over." Jackie kept crying off and on for a few more days, but that was pretty much it until this afternoon when Cracker Jack and Buster must have gotten kinda crazy from boredom and dug up a member of their very own family.

I thought maybe they had been missing Beau, but Hayden said, "No." He said they could smell Beau under all that dirt and that is what drove them crazy and made them dig Beau up and drag him around the yard and leave him right where I found him. I think he was on his side with his legs sticking straight out the front and back. His whole body looked stiff and smaller as if it had been shrinking underneath his fur, which was still there but was dull and dirty and worn down in some places and clumped together in others. But most of all he stunk. He smelled terrible, worse than the worst dog-doo, or water that's been sitting in a ditch for a long time, or a full garbage can on a hot day, or even the inside of Hayden's oldest pair of sneakers. I could smell Beau from the mailbox, as soon as I was off the bottom steps of the bus.

I didn't get too close. But my eyes looked and looked while I walked up the driveway to the house. I even stood there for just a few minutes trying to see everything without getting any closer. I couldn't really make out his eyes. His whole head was just sort of a blur. It may have been turned toward the ground anyway.

It wasn't until I was upstairs in our bathroom washing Cracker Jack in the bathtub that I started to cry. Cracker Jack and Buster both smelled to high heaven. They must have rubbed themselves all over Beau and the dirt from his grave. It was gross. It got all over me too while I was trying to wash it off Cracker Jack. It was strong and sweet and rotten and it clung to everything and filled the air. Soap and water didn't hardly do a thing to get rid of it. It was so bad I put my nose inside the neck of my T-shirt, but I could still smell it. I tried breathing through my mouth, but then I tasted it. I hated Cracker Jack right then. I hated him for what he'd dug up and gotten me into. I could feel that smell getting into everything. It was soaking into the pores of my skin, my hair, my mouth. I started to feel sick—like I might throw up. I was afraid I'd never get away from it. When I told Cracker Jack how bad he'd been, he just rolled his eyes up at me and licked the water dripping down the sides of his face.

Daddy reburied Beau in the same place, this time with a pile of rocks all over his grave instead of just one to mark the top. I asked Daddy if this wasn't some very bad luck, to have this happen. But he said, "Baby, all this is a case of dogs being dogs. It's not lucky or unlucky. It's just nature, and there's no escaping that."

So now I'm confused. I don't know what the difference is between luck and nature and what my Mama calls "coincidence." I have had my own bath and I'm lying here in bed trying to go to sleep. I've said all my prayers, twice. But I don't know if it'll do any good. I can hear Jackie breathing heavy, like she's already asleep. When I get up and go over to the window above my desk I can see the garden. The mound of rocks over Beau's grave and the birdbath glow in the dark. The street-light at the circle casts the same strange glow as our hall night-light. Some things are real bright and others disappear into the night. Our mailbox is a dark shadow waiting at the end of the driveway. I breathe in real deep and try to fill my head with the smell of cut grass and fall leaves, but on the edge of that smell I catch a whiff of Beau. I close my eyes real tight and pray to God for Him to let everything that's buried stay that way. When I get back in bed I reach under my pillow to find my piece of fool's gold—the one that's the size of a baby tooth. I pick it up and rub my finger along the rough rock until I can feel the smooth nugget of gold.

Mama and Daddy don't know how much Jackie and I know about the Claytons. They have no idea what else we've heard, like how she saw him doing kissy-kissy with his secretary. That he came home and sat down in his easy chair and was drinking bourbon when she shot him. Tommy said Mr. Clayton's brains splattered all over the wall and that they couldn't get the stain off, no matter how much they scrubbed. Angie said she heard the house is haunted now and that Mike has been moved to the orphanage.

Teenie and Mama agree that the story of the Claytons is about tragedy and loneliness. But if anybody ever asked me, I'd say it was all about bad luck. I'd say, you just never know what a rock might be holding down. It might be hiding a treasure or the world's worst smell. I'd say Mr. and Mrs. Clayton were two people who never stopped to look. Maybe they didn't believe in fool's gold and never bothered to search for some. Maybe they never even noticed all the cracks in their sidewalk, a river of bad luck running right up to their front door.

TATE GIBSON

one of the Claytons' next-door neighbors

After downing a few, my friend Jimmy Needham likes to talk about questions. He'll turn the topic of conversation to whatever it is that's on his mind and worry us with it till we've plumb talked it to death but still managed to come up with no kind of agreed-upon solution. That's Jimmy's whole point—that there are no real answers—only questions leading to more questions. Jimmy calls this "probing reality" and says it is the fundamental force that drives the philosophical man. Philosophy, Jimmy says, is a rarefied art form—a thinking man's game and a sign of true civilization. He's sure life as we know it is going straight to hell because there are so few people who really understand and appreciate a philosopher when they meet one. Jimmy wholeheartedly believes that if the world really cared about saving itself, it's philosophers they'd put on the top of our endangered species list. But my wife Tilley thinks Jimmy is obnoxious. She says he makes a sport out of trying to mess with our minds. "Why do you want to drink with somebody like that, Tate?" she asks. "What is it in you that makes you want to do such a thing?"

"I've never known a real philosopher before," I say. "Besides some-times I think he might be on to something, you know?"

"Philosopher, my fanny," Tilley says. "The man's a banker."

"But philosophy is what he studied in college," I say. "It's his true calling."

This always makes Tilley worry about our finances. "It may be his calling but that's not what he's getting paid to do. Maybe he's not thinking enough about the money he's paid to worry over," she says. "Maybe we should consider moving our savings. It's one thing to put up with his being called to pontification every Friday night, but I don't want it to cost us anything."

Tilley and I have had this same exact conversation many times, and we went over it all again just yesterday evening while we got ready for Jimmy and his bride Barbara Rose to come over for Friday happy hour at our house. Our two kids, Ruthie and Glenn, were both already on spend-the-nights at their friends' houses. Tilley was arranging cheese straws on an hors d'oeuvres plate while I filled the ice bucket. Her brows were knitted and she looked somehow irritated with each squiggle of stiff cheese as she lifted it from the storage tin to the glass plate in front of her.

Tilley takes pride in her cheese straws. They are good. Her mother taught her how to make them and I've always said that was the one positive contribution Tilley's mother has made to our marriage. Despite my mother-in-law's influence, Tilley is a sporty, good-natured woman— a fun-loving happy-go-lucky kind of gal. This kind of talk was not in her nature. I could tell from the set of her shoulders that our Friday evening drinking sessions with Jimmy and Barbara Rose were numbered.

This feeling returned later that evening when Jimmy steered us to the subject of dying, when he asked me, "Tate, what kind of death is it you fear most? What kind of dying wakes you up in the middle of the night, makes you break out in a cold sweat, and sets your heart to racing so fast you can't go back to sleep?" His question caught Barbara Rose mid-sip and sent her drink down the wrong way.

Barbara Rose is Jimmy's much-younger second wife. After he and Penny split up a couple of years ago, Jimmy said he aimed to re-explore the philosophy of youth. He bought a used motorcycle and married Barbara Rose a year later. I don't think Barbara Rose is even thirty yet. Besides being so young, she has that pale skin that's quick to flush, so when she started choking her face got really red. Tilley reached over and patted Barbara Rose's back until she was able to catch her breath. "Jimmy, darling, do we *have* to talk about dying tonight?" she finally got out.

"It is a fact of life, sugar. Of course it's one that's gonna concern this old coot a whole lot sooner than a sweet young thing like yourself." Jimmy reached over and gave Barbara Rose's thigh a squeeze.

"But we're still newlyweds. We shouldn't have to worry about that yet."

"Well, now, I really want y'all to think about this," Jimmy insisted. "Of course, we're all afraid of dying. It's the one thing that unites us each and every one—lovers and enemies, best friends and strangers, capitalists and communists—whether we want to admit it or not. But the way of going that most terrifies us—now that can really say something about a man, something about his own individual person if you know what I mean." Jimmy sat back as if he were completely satisfied, as if he'd just rolled out a big red carpet and invited us to join him in some kind of spectacular once-in-a-lifetime opportunity.

He smiled and started to chew on a corner of his mustache. His eyes droop at the corners. Like a hound dog's, Tilley says. Usually this makes him look sort of sad, but right then, they gleamed with excitement. I've never seen somebody so looking forward to talking about their own death. He let a little silence fall so we could all savor the moment. Tilley made a point of catching my eye and tossing back a huge gulp of her drink. I knew what that gulp meant.

Murder, drowning, accident, and old age were some of our options. The four of us were sitting around our kitchen table drinking Jack Daniel's Green Label. The women were mixing theirs with ginger ale and adding ice, but me and Jimmy take our bourbon straight up. Whenever I turn to the bar and ask what'll it be, Jimmy always says, "Now, son, you know how I feel about wasting water when you've got the good stuff." Many times Jimmy has suggested his drinking philosophy is simply a reflection of his concern for the environment. "Only empty bottles mark my trail, nothing else," he says. "The only rocks I turn over are all right here." And then he'll tap at the side of his forehead and smile a little satisfied smile that's meant more for himself than anybody else.

I imagine it was the new neighbors moving in next door that must have triggered Jimmy's thinking in the direction he was so set on. The house had stood empty for almost a year since Regina Clayton killed her husband Michael and then herself right there, right next door, right in their sunken living room. Michael was sitting in his leather La-Z-Boy. I have one just like it. Tried his out one evening right after they bought it and liked it so much Tilley got me one when she redid our family room. You can't find a more comfortable seat. Though I don't imagine Michael Clayton was *relaxing* when his wife pointed his own handgun right at him, when he realized she was actually aiming to shoot. Tilley says he shouldn't have been all that surprised. "What did he expect after all that he'd done to her?" she said. "A woman has her limits just like a man. Just because we give birth doesn't mean we can't kill. In fact, I'd say if a woman has given birth—*look out*. Don't dare test her patience any further."

Last night when I went out to greet Jimmy and Barbara Rose as they pulled up in the driveway, you couldn't help but notice the moving van next door, which got us all talking about the Claytons and the new people who were moving in. They're a young couple from Winston-Salem. Jimmy had met Robert that day at the bank. Bobbie they call him—Bobbie White. He's going to work in Jimmy's office, fresh out of the Wachovia training program. They have one little girl, maybe five or six years old. She had already drawn a set of crooked boxes with chalk down the front walk and was trying to jump in and out of them as the movers unloaded. I was watching her skinny pigtails bounce up and down as she hopped after two men who were struggling with the Whites' heavy mattress, when Barbara Rose whispered, "I don't think I could live in that house."

I, myself, have thought the same exact thing. Sometimes I wonder if we should even keep on living next door. I raised my eyebrows, gave Barbara Rose a little nod, and tried to stop the shudder that shifted down my back. My daddy always told me he never trusted a superstitious man. I certainly wasn't going to own up to any such nonsense in front of Jimmy, but the truth is I had asked Tilley months ago if she wouldn't like to move.

"Don't be silly," Tilley had said. "Our house has been struck by lightning and murder has been committed next door—what else could happen around here? We've got to be living in the safest place in the world. We've weathered our storm. If we moved, we'd have to wonder about when was the last time that place had been hit. No sir, I'm staying put."

Jimmy waited until we got inside before he made any kind of comment. "Hey, Tilley!" he called as soon as he stepped through the door. "Guess what! My wife's afraid of ghosts. Oooooooooooooo!"

"It's not ghosts I'm afraid of," Barbara Rose said.

"The goblins'll gitcha!" cried Jimmy.

"Not ghosts or goblins," Barbara Rose tried to continue.

"Don't worry, baby. I'll protect you," Jimmy said as he pulled Barbara Rose into his arms. "I've never seen this side of you before, my spooky little sweetheart. But it's all right, darling, Daddy's here."

Barbara Rose giggled. "It's really more about karma than anything else, Jimmy," she said. "Now stop, you're embarrassing me."

"Oh my marvelous mystery girl," Jimmy crooned while he folded Barbara Rose backward over his right arm in a daring dip. "My marvelously beautiful mystery girl. Oh baby, I love you so much it's killing me!"

I worried Jimmy would drop her, but he didn't. I guess you lift weights regular if you're trying to keep up with a younger woman. Their shenanigans were embarrassing me too. Jimmy was being so lovey-dovey, I felt like I shouldn't be watching. But they were doing it all right in the middle of our kitchen. It was my house. Where was I supposed to go? After Jimmy had pressed a few noisy kisses on the pale underside of Barbara Rose's upturned chin, I cleared my throat and said, "How about a toddy everybody!"

"Ah yes, it is time to celebrate," Jimmy said as he lifted Barbara Rose to her feet. "I know my happy hour has arrived—hasn't it, darling?"

Barbara Rose had the decency to look a little guilty. She smoothed the front of her blouse and patted her hair back into place. "If you say so," she said. "You'd know more about those kinds of things than I do."

"What's all this about ghosts?" asked Tilley. The corners of her lips were bent upwards in an almost-smile that made me afraid she thought Jimmy's antics were actually romantic and that soon she'd be after me to dip her.

"I just said I didn't think I could live in that house next door. The idea of sitting in that living room and watching television every night right where it all happened—it's too creepy. I don't even like moving in where other people have lived, much less died."

"Here's a drink to calm your nerves," said Jimmy as he handed Barbara Rose an extra tall one. "By the way, sorry we're late, folks. Barbara Rose got hung up a little at the doctor's."

"Oh, of course," Tilley said. "Y'all have a seat. Hope everything's all right?"

Barbara Rose hesitated for a moment. She looked nervous—caught somehow. "Annual check up," she said and then quickly switched the subject back to the neighbors' house. "It's bad enough having to scrub off and paint over the imprint somebody else leaves behind," Barbara Rose continued as she pulled out a chair and sat down. She placed her drink carefully on a cocktail napkin and then sat with her eyes still on the glass as if she were just waiting for it to start to sweat. "I've heard those stories about blood stains that won't wash off and keep bleeding through anything you try to cover them up with. How do you get rid of that? How do you ever make it your place instead of theirs?" She looked up from her drink.

For a minute Tilley locked eyes with Barbara Rose and something passed silently between the two. Then Tilley pushed the plate of cheese straws in Barbara Rose's direction and said, "I think I know what you mean."

"You're not getting superstitious on us too, are you Tilley?" asked Jimmy.

"No, I'm not." Tilley sat back in her chair and let out a sound that was somewhere between a snort and a chuckle. "But I can appreciate Barbara Rose's position. Tate well knows that I, myself, subscribe more to a theory of probability. If something unlikely happens in one particular place, how likely is it to happen again in that same exact spot?"

"You mean like with that bolt of lightning that blew up y'all's TV set a few summers ago?" Barbara Rose asked.

"Yes," said Tilley, "that's it exactly."

It was an eighteen-inch brand-new RCA. I nearly pissed my pants when that ball of fire busted through the screen and rolled across the living room. It scorched the shag carpeting and left a long black trail like the skid marks you see on the highway when there's been an accident. The resulting fire led to Tilley's redecoration of the downstairs and my new La-Z-Boy. Tilley was proud of her handiness with the fire extinguisher. She told everyone the damage was only cosmetic, nothing structural, only what could easily be fixed.

"Now when it storms do you leave the TV going if it's already on? Or do you shut it off and unplug it?" Barbara Rose had sucked down her drink. She rattled the ice in her glass as she questioned Tilley.

"I'd probably let the kids leave it on if it was up to me," Tilley said, "since the damage is already done. Tate won't let us though. But all this is really not the point, is it? If you want to get really philosophical, then the lightning and the Claytons' deaths are not the same thing at all. There's a big difference between living with the chance of the same thing happening again, and living with whatever it was that has already happened. Am I right?"

Jimmy didn't give Barbara Rose a chance to answer. He jumped right in and started talking about how it all boiled down to fear and death which, he added, is what everything boils down to eventually. This was when he brought up the whole thing about dying, about what way of dying it was that scared the devil out of us. After Barbara Rose's coughing spell and her failure to persuade Jimmy to pick another topic of conversation, I poured us all another round of drinks. Doubles—I made them all doubles.

"Well Tate? You haven't answered my question, boy," Jimmy said as I sat back down at the table.

"Hmmmm," I said. "Let's see . . . Michael Clayton's way of going doesn't strike me as a real happy send-off, but I imagine it was over pretty quick. That flash he must of had right as he realized she was going to do it, but she hadn't actually pulled the trigger yet—I can't say I envy him that. I guess you could say when all's said and done, it's the painful struggles against dying that worry me most, especially if they're brought on by some kind of surprise. Like the water-skier you always hear about who fell in a nest of cottonmouths—that gives me the willies. But then I don't water-ski . . ."

"Isn't that one of those urban myths?" said Jimmy. "Does anybody actually know somebody who died that way?"

"My best friend from high school," said Barbara Rose. "Her neighbor lost a second cousin that way."

"Well then," I continued, "there's also the story my daddy told me about the summer he worked on a road crew. It was Highway 54 they were putting in. Some guy was running one of those big mowers clearing a field near the old Alston plantation. Evidently the mower blade sliced a hornets' nest clean in two. I think they were hornets— could have been dirt daubers or yellow jackets. But they were plenty potent and pissed off too. Daddy said they swarmed the man's head. No matter how hard that poor feller ran, they stuck right on him. Said he looked something like a dark thundercloud that had grown a pair of moving boots and flapping arms."

"Sounds pretty bad," Jimmy said.

"Daddy said it was watching the man being completely filled up with something determined to kill him that has always stuck in his mind. Those hornets didn't just cover him, they crawled in him—down his shirt collar and up his pant legs. They filled up his boots and gloves. They stung his eyeballs and lids, burrowed up his nose, funneled into his ears, poured into his mouth . . ."

"Stop, Tate. That is enough," Tilley said. "We get the picture."

"Bzzzzzzzz," Jimmy held up a cheese straw and moved it in a crooked line to the edge of Barbara Rose's lips. "Pretty bad indeed," he said. Barbara Rose shook her head back and forth and refused to bite. Jimmy shrugged and popped the thing in his own mouth. He made loud chewing noises and smacked his lips after he swallowed. "Mmmm . . . tasty," he announced. "Sounds to me like Tate here is afraid of the enemy within, being filled up with poison and pain. Is that what gets your goat, too, Tilley?"

"Pointlessness. That bothers me a lot," Tilley said as if that were all she had to say on the subject.

But Jimmy didn't take the hint. "Ahhh, now that's an interesting perspective, Mrs. Gibson. Bartender," he said to me, "how about another little drinky-poo? Your wife has already sweetened the discussion, it's the least you could do." I got up and brought the bottle of bourbon to the table and topped off both our drinks. I left the cap off the bottle. It didn't seem worth the effort to screw it back on.

"Yeah, yeah, yeah . . . pointlessness. Now what exactly is it that you mean by that, Tilley? Can you give the rest of us some kind of example?" Jimmy asked. Beside him, Barbara Rose was frowning while she picked at a hangnail. She bit at it, rubbed it, bit at it again.

"Isn't pointlessness self-explanatory?" Tilley asked.

"We don't want there to be any room for misunderstanding," answered Jimmy. "In all my experience I've always found philosophical discussions flourish best when each contributor is able to elucidate his—or *her*—point with an illustration taken from life experience or perhaps from observations of the natural world. Plato—you can't conceive the many without the one." All the while Jimmy was talking, Barbara Rose acted as if no one else was in the room, as if she were completely engrossed with this hangnail situation and nothing else. She seemed outraged and furious with the tricky little piece of skin that she couldn't quite catch between her teeth.

"That Plato, he was some kind of good old boy, now wasn't he," I interrupted.

Tilley can't stand it when Jimmy starts in on the quotes. This kind of thing makes her roll her eyes behind his back and ask me later if he doesn't have any ideas of his own. "Let's all tip our glasses right now to Pluto—I mean Plato," I said. "A true gentleman and a scholar." Everybody took a swig. Even Barbara Rose stopped all that business with her nail long enough to choke down a big one. Afterwards, it seemed she gave up on doing anything about it. She stopped the biting and, instead, proceeded to use one nail to push back all her cuticles on one hand and then to switch over and work frantically on the other.

"Okay, okay," Tilley said, "I've got you an example." Her eyes were still smarting from the stiff drink she'd just taken. "There was this bird I saw the other day. A pretty, bright-red male cardinal." A light sheen of sweat had broken out across her upper lip and her posture had relaxed into a loose-jointed slouch. These were all signs that Tilley was getting snockered, but when I got up and mixed her and Barbara Rose fresh drinks I made Tilley's another double anyway. I felt bad. I knew she'd be feeling it tomorrow. "At first he was just sitting on a branch outside our bedroom window," Tilley nodded her thanks as I set the new drink down on the table by her left hand. "He sang a little and I thought it sounded so pretty. He was looking straight at our window, almost as if he were looking right in and singing me a pretty little bird serenade. He looked so cocky and fresh. I could have sworn he was flirting. Then he started putting on a show. He puffed up his chest and ruffled his feathers and hopped back and forth, tilting his head from side to side.

"I thought it was so cute when he started getting all hepped up like that. But then he flew straight off the branch and made a direct beeline for the window. There was a horrible thud and he bounced off the glass. Somehow he recovered and made it back to that same branch he had been sitting on before. But instead of having the sense knocked into him, he seemed to have been knocked senseless because he started doing the same thing over and over and over again. He'd fling himself at the window, bounce off, regroup, and then do it all over again, harder. He didn't seem to get what was happening to him at all. Each time just made him more determined until finally, instead of bouncing off, he dropped to the grass below." Tilley's eyes fluttered as she unknowingly sipped from her second double. "That's what I mean by pointlessness. He was dead, but his dying didn't mean anything. What was the point? What was the reason?"

"Now hold on there, partner," Jimmy said. "Whoa now. Wait just a minute. It may have appeared on the surface of things that there was no reason for that bird to die, not to you. But what about to him? Now, if we really examine this situation, plumb its depths, mine the possibilities, we may rise up enlightened. That's the beauty of philosophy."

"Just tell her," Barbara Rose mumbled without looking up. She was scraping hard at the cuticle on her ring finger, so she didn't see the look of annoyance that Jimmy cast her way.

"Tell me what?" asked Tilley.

"That bird wasn't singing at you," Barbara Rose explained as if she were apologizing to Tilley. "I hate to tell you this, but he didn't even see you."

"Protecting his territory," announced Jimmy, "a perfectly natural instinct for any male species. He—"

"He saw his own reflection," Barbara Rose interjected mournfully. I noticed then that she had stopped working on her nails and seemed a little let down but doggedly determined, like she was finally ready to face a battle she hadn't started and knew she was going to lose. "He was fighting himself. That glass was a mirror. He didn't understand the only thing he was hitting was himself."

"He did, however, understand the all-powerful instinct to survive," Jimmy insisted.

"It wasn't working very well," said Tilley.

"It's true. Nature does work in strange and mysterious ways," Jimmy continued. "All of God's creatures don't have the same power of reasoning that man does. This is what lifts us above the birds and the bees. We have the power to examine our instincts and to question the meaning of our and others' actions. Cause and effect. Deductive thinking. Problem solving. These are all tools that we can use to unlock the mysteries of the universe. If we apply them to Mr. Cardinal's situation, his death is understandable. He thought he saw another male bird challenging his place, threatening to compete with his driving instinct to produce as many progeny as possible before dying. There is reason. There is meaning. See? Case in point, once again, we return to the fear of death."

"Makes you think a little of Michael Clayton, doesn't it," I said.

"Meaning that he was responsible for killing himself?" suggested Tilley.

"Tate understands my point exactly," said Jimmy. I had lost track of the number of times I had refilled our glasses. While Jimmy's mind seemed to be off and running, my thoughts were becoming dull and befuddled. His words and ideas buzzed around my head. I was having trouble fighting them off. At that moment I wasn't exactly sure just what my own point had been.

"Plato has explained the most terrible death for all of humanity," the hum of Jimmy's brain continued. "'The life which is unexamined is not worth living.' This, my friends, says it all. This is where buddy Michael went wrong. If he had stopped to think about what he was doing, to examine his actions, to understand the nature of his instincts and the effect they were having on his mate—he might have figured out a way to prevent them from leading to his own demise. This is the shame of this situation. Michael Clayton's life was a waste because he failed to philosophize. Only thinking men are able to swing above the beasts in the forest."

"But what about Regina? What about her life?" asked Tilley. "She obviously gave it some thought. She had a reason for ending it, believe you me, but that reason doesn't do much to give her whole life meaning."

"Regina is the one who suffered the worst of all possible deaths," said Barbara Rose, as her eyes looked off into an unfocused, far-away distance. "Unloved. The woman wasn't loved."

"But her son," said Tilley, "he was bound to have loved her. I'm sure. And her parents, her family."

"You know that's not the same." Barbara Rose shifted her gaze to Tilley's face and spoke in the same gently apologetic tone she had used to tell Tilley about the bird. "That kind of love is important, but it's not the most important kind. She died thinking she had never had that. He ruined everything for her when he followed that senseless male instinct to boink anything that moves."

"Boink?" said Jimmy, suddenly looking offended.

"Boink," answered Barbara Rose. "Like two pigs rutting in the mud. That's all it was."

"But that's instinct," said Jimmy. "That doesn't have anything to do with love. He could still have loved Regina."

"If he loved her so much, then why couldn't he fulfill that instinct with her, his wife?" Barbara Rose emphasized her point by knocking against the table with the bottom of her glass. "You know there are some birds that mate for life. When their mate dies, they never *do it* again. Why didn't Michael have that instinct? Why didn't he realize how lucky he was? Regina loved him. Doesn't anybody realize how rare that is? In your lifetime, you have a better chance of being struck by lightning that you do actually finding real, true love—love with a capital *L*—Romeo and Juliet kind of love."

"I'm not sure that kind of love even exists," Tilley managed to slur out of the corner of her mouth. My normally perky wife was drowning in the conversation. She was slouched so far down in her seat it looked as if she were caught in a whirlpool that was sucking her under the kitchen table.

The conversation had begun to move in a very dangerous direction. The humming around my head had built to a dull roar. I was starting to get a headache. "Maybe he really cared for both of them," I said. "Maybe he loved Regina and the other woman."

"Cindy what's-her-name? I don't think so." Tilley shook her head, which struggled to stay afloat, right above her half-empty glass.

"It's possible," said Jimmy. "You don't know what goes on between two people."

"Love with a capital *L* can only be had with one other person." Barbara Rose sounded as if she had been studying up on this. "Only one. A person can only have one soul mate, only one person they're meant to be with and want to be with. If you think you've found that with someone else then you didn't really have it with the person who came before."

"I'm not sure I agree with you there, not sure about that at all," Jimmy said.

"What do you mean? It's true!" said Barbara Rose. She looked as if she were choking on Jimmy's words. Her eyes watered and her face turned beet red. "Are you telling me you Loved Penny? That I'm not the Love of your life, just some young thing you're instinctually boinking to ward off death?"

It was Jimmy's turn to stare at his own drink. It was empty. It had grown dark outside. The light coming from above the table poured down on us like warm honey. Half of Jimmy's face was lost in shadow. Even the silence buzzed in my ears and I wondered if anyone else could hear it. "Love is not such a simple thing." Jimmy's words flew out his mouth and joined the others circling around our heads. "It's not an absolute. It's based on perceptions, which can change. I thought I loved Penny for many years. So I did love her. But then I realized she wasn't the person I thought she was. So I didn't love her anymore, but I had still loved her all those years before. The change in my perception couldn't change what I had already felt—now could it?"

"So it's kind of like the bird," said Tilley.

"Yes," Jimmy replied in a voice grown soft, tender, thankful even. "Even though what he saw was his own reflection, for him it was another bird. He saw a threat and fought it. And because he did so, it indeed became a threat. After all, it killed him in the end, didn't it?"

"No, no, no," Barbara Rose moaned. She had put her head down on the table and was rocking her forehead back and forth across her folded arms. "Don't tell me Love is an illusion. That can't be true. I hate that." Watching her reminded me of similar tantrums thrown by our children when Tilley says they haven't eaten enough of their supper to get dessert. "It's not fair! I don't believe it! I won't believe it!" When Barbara Rose lifted her head, I could see she was all-out crying—just like one of the kids. The force of her grief and its messiness took me by surprise. Her face was all screwed up. Her mouth opened wide. She seemed to speak without having to move her lips and tongue. It was as if the words were coming out all by themselves, as if they had a life of their own. Each utterance, a stinging dart of poison, was launched from the gaping black hole of her mouth directly toward her husband's head and chest. "What if I'm not who you think I am? What then? No one should be allowed to just change their mind about who they love. Just who is it that you think I am anyway? What is it that you see when you look at me? Tell me, tell me now. I want to know right this minute!"

Jimmy took a moment before he answered. "You are the woman I love. You're the woman I've chosen to spend the rest of my life with. What more can I say?"

"What about the rest of *my* life? What if your sweet young thing, your marvelous mystery girl, has a big surprise for you that she found out about at the doctor's today and it's not a baby. It is growing inside, but it's not new life. It's death. You traded in your prize for what was behind door number two. And guess what, mister, you win the clunker, a twenty-eight-year-old model eaten up with breast cancer. How do you like that? What a deal! It must be your lucky day." Barbara Rose stopped crying and seemed to regain control over her own mouth. She hiccuped a couple of times and used her cocktail napkin to wipe her nose. Then she leaned back in her chair and closed her eyes.

For once, Jimmy was truly speechless. His face looked puffy and tired. He acted stunned and disoriented. All I could think to do was to offer everyone a drink, but I knew that now when we really needed them, no one could stomach another drop.

"Does anyone want to hear my philosophy?" Tilley asked. "Sometimes you can ask too many questions. Maybe we should all just take a minute to ponder that."

Barbara Rose nodded in agreement. "Plato meet Pandora," she whispered, with her right hand over her left breast as if she were pledging allegiance. Then both women let the silence fall again, as if they were satisfied that we had finally found the right question to consider.

The buzzing in my head was killing me. It was all I could hear, all I could think about. I kept worrying that I had forgotten something, something about the buzzing. The evening's swarm of words hummed across my brain as scenes from the day flashed through my mind. I found myself picturing the little girl who had been playing hopscotch next door. I was sure she had since gone inside, had supper, been tucked into bed, but for some curious reason all I could see was her sturdy little body hopping up and down as if she were still caught up in her game, still struggling to avoid the lines she had made earlier—imaginary obstacles that had become invisible in the dark.

CINDY WORTHINGTON

the other woman

1978

Have you ever noticed that in romance novels no one ever gets cystitis or VD? The hero never has bad breath or BO, and the heroine never has gas or gets her period at an inopportune time. Am I being too frank? Do I disgust you? Are you appalled? If the answer is yes, well then, gentle reader, turn back now, for true romance is not for the faint of heart. It is nestled between the smudged pages of a lurid paperback that romance offers the clearest rewards. For no matter how badly the hero and heroine mistreat each other, destiny wins out in the end and they both fall madly, passionately, and undeniably head-over-heels in love. And no matter how many close calls or brushes with death—duels fought, hostages held, falls from spooked horses suffered, mysterious fevers endured—neither of them *ever* dies. Sure they have their troubles—the fickle winds of fortune, war, disgrace, lost identities, societal pressures, painful misunderstandings, evil step-brothers, and wayward hearts— but the goodness of the heroine *always* wins her love in the end. No matter what, they always end up together, riding off into the sunset to live out the rest of their days happily ever after, deliriously in love and lust with the perfection of their mate.

Take, for instance, the story I've just finished reading, *Bird of Paradise*. Over the course of 456 pages, the heroine was kidnapped twice, locked in a dungeon, beaten with a whip, stripped of her clothes half a dozen times, gave birth to her first child unassisted in the jungle, and ravished too many times to count. Yet, she held on, fought for her love in the torrid heat of the Amazon, escaped a tribe of mean-spirited head-hunters, and managed to become even more beautiful by the end of the book than she was in the beginning. The adventures of Angeline, the raven-haired, emerald-eyed exotic beauty of this tale, prove that there is no telling, really, just how much trouble a simple story can get you in.

Of course, as a *fallen woman*, I know a lot about this too. I am perfectly aware of what this town thinks about me—the scarlet harlot who slept with Michael Clayton and drove his wife to kill him. I've felt the condemning stares, the sly glances, the speculating eyes. I know that there are those hypocrites who are busy trying to figure out how they can do (or keep doing) the same thing and not get caught, as well as the righteous others who wonder, *How could she?* I'm not sure I have good advice for the first group. But for the second, my answer is: just use a little imagination. It's not all that hard to figure out.

If I were to write my own saga it would be titled *My Romance With Romance*. For starters, it would be set in the lush, verdant land of the South, home of miscreants and gentleman, sexpots and ladies. A place where the powerful heat and humidity, notorious for sapping the strength of outsiders, is only a slight reflection of the true natures of the men and women who inhabit it. It would be a modern day story, spanning the sixties and seventies, riding the wave of the sexual revolution that swept across America and unleashed a storm of passion in its wake.

In keeping with tradition, after setting the scene—painting the backdrop so to speak—the story must begin with a description of our heroine as well . . .

1962, Riley, North Carolina—She was a young and foolish girl full of fiery spirit and grace. At fifteen, she had the temperament and beauty of an untamed colt. Her long, shapely legs, luxurious mane of burnished chestnut hair, and flashing sapphire eyes were already attracting the attentions of many would-be suitors, despite her obvious youth. She was willful, spoiled, an unrepentant flirt able to lift up and crush a male ego in the single blink of a darkly lashed eye. It was believed she had inherited her looks from her mother, a debutante from South Carolina, famous for her beauty and charm, who had died tragically after the birth of her only child. Everyone knew she was the only soft spot in her father's otherwise forbidding armor. A powerful landowner, who many feared and all respected, he was unable to deny her anything, spending lavishly and granting her every wish.

Okay, okay, it wasn't really exactly like that. I do have reddish, golden brown hair and it's natural, so it was that way when I was fifteen. My eyes are blue and I was skinny. But I'm only 5'4", so my legs were only so long even back then. I do have dimples though, and I didn't even mention them. They're probably my best feature. They're deep indentions in the center of both cheeks. When I was little, my mother told me I must have been kissed by an angel. Yes, that's right, my mother. It was my father who was the no-show, not my mother. She always insisted that they were married and that he died during World War II, a daring Navy pilot shot down defending his country, who would never see the child he fought so hard to protect. However, I was unable to pin her down on the actual details and, honestly, never could get all the dates to match up.

All I really ever knew was that it was just me and Mama for as long as I could remember, living in a shabby little mill house only about one step up from trailer trash. My mother was a nurse and looked about as far as you can get from a debutante. She didn't look *bad*. She just looked like a mother and *not* a glamorous one. She wore her hair chopped off in a practical bob and had the chapped, rough hands that mark those of her profession. The only makeup she ever wore was a thick coat of waxy lipstick. And her clothes weren't anything special—we couldn't afford it.

I was hardly beauty-queen material myself. I was such a gawky teen, painfully shy, with wild bushy hair and horn-rimmed glasses that left a red mark on the bridge of my nose. Far from popular, I was one of those people no one else ever notices. Once I was out sick from school for two weeks with mono and no one said anything about me being gone for so long when I got back, not even the people who sat next to me in class. Not even my lab partner, Sue Alston. That's just how it was. Back then, there wasn't enough of me to make a side character, the heroine's best friend or worst enemy, not even the hero's undeveloped little sister. I wouldn't have rated a character sketch in one of the crowd scenes, but could have easily been swept away in a clump of nonentities destined to remain forever in the background. *The gathering buzzed with amazement when the dashing couple finally made their dramatic entrance.* That was me lost in there, in case you missed me. An insignificant part of the crowd, featureless and nondescript, my nameless face just a pink blob that no one could see, much less remember.

It was right around fifteen that I discovered my mother's cache of romance books tucked away in the back corner of her closet. They were piled in a brown paper grocery bag, hidden behind the curtain of her drab winter coat. What was I doing snooping in my mother's things? I don't know; it was something to do in the afternoons. Like I said, I didn't exactly have an active social life to keep me busy. And Mama often worked the late shift. Lots of times she didn't get home until after I had already gone to bed. So I'd come straight home and do my homework, but then what? Usually Mama left a casserole for me to stick in the oven to warm up for supper, and I'd have a couple of chores to do. But all that only took minutes. Then I was left with staring at the TV or listening to the radio. Often the liveliness of the canned voices only made me feel the quietness of our own house even more. Silence and nothingness would drift over me like a thick gray cloud of my mother's cigarette smoke. Even a long, hot bath did nothing to get rid of its stubborn scent that clung to my skin and hair.

So, I started snooping. Maybe I was looking for clues to my mother's past. Or maybe I was curious about my own future. But for whatever reason, tiptoeing through my mother's possessions made me feel more alive. There was always a sense of danger and the possibility of discovering something unexpected. At first all I did was examine the inside of her jewelry box and the drawer in her bedside table. The only thing of interest that I found was a small silver heart-shaped locket that held a fuzzy black-and-white picture of a swarthy-looking man with dark hair and an impossible-to-read expression on his half-turned face. I visited the locket often but needed the thrill of conquering new territory, which led me to Mama's closet and the books. I can remember being immediately captivated by this treasure—the initial shock of discovery, followed by the rush that accompanies the sampling of forbidden fruit. I must have sat there on the floor for hours reading and rereading all the jacket covers until my feet and legs went numb and my whole body was left tingling with the anticipation of first love.

Initially, I dared only to *borrow* the books by Barbara Cartland. They were small, so I didn't think she'd notice if just one little book was missing. I could almost read one a night. I'd tuck it under my mattress before going to sleep and switch it for a new one the next afternoon. I think the very first story I read was set in colonial India. The central characters were an English lord and an Indian princess. The lord saved the princess who had been captured and enslaved by a wicked king. The princess was so beautiful the king had not been able to resist the temptation of stealing her for his harem. The cover was white with a framed color portrait on the front of the English lord leaning over the princess. He was handsome and noble looking with a strong nose and chin and tawny blond hair that brushed the collar of his shirt. He looked like he was in the middle of swooping down to eat her up. She was wrapped in a sari and veil. Her huge luminous dark eyes beckoned from the filmy frame of her exotic headdress.

There was hardly any real sex in these stories, but the promise of it was as potent as any strong perfume. The heroines were all fragile waifs, mysterious beauties who spent most of their time swooning, blushing and stuttering. Rarely did they come up with the courage and wherewithal to complete a full statement. Instead their speech was riddled with half-whispered words, gasps of alarm, and sighed salutations that were strung together with the inevitable thread of . . . All these girls were shy and retiring with a gentle inner beauty that won over the adoration and devotion of a handsome, debonair, and wealthy lover. Their stories uplifted and inspired me. Soon I was experimenting with thick black eyeliner and a collection of scarves I bought with my allowance at the thrift shop. I also got busy practicing the art of fluttering my eyelashes and letting them lie across my cheeks.

Chase Worthington became the focus of my new daydreams. He sat next to me in homeroom and English class. He was good-looking— already tall, dark, and handsome at sixteen. You knew it was only going to get better. He had these really intense eyes that were always half-closed and looked like they could strip you naked in just one casual glance. He made girls nervous. They'd giggle whenever he looked their way and whisper to each other about "bedroom eyes." He played basketball and sometimes drove his older brother's motorcycle without a helmet. He was a total enigma. I became completely and utterly distracted every time he came within a twenty-foot radius. What with all the batting and lowering of my eyes and trying to emit the all-powerful aura of fragility and irresistible sweetness, I had a hard time that year keeping up in English, which was normally my best subject. One day, my teacher, Mrs. Norman, must have become distracted by my antics as well, for she stopped class to ask me if I had gotten something stuck in my eye and needed to be excused to go to the restroom to flush it out. I was mortified, but remained determined. Despite my unwavering commitment to these tactics, however, Chase appeared to remain oblivious to my existence. Then one morning, the first day I had shown up at school sporting a new *beauty mark* I had placed high on my cheek right below the corner of my left eye, he finally spoke to me . . .

"Hey, there," he said in a lowered voice that scratched roughly across the delicate shell-pink swirl of her exposed ear. He leaned toward her as he spoke, and she couldn't help but notice the intoxicating male scent that immediately assailed her senses.

"Hi," she breathed. A becoming blush spread across her pale cheeks.

She could feel the heat of his gaze as he lowered it gradually across the planes of her face. She was overwhelmed and confused by the strength of her own body's response to the nearness of his. Her throat had gone dry, her heart was pounding frantically beneath the shallow rise of her flushed chest, and her stomach felt weak and trembly.

"Isn't your name Cindy?" he asked in a drawling voice that faintly mocked her.

She was sure he knew of her discomfort, that it was all too obvious the effect he was having on her. She didn't think she could stand it. Lost in the dangerous dance between moth and flame, her gaze fluttered beneath his. "Yes?" she replied, afraid that she was acquiescing to more than his question. "That . . . is . . . my name."

"Well, Cindy, I know we haven't known each other very well for long, but would you mind doing me a bit of a favor? I'm kind of in a jam and if you'd be an angel you could really help me out. I'd be forever grateful," he declared with one long-fingered hand pressed across his chest and the flash of a brilliant white smile.

What this was leading up to she could not imagine. She felt overcome and woozy, as if she might faint any minute. But she mustn't. She had to fight to control herself. She couldn't give in. She mustn't let him have his way with her. "Okay," she whispered. "I'll help . . . if I can."

"Thanks," he said and reached over and nonchalantly grabbed her wrist. His large hand easily encircled the tiny bones of her arm. She was horrified that he might feel her rapid pulse which leapt desperately against his negligent touch. Then he reached forward with his other hand and dropped a folded piece of paper onto her outstretched palm. A note . . . for her? What did it proclaim? . . . Undying love? . . . Devotion? . . . An insistent plea that she be his at last? His voice pierced her disheveled thoughts, "You're a doll. Could you pass this over to Serena for me?"

Serena? Serena Gupton? The beautiful idiot with big blonde hair and eyes so cold and empty they always made me think of being locked in a freezer? Cold, icy tentacles clutched at my heart. I remember being mad at myself. I should have known. Had I really believed Chase Worthington was going to just fall into my lap one day? With as much good grace as I could muster, I handed over the note to Serena, who just so happened to be patiently waiting in the seat next to me on the other side. She smirked at me as she ripped the note from my grasp and then favored Chase with what I'm sure she thought was a beguiling little grin. It looked more like a bizarre facial twitch to me, but I was hardly in the mood to be generous at the time.

I tried to find consolation in the fact that he did know my name and he hadn't been too grossed out to touch me. Besides, all good romantic heroines come across some *other* woman at some point in their story. I convinced myself Serena was that *other* woman, and I would have to refuse to be intimidated by her. I decided not to be thrown off, but to consider Serena as just one of those tests the heroine always has to face before she gets her man. And, of course, he was worth it. For a long, long time after that day, I spent countless hours reliving the moment when his hand circled my wrist, when he looked at me with those smoky, sultry eyes, when the sound of my own name touched his lips.

I hadn't given up, but I did realize I needed to do more research. It was in this way that my romance reading progressed from Barbara Cartland to Harlequins. The Harlequin heroines talked more and tended to be less *exotic*. Instead of being wafer thin, they had slender or trim figures, spoke in complete sentences, often showed signs of being spunky, and, for the most part, had to work for a living. One of my favorites in this category was the makeover. There was one story, in particular, I remember that had an orphaned young woman who went to work on a horse farm as a Girl Friday for a wealthy older man. Of course, the man was to-die-for, gorgeous beyond belief, and able to see past the woman's primly drab exterior. He spent the entire book slowly unveiling her beauty. The glasses were the first to go, right before he rocked her world with her first "real" kiss. (I must say, the kisses in Harlequins were much juicier.)

The "awakening" kiss was followed up several tension-filled chapters later with a much more lengthy onslaught that included blazing a trail of searing kisses across her face and neck as well as quite a bit of groping. It was during the groping that he pulled the pins from her hair, releasing it from the confines of its tight little bun and letting it spill through his rough hands and down her back and shoulders. After this climactic scene, it was only a matter of time before she agreed to go out for a special dinner with him. He surprised her with the gift of a sexy slinky dress that was oh-so-revealing of all her previously hidden charms. And she threw caution to the wind and wore the dress despite the way it clung to her every curve and left no doubt as to her very delectable assets. In keeping with the dress, she left her hair down and even applied a subtle touch of eye shadow across her lids and lip gloss across her kiss-swollen lips. The glasses had long disappeared. She didn't really need them anyway; she had just worn them because she thought they made her look more mature and capable. The finishing touches to her transformation occurred in the final scene when she discovered both diamond ring and full-length mink under the Christmas tree. And so there you have it—voila—a real life Cinderella story complete with dramatic makeover, handsome prince, and happy ending. Who wouldn't want that?

I was completely sold. I was ready to go to the ball and dazzle everybody with my unheralded beauty. I wanted everyone to say, "Who is that? She's exquisite!" And, most importantly, I wanted to win the love and admiration of my very own handsome, and sexy, Prince Charming.

So I got a job after school and on Saturdays at Woolworth's. Work did cut into my reading time a little, but it was a necessary sacrifice. The first thing I did was to buy contacts. The only time I let myself use my glasses was when I read at night. For a while I kept touching my finger to the bridge of my nose as if my heavy frames still needed to be constantly propped up. But eventually, I broke that habit and the red mark they had always left there disappeared.

Next, I paid for a new layered haircut at Ida May's and she showed me how to style it so that it would curl instead of frizz. I'll never forget that day in Ida May's shop when she finished cutting and blowing it dry for the very first time. "My goodness, honey, this new 'do does wonders, if I say so myself!" Ida May had exclaimed. "Now take a look and tell me what you think," she said as she turned my chair so I faced the big three-way mirror that hung over the speckled pink countertop. I did look different. Without the glasses and the poufy halo, I looked a whole lot less like a geeky nerd and a whole lot more like a girl with potential—real potential—big-blue-eyed and loose-curly-auburn-hair potential. I couldn't help but share a little secret smile with the girl who stared back at me. I felt as if I had just discovered my long-lost twin, only she was pretty and popular. Now that I'd found her, I had reason to hope that I just might actually be getting somewhere. I bought a heart-shaped silver locket of my own to celebrate and started wearing it all the time, even though it was empty.

You can be sure I didn't stop there to rest on my laurels. I bought fashion magazines and makeup and clothes. I worked on my posture by walking around the house with my heavy English textbook balanced precariously on my head. I practiced dancing in front of my closet mirror until I thought I could do it in public without making a total fool of myself. Good old Mother Nature even did her part—my figure finally blossomed so I actually had something to put in a two-piece bathing suit and my complexion cleared up. Now, none of this happened overnight, by any means. I was well into college before I felt like the new me actually existed. And even then, when I looked at old pictures of myself, they made me feel guilty and slightly queasy, as if they were evidence I was really an imposter.

Still, I made friends at UNCG. I went on dates. Kissed a few boys. Got to slow dance under the swirling lights of a disco ball. French kisses, holding hands, the suggestive brushes of thighs and chests beneath layers of clothing—that was about as far as I went. My girlfriends teased me about being a twenty-year-old virgin. "You need to get with it, Cin," they'd say. "You are way too uptight, baby. This is not Victorian England. You are living in America, and it's the sixties. Go ahead—live a little! Try it—you'll like it!"

But my mother had long indoctrinated me into thinking that love, especially if it involved *sex*, was not to be shared casually. In commenting on the misdeeds of what she termed "slutty" girls, she proclaimed that loose girls only hurt themselves in the end by ruining their chances for marriage. She always ended her warning with a question that she stated in the same ringing tones she used for the Golden Rule: "Why buy the cow when you can get the milk for free?"

I tried not to blame my mother for trying to lay a major guilt trip on me, seeings how the circumstances of my own conception and birth were so murky. Besides, what had made the biggest impression on me, what was really holding me back, was that in almost every romance I had read up to that point, the heroine was "deflowered" by the man who became her ultimate love. The bottom line was, I hadn't dated anybody who I believed had true romance hero potential.

During my later teens, I had sampled some of the thicker romance sagas. These books were *pumped up* with more, more, more—especially more violence and more *sex*. Their covers were bright, lurid pictures of men who were muscularly passionate and women who were so voluptuous they appeared about to burst out the top of their bodices at any minute—a not-so-subtle hint of what was to come in the pages that followed. For inevitably, in these stories, bodices were ripped and virgin territory was taken. No matter how many times the heroine ended up having sex during the course of her adventures, she began the book as a virgin. This plundering of virgin flesh was often one of the first major acts of the hero. And, strangely enough, it didn't matter if invasion was done by force or not. Being her "first" always had an amazingly powerful effect on the man. Initially he may have taken her by force, but nevertheless she always ended up breathless with sexual satisfaction, the key to his heart dangling from her dainty white hand.

To my friends, I may have appeared to be hopelessly old fashioned, an incurable romantic foolishly holding out and saving *it* for my wedding night. But I thought of myself as lying in wait, a tender trap primed to snap when the right man came my way. I was still waiting for the right catch when I spent the summer of 1967 down at Atlantic Beach living in a cottage on the Gold Coast with a house full of twenty- and twenty-one-year-old girls. The huge gray-shingled cottage belonged to Patricia Horne's family. Tricia, one of my suitemates, had convinced her folks that she and her friends needed a break before getting back to the grind of senior year or, even more trying, facing the cruelties of job hunting in the real world. I couldn't believe they gave in to her demands, but living there was wonderful—no chaperones, no check-ins, no rules, no regulations—one endless house party.

To cover expenses, I waitressed at a restaurant in Morehead City. But I had plenty of time to take advantage of it all. There were long hot days spent on the beach lounging and basking in the sunshine. Laying out was the perfect time for romance reading—the intense heat of the blazing sun heightened the seductive power of the steamy pages until I reveled in every trickle of sweat that rolled across my oiled skin, delighted in the subtle touch of the ocean breeze as it caressed my body, and was driven nearly wild by the constant irritant of sand and salt as it coated me, tickling, grinding, and clinging its way across every curve, every bend, every sticky fleshy inch. Whew! It was hot!

Then each evening, as the sun dipped slowly into the liquid horizon, we'd all rouse ourselves and take long tepid showers and get ready to go out. When I didn't have to work, I slipped out into the balmy night with the rest of them. We drank beer, danced, laughed, and flirted our way up and down the coastline. We collected boys like shells, casually picking up new ones when they caught our fancy and just as easily tossing the old ones aside when they no longer held our interest. I had never felt so alluring or powerful. It was as if I had unknowingly tapped into something that made guys fall all over themselves to get to me—*me*, the former nondescript pink blob in the crowd. The awareness of possessing this unknown something and its power over the male species was as heady a rush as I had ever experienced.

But still, I waited . . . until one night when I was sitting at a table with a group of friends and this guy came up to me. He had singled me out and just walked right up, as if he'd seen something he wanted and was just going to get it. He made no attempt to hide the fact that he found me attractive, but, at the same time, he seemed to be the one who was very much in control. He was older—a lot older. The first thing I noticed when he loomed over me was that his was the body of a man, not a boy. He was tall, the bulk of his broad shoulders and deep chest was massive and imposing. He had dark eyes, recklessly wind-tossed brown hair, and a square jawline that already showed the shadow of a heavy, scratchy beard. I don't know if it was his age, or if I was convinced by the way he'd lift an eyebrow and quirk the corner of his mouth, but I was sure he knew something that I didn't—a lot of somethings, actually. So when he asked me out and I felt the tiptoe of anticipation climb up my spine and lift the hair at the nape of my neck, I said yes.

For the next two weeks, he wooed me like mad, took me to bars and restaurants, and introduced me to all his older friends. Whenever we were out in public, he did all these little things that marked me as his. He would steer me with one hand placed in the small of my back or stand with one arm draped around my shoulders. He made a habit of bending over to whisper something in my ear or to tuck a lock of my hair behind it. He was constantly finding some excuse to touch me, to claim me, again and again. And when we weren't physically touching, his eyes held me in a grip that was even tighter and more compelling than that of his hand.

As each night passed, I got the feeling he was reeling me in, slowly but surely, drawing me toward him, closer and closer. Then instead of going out one evening, he asked me over to his place for dinner. He cooked for me. There was candlelight and wine. He had left all the windows open so that the breeze pushed and pulled at the billowing white curtains and filled the house with the lulling murmur of waves crashing along the shore. We went for late-night walks on the beach. We had a nighttime picnic and ended up lying on the blanket, my head cushioned against his shoulder while he pointed out different constellations in the night sky. And have I mentioned that his kisses were phenomenal? They started off as fairly non-threatening but intriguingly soft touches of lip to lip and grew into slow, erotic explorations that tormented me in a way I had never imagined possible as he used them to show exactly what he really wanted to do to me. And then there was the night he took me on a surprise boat ride in the moonlight . . .

As the boat slid across the smooth, glassy surface of the sound, the wind ran through her hair with insistent fingers, loosening her knotted scarf until the sun-bleached tresses broke free of their silken confines and flew in a wild, tousled mass that glinted under the glow of the night sky like rough waters in a deep sea. He was a dark silhouette at the helm as he drove recklessly forward in a powerful push that repeatedly lifted the boat until it skimmed the air and then slammed downward in a bone-jarring thrust.

She was mesmerized. The thin line of scattered lights that twinkled along the shoreline was a distant reminder of the carefully civilized life she so desperately wanted to escape. The rush of wind, the salty spray of water, the rhythmic pounding of her body, the glorious sensation of unchartered flight . . . she wanted it to go on forever.

But, finally, he slowed the boat and brought it to a gently rocking stop in the middle of the dark and deserted waters. They had a perfect view before them of the bridge, a dramatic arch against the star-laden sky.

"You're wet," he whispered as his warm fingers flicked across her damp cheek. She couldn't stop the shiver that raced along her nerve endings in response to even his slightest touch.

"You must be cold too. The least I can do is help warm you up," he said before slanting his mouth across her delicately parted lips. As he deepened the intensity of the kiss, his tongue tempted and teased every corner of her mouth, and his hands made their way up her narrow ribcage. His tantalizing onslaught ravaged her senses and sent her mind

reeling in an intoxicating swirl of physical delight. "So beautiful, so sweet," he murmured. Her back arched in response. She was on fire, a bundle of raw, needy nerves that craved his every touch. He pressed the length of his body against hers as they lay across the seat cushions.

"I want you," he moaned. His breath was ragged. His jaw clenched as he demanded, "I've got to have you." She thrilled at the force of his words and felt the ache of desire that threatened to consume her spread across her lower body. She knew then that she had been waiting for this moment since the first time she met him, since the first time her eyes had locked with his across the dimly lit bar, since the first time his hand had grazed hers when he introduced himself and handed her a fresh drink. Their meeting had sparked a flame that had been building ever since and that would take a lifetime to extinguish. But first, somehow she had to manage to hold on to a shred of sanity before things went any further.

"Stop. You've got to stop. I have to tell you," she said. "I haven't done this before. I've never been with anyone."

"That's okay, honey. It just so happens I'm a very good teacher." He continued raining kisses across her face.

"But, but, I was planning to wait," she weakly protested.

"Wait?" he said, his voice suddenly still and heavy as it filled the darkness. "For what?"

"For marriage," she answered in a nervous whisper. "For my wedding night."

An ironic chuckle escaped his lips as he began shaking his head back and forth. "You'd get married to somebody without ever sleeping with them first?" he asked in amazement.

"Yes," she said. She knew she was naïve, but she hoped against hope that he would find some way to reassure her, to overcome her doubts, and to make what she wanted with every fiber of her being possible at last.

She could feel his eyes boring into hers but their expression was lost *to her in the shadows. One corner of his sensually curved lips tilted upward. And then, the lips which had wreaked such havoc, turning her into a wanton who craved nothing but release, parted and he said, "You would buy a car without test driving it first?"*

Test driving it. That's what he said. Can you believe it? In the middle of the ultimate seduction scene, Prince Charming started sounding like a used car salesman. Hosing me down with a blast of cold water would have been almost as effective. So much for destiny. After that unpleasant little dose of reality, I couldn't get far enough away from him. I think I used the I've-suddenly-gotten-a-splitting-headache routine. I knew he didn't believe me, but at that point what did it matter anyway? I spent the ride back silently debating how many girls he'd said that stuff to before. Had that pitch ever actually worked? The thing was, I could tell that he had the nerve to be mad at *me* because *his* stupid line ruined everything. So I wasn't terribly surprised when I never saw or heard from him again.

I felt even worse about it when one of my friends told me she heard that the whole time he was going out with me he'd been engaged to some girl who'd gone to Europe for the summer. At the time, I tried to pass it off as being no big deal. But not only was it an incredible blow to my ego, it also shook me up to realize I'd almost wasted my virginity on some guy who was in love with someone else, and that, unknowingly, I'd been cast in the role of the other woman, a relatively cheap lay instead of the love of his life.

At the end of that summer, I went back home feeling slightly tainted. Even though I hadn't lost "it," something equally important had escaped me. I felt more mature and believed I had a newly acquired air of worldliness about me. Maybe it was that hard-won edge of sophistication, or maybe it was the sudden impact of my long-term makeover; but whatever the reason, when Chase Worthington saw me at a back-to-school bash there was something decidedly different in the gleam of recognition he flashed my way.

I have to say my first glance of him nearly took my breath away. If he had been good-looking in high school, he had become devastatingly handsome in college. He had filled out some, but still had that lean-hipped bad-boy swagger that made my pulse race. And those eyes—*mm-mm*—if anything they had become even more powerful. They were the eyes of a pirate, a libertine, a rake. And when he let them linger suggestively along the contours of my curvy figure, I felt my insides melt to mush.

I was careful, though, when he started to walk in my direction. Under the guise of tossing my hair, I glanced quickly to see if Serena Gupton was anywhere in the near vicinity. But she wasn't. And he did ask me to dance. In fact, he talked to me all the rest of the night. And he called the next day and the day after that. And when I went back to UNCG for my senior year and he to Wake Forest, he kept calling. We dated for months until one night in the late spring when we were both really drunk and he wanted to *do it* so bad that he convinced me to run off and get married.

So we eloped right before graduation. We only got as far as the first county in South Carolina. It was in a cheap motel at South of the Border that I lost my virginity sprawled across the already stained sheets of a bed that would actually rock if you put in enough quarters. It wasn't exactly what I had had in mind, but getting caught up and swept away by the rush of it all did seem kind of romantic. While the first time did hurt more than the books had ever suggested, it was a relief to finally have that done and over with and to move on to trying to get the hang of it. We "practiced" in that nasty room for three straight days until I got a raging bladder infection and had to go home to see the doctor.

After graduation, we moved back to Riley and Chase went to work for his daddy's real estate company. My mother took the news of our marriage pretty well, but Chase's parents were clearly disappointed. I don't think they've ever really approved of me, even long before the scandal with Michael Clayton. It was as if his mother could see straight through me to the poor, unattractive little girl that I really was and that she couldn't forgive me for being. Even after I gave birth to two healthy grandchildren, my status has always been questionable in their house.

However lots of times in romances there is an estrangement of some sort from the parents of either or both the hero and heroine, so at first I didn't let it bother me too much. These things were supposed to work out in the end. Of course, I kept reading every chance I got. When I put the kids down for naps, I'd read. When I had to get up in the night to breast-feed and had trouble going back to sleep, I'd read some more. While I washed diapers and mixed formula, I read about lush beauties caught against the hardened frames of their fiercely determined roguish lovers. In a life full of crying babies, burnt suppers, and dirty bathrooms, it was a relief to escape to a place where people had all the time and energy in the world for each other.

I couldn't help but notice that often in the stories the heroine didn't have a baby until the very end. The last scene would be one of family contentment—two passionate lovers delighted with the cooing, gurgling cherub that was proof and product of their consummated love. And if the story did continue after the first baby's arrival, it never mentioned any real problems with having both kids and a very active sex life. The guy never seemed all that put out or frustrated by the demands of his own child. The woman always bounced back quickly from giving birth. She was always just as tight and desirable and responsive as she'd ever been. Never did she even feel like screaming, "If one more person touches me or wants something from me, I'm outta here!" And never did he leave her at home by herself, night after night coming in smelling of liquor and strange perfume.

By the time Christopher was five and Charity was three, I decided to do something about the way things were going. I decided all Chase and I really needed was to get a little romance back in our lives. I had just finished *Sweet Savage Love* by Rosemary Rogers, one of my all-time favorites. The savagery of the story had kind of shocked me. I had been surprised by the lengths the heroine had to go to "win" the hero, and by the way the hero continued his dalliances with other women long after he'd married the heroine. But Ginette's determination to seduce her roving husband, despite everything, inspired me. I particularly liked the way she fought for her love and wooed his affections by learning to dance like a sexy gypsy.

So, with that in mind, I got my mother to take the kids for the night and told Chase he had to come home on time for dinner because his parents would be there. I closed the curtains and turned out the lights and got out every candle we owned and placed them all over the living room. I threw piles of pillows on the floor, poured two generous glasses of red wine, and put the record I'd checked out from the library's folk music collection on the stereo. I was proud of myself—nervous but proud. I'd worked hard on my outfit—a flowy skirt with the elastic waistline pulled down to my hips and one of Chase's white shirts, unbuttoned and gathered up instead and tied at the base of a plunging neckline between my breasts. No bra. No underwear. I was going all out. I let my hair dry naturally and fixed it so that a wild mass of curls tumbled down my back and loose wispy tendrils framed my face. I wore big gold hoop earrings and a delicate chain around my ankle.

It was all ready way too early, but I downed a few glasses of wine while I waited. I knew I had to be relaxed and slightly careless if I was going to pull it off. Still, I almost lost my nerve when I heard his car pull up in the driveway. But by the time his key turned in the lock, I was ready. And when he entered the doorway of the living room, when I saw him standing there, his jacket flung casually over one brawny shoulder, his white collar open against the tanned muscular column of his neck, his hair slightly rumpled as if he'd just run his long fingers distractedly through it, I began to dance . . .

The jeweled flash of her eyes, the enticing cleft that divided her generous bosom, the smooth creamy expanse of her bare belly beckoned and bewitched as she swayed across the room. At first her moves were full of provocative challenge—the flick of her wrist, the twist of her hips, the boldness of her gaze—each purposefully orchestrated to taunt and tantalize. And with each voluptuous gesture, the air between them thickened, growing charged with the electric force of their longing.

The primal beat of the music took possession of her slim figure and her sultry performance intensified as she lifted her arms over her head and ran her hands in inviting caresses down the length of her own body. Her feet turned in an ever-tightening circle that caused her skirt to flare out in a widening sweep, revealing teasing glimpses of slender calves and shapely thighs.

After completely losing herself in a frenzied spiral of unleashed desire, she ended the dance with a dramatic flourish—her head thrown back, her eyes closed, her body bent in an alluring offer of supplication. Slowly, she raised her head. She was flushed and triumphant. Her eyes were dark, liquid pools that drew him into their irresistible depths. She was a coquette, a temptress, a gypsy. Never had there been such a woman, a woman who burned with such passion and fire.

He remained motionless, staring broodily down at her. He was leaning against the wall, his arms crossed in front of his broad chest. The muscles had tightened in his face, hardening his jawline and thinning his lips. The expression in his heavy-lidded eyes remained enigmatic. But she knew. She could feel the tongues of desire as they leapt and sizzled between them. Without moving an inch, he radiated the overpowering force of his need for her. Any second, he would reach with lightening strength and crush her in the steely arms of his embrace. She could already feel the rough heat of his hands stroking her skin, the probing thrust of his tongue as it plundered her mouth, and the crisp texture of his hair as her fingers threaded their way through it.

He shifted slightly and lifted his chiseled lips in a sardonic smile. The arrogant lines of his face remained harsh and unrelenting as his voice sliced through the vibrating air with a violent potency, "What in the hell do you think you're doing?"

Instead of being turned on, Chase had gotten pissed off. He had been angry that I had "tricked" him about dinner with his parents and further irritated to discover that I hadn't actually fixed anything to eat— not in the way of real food—that is. It was only after I'd thrown together several ham sandwiches and plied him with plenty of wine that he *relented* to having sex on the floor of the living room. I tried to make the most of it. And afterwards, I even told him about several other scenarios I had dreamt up for us that I thought would be fun and exciting. I said, "Come on, it'll spice things up a little. You can be a ship captain and I'll be your wench. We can pretend we've never had sex before. I'll even get you an eye patch." He laughed at that one and said I'd obviously been spending too much time reading "trash."

But he didn't come right out and say, "No." So I kept trying to spring little surprises on him. It was the handcuffs that actually did the whole thing in. He got so mad when I cuffed his arms to the head-board, and then realized I couldn't find the key, that I lost my nerve. I pretty much gave up after that and decided to go back to work instead.

By this time, Chase was making enough money to pay for someone else to clean the house and look after the kids some. Christopher started kindergarten and Charity became obsessed with following Eunice around while she dusted and ironed. So it wasn't long before it dawned on me that I needed something to keep me busy. I could type, file, answer phones. Suddenly, the idea of having some other place to go every day—some place where I could be a real working woman instead of a frustrated, horny mom stuck at home with a never-ending pile of dirty laundry—appealed to me. I swear. I did not start off looking for romance, just a job.

Chase thought it was a good idea too. He was actually the one who found the job for me. You see, Michael Clayton did some accounting work for Worthington Realty and he mentioned to Chase that he was looking for someone to help out in his office part-time. Chase told Michael he thought I might be the person Michael was looking for. Looking back, it does seem pretty ironic, doesn't it? But at the begin-ning, it was all so innocent. Yeah, I know, that's what they all say, but this time it was really true.

Before I started working for Michael I didn't know all that much about him. I knew he was married, had one son, and lived at the coun-try club. And, of course, I could see with my own eyes that he was pretty handsome—in that craggy, older-man kind of way. He had dark hair that was going a little gray at the temples and a nice solid build.

He wasn't as tall as Chase, but he wasn't short either. If you want to know the truth, the sexiest things about him were the lines on his face. He had that Marlboro Man look with crinkly lines that radiated from the corners of his eyes as if he'd spent long hours squinting in the sun, and (these were really my undoing) two crescent-shaped creases that framed the outer corners of his mouth. You could just look at him and tell that he had been around long enough to know what he wanted and how to get it. I have to admit, I was drawn to that.

While he was extremely charming, Michael—or Mr. Clayton as I started off calling him—was old enough to be intimidating. I didn't really mind that though. It kept me on my toes and added a little edge of excitement to what otherwise could have become very mundane duties. As it was, I enjoyed playing secretary. I started wearing my hair pulled back in a sleek knot at the nape of my neck. I liked wearing hose and heels and short straight skirts that "said" no-nonsense but showed off my legs all the same. I switched from Opium perfume to Chanel No. 5 and began favoring rich red lipsticks and liquid eyeliner.

But then I started hearing things about Michael, about how he was practically notorious for having affairs and how the town was just loaded with his conquests. I didn't believe it at first because I knew how much this town liked to talk. Around here, they'll go ahead and make things up if they don't have something juicy to gossip about. So I took it all with a grain of salt until I, myself, started noticing that Michael kept kind of strange, disjointed hours and that his wife, Regina, always sounded strained when she called for him at the office.

And then Michael started making comments about Regina. Little things at first that I guess were supposed to be more compliments to me than criticisms of her. Things like how much he admired my working, that he thought that was just great that I showed such ini-tiative and he bet my husband was real proud, and how much he wished his own wife would do something like that with herself. Later, the things he said became more revealing of Regina. He would shake his head and tell me how reclusive she was, how she never liked to go out and how unhealthy he thought it was to spend so much time alone. "But what can I do?" he'd turn to me and ask with a winsome smile to lighten the weight of his question.

Meanwhile, he kept being really nice to me. He was full of compliments. Anytime I wore something new or different, he noticed. He was always noticing things about me, things Chase never paid attention to. Michael even tried to get to know me better. He'd play this game of trying to figure out what my favorite color or food or music was. And he'd make these guesses about what I was really like. He'd say stuff like, "I bet you're the kind of woman who likes to be wined and dined. I bet you like to get all gussied up and go out for a night on the town, now don't you?"

He just seemed so lonely—a charming man with a hidden, secretive past. Before I even realized what I was doing, I had cast him in the role of *Lord Raven*, a dashingly seductive older man whose dark side was the result of being tragically saddled with a crazy wife. After all, it was not unusual for a romance to begin with a hero of ill repute, whose bad reputation was really the result of a misunderstanding. Oftentimes, this kind of hero was scarred or *masked* to hide his identity, and sometimes both. His true love was always the one person who was able to see past whatever marked him on the outside and into the nature of the real man that lay beneath the surface. Her passion for and devotion to him healed his scars. And, in the end, his honor was restored as well. All this happened because she dared to believe, despite what other people said and how things may have *looked* at the time.

I practically fell into this role. I had almost no difficulty convincing myself that Michael was really *good* and that he had fallen in love with me, but was trying to deny it because of the impossibility of our situation. So when he put the moves on me one night when I stayed late to help during tax season, I took it all as further confirmation of my own understanding. That first time was not bad, not bad at all. He took his time—pulling the pins from my hair, lots of deeply searching kisses—all that good, romantic stuff. And, I have to say, the novelty of office sex was a powerful aphrodisiac. Doing something so messy and uncivilized in the midst of a formal business setting made me feel like an unwilling slave bound by her master to commit forbidden and unspeakable acts.

Did my conscience bother me while all this was going on? Not really. After all Chase had been keeping suspicious late-night hours for years. I figured he was finally getting what he deserved. And Regina was just a shadowy figure in my mind. The less I thought about her, the less real she seemed. It may seem twisted to you, but I considered *her* the other woman, not myself. I deserved to be the heroine because I was the one who believed in Michael.

At least that's how I thought it was supposed to work until the day Regina walked in on us. And yes, the stories are true; we were having sex on his desk. There aren't really all that many choices in an office. I was quite disenchanted with the awkward gymnastics on hard, uncomfortable surfaces that had become routine by then. It's difficult to remain lost in the unleashing of primal urges when a stapler is biting into your shoulder blade and your panty hose are hanging in a constricting wad around your ankles. Of course, we had locked the outer door of the office and had never imagined Regina would show up with a key. She had never dropped by before while I was working there.

My eyes were closed in concentration when I heard Michael cry out, "Regina!" in a voice that sounded horrified and amazed, as if he'd made a sudden and terrible discovery. His head was turned and he was looking over his right shoulder when my eyes flew open and saw her standing in the doorway. My gaze glanced off Michael's strong profile and focused on the woman hovering in the background. I noticed first the outline of her figure. She was tall and trim, not slender but athletic. Her dark hair was a little mussed, her crystal blue eyes widened with pain and surprise in the pale oval of her face.

And as I looked, really looked at her for the first time, the worst thing I discovered was that she didn't look crazy at all—devastated but very sane. That was when I began to fully understand what I'd done. I didn't have to look into her eyes to see the years spent folding his laundry, making his bed, cooking his dinners and waiting for him to come home and eat them. And when Michael's frozen body slumped in defeat, I realized just how far I had allowed myself to travel down the path of romantic fantasy.

She was gone in a second. Michael and I were already fumbling with our clothes when I heard the soft click of the outer door as she left the building. I kept my head down, my attention directed on fastening all the buttons down the front of my blouse and nothing else. My hands shook and I refused to look Michael in the face. I never made eye contact with him again. I was so ashamed and in such a mad rush to leave the scene of my crime that I just grabbed my pocketbook and ran. For once, Michael was at a loss for words. As I left, I caught a glimpse of him sitting silently deflated in his desk chair.

I rushed home and took a long hot shower and tried to wash off the whole nasty, sordid affair. Lost in the pages of my worst nightmare, I instinctually reached out for something to help me find my way. That was how I ended up spending the rest of the afternoon and most of the evening rereading *The Wolf and the Dove* by Kathleen E. Woodiwiss. I had read that book so many times, it had fallen apart. He was so strong and honorable and loved her so much, and she was so good and beautiful and smart about getting him to admit it. I wanted to bury myself in their medieval world of vanquished evil knights and restorative love and never come out.

It wasn't until the next morning that Chase told me Regina had killed Michael and shot herself. And then later that afternoon Chase broke the news that Regina had died in the hospital as well. When Chase told me, he spoke in a flat emotionless voice and kept his eyes on the cover of the book I was holding in my hand. He never accused me or even tried to talk about what had happened. To this day, he still hasn't.

It's hard for me to think about how bad I felt. I don't really want to remember. Let it suffice to say that there is nothing worse than realizing you've done something so hideous and it's too late to turn back now. You've done it and nothing can ever change that. I tried to block it out, forget it, pretend that it was my evil twin who had done it and not the real me. I had read stories about twin sisters—one good, the other promiscuous. The good sister was always being mistakenly blamed and judged by the bad sister's actions. The hero who falls for the good sister does so even before he finds out she's really good after all. I longed for the righteous indignation of that good twin, though I would have even settled for the lack of conscience of the bad one.

Somehow I thought if I read enough of these stories I would figure out where I had gone wrong. So basically, all I did for a long time was read one romance right after the other. I figured this was a guilty pleasure that couldn't hurt anyone. In those books I was safe. I could lose my virginity, find and discover new love, face all kinds of torment and demons, without ever having to confront a single, solitary soul.

Nothing compares to a romance novel when it comes to giving me the sense of entering an entirely different world and somebody else's life. When I'm reading, I can hear everything that's going on around me—Eunice vacuuming in the hall downstairs, the phone ringing, the children screaming—but it all fades into the background while the story unfolds before me. It's as if I'm living *there* where the story is taking place and real life is just a distant hum, the drone of the TV someone else is watching.

Not only are romances a great escape, but they are also powerfully addictive. Reading a romance is like good sex. While you're doing it, you can hardly wait to get to the end, yet you don't want it to ever end—and as soon as it's over you can't wait to do it again. It's a heady, consuming rush and I needed that. I desperately needed something—anything—to get me through that time, to help carry me from one day to the next.

Things went on like this for about a full year. Chase spent even more nights out late, and we hardly went anywhere as a couple. I couldn't much blame him, really. But gradually, I tried to do more stuff with the kids and make myself get out for their sake. One thing too was that people tried not to say too much in front of Charity and Christopher, so that made it a little easier. Over the past summer, I took them with me wherever I went—to the drugstore, the grocery store, the hairdresser's, the swimming pool. And when we went as a family to the Fourth of July picnic at the country club, I spent all my time taking care of them. It was like traveling in a bubble. I just didn't see anyone or acknowledge anything that was outside of what I thought was safe. While I watched the kids swim, filled their plates with food, washed their sticky fingers and faces, I played over in my mind different scenes from the books I had read most recently. And I got through it all right. I figured, if I was careful, I could keep up that bubble for a long time.

But then just last week, Chase surprised me. He announced that we were going to go to a party this weekend. A new couple who had just moved to town and bought a house on the golf course was having the party. It was an adult thing, he said, a masquerade party. He said he would handle the costumes and had already made arrangements to pick them up from a rental shop in Chapel Hill. I didn't know what to think. Part of me wanted to be hopeful. But another part worried about who would be there and what I would do with myself without the children to keep me distracted. And I couldn't tell how Chase really felt about it. It was his idea, but there was something about it all that made me uneasy.

This brings us up to yesterday, Saturday, the day of the party. Chase drove to Chapel Hill in the morning and picked up the costumes. I was reading upstairs on the chaise lounge in my room when he got back. He made a sweeping bow and said, "For you, Madame," and draped the clothes bag over my legs. And then he stood back to watch my reaction as I unzipped the bag. I couldn't stop my jaw from dropping in disbelief when I saw what he had chosen. It was a shimmering blue ball gown, complete with dramatically full skirt, cinched waist, and daring décolletage that looked as if it had been made for the heroine of a historical romance. When Chase saw my reaction, his eyes dropped all the way closed for a second, his dark eyelashes fanned against his high cheekbones, and a slow, wicked grin spread across his face. "I figured this would be right up your alley," he said before turning away.

I spent most of the afternoon getting ready. I coaxed my hair into a cascade of ringlets on top of my head. I wore delicate, antique-looking drop earrings and my old silver locket. My mask was beautiful. It was daintily cut with eyes that slanted in an upward tilt. The background was the same blue as my gown, but it was covered in iridescent beads and sequins. I took a lot of time with my makeup, even though I knew the mask would cover some. I applied lots of dark mascara and loose white powder. Then I added red lipstick that contrasted sharply with my pale, powdered skin and, on impulse for old times' sake, a playful beauty mark right above the corner of my mouth.

I hadn't been that excited in a long time. Chase had even taken care of the kids for the evening. He'd gotten his mother to agree to have them over to spend the night. Just before they left, they came upstairs to see how I looked. They were so sweet. Both of them sucked in their breaths and held them for a minute before ooooing and ahhhing like they did when they saw fireworks magically light up the sky on the Fourth of July. Charity's little-girl voice exclaimed, "Just like Cinderella, Mommy!"

Chase looked very handsome as well. His costume matched mine. His long jacket was the same color blue and his tight-fitting buff-colored pants stopped just below the knee. The snowy white shirt and cravat gleamed brilliantly against his dark skin. His mask was also blue, but bolder and unadorned. It added an air of enticing mystery. In fact, the combination of courtly dress and roughly masculine physique was quite impressive. I felt my own breath catch in my throat when I looked at him. He was the epitome of an eighteenth-century gentle-man Don Juan, and he was *my* date.

He held all the doors for me and helped me in and out of the car. As we made our way up the path to the front door, he walked beside me and lightly cradled my left elbow in his hand. To all eyes, he would have appeared to be a devoted and solicitous lover. But when we stepped in the foyer, Chase didn't even look at me before he tossed our car keys in a large clear glass bowl that sat on a fern stand right by the front door. It took a minute for me to realize what he had done. The bottom of the bowl was already filled with clusters of keys bound by an assortment of key chains.

Chase had brought me to a *key* party. I had heard rumors about them, that at the end of the night each man would draw a set of keys from the bowl and go home with the woman who *went* with that set.

I tried not to let my emotions show. I kept a smile on my face and carefully acknowledged the hosts, who were dressed as Jack and Jill, before I headed to the bar. After a few gimlets, I switched to champagne because I thought I needed something bubbly and effervescent. But I might as well have been drinking water; I couldn't feel a thing from the alcohol. As I wandered around the house, I felt an intense panic rise up from the pit of my stomach and invade my chest. Everything inside me constricted. I couldn't think. I couldn't feel. I didn't know what to do.

Chase had disappeared. I didn't see anybody I was sure I knew. For a minute I thought, *Maybe that's Jack Joyner over there in the cowboy outfit—he has a mustache like that.* But then the cowboy laughed and it sounded all wrong. And I thought, *No way, what would a banker be doing here anyway?* So I looked in the other direction and spied a beefy sailor who was using one hand to grab at the rear end of a big-boned mermaid. The sailor was making a joke about his wooden leg and the mermaid giggled while she adjusted her red wig, which fell in a tangle of ratty curls well past her waistline. There was something about their body shapes that reminded me of Richard and Lorna Everette, but I couldn't be sure. And, frankly, the thought of Richard's fat fingers touching me made me sick.

Frantically, I kept searching the crowd but it was getting late. I saw a doctor dressed in green scrubs walk up to a French maid and dangle a set of keys in front of her eyes. "I gotta cure for what ails you," he said while he slipped one finger in the waistband of her frilly white apron and started pulling her toward the door. That was when I decided I wasn't going to stick around. I had to get out of there. I made some ridiculous comment to the bartender about needing fresh air and escaped out the back. The house was big and modern with sliding glass doors all across the living area that opened onto a stone patio. There was a swimming pool and then the golf course beyond. I pretended to be enjoying a nice, leisurely stroll while I admired their elaborately landscaped gardens. But when I reached the edge of the yard, which was separated from the golf course by a thin stand of trees, I picked up my skirts and dove into the darkness.

Instinctively, I ran along the edges of the neighbors' yards, as if the clumps of trees and shrubs that grew there offered some kind of protection. I didn't know how I'd get home. I wasn't thinking very clearly, except about what was waiting for me back at that party. I could hear music and laughter spilling down the golf course after me and tried to run faster. The tight stays in the bodice of my dress made breathing difficult. But I wasn't going to let anything stop me. I was determined to keep running until the only thing I could hear was the sound of my own gasping breath. The stitch in my side had become a sharp burning pain when I was brought to a halt by a sudden yank on my shoulder . . .

She let out a muffled cry of alarm when she felt the tender flesh of her bare shoulders and upper arms caught in a hard and merciless grip. Her body felt as if it were being twisted in a steely vise as she was forced to turn around to confront her assailant. Fear raced through her veins when she looked up into the face that loomed above hers in the darkness. His head and face were obscured by a black wide-brimmed hat pulled low on his forehead and a large black mask. The severe features of the mask revealed nothing. A hawk-like nose jutted insolently from below the narrow slits that hid his eyes. And when the black cloak that hung from his wide shoulders spread into two velvety wings as his arms enclosed her in a stifling embrace, she couldn't help but think of herself as helpless prey.

There was no mistaking the raw, animal heat that emanated from his body, but she felt, rather than saw, the glint of his gaze rake her vulnerable flesh as he easily plucked the jeweled mask from her own visage. She gasped in outrage and began to beat her fists ineffectually against his unyielding chest. With little wasted motion, he captured her wrists and held them in one gloved hand behind her back. The other hand reached for her heaving bosom and grasped the plunging neckline of her gown, ripping it in one quick gesture all the way to the waist. She felt the shock of cool, night air touching her heated skin.

Without a moment's hesitation, he pushed her down to the ground. Her arms were pinned together above her head and her skirts shoved up around her hips. She could feel the moistness of the grass beneath her begin to seep into her clothing. She moaned in desperate denial. "No, no," she pleaded. But to no avail, for quickly and efficiently he stripped her of her undergarments and she could feel the full weight of him crushing her slight form.

A strangled expletive exploded from his lips as he bore down relentlessly, foraging deep into her innermost recesses. The writhing of her tortured body only seemed to heighten his determination to demand and possess. She felt as if she had been taken by a wild and uncontrollable force of nature. Never in her life had she ever had such a mind-shattering experience. Her senses were devastated as his engorged flesh continued its violent conquest of the inner core of her being.

Truth be told, instead of feeling overwhelmingly ravished, I felt dried up and hurt. When you haven't lost yourself in ecstasy, then all you end up feeling is exposed, used, betrayed. And that was what overwhelmed me—the sense of being betrayed—betrayed by myself, betrayed by my husband, betrayed by romance. The whole time I was trapped there, I tried not to look at him because there was something familiar about him. I was terrified of looking too closely for fear that I would recognize him and be forced to remember what he did to me every time I ran into him. On the street, at the post office, by the go-fish booth at the elementary school fall carnival—there he could be and he would give me that knowing look and I'd have to live with it.

So I kept my head turned and my eyes closed. And when he was finished, he tossed the keys on my stomach and left me lying there without speaking a single word. Somehow, I managed to drag myself back to the car and drive home. I was grateful Christopher and Charity were at their grandparents' house. I took a hot shower, got cleaned up, and put on an old sweat suit. I was too keyed up to sleep, so I reached for a new romance out of habit. Chase never made it home last night.

It's afternoon now and I've spent most of the day sitting on a lounge chair in the backyard, finishing *Bird of Paradise*. Despite last night, I still managed to enjoy the book. And now that I've finished it, that old familiar surge of pleasure filled with bittersweet longing washes over me. *Bird of Paradise* was a second-chance romance. I have read a lot of these stories. Sometimes the *first love* has died, sometimes the lovers have been cruelly separated, but almost all of them involve some kind of initial *fall* for the hero or heroine and a chance to recover and find happiness in the end. Through the whole story, you, the reader, often just want to shake the heroine and say, "It's so obvious he loves you!" But, of course, you can't. Part of the drama and excitement is waiting for her to figure it out.

How do I know if I am not that same kind of *blinded* heroine—the kind that doesn't see love when it's right in front of her? But I'm afraid that's just wishful thinking. I'd like to believe that I'm caught mid-way, stalled somewhere around Chapter 15, in the story of a second-chance romance and that all I have to do is just keep going and everything will work out. But it could be that my story is already over, or that I'm simply stuck being the *other woman*. No matter how hard I try, I can't see my situation objectively.

The lulling warmth of the sun makes me drowsy. So I lean my head back and close my eyes. But suddenly a cool shadow falls across my head and shoulders and I see the face of the masked man staring back at me. Frightened, I open my eyes and find Chase standing in front of me with his back to the sun. He's looking down at me and the expression of his features is lost in the shade. I don't know what to say. He takes a deep breath as if he is getting ready to speak, and a fierce lonely cry splits the silence. Something rustles inside my heart and reminds me of unseen footsteps crunching through dry autumn leaves.

I look over Chase's head and see the black outline of a large bird in mid-swoop. "A hawk," I say and try to follow its path.

"Nah," Chase answers without bothering to look. "Turkey buzzard, I bet."

But I become more convinced it is a hawk as I watch the pattern of its flight as it circles and banks in the patch of golden sky above. The book slips from my grasp and the hawk floats further and further out into the horizon until it becomes a tiny black dot—a period marking the end of a sentence that spans the sky. And when it vanishes behind a single dark cloud, I know it represents a place so far, far away that it is lost in the edge between light and darkness. A place so beyond reach, I can't imagine ever finding myself there.

MIKE JR.

Michael and Regina's son

August 2007

Picture this, a young boy caught standing in an open doorway, his black-and-white image frozen in the center of the photograph. He is crossing the threshold, bent on entering a dim interior. A soft halo hovers along the top of his head and narrow shoulders, but his features are depicted in clear, focused detail. He holds one arm extended toward the camera. His palm is cupped and turned, cradling an unseen object. His eyes are two dark-rimmed full moons that shine with liquid light. He stares upward, beseeching the viewer to take a closer look.

The boy appears to be about eight or nine. His build is sturdy but slight. He wears a white T-shirt and the open, triangular smile of genuine childish delight. The stiff stand of his fuzzy crew cut adds to his look of surprise, and there is a careless smudge of dirt balanced on the tip of his freckled nose. Behind him is the scratchy gray outline of a screened door that is tilted open and bleached by the blinding blast of outdoor light. The entire scene is surrounded by a circle of undeveloped darkness that bleeds a smoky fog from the corners inward. So it appears that the boy is about to enter a long dark tunnel with his hand outstretched as if making a sacred offering to the gods.

The boy is me. I am the boy. At least I was about thirty years ago. This photograph marks the first page of my family photo album and a time in my life that was full of wonder and discovery.

No one else thought I'd find one. And I can't say how the idea got in my head, but it did. And I just about drove my parents nuts during the search.

"Is this an arrowhead?"

"No."

"Is *this* an arrowhead?"

"No, that's just a pointed piece of gravel."

"How about this one?"

"Not quite. Remember they're pointed, shaped like a triangle."

"Okay. Like this?"

"Even more like a triangle."

"How will I know when I see one?"

"You'll know," my mother promised.

But I don't think she actually *believed.* I kept looking anyway. It became an obsession. At times I got discouraged for a day or two. But then a pointed rock would catch my eye and the hunt would be on again. I never really thought I wouldn't find one. I just thought it was taking longer and was harder to do than I had expected.

Of course, I wasn't even looking when I actually found it. Mom had me helping her plant bulbs in the backyard. She was in the kitchen fixing our lunch, tomato soup and open-face cheese melts. I was supposed to be turning over the soil, loosening it so the bulbs could breathe, she said. The dirt was hard packed and I was tired, bored really with what I thought wasn't much of a fun thing to do. So I was sitting there, biding my time until I got called in to wash my hands and mindlessly digging a small hole when the tip of the trowel hit against something hard and I heard the flinty sound of metal scraping rock. Oh, how I remember that instant flash of recognition. *This is it! I've found one!*

And when I brushed the dirt from it, all doubts crumbled away as well. This wasn't just a long crude triangle that said, "Yeah, *maybe*. I *could* have been an arrowhead once." This one was perfect. Made of greenish-gray stone, it had a compact head and narrow stem. It wasn't just a pointed rock that some lazy Indian picked up casually and said, "I can use this." Someone's hands had worked to chisel its shape and define its edges.

Nearly breathless with excitement, I ran toward the house, yelling to my mother through the kitchen window. She met me at the door, camera in hand. "Smile for the birdie," she would have said. "Smile." And then gently triggered the snap of the shutter, the pop of the flash.

"Is *this* an arrowhead?" I demanded.

"Why yes, honey, it is," Mom said. "It is an arrowhead. Where'd you find it?"

"In the dirt where you had me digging," I said. "You know there might be a whole burial ground out there."

For a while afterwards, I entertained fantasies of leading an excavation of the entire backyard, but Mom just laughed every time I mentioned it. I knew she'd never want to mess up her garden. However I did get her to help me tie a piece of rawhide around the base of the arrowhead so I could wear it around my neck. I refused to take it off for baths or church, not for anything. I wore it to bed every night and wished it would make me dream the adventures of a daring Indian brave who spent every day taming the wilderness, fighting to survive, defending the fierce nobility of his people.

I still have that arrowhead today. I've lost the rawhide strip, and when I look at it it seems diminished in some way. I'm always surprised at its smallness. My hands are large now, but if I position its point in the center of my palm and squeeze my hand into a tight fist I can still imagine it sailing through an arc of air, destined to meet living flesh with purpose and hope.

As I sit here in my favorite cracked leather chair staring into the eyes of my former self, everything that belongs to my current surroundings—the faint sounds of city traffic, the blur of the Los Angeles skyline that fills the picture windows of my sparsely furnished apartment, the bookcases and framed photographs that line the walls of my living room, even the geometric pattern of the oriental rug and the gentle breathing of the dog that lies at my feet—all of it falls away and I find myself dropping down a rabbit hole that leads to a different place and time, one that never ceases to be more real to me than the one I leave behind.

The past calls in a voice full of the haunting melodies of my youth— the elusive refrain of a whip-poor-will echoing in the softened heat of early dusk; mothers calling children to supper; the distant, rhythmic pounding of a basketball as it bounces on pavement and occasionally strikes against a wooden backboard; fathers yelling "fore" to clear the fairway; golf carts full of joking men that come to sudden, squeaking halts; the whoosh and ping of carefully aimed shots; the rattle of clubs as the cart rolls away. As the sounds ring hollowly in my ear, the scent of nostalgia wafts over me, smelling of sweaty leather, pine sap, and my mother's earthy scent—the crisp green of wet grass, the richness of black soil, and the clean perfume of Dove soap. And I am filled with a sense of loss and longing, the unmistakably familiar pangs of homesickness, that childhood disease brought on by strange beds and foreign circumstances. Such is the power of photographs, those small stamps of encapsulated time that drown us slowly, image by image, in a bottomless well of remembrance.

The album I hold open in front of me is my Book of Before. When I look at the awkward Victorian portraits of my grandparents as children, I think that was *before*—before Grandpa Clayton ever went to war and got that bum knee, before he ever met Grandma Clayton and they had three sons, before he even started school in the one-room schoolhouse where he got switched at least every other day for mischief. This layering of befores overwhelms me with the density of time. I have difficulty linking the image of a curly-headed blonde baby dressed up in an embroidered white gown and laced shoes with the grizzled old man I knew who liked to tell dirty jokes and work crossword puzzles.

That same sense of *before* permeates every picture. That was before we got Grandma Marshall's old dining room table, when I was still sitting in a highchair with a dirty bib around my neck. That was before Uncle Ron married Aunt Sue, before she put on weight and lost her girlish figure, before he shaved off his mustache. That was before I got my first bicycle—a blue Schwinn with wide sturdy tires—and broke my left arm for the first time. This is one of the things photographs do. They offer us *before*—before cars, before airplanes, before the war, before the bomb, before color . . . But for me, there is a particular before that is the same in all the pictures of this album. Because they were all taken *before* my mother killed my father and herself, before I had to go live with my mother's only sister, Aunt May. Before there was a permanent *before*, an inescapable line drawn through all our lives.

This is largely what I do in my spare time. My two children live across the continent, tucked safely away in the suburbs of Charlotte, North Carolina, with my ex-wife and her second husband, George. So when I'm not busy teaching college history, I spend my time attempting to take artistic pictures of strangers that I blow up and hang as large black-and-white still lifes around my apartment, and I sift and sort through these old images of before. Looking for clues. Answers. Understanding.

As a history professor, I teach my students to be wary of my subject. I urge them to question facts and records, to read between the lines in the negative space of what hasn't been said. I warn them of those who rearrange and reorder to achieve a tidy story that sums it all up, ties everything together in a neat package that makes perfect sense and is easy to digest. Even so, in my secret, private life, I attempt the very thing I warn my students against. I contemplate and study the alchemy of revisionist history. For how could I be satisfied with the historical facts of my parents' lives? Simple dates, birth certificates, wedding license, newspaper clippings, tombstones, don't begin to tell the story. Mother meets Father. Father marries Mother. Mother gives birth to Father's child. Father cheats on Mother. Mother kills Father and commits suicide. What's the significance of this chain of events? Where's cause and effect? Who is to blame? Who would history label Hero, and who Villain?

Frequently, my students ask, "Why, Professor Clayton? Why did that happen?" And I answer, "I don't know. You tell me." I lecture them about the evils of passive acceptance. "Look harder," I say. "Dig. Follow your hunches. Study the evidence. Draw your own conclusions." I offer them loads of primary sources—photographs, diaries, letters—and the challenge to come up with their own interpretation of events. But, it all comes with a warning: "Be prepared," I caution. "The answers aren't always what you want or expect them to be."

I am reminded of my own warning as I shift pieces of my family's history around in my mind as if they are parts of a puzzle waiting for the right match to reveal a whole and complete picture. Often, I imagine myself lost in a game of solitaire, shuffling and reshuffling the stack of images I've been dealt and hoping that, this time, with a bit of luck, I can get them all to fall into place and finally win the game. I think of my students, their youthful outrage, and how they would scorn the hypocrisy of my teachings should they discover their professor's juvenile refusal to accept the obvious and his insanely persistent attempts to reshape the story of the past into one that suits him better. The only rejoinder that comes to my preoccupied mind is the handy old adage, "Do as I say, not as I do."

I repeat the words of my feeble comeback under my breath as I quickly turn the sparsely covered pages that record the time of my grandparents' youth and reach the pictures that mark the births of my own parents. A moment's hesitancy is natural, I suppose, at this point. It's time to begin again, a new shuffling. My eyes linger on the two plump, downy-haired babies cradled in my lap. They look so innocent, so sweet and untouched, that for a second I actually believe this time I may be able to construct a house of cards that won't fall apart, one that will remain standing even when the winds of whispered truths begin to erode its foundation.

Regina Ann Marshall has the sturdy body and sparkling eyes of a healthy, happy baby. She wears one of those little girl dresses made with stitched designs across the front that draw the fabric into a pattern of puckers. Smocking, I think it's called. My ex-wife, Helen, had a penchant for dressing our own little girl in them. My mother's has ducks embroidered in a waddling line that begins and ends within a frame of chubby arms revealed beneath cap sleeves. The picture is hand-tinted. Her soft brown baby hair is pulled into a wispy sprout on the top of her head and tied with a ribbon. Grandmother Marshall must have liked the effect, because this little fountain spills jauntily from my mother's head in many of the pictures of her early years. I can imagine my mom's grimace in looking back at the silly way Grandmother Mimi dressed her. Mom grew into a statuesque woman, with the strong bones and athletic build of a Greek goddess. I always remember her wearing clothes that had clean, simple lines. She wouldn't have been caught dead in something she dismissed as "too froufrou."

Her eyes are the clear, guileless blue of a wide Carolina sky on a cloudless day. The rims of her irises have yet to darken, just as my own and my daughter's have. But, I do have to wonder if the person who tinted the picture just colored them in the standard shade he used for all the blue-eyed babies. There is a certain generic quality that encompasses all baby pictures. At that age, your face has none of the moles, wrinkles, lines, and other blemishes that end up distinguishing it later on. A baby's face still looks unshaped and newly formed. Light, barely fuzzy eyebrows above bright enchanted eyes, pug nose, full cheeks, sharp little chips of brand-new teeth—they could belong to anybody.

My mother's childish gaze is steady, her expression almost serious except for the naïve, gentle wonder with which she contemplates the elusive eye hiding behind its shiny glass lens. I search her unblemished face. There is no sign yet of the high slant of her cheekbones, the dramatic rise of her dark eyebrows, the freckles that scattered across her long nose. It was years before she would be bitten by a dog and left with a faint pink scar that ran from under her nose through the line of her top lip. "She was a sweet pea, a real doll-baby," Aunt Myrna, my grandmother's younger sister, always claimed. "Never gave us a moment's trouble. Now, your Aunt May, she was another story . . ."

But by the time I went to live with Aunt May, her rebellious youth was over, the only sign of its passing a certain resoluteness with which she held her shoulders and an occasional bark of wild laughter that would escape unexpectedly when she was particularly surprised by something she found to be dark and dangerously funny.

My mother was the eldest of two daughters born into an upper-class family that believed in the Southern tradition of maintaining appearances. My Grandmother Mimi's father was a genteel farmer who owned more land than he knew what to do with, a condition that lead to my Grandfather Marshall having to spend most of his adult life proving his worth to his wife's family. He came from more humble beginnings but showed a particular talent for selling insurance. It was said his talent depended on his storytelling abilities, which he used to relate disasters of the uninsured to potential clients. Grandfather Marshall refused to discuss his tricks of the trade, but loved to joke that he had "made a killing selling life insurance." My mother and her sister, May, grew up with a father who traveled for his job much of the time and a mother who lavished attention on them to make up for his absence. Aunt May always said she felt like she didn't really know her own father, but Grandmother Mimi insisted their children were of the utmost importance to her husband. "The light of his life, she sure was," Grandma Mimi would say of my mother. "He would have given her the sun and the moon if he could. Of course, she never asked, not my Regina. She would never have done something like that."

Quietly accepting, undemanding, dependable, loving, thoughtful—all words used to describe the Regina of before. I look again into my mom's eyes and search her face for the kind of potential she revealed in the end. Nothing. I let my gaze wander across the page, isolating body parts as if they may reveal more in the abstract. I drift from ear to chin to shoulder to hand. Her right hand clutches a fluffy woolen lamb, a favored toy she called Woolsey. I remember it dingy and well-worn sitting on a shelf in my own room. I try to imagine that hand growing into the hand of my mother, the same hand that smoothed and tucked and caressed its way through my childhood. The same hand that pulled the trigger that ended it. Impossible, I think, as I note each dimpled knuckle.

My father, Michael Charles Clayton, faces my mother on the opposite page. But the look he presents is hardly a challenging one. Dressed in a miniature suit, with his potbelly straining like an old man's against the buttons of a tailored jacket, he looks as if he's fully aware of the incongruity of his attire and finds it to be a source of gleeful merriment. The black-and-white photo has appropriately preserved him in the midst of full laughter, for the Clayton boys were known for coming from a long line of men of easy good humor, who took great amusement from a never-ending series of pranks, ribald stories, and general buffoonery. The Claytons were solid members of the working class who prided themselves on being "full of the salt of the earth." Grandma Clayton said that wasn't all they were full of, but the smile of satisfaction that always accompanied her comment told me she wouldn't have had it any other way.

Grandfather Clayton, Pap, prided himself on his ability to enjoy life regardless of the circumstances. Many of his stories began with disturbing realities—someone who was sick or dead, or who lost his job and didn't have a dime to his name, or whose wife and children had up and left him—but they always ended with a joke and a long stretch of chuckling laughter that denied the seriousness of their beginnings.

While I don't have the pictures of my uncles, I do know that each of them was photographed at approximately the same age and in the same suit. First was Uncle Ron, then Uncle Jimmy, and then my father, the youngest, who my uncles claimed was spoiled rotten. "He had Mama wrapped around his little finger from the day he was born," Uncle Ron always insisted with a begrudging grin. "When the three of us were caught red-handed doing something we weren't supposed to, Mama would switch me and Jimmy even harder for leading her baby astray. Somehow, Michael always ended up with milk and cookies in the kitchen while our hides got tanned but good." Uncle Ron and Uncle Jimmy may have had trouble getting by Grandma Clayton, but none of them had any difficulty charming almost every other woman they ever encountered. While they could be crude and crass in the company of men, they could be equally polite and chivalrous in their encounters with the opposite sex. It didn't matter if the woman was a crotchety old neighbor lady or an awkward teen, they knew just what it would take to put her right up there on top of the world.

While I failed to inherit their smooth, easy charm, there is no doubt that I am my father's son. Except for the eyes and the broad, square shape of his face, it would be easy to mistake my father's baby picture for my own. We had the same dark hair, the same cowlick that popped up in the back at the end of our side part, the same curve in our smile, the same shaped ears. One of the things I tell my students is to watch for patterns in history, bits and pieces of repetition. We hold lively debates over whether or not history does, in fact, repeat itself. I think of this each time as I watch my father grow older in the pictures that follow and it is like watching myself grow up. We had the same compact medium build. Both of us grew to a fairly broad-shouldered 5'11" and tended to collect any extra weight around the middle. Our hands were the same thick, blocky palms with slender, almost fragile-looking fingers. My face has even adopted the same exact lines that creased my father's. Deep curves punctuate the corners of my mouth and rays of crow's feet have already begun to collect around each eye.

I have to admit I am not completely comfortable with this marked resemblance, with being just a slightly narrower, blue-eyed version of him. When I flip through especially the black-and-white pictures of him, there are times that I am taken aback by the feeling that I have stumbled on a permutation of myself, another life I have lived and already forgotten. And as I get closer to the age he was when he died, I worry that for the rest of my life whenever I am confronted with my own reflection it will be with the eerie sense of staring into an altered reality where my father actually succeeded in living into old age and I ceased to exist. I guess it's proof of my own contradictory nature that I was both disappointed and relieved when my own son, Jonathan, turned out to look just like my ex-wife's father—tall, gangly, and very blond.

Strangely enough, even without my encouragement, Jonathan has developed a passion for knock-knock jokes. Every time I talk to him or see him in person, he greets me with a new one and I hear in his young, excited voice echoes of my father calling out a greeting to one of his old buddies: "Hey now, ya heard the one about . . ."

This was one of the main ways my father communicated with his friends. They didn't discuss their problems or what was going on in their lives or any subject for that matter in any real depth. They exchanged jokes, spoke in one-liners, slapped each other on the back, and went on their merry ways. My father had a knack for incorporating the basic plots of his favorite jokes into stories that he made up about his own life. These stories were so detailed and presented so casually, you never knew when one of them was being thrown in.

He was also quite inventive in making up his own tall tales—the more outrageous, the better. He usually began with some kind of un-believable claim, often posed in the form of a question. "Did I ever tell you about the time I had to wrestle a cross-eyed, three-legged man? Would you believe I'm late for supper because I had to help an animal trainer find his lost tiger? Do you think you could lift a rail-road car if you had to?" There was an entire collection of these tales that starred my heroic father. There were ones from his childhood that included my uncles and ones that detailed his leaving the nest and making his own way and new ones all the time that he presented like shiny new toys for me to admire and enjoy.

Somehow he made these stories work, even when it was obvious they couldn't possibly be true. I don't think anyone ever questioned their veracity; everybody just went along with it. Maybe it was because he was able to convince us all that we wanted it to be so.

A case in point is the ball my father is preparing to throw in his baby picture. His right forearm is raised and drawn back as if he is getting ready to slingshot it across the room. He always declared that that ball was a golf ball and foretold his love and devotion to the game. "I was born to play golf," he would insist. "I dreamt of hitting 'em long and straight when I was still in the womb. Carried a club before I could walk." Now this was from a man who couldn't have been introduced to the idea of actually playing golf, himself, until he was at least in his teens. While my mother was raised on golf lessons at the country club, my father's family didn't have that kind of money. There are no pictures of my father with clubs of any kind until after he was married to my mother. Also, if you look closely at the ball in the picture, between the stretch of my father's little fingers, you can see that the ball is completely smooth. It has none of the regular indentations that wrap around the surface of a golf ball. Still, when I look at the sparkling gleam in his eyes and allow myself to become lost in the power of their devil-may-care daring, I almost find myself believing every word he ever tossed my way.

There aren't a lot of pictures from my father's childhood. There are a few group shots of the family gathered around the Christmas tree in their Sunday best and arranged awkwardly in stilted poses on the front porch. For some reason the Claytons almost always adopted serious, even grim faces for the camera, as if they could find nothing humorous in an occasion that recorded their own mortality. Typically, on every Clayton face there is an expression of distrust, suspicion, as if they don't really know the person who's taking the shot.

But when the boys are pictured by themselves, they don't take it nearly as seriously. There's one of the three of them dressed in choir robes, their mouths poised in the rounded *o*'s of song. Someone has penned, "We're no angels!" in a loopy sprawl across the bottom of the photograph. One of my favorites was taken after they had reached their audacious, wiry teens. Ron and my dad are sitting next to each other on the porch glider and Jimmy is on the right in an old rocker. A dead buck is stretched out at their feet. Each of them holds his gun by the barrel in one hand, butt balanced on the floor, end pointed toward the ceiling. In the other hand they're holding half-empty soda bottles. They're grinning—wide, tight grins—and appear to have just toasted the photographer, or maybe the dead deer. Anyway, you can tell it's a celebration, and there's something about the fierceness of the pride and joy that radiates from my father that tells me that this particular time, he was the one to have been lucky enough to kill it.

The skimpy coverage of my father's youth is even more noticeable as I turn a few pages and reach the thick section dedicated to my mother's childhood and early teen years. I decide to take a break. I get up and stretch a little and pour myself another cup of coffee. Sherman, my faithful yellow lab, follows me into the kitchen and promptly sits at his empty food bowl. He looks up with the cajoling expectant expression that suggests it's suppertime. His tail brushes against the wooden floor in a slow, hopeful wag. But I just pat his head and shake my head no before going back to my seat and returning to my parents' past, which lies there, waiting.

There are pages and pages of my mother and Aunt May—holidays, birthdays, garden shots, and lots and lots of studio portraits. Right before my eyes, my mother grows from a ruffled and bowed cherub into a wholesome, clear-eyed young girl. I particularly enjoy watching her progress in Grandmother Mimi's garden. First she's caught in the staggering stance of a toddler, white dress, white shoes, and lacy white socks, lurching unsteadily along a dirt path. She appears bent on reaching a clump of spiky iris leaves, swords of spring, with such keen edges they appear to be slicing their way through earth and air. A year or two later, she sits beside my grandmother on a thick lawn of carefully mowed grass. My mother is squirming within my grandmother's embrace. Something or someone has gotten her attention away from the camera. Her hair is longer, curled in ringlets that brush her shoulders. The topknot is gone, but the bow is bigger and pinned to one side of her head. Mimi is young, her face soft, yet maternally knowing. There is a gentle smile on her dark, full lips. She looks directly into the camera and has drawn her child almost into her lap, despite my mother's resistance. One of Mimi's arms is wrapped protectively around Mom's shoulder. Her painted nails stand out in sharp contrast against the pale skin of my mother's knee.

It's a matter of only a few seasons before Mom reaches skinny-legged adolescence. She stands self-consciously before a birdbath with her arms held behind her, out of sight. She hangs from the split rail fence that runs along the back of the garden. Her dress is plaid trimmed in rickrack, her hair hidden by a matching scarf. She tests the reach of her newly lengthened limbs as she tries for a plum that dangles from a tree's lower branch. I know my mother loved this garden. She called it the garden of her youth and said she felt they had grown up together.

By the time she is pictured as a young woman, reclining in the grass in roughly the same position that her mother was photographed holding her years previously, it almost looks like a different place. There is an arbor in the background that has been completely covered by a wild tangle of climbing roses. Established beds of an assortment of shrubs and flowers border the grass. The young maple that was planted right after my mother's birth now dominates the left side of the picture in its maturity. Only the back of the house, just a segment of it visible in the distance, looks the same. My mother's legs are drawn together in a bent curve. She leans on one arm; her left hand lost in the grass. The right hand holds a spade loosely in her lap. She's become a full-fledged gardener by this point, spending her afternoons digging and her evenings poring over seed catalogs and carefully drawn diagrams. True to her obsession, she's dressed in dungarees and a sleeveless blouse. Her hair is pulled back by a bandanna that covers it in a pointed triangle, but a few wayward strands have escaped and float around her upturned face. Her eyes reflect the outdoor light with a strange, unearthly glow. There is a dreamy, wistful look about her expression as she gazes off into a far horizon. It's as if she can see into the future, and I wonder just what it is she thinks she'll find there. Is she dreaming of a new garden, one she's never seen? Does she long to use the lessons she's learned from Mother Nature on a plotted piece of the world that she can call her own? Or does her loose grip on the spade handle mean that she's not even thinking of seeds and soil, that she's simply dreaming of love?

In an attempt to help my students manage the enormity of history's sweep, I suggest they make a detailed timeline of the period we are studying. It is essentially a map of the past. I tell them to include only the historic moments, the landmarks that defined the collective journey of our civilization during that time.

Some are more obvious than others. As I fill in the map of my own family's history it is relatively easy for me to pinpoint my parents' first meeting as one of those watershed moments. In their early teens, they stand hip-to-hip on the edge of a lake's thin strip of sandy shore. They appear to be completely oblivious to the significance of the occasion. My father wears swimming trunks and a white rubber cap that isn't pulled down properly so it appears he has a puffy white dome riding the top of his head. His arms hang loosely at his sides. He is skinny and only slightly taller than my mother. His face is turned downward towards hers, and he is in the middle of telling her something. She reacts in mock outrage, her jaw dropped in mute disbelief and her hands propped on hips cocked in a saucy tilt. The top of her bathing suit is covered by a sleeveless blouse, but the bottom peeks out from underneath. Angled behind them, the wooden planks of a rickety dock lead to deep water and an empty boat, its abandoned oars positioned in a stiff salute.

Both lifeguards and camp counselors at a summer church camp, they meet here for the first time, on the man-made beach of a freshwater lake surrounded by a forest of pine trees. He is fifteen and she fourteen. Even though they've both lived in the same general area on the edge of Charlotte all their lives, they haven't gone to the same schools or known the same people. They don't even belong to the same church.

My father has been roped into going to this camp by a buddy of his who promised it would be a great place to meet some new girls. And so he does, including my mother who has been a camper here—roasting marshmallows, fishing, boating, swimming in the shallows of this lake—for many years. "I don't care what everybody else says. They loved each other. I know it," my Aunt May has repeatedly insisted. "I knew it from the day she came back from camp. You know I hated going. I think that was the year I faked chicken pox to get out of it. Anyway, there was something different about her when she came home, a spark of new life, excitement, wonder, what have you, as if she'd found a secret treasure washed up on that pitiful little beach. I was too young to understand at the time, but I was smart enough to know that she'd gone somewhere I couldn't follow. And it made me mad. So I hounded her, chased her around, chanting, 'Gina's in love. Gina's in love,' until Mother made me stop. I was obnoxious but not stupid." Aunt May's observations have always made me wish I could have been there to see my mother blossom in the bright light of my father's warm sun. In my mind's eye, when I pull back and envision the picture of their meeting as an aerial shot, their two figures merge into a single dot, just one of many poised on the outer rim of a large unblinking eye that stares blindly out of a fuzzy wilderness.

"He was a sweet talker, plain and simple," Aunt May has also said more than once, "and not bad looking either. Your mother had never met someone like that and she liked it." It would seem that the photos of my parents' courtship prove her right, because as I scan these pictures, I notice that in just about every one of them my father's mouth is frozen open in mid-speech. From the position of their bodies, the tilt of the heads, it is easy to gather that theirs is a private conversation, the ongoing exchange of a new language that only the two of them can understand.

Whenever I asked my father about meeting my mother and falling in love, he'd tell a funny anecdote or story about some scrape he'd gotten himself into trying to impress her. But these were more of his adventures and revealed little to nothing about his personal feelings for her. She simply became the princess or the prize and was described in the appropriate hyperbolic cliché: "She was the prettiest girl at the dance, no one could hold a candle to her. When I first saw your mother, I thought I had died and gone to heaven."

In turn, my mother clung to her typical reticence whenever I posed a similar question to her. All she would ever say was, "Your father knows how to stand out in a crowd. I guess just about any girl would have had him, but he chose me."

Sweet talker; prettiest girl at the dance; thought I'd died and gone to heaven; stand out in a crowd; any girl, any girl, any girl; but he chose me, chose me, chose me—these old phrases run in a rippling refrain through my head as I look at the picture of my parents dancing at my mother's debut. I can almost see them as strains of superimposed words floating in a gently swirling funnel around the dancing couple—*sweet talker thought I'd died and gone to heaven but he chose me.*

I love this photograph. It has all the sparkle and glamour of a fairy-tale ending. My parents could be movie stars moving in choreographed splendor against a backdrop of blurry, out-of-focus extras. For who could deny them the spotlight? My father cuts a sharp, debonair figure in his tuxedo; my mother is a radiant, stately beauty in frothy white. They waltz, the bare curve of her back to the camera, her profile raised to meet his gaze. Lifted with the graceful ease of a ballerina, her hands and arms are covered in long kid gloves that reach her elbows. There is a sense of arrested motion in this picture; you can almost feel the force of his pull as he guides her through the next turn. Her skirts sway with the bending, twirling magic of freshly spun cotton candy following the command of a masterful hand. He looks down, either into her eyes or her cleavage, and there's a half-smile on his parted lips. I like to believe they're sharing something, a joke or a misstep or the rush of their over-whelming happiness, that both are content and fulfilled in that moment with him confidently leading her around the next bend. The way she is enfolded in his embrace makes me think of a bright and lovely lily rising up and shining forth out of the darkness.

Engagement pictures follow soon after. There is one of Mom in a sweater set and tweed skirt, flashing a diamond and a big smile for the camera. There are a few pictures of them at engagement parties and bridal showers. And then there's the wedding, more than a dozen glossy eight-by-tens that record the day of their official union. The last one is of them sitting together encapsulated in the backseat of their limo. He looks at the camera while she looks at him, as if he's ready to face the world and his future out there, while she is delighted to have discovered her world and future sitting right there by her side. His smile is happy but a little stiff, hers wide and adoring. They are a team, a couple, a pair, a match. His left arm and hand rest alongside her bouquet of white flowers and trailing ivy on the buoyant mound of her skirt. Her veil is a filmy cloud that hovers behind her and reaches out to brush along his tuxedoed shoulder. Theirs is a portrait of wholesome, youthful assurance that they have indeed chosen the road they are on and that it leads in the right direction.

The promise of their confidence reminds me of a time when I was little, riding in the backseat of our station wagon up a twisty mountain in the middle of a rainstorm on a dark night. It was pitch black and the fall leaves had covered the lines so there was nothing to keep my father oriented as he drove, to stop us from all rolling off the edge of a cliff. I remember they rode with their windows down and their heads out, despite the cold, drenching rain. I could hear the panic in my mother's voice and the tension in my father's. And while I knew we were in danger, I stretched out on the seat cushions and fell asleep, lulled by the steady push and pull of their conversation and the sense that the intensity of their combined determination would keep us on the right track even though the road before us had seemingly vanished, without leaving a trace of any kind.

After their "Just Married" photo, there are fewer and fewer pictures of them together. Some of them are disjointed and strangely surreal. One that jumps out on the page is of them at a party. The picture is of poor quality; its smudged color appears to be draining out of it. The flash of the camera has illuminated their images but blacked out everything else in the frame. So they look oddly like cutouts carelessly left floating on a background of oily black. From the lei hanging around my father's neck and the bright Hawaiian print of my mother's dress, I gather they are at a luau. They are standing apart, without touching. My father is animatedly talking to someone off camera on his right, while my mother's unmoored gaze wanders off in the opposite direction. There is something precarious about her two-handed grip on an umbrella-topped half coconut that makes her look anxious and vulnerable.

There are only a few more pages of photos until I arrive on the scene, and then there aren't any more pictures of just the two of them alone. Instead, there are photos of each of them with me, tons of me by myself, and the regular scattering of family group shots taken during all the traditional gatherings. Christmastime was the most frequently documented holiday, with annual pictures of hanging the stockings, discovering Santa's presents, opening gifts, Grandpa Clayton ceremoniously lighting the Yule log, grandchildren lined up along the staircase each holding a favored gift, and someone getting a surprise kiss under the mistletoe.

Christmas was a much more formal occasion at Mimi's house. The Marshalls made a great to-do about sitting down to a multiple-course meal with all the best china and recently polished family silver. Year after year, someone took pictures of the Marshall table covered in a lace cloth and laden with food and dishes, silver or crystal candelabra, elaborate flower arrangements, and goblets stained in brilliant hues of red, blue, green, and gold. The emphasis in these pictures is always on the table itself rather than the people gathered around it. It's almost as if the people are an afterthought, the background this time for the tabled display. In one of these photos, my parents are incidentally caught within the frame. They are sitting next to each other. And I stand between them. I am dressed in a little red jacket; my precisely groomed head just reaches their shoulders.

Evidently, I have made the trek from the children's table, customarily set up out of earshot in the den, to petition for some important cause. There is a quizzical expression on my face as I watch for my mother's reaction. I have presented my case and am waiting to hear what the answer will be. She is the only one listening. Once again my father is busy talking, telling a tale no doubt to entertain the crowd. I can almost hear him, the laughter, the chink of silverware against fragile bone china. And I can't help noting their plates. His is graced with a generous wedge of pecan pie. Hers is pushed aside, completely clean and empty. Her cup and saucer have been pulled toward her where the dessert plate should be. Her right hand is in her lap, under the table by my side. In her left, she balances a cigarette between her middle and index fingers, holding the tickle of its thin trail of smoke away from me.

Mixed in with the Christmas photos is a host of other childhood scenes. There are the obligatory school portraits, chaotic birthday scenes, sandy poses by the ocean, and blurry action shots that document the graduating thrill of first rides on tricycle, two-wheeler, ten-speed. For all intents and purposes, such a life and such a careful recording of it would appear to give testimony to a child who was more than casually loved. I often wondered why my parents had only me, why they never even mentioned the idea of raising other children. I do remember a spell my mother went through when she seemed sad all the time and cried by herself a lot. I must have been around six or seven because I remember coming home from school and finding her sitting alone in the dark house, holding a crumpled tissue or an empty coffee cup, with tears running down her face. Each time, she made me promise not to tell my father. She said it was just a silly girl thing and she'd get over it soon. I never knew if she was upset because I'd left her for Mrs. Nelson, my much-adored first-grade teacher, or because she wished she had some other little children to keep her company during the day.

There are also plenty of pictures that attest to the prominence sports were given in my early life. Baseball, basketball, football, swimming, hunting, fishing—they are all there. But golf is there the most. It was natural, I suppose. We lived on the golf course and both of my parents were avid golfers. Yet they never played together. Sometimes I played with each of them, but never both of them at the same time. My father played all out, talking to himself and the ball the entire round. If his game was "on," he was loads of fun. If not, he sulked and was in a foul mood that only got darker with each hooked drive and missed putt. My mother, on the other hand, played evenly and smoothly with a calm assurance that made the game almost a meditation. I never saw her get upset on the course. And she never critiqued my swing or offered any kind of unsolicited advice. Mostly she just said things like, "Nice shot!" and "Well done, honey, you're growing up to be a fine golfer." Or she'd just talk about what a beautiful day it was and how good it felt to be outside in the sun.

As I near the end of the album, I am increasingly aware of the weight of accumulated pages as it shifts from right to left. The dog whines softly in his sleep. His feet twitch as he chases elusive quarry in his dreams. Frequently I advise my students to try to place themselves in history, to try to imagine themselves as a real, living and breathing part of some significant moment in time. "Forget about being a fly on the wall," I tell them. "Be somebody. Pick a person who was there. Recreate in your mind the steps that person took that led him or her to end up in those circumstances. Try to understand their motivations, what drove them to do what they did. Understand the forces at play by becoming part of them," I say.

But when I try to do this with the last moments in my parents' lives, when I try to be there for the history-making moment of my father's murder and my mother's suicide, I just . . . I can't. I can't see my father's face from my mother's point of view and pull the trigger. I can't watch from inside my father as my mother aims the gun at his head. Instead,

I return again and again to a bizarre tableau of my own imagining. In this fantasy scene, my parents have joined forces and are determinedly attempting to take my picture. I appear to be the same young boy who is in the arrowhead photograph. My father's head is lost under a black cloth draped around a cumbersome, old-timey camera that sits on a huge tripod. My father cries, "Smile for the birdie!" and holds a feathered stick aloft to win my smile, while my mother stands silently to one side, patiently waiting to squeeze the flash.

One of the last actual images in my Book of Before is of my mother and me. It was taken in the fall, less than a year before their deaths. We had been raking leaves in the backyard and are standing together behind an impressive pile, a trophy of sorts for our efforts. I am twelve in this picture and still haven't grown quite tall enough to look eye-to-eye with my mother. My features are beginning to sharpen, to gain the definition that comes with adolescence. I am wearing a gray sweatshirt, blue jeans, and dirty white Converse sneakers. My left hand is holding the handle of a rake, while my right arm encircles my mother's waist. She's dressed in khakis and a thick red cardigan. There is a leaf clinging to her right shoulder, but her head is turned to the left to look down at me. She smiles with her lips closed, her chin tucked inward and her head tilted in contemplation. The look on her face is both a blessing and a prayer. My own expression is equally ambiguous. My face is pointed straight at the camera but my eyes are cut toward my mother. And there is a half-smile on my lips that could be read as shy admiration or as sly consideration.

That's the difficulty with having to rely on photographs for knowing. Convincing yourself to believe is so hard when seeing truly is next to impossible. What's the lie? And what is lying there begging to be finally seen as the truth? I lift my chin and let my head drop back on the headrest of my chair. I let the images from the album sift through my mind. They float and tumble, a cascading drift of falling leaves. I realize that I'm staring at one of the large, black-and-white portraits I have hanging on my walls. It's of a collection of people riding a ferry. The focus of the shot is a young dark-haired woman and her towheaded, chubby-cheeked little boy; in fact, I think of this picture as a modern Madonna and Child. They are both graced with beautifully ripe skin and full lips and an attitude of peaceful unity.

As I wonder anew at their small still circle of two in the midst of the fidgety crowd, a murky sense of guilt begins to filter through and rise up along the surface of my blurry vision. It's as if I'm watching the emergence of a new image as it slowly blooms on the page while submerged in a liquid bath of developer in my darkroom. Point by point, grain by grain—it is a painstaking process of accumulation not unlike that of the gradual trickling shift of sand through an hourglass. I glance back down at the photo in my lap as the piercing light of recognition bores through my vision. I've been hit by my own weapons, eyes that are two sharp arrows with points that could easily rend the tenderly beating pulp of a human heart.

They say a picture is worth a thousand words, but I have to wonder. How can one picture possibly take the place of so many things left unsaid, of even the simplest forms of speech, straightforward declarations like "I'm sorry" or "I love you"? For no matter how much I plead with my mother's image to tell what she sees staring back at her—a reflection of her own eyes or my father's face—her lips remain locked, frozen in an upward bend, a haunting portrait of a slight, secretive smile.

MICHAEL CLAYTON

Friday, August 1977

There was a time in my life, when I was still just a boy, that there wasn't anything in this whole wide world I wouldn't do for my mama. You might say I was blessed, or cursed for that matter, with a precociousness for loving women. But at that point in time, all that loving centered on one female and one female only, my sweet, sweet mama. Some of my best first memories are of toddling over to grab hold of the reassuring swell of her thigh and of being pressed against the cushioned softness of her chest when she hugged me tight. That sense of rightness—knowing it and she were both always there, always within my reach—meant the whole world to me. That is, until I tripped over one of Misty Holland's miniature Buster Browns in third grade and fell hard and fast for her ornery blonde self in less time than it takes a person to say, "Sorry."

However, Misty, the new girl in our school and the prettiest little thing you ever saw this side of the Mississippi, was nowhere near intending to apologize. She pointed the scuffed toe of her shoe, dangled it right above my nose, and said, "That story you told was a lie, Michael Clayton."

I was still sprawled facedown on the dirty floor in the hallway. It was recess. She had ambushed me on my way out to play. "What do you mean, a lie?" I said.

"Liar, liar, pants on fire," she taunted. Her blue eyes spit sparks and her face was flushed an angry red. She was mad, full of righteous indignation.

I was downright thrilled. I'd never seen somebody get so riled up about one of my stories. It was obvious she wasn't from around here. No one questioned *the truth* of the stories we shared during "Show and Tell." That was the fun of it. Besides, I had a reputation. My classmates loved my stories. In fact, the one I'd told that day about the time I chased a rainbow and was tricked by a wily leprechaun named Bubba Jack was one I'd told a thousand times before. I told it by request. Even my teacher loved that one, said she could eat it up with a spoon. But not our girl Misty, she was having none of that.

"You never saw no such thing as a little green man singing and dancing in the woods behind your house," she said.

"Of course, I did." I got up and began dusting off the knees of my pants. "Think I could make something like that up?"

"You had to of," said Misty. "Everybody knows real leprechauns are Irish. They don't have names like Bubba Jack."

"They do if they live around here," I said.

"They do not. That's a redneck name. Leprechauns are magic."

"How do you know?" I asked. "You ever met a real leprechaun?"

"No," she said, "but I've read about them."

"And just how did you think those stories got written? Huh? Ever stop to wonder about that?"

"Well, no, not really," Misty was willing to admit.

"See what I'm saying? Somebody had to have met up with one some time or other. Or else, there wouldn't be any of those stories. I just happen to be one of those people."

"But you could be just be making it all up," she said. And it was then, right then, in just those few little seconds it took for her to say her answer that I heard the barest beginnings of a waver—that ever-so-slight mixture of disbelief and hope riding the upward inflection of her voice told me exactly what I wanted to hear. Her lips may have been saying, "No." But her heart was saying, "Yes. Puuuullllease, pretty please with gumdrops on top, please, please, please, be *yes*." She was begging me to make it all true, had her hopes and dreams pinned on me. She didn't just *want* to believe, she *needed* to. My story was that important. An enormous sense of power came over me. I thought my heart would explode with the brilliant force of a firecracker as it paints the night sky in bits of burning light. I loved this girl. My mind raced with the thought of it. I would make her believe. I could and I would.

"But if I was making it all up, how would I know that leprechauns like licorice?" I reasoned.

"They do?" she asked. I couldn't help but be charmed by the way her fair little brow wrinkled when she was puzzled.

"Yeah, that's how I got Bubba Jack to come out and talk to me. And did you know that most everything else they eat is green, including spinach and Brussels sprouts, and that if they stop eating all that green stuff they start to fade and lose their magic?"

"Right. Sure," she said. I could tell I was starting to lose her.

"But it's true," I said. "They also get along really well with the giants but can't stand fairies of any kind."

"You're making this all up. I need some kind of proof," said Misty as if she were tired of being bothered by it all.

"Proof?"

"Yep. That's right. You heard me."

"Okay," I said. "I've got proof."

"Let's see it," she demanded.

"I—I don't have it with me," I said. "But I'll get it and bring it to school. Tomorrow." Immediately after making this foolish promise, I realized my mistake. I didn't have any proof and didn't know what exactly I might be able to scrounge up that would count in Misty's eyes. I was young and prone to making mistakes of this sort. Talk now and think later was already my modus operandi. And, well, that kind of thinking *may* get you out of trouble and, then again, it *may not*.

All that afternoon through times tables and spelling and a cursive writing lesson, I worried over the fix I had gotten myself in. How many times had I heard my father say, "A man is his reputation" and "All you can ever really call your own is your own good name"? If I was labeled a liar, well there was just no telling what would happen to me. It'd be all she wrote. I would be washed up and a laughingstock at the tender age of nine. And, most importantly, the storytelling fun would be over. I just couldn't see letting that happen. No way, no how. I had to do something.

I was still thinking on it when I started walking the old dirt road that led to our house. I was panicked but inspired at the same time. After all, there's nothing quite like a good challenge to get your juices flowing. 'Long about the time I started considering asking my two older brothers for help, I noticed somebody walking toward me on the other side of the road. When we got closer, I could see it was a man, a scruffy sort, with a burlap sack thrown over one shoulder and a thick walking stick held in his other hand. I didn't recognize him, which was unusual. We didn't have many visitors in our neck of the woods, and I knew most everybody there was.

"Howdy there partner, how-day-do!" he called out and raised the brim of his cap in a jaunty salute.

"Hey, mister," I said. "How are you today?"

"Well, now, I'm just fine," he answered. "Usually I'm lucky to be feeling fair to middling on account of all my troubles and all, but today, today, I'm about as good as a man can get."

"Good, good, glad to hear it," I said, wondering all the while what he could possibly be feeling so good about as I took note of the dirty rings around his neck. He had stopped and pulled out a faded bandanna and was proceeding to wipe at his face with it. So out of politeness, I stopped too. We faced each other across the road. He was tall and lean. His eyes were fierce and so pale they looked like polished quartz when you hold it to the light. But the rest of him was worn to the point of exhaustion. I wasn't afraid. The cuffs of his jacket were frayed. His trousers were torn, his shoes scuffed and dusty. One was tied with a piece of knotted twine. Looked like a vagabond to me, like he had just rolled off a freight train and was desperate for a meal. What did a feller like that have to be so grateful for? I couldn't help questioning his apparent enthusiasm.

"Windfall," he said as if reading my mind. He carefully refolded his handkerchief and slid it back out of sight. "My ship has finally come in." He grunted as he repositioned the sack on his back. "Yes indeedy. 'The meek shall inherit the earth' is what the Good Book says. And I have finally gotten my fair share—what was owed to me, my piece, my birthright, mine fair and square—no ifs, ands, or buts about it. I have finally received my due and not one moment too soon. And I am grateful. Thank you, Lord," he said with his head tilted back so he could address the sky. "Thank you. Thank you for seeing fit to bestow upon me, for giving unto me this day, O Lord. I thank ye kindly for that."

Then he doffed his cap and made a sweeping bow so deep that the ends of his long beard tickled the ground. "Seamus Patrick O'Malley at your service, me wee laddie," he said, "but, by all means, you may henceforth refer to this bag o' bones as Paddy." He had righted himself by the end of his introduction and re-covered the crown of his balding head. "You see sonny boy, what you've got here is living proof that if only you believe, truly believe, the good Lord above will provide. He may make you work for it, but in the end you'll get what you deserve. Me, I came by it the hard way, but I came by it all the same."

"Came by what, exactly?" I asked.

"Ah, curious are we?" he asked as he cast a furtive look over both his shoulders. "I'll not be spreading the word too loudly. I've never been one to invite trouble, if you know what I mean. But you, you look to be a proper sort of lad. I bet your mama has taught you right. Wash behind your ears every night, do you?"

"Yes, yes sir," I nodded in vigorous agreement.

"Well, then. Step on over here my trustworthy young man and I'll show you just exactly what I mean."

I didn't need any further encouragement. I trotted right over. Mr. O'Malley dropped the sack from his shoulder to a clump of stubby weeds growing on the edge of the road. He began loosening the knot at the top of the bag, his knobby fingers making quick work of it. But then with one hand closed around the neck of the sack, he raised the other in caution. "Wait a minute, now, lad," he said. "This treasure of mine needs a fair introduction."

"You're going to introduce us?" I was a bit taken aback. I stared at the rough fabric searching for any signs of movement. And what do you think I saw? Nothing. I strained my ears trying to listen for strange noises, muffled cries. Again, nothing. The sack didn't even appear to be all that full, just a few soft lumps lying mutely in the sun.

"Aye," Paddy replied. "Every treasure has its own tale, don't you know?"

"Oh sure, okay," I said.

We both crouched down on our haunches with the bag sitting between us as if we'd gathered around a warming fire. "Well now then," Paddy began, "It was many a year ago that my family first made their way across the ocean to this great land of ours—long, long before your time or your father's or his'n before that. It was during the glory days of the O'Malley clan when all the O'Malleys lived on the emerald coast of Ireland, they did, in great castles. All the women were great ladies in rich robes of fur and velvet, and all the men were great men, courageous warriors, who fought daring battles and won." Paddy gazed off into the distance as if he could see all those old O'Malleys still decked out in their good clothes and living high on the hog over in Ireland. His voice had grown soft and wistful like my teacher's did when she read us stories of King Arthur and the knights of the Round Table.

"It was in this way that they earned their great, great riches, hoards of gold and silver and piles of jewels of every description. But several of the neighboring clans grew jealous, as some are bound to do, and plotted to loot the O'Malleys' castle and dishonor their women," Paddy continued, drawing his wild eyebrows together in a dramatic bank of unruly dark clouds that warned of a coming storm. "Now, the O'Malley men had never been ones to shrink from a battle. But they were wise men as well. They knew when they were outnumbered and decided to escape with their family and wealth intact. So, they did. They disappeared in the middle of the night, boarded a ship for the Americas, and brought all their riches, twenty-five trunk loads, to safety in the New World.

"And it was many years they prospered here in America. After choosing to settle in the piedmont of North Carolina, they bought land aplenty, raised fine livestock and even finer children, and enjoyed many a well-spent day of good health and prosperity. Even during the great

Revolution, the O'Malleys fared well, with nary a scratch collected amongst the lot of them. Though it wasn't from a lack of action on their part, mind you. No sir. The O'Malleys earned an equally noble reputation fighting to win our nation's independence as they did in their homeland. Aye, it was said one O'Malley against three of those English dandies was still considered an unfair match—for the Crown, that is. No, no, it wasn't the Revolution that did in the O'Malleys. It was the War Between the States that proved our undoing.

"You see, the men were all off fighting. Even the youngest, young Michael Todd O'Malley, just turned twelve years of age, had gone off to do his duty. So it wasn't but women and girls left to defend their home when the Yankee brigade tore a path through their land, burning and stealing everything they could lay their hands on. Now old Ma O'Malley, when she heard the Yanks were coming, she decided to tear a page out of the family history and make off with the money and women before they could get there. But all the family's horses were being used in the war and there was no way the women could carry trunk loads of gold and silver and make good their escape. So Ma grabbed a leather pouch and filled it with pure gold nuggets and buried it in a secret hiding place on the property before they ran off. She knew that if they were caught with anything of value it would be taken from them, so this was the best she could do.

"Well, and to make a long story short, the O'Malley women survived, but barely. They were trapped in their hiding place out in the woods. All around them, murder and destruction raged on for days. Their meager supply of food had long run out before they felt it was safe enough to return home. They were weak and ragged when finally they reached the charred remains of the old home place. A blackened chimney and hearth were all that was left. The house and barns had been torched and the crops ruint. There was just one runty biddy, hardly a feather left to call its own, found scratching in the bushes. That was it. These were dire straits. Dire straits indeed—the like of which old Ma had never seen.

"Her mind reeling from the shock of it all, old Ma sat down on a piece of crumbling hearth to try and get a hold of herself. But before she could take more than three deep breaths, young Michael Todd came running up with the devastating news that all the rest of the O'Malley men had met their deaths in battle the day before. Wiped out in one fell stroke. Dead and gone.

"This was the final blow. Old Ma's mind went spinning right out of control and she never did get it reeled back in. Never could remember where she'd buried that gold. No matter how much the other women cajoled and begged, she'd just shake her head and cackle in that high lonesome sound of wind whipping through the trees. Bits and pieces of nonsense, fragments of nursery rhymes and old sea chants, were all that passed through the old woman's lips till her dying day."

Paddy's tone had shifted from ominous to angry to mournful. So convinced was I by the tragedy of his loss, I couldn't help but put out a hand and pat him reassuringly on the forearm. I was afraid he was going to cry any minute. I had forgotten about his recent good fortune and all, so I was startled when he suddenly grabbed a leather pouch from his bag and let out a whoop of joy as he tossed it high in the air.

"And for all those years since, not one of the O'Malleys has ever been able to figure out that crazy old woman's mind. Not a single dagburn one of 'em, that is, until Seamus Patrick, the very last male in the O'Malley line." Paddy caught the pouch and gently cradled it in his dirty hands. His voice was gleeful and triumphant. "Seamus Patrick, the one they call good-for-nothing, has managed to rule the day!"

Paddy began chuckling his delight as he used one hand to loosen the opening of the pouch. "Hahaha," he crowed, "hahaha. Now, take a look at this, my boy. Does this look like a pile of nothing?" he asked as he held out the small bag so's I could see what was inside.

From the outside, the brown leather pouch had reminded me of my own that I used for keeping marbles. But when I stood up so I could bend down over the opening for a better look, my curious gaze was met by a pile of glittering gold, nestled right where my own ordinary collection of colored glass would be.

"Golly!" I couldn't help but reveal my amazed admiration. "Wow!" There was no denying the roughly gleaming treasure that shone dully from the darkened depths. I felt like Ali Baba, standing for the first time before an underground reservoir of vast and untold riches. "That's really something," I breathed.

"Mine, all mine," Paddy said with obvious satisfaction. "Do you want to touch a piece?" he offered.

"Sure," I said and put out an eager hand. Paddy made a careful selection of a smaller piece and gave me a thoughtful, considering look before placing it in the center of my outstretched palm. Gold. It was gold. Not an insignificant smattering of dust. Or even a little nugget that might be exciting, all right, but probably wouldn't be worth all that much. This was heavy, solid, with the rugged outline of a craggy stone mountain. And Paddy had a whole pile of them. This was manly treasure—a proclamation to the world. That was when it started to sink in—*gold*—as in the precious yellow stuff. Gold, as in pots of. Gold, as in rainbows and leprechauns. God had answered my prayers. I did believe! I did! Just one of those pieces could prove everything to Miss Misty Holland. Just one was all it would take.

I knew it would be tricky getting Paddy to let me borrow so much as the dusting from inside that pouch. But I had to try. So I did. And Paddy refused flat out. He was adamant. Said he wasn't sticking around, had places to go, people to see. Which, of course, I could understand. But still I tried some more. I told him all about my predicament. Told him, I too, was facing those who doubted my real worth. Finally, just as I was beginning to run out of argument, I started to see that maybe, just maybe, I was beginning to get somewhere. With great reluctance, Paddy said he did have to be on his way but . . . seeings as how he had so much and he was feeling a tad on the generous side, he just might be willing to consider selling me that there small piece that I still had in my hand.

Hot dog! The next hurdle was agreeing on the price. All I had on me was a nickel—just a drop in the bucket, I knew. I wasn't very good about saving up. Always spent just as fast as I got. My brothers weren't much better. But my mother, now she was a saver. A life-saver. We all knew about the money she kept stowed away in a cookie jar on the kitchen counter. It was white with a little blue bird painted on it. She called it her nest egg.

As soon as I thought of that money just sitting there with nothing better to do, I told Paddy I might very well could come up with some more cash. Paddy begrudgingly agreed to wait while I ran home. "I guess a man don't go walking around every day with the price of gold in his pocket," he said. "Go on," he waved. "I'll reckon I can rest my bones right here for a spell."

So I skedaddled on home as fast as my legs could go and was relieved when I got to the kitchen and nobody was there. I didn't even stop to catch my breath, just lifted the lid on that jar and snatched up all the bills and loose change and let the door slam on my way back out. I was on a mission. Plus, the way I figured it, gold was bound to be worth tons more than that little crumpled handful of paper money and coins. As soon as I got back from showing Misty my proof at school the next day, I'd give the gold over to my mama and explain everything. So it wasn't like I was stealing at all. Borrowing was all I was doing. And in the end, my mama would probably thank me for all I had done.

But honestly, I didn't waste a whole lot of time trying to reason things out. I was gold-struck and could barely contain the molten rush of adrenaline that gushed through my veins. After all, by some incredible turn of fate, by some miracle, Paddy's good fortune had become mine.

He was still patiently waiting when I returned. In fact, he had dozed off. I had to rouse him before we could make our exchange. I hadn't even bothered to try to count the money, just handed it over in a hurry, hoping against hope that it would be enough. It was. Paddy counted it out to himself, briefly looked down at me with lifted eyebrows and then tossed me my new piece of gold. We shook hands. He shouldered his sack and was quickly on his way. "Good luck, laddie," he called just before stepping off the road and slipping through a patch of particularly dense woods. As his silhouette disappeared in the dusk, I breathed a sigh of relief. That was that.

Course, I was fit to be tied all evening, thought the next day would never get there. But it did, soon enough. The morning dawned beautiful and bright with a great big yellow sun that promised nothing but good that whole day long. I went off to school with a song in my heart and that gold piece threatening to burn clean through my pocket any minute.

I was fair to busting by the time the bell rang for recess. This was the first chance I had to show my stuff. But I had to play it right, so I took my time getting to the playground. A small crowd was gathered when I got there. "Witnesses," Misty called them. But I wasn't scared. I had all the proof I needed. I couldn't stop from smiling. I was the man in charge. I imagined myself dressed in knight's armor about to present a hard-won trophy to his lady before the king's court. Heroes have to get used to this kind of thing.

"Well, have you got it?" Misty asked.

"Of course," I said. "I told you I would."

"Let's see then," she said.

"What you waiting for?" urged a voice from the crowd.

"Show us now," said another.

I could feel them closing in around me. But I didn't want to be rushed. I wanted to enjoy the suspense of it all. I made a dramatic bow, my right hand on my chest, my left raised out from my side. I already had the gold in my right hand. So when I stood back up, I slowly unbent my right arm and announced, "Ta-da!" before opening my clenched fist to reveal the treasure.

"Ahhhhhh." There was a collective gasp and one second of the truest pleasure I had ever known. But quicker than lightening, Misty plucked the gold from my hand. She held it up to one eye and began examining it mercilessly.

"So this is it," she said.

"Yeah," I answered.

She quit looking at the gold long enough to stare me straight in the face. "You got this from a leprechaun? A piece of gold—from his pot?"

"Yeah," I affirmed in a voice of vindicated innocence, "just like I told it."

"Hmmm," she said. "Gold, real gold," she muttered under her breath while she turned the small piece over in her hand. She smelled it, drawing in with all her might, and then licked it with a quick flash of an eager pink tongue just like a kitten drinks from a saucer of fresh milk. Still, the battle with indecision raged on. When she balanced it between thumb and forefinger and raised it to the light, I heard several whistles of admiration. It glistened and shone, not with the shiny brightness of a new coin, but with the dull, rich gleam of ancient wealth and power. How could she doubt? The truth was obvious. It was gold. And it was beautiful.

"I bet that could buy anything," someone suggested right before Misty ran to the steps of the school building and raked the gold piece across the bottom step.

"Ha," she said when she looked to see the damage. "Nothing is more like it. All it is, is painted gravel," she announced. Obviously disgusted, she tossed the rock in my direction and left without another word.

Before the day was over, Misty and Angus Matthews were boyfriend and girlfriend, and she was wearing a cheap dime-store ring and a wide flashy smile. Neither one fit worth a damn, but evidently Angus was responsible for producing both. Misty was practically frantic, showing off to anybody who'd give her the time of day. It was as if some other girl had taken over her body. Gone was the tough little spitfire with the sharp blue eyes. In her place was a simp, who giggled uncontrollably as if she were pleased as punch over how everything had worked itself out. But I could tell it was all a lie. Even the ring didn't look real.

Fortunately for me, most of my friends took me for a fool and not a fibber. I even managed to incorporate the fake gold into my tale of Bubba Jack, who now everyone agreed was the trickiest old leprechaun that ever lived. So my heart may have been temporarily busted, my confidence more than a bit shaken, but my reputation, such as it was, was still fairly intact as I made my way toward home that afternoon. You win some; you lose some. I was trying to be a good sport about it all until I remembered my mama's now empty nest egg. The sudden weight of my conscience hit me like a ton of bricks, nearly knocked me to my knees. I had taken all my mother's money and didn't have thing one to show for it. A piece of painted gravel with a big jagged scratch that revealed its mortifying and true nature? How was I ever going to explain?

I dragged my feet the whole way as if my legs had been weighted with heavy metal chains. My triumphant armor had vanished. I was a criminal sentenced to a fate worse than death, but only what I justly deserved. I considered running away and joining the circus. But the minute I pictured myself taming lions and making daring flips on the trapeze, I was filled with a terrifying sense of loss. I plumb couldn't stand the thought of being without the one person I was most afraid of facing.

I knew my worst fears had been realized when I stepped into the kitchen and found Mama waiting at the table for me. The empty jar was waiting there, too, right on the table in front of her. The lid was off. It was lying there accusingly on the checkered oilcloth. Jar, lid, and Mama—I faced them all with the overwhelming terror of a blindfolded man before a firing squad. I knew I was going to get it. I knew I was guilty as charged. And what was even worse, I knew she knew it too.

"Michael?" Mama said in a voice overrun with bewildered sorrow. "Did you take my money? All of it? You wouldn't do anything like that, would you?"

"No ma'am," I said. "Not exactly . . ." I couldn't bear to meet her eyes. I stared at the little blue bird painted on the side of the cookie jar instead. I was sure if that bird could speak, it too would ask why I had done such an unforgivable thing as to rob its nest. I couldn't let my eyes up from that bird even when I thought I heard the whisper of wings and felt the shivery shadow of footsteps falling across my grave.

"Are you in some kind of trouble?" Mama asked, "some kind of trouble at school?"

My eyes flew to her face. In that moment, my love for her was so strong, it surged in a shooting pain that leapt through my chest. "Yes," I said, "that's right. But only it's not me that's in trouble, it's somebody else. Another boy. One of my classmates. There's this bully who won't let him alone, threatens to beat him up every day unless he pays up. And the boy, he doesn't have it any better at home, you see. His daddy uses any old excuse he can muster to beat up on the boy himself. So either way, the boy gets it—because of the money or because he can't stand up against old Angus Matthews" (his name slipped out before I even realized it was going to). At first my speech was stilted and searching, but I was picking up speed, rounding the curve. I could do this. I knew I could.

"What could I do?" I asked. "You always told me to 'Do unto others'—the Golden Rule and all that. Besides, I was hoping to get a job and make all the money back before you even noticed it was gone. I didn't want you to worry, Mama, not for one minute."

"Oh Michael," she said at the end of my pathetic little tale. "You're telling me the truth, aren't you? You're not telling me a story, now are you? You wouldn't do a thing like that, would you, Michael? Not when it really counts. Not to your own mother." It was almost as if she were carrying on two conversations, one with me and one with herself. I could hear that same desperate need to believe that had been Misty's when she challenged me to prove my leprechaun story. Only this time, she wasn't asking for concrete proof, just my word was all. That was it. All's I had to do was stand by my story. All I had to do was produce some of that magic make-believe and we'd all be saved.

"No ma'am," I said. "I wouldn't lie to you, not for all the tea in China. Why would I do such a thing? What good reason would I have to lie to the person I love the very best?"

The smoothing of her worried brow, the tender look of love and gratefulness that filled her face, and my own heady sense of power from having delivered the soothing balm that eased her pain—it all comes flooding back to me as I sit here so many years later facing my wife who has asked so many of these same questions before. A lifetime of telling stories, yet that leprechaun story is still as fresh in my mind as if it had happened just yesterday. The years have been so full of tales, it's a wonder they haven't all gotten jumbled in my mind. But Regina's insistence—the fury in her voice, the gun that trembles threateningly in her hand—brings me back to the present.

"Tell me the truth, Michael," she says. "Damn it all. For once in your life, tell me the truth." Of course, I'm guilty. We all know that. Nothing has changed.

"I love you," I say.

"That's not what I'm asking," she answers in a voice that threatens to break under mounting pressure.

"But it's true," I insist.

"Tell me what else is true, Michael. Just this once. For heaven sakes!"

The ice in my drink is making the glass sweat. As the moisture seeps into my palm, I feel the enticing prickle of inspiration. This is a hell of a situation, I think. Talk about drama. What a story it will make. But first, I have to come up with something for Regina. Something good . . .

"Stop. Stop right now," she demands. "I know what you're doing. I know what's going on. I can see it in your face, your lying two-timing face, you bastard!" she yells.

Come on, Michael, think. Come on, buddy, you've done this before. I've got to do some quick thinking and even faster talking, but all that comes to mind is how much I've screwed up, how much I have to make up to Regina, how much I've stolen from her. You know it's really kind of funny. The real truth, the one I've always known all along, the truth no one ever wants to be the one to say—is that there's plenty of gold to be had. Plenty enough to line all our pockets and to fill a life's worth of treasure chests if only you're able and willing to turn all the scratches so no one will see. And hold on. Hold on for dear life. That's the tricky part, holding on to leprechaun luck and making it yours no matter what. Because as long as you've got it on your side, you can go and do most anything. But if somehow it gets loose, manages to slip away . . . Well, let it suffice to say, you're gonna find yourself having a real, real hard time ever getting it back.

I try to moisten my lips, which have gone surprisingly dry despite the drink. I shake my head softly and have to give Regina a little smile. "Ta-da," I say. For it's all I have to offer. I couldn't tell her the truth. Not even if I wanted to.

REGINA CLAYTON

My mother was a sewing sorceress, an enchantress who cast spells with needle and thread. She didn't care for cooking, neglected the garden, had little time for playing cards or the piano. She seldom shopped and rarely entertained. She stitched instead. She crocheted. She patchworked. She quilted. She appliqued. Bedspreads, doilies, tablemats, cloths, and napkins. She sewed all kinds of clothes. She basted and darned. She knitted. She hemstitched and tatted. She even made yards and yards of intricate white lace. There was nothing she couldn't do with a needle, no task too large or small. My aunts claimed this was why she had married our father. She was determined to repair all his tears, to mend all his holes with such fine stitches that even he would forget they'd ever been there.

Embroidery was her specialty. In her hands this homespun craft was elevated to high art. *Arrowhead, Basket, Buttonhole, Chain.* She painted pictures on fabric, textured tapestries of silken thread. *Cross, Diamond, Eyelet, Feather.* Fine linen scenes laden with heavy vines, lush flowers, juicy ripe fruit. *Fern, Herringbone, Knot,* and *Ladder.* Birds flew. Fish swam. Sunlight shone on leaves that trembled in a quiet breeze. *Satin, Scroll, Seed, Shadow, Sheaf, Split,* and *Star.* To run your hand across my mother's work was to touch the world of her imagination. It was an odd landscape where the fantastic mixed with the ordinary, where fiction and reality often lived side by side. The two little girls next to the unicorn drinking from a small wave-stitched stream were my sister, May, and I wearing matching blue dresses we recognized. And that was our house, sewn brick by brick, a familiar pink rectangle placed under a colossal columnar canopy of wild, leafy green. While a tiny red axe was propped against the vine's thick trunk, our father's white Ford sat nearby, determinedly sewn into a thorn-stitched driveway and further proof of my mother's fantasy. For my father was rarely home. He traveled for work, was usually gone for long stretches of time. So we grew accustomed to this—my mother, my sister, and I—to living in a world that was largely of our own making.

My mother's sewing punctuated the order of our lives. Mornings were spent on practicalities, mending and making new clothes. Afternoons, she devoted to more ambitious projects—sets of monogrammed linen sheets with tatted borders and an assortment of quilts, some she kept and some she gave away. Evenings, after suppertime, she embroidered. After May and I were properly bathed and dressed in our old-fashioned nightgowns of sheer white lawn painstakingly adorned with delicate tucks, miniature knots, flowers, and pale blue ribbons threaded through handmade lace, we would tiptoe down the long dark hall to find her. Our gowns so light and full, it was easy to pretend we were something else: ghosts of girls haunting the house in which they'd lived long ago, unleashed smoke rising in a swirling stream from a genie's bottle, or puffy clouds racing the North Wind along the vast corridor of a starry sky.

We would find her, bent over a square of fabric stretched taut in a wooden oval frame, sewing in her room. We called it her room even though it was of course also my father's. But here again, there were so few signs of his existence—a handful of loose change in a china dish, a man's set of silver brushes lying untouched on the bureau, the smooth, unwrinkled side of the large four-poster bed. Sometimes it was all too easy to believe he wasn't real, that he was a story we'd made up, a figment of our collective imagination.

Our mother's presence, however, was everywhere in that room. Her embroidery covered the curtains, the upholstery, the bedspread, and turned her private chamber into a feminine bower made even more lovely contrasted against the mahogany curves of the furniture that shone with a polished gleam in the lamplight. Entering that room was like floating into a moonlit garden. We were swans gliding over cool, glassy water that ran through a tunnel and opened at the end into an extraordinary world of blossoming beauty. We'd come to a fluttering stop in a small pool at my mother's feet, expectant and eager.

It was story time, you see. My mother told us all kinds of stories every night while she sewed. She sat in one armchair while we shared the other. Every time, before she began telling the tale, she'd stop sewing for a moment and stare intently into the round embroidery hoop as if she were looking into a magic mirror and would find the story there waiting for her among the threads.

The stories my mother found in her embroidery were fantastic tales of curses and charms, broken spells and bizarre transformations, of impossible tasks that led to long journeys in strange lands. *Jack and the Beanstalk, Hansel and Gretel, Goldilocks and the Three Bears.* There were witches and fairies, giants and dwarfs, animals that talked and mermaids who couldn't. *The Goose Girl, Thumbelina, The Ugly Duckling.* And, of course, lots and lots of princesses with long dark hair and bright blue eyes just like mine and May's.

Many of the stories we knew quite well. *Cinderella, Snow White,*

Rapunzel. But she often modified these. Sometimes, she'd put us in them or she'd change the ending, mix everything up and turn it into something new, something different, something I guess she thought of as her own. *The Nightingale* was one of these. I didn't care so much for it, but as one of her favorites she told it often

There once was a family of nightingales that lived in an enchanted forest in the branches of a wild plum tree. Mother and Father Nightingale were proud of their little family. They'd worked so hard to raise their nest full of babies and they'd done a fine job. They'd taught their children how to fly, to find food, to build the best nests, and most importantly, how to sing. But now their work was done. It was time for the young birds to leave the nest, to test their wings, finally, on their very own. On the day they had all been waiting for, the four young nightingales gathered in a line on one of the tree's branches to say goodbye. Each was anxious to be off, but their mother insisted on giving them one last thing before she could let them go.

Her gift was a large seed, the color of ripe apricots. There were four of them and they glowed with the gentle light of a setting sun. She placed one in the beak of each of her children and said, "Take great care with these for they are the seeds of Happiness. They are precious and rare. But your father and I cannot tell you what to do with them. That is for you to decide." And with that, the young birds were free to be on their way.

Each took a different path through the forest. The eldest promptly swallowed his seed and flew north where he quickly found a mate and built a mighty nest high in the topmost branches of the tallest fir. At the close of each day, he sang rich, throaty songs in praise of his good fortune.

The second eldest flew to the east. When he reached the edge of the sea, he buried his seed in the sand. The seed grew into a lovely fruit tree that offered both shelter and food and allowed him to live forever surrounded by balmy ocean breezes and sparkling blue water. Inspired, his songs rippled endlessly across the changing tides in a haunting refrain of adulation.

The third son flew west. There he used his seed to win the love of a beautiful mate. They each ate half the seed and then built their nest on the edge of a small village where the nightingale couple became famous for the passionate songs they delivered, much to their neighbors' amazement and delight, every evening at twilight.

The fourth and youngest nightingale was a female. She flew south. But she didn't know what to do with her seed once she got there. She held it inside her beak for three days while she tried to decide. At the end of the three days, she was weak from hunger and realized she'd have to find a new hiding place for her seed so she could search for food. She was so busy looking for a good place to put her seed that she didn't notice she was being stalked by a young boy from the king's court. The boy was not fooled by the nightingale's modest appearance. He knew the power of a nightingale's song and that he would be richly rewarded for it. So he scooped the little gray bird up in a finely woven net and shouted in delight. His pounding steps shook the nightingale as he ran toward the castle. There was nothing she could do. Her wings were bound so tightly by the net's fine webbing she knew she couldn't escape. Neither could she cry out in alarm, nor plead for help or rescue because she still had her precious seed of Happiness hidden within her beak.

The king was young and handsome but lacked charm and understanding. He was, indeed, very pleased when the boy presented him with the nightingale. Such birds were scarce and highly coveted. So he had the nightingale locked in an ornate gold cage and told the court to announce her arrival. Word spread quickly throughout the kingdom and that night a large crowd gathered beneath the castle tower to hear her lovely song. But the nightingale couldn't sing without revealing her seed. She was sure the king would take that too. Then, she would have lost her freedom and her happiness. So she remained silent. And when the evening had passed darkly into night and the moon had risen high in the sky, the eager audience gave up and went home in disappointment.

The king did not want his people to think he couldn't command a song from such an insignificant little bird. So the next morning he tried to bargain with her. "Nightingale," he said, "I will release you if you will sing for me tonight." He wasn't planning on letting her go the very next day, but sometime in the future. The nightingale's heart was filled with hope when she first heard the king's promise. But then she remembered her seed and the reason for her silence. What was freedom without happiness? So once again that evening she refused to sing.

This made the king angry. He knew the little bird had had nothing to eat or drink. So he tempted her with seeds and berries and fresh water from an underground spring. But the bird refused to give in. "Just one song," he coaxed, "one song that none of my people will ever forget." But still, the nightingale remained silent. For again, what was fame and fortune without happiness?

The very next morning the king had a black cloth draped over the nightingale's cage. "I condemn you to live without food and light until you sing," he said. The poor nightingale was plunged into despair. She was so weak and hungry. She knew that she would die soon without anything to sustain her. So that evening as the sun began to slip toward the horizon and the edge of light beyond the cage curtain began to fade, the nightingale opened her beak and let the seed drop to the cage floor. She pretended she was perched on the ledge of the tower window. She imagined she could look out and see the whole wide world spread out before her. And then she began to sing.

The first notes trembled in the air, round and full, and then fell, a sprinkle of tear-shaped kisses scattered across the parched land. No one was waiting to hear the bird sing. But as soon as the first notes sounded, everyone—young and old, rich and poor, inside the castle and far beyond the castle walls—stopped to listen. As the notes began to collect and build, people thought of the secret, dappled light that dances through a dimly lit forest and of the pungent, purple juice that runs from the wounded flesh of a ripe plum. Then the notes crystallized. They turned sharp and clear, a brilliant scattering of diamonds that climbed so high those who heard them imagined lofty perches on snowcapped mountains and the cool sweep of wind combed with the fresh scent of pine.

The song shifted yet again and became a playful dance of sunlit sparkles on a sapphire sea. And then it changed once more and spoke of the ruby richness of passion and love. And then as it began to unwind, the nightingale's voice reminded the people of the earth's diminishing warmth beneath their feet. Night was drawing nigh, pulling a curtain of darkness across their sky. The song was simple and sweet and led them to think of home and the forgotten beauty of their own familiar sounds: the click of the door latch, a welcoming call, the crackle of a fire, an upwelling bubble of laughter, the tender hum of a well-worn lullaby. All of these were woven into a melody that the people heard with such complete and utter delight that many continued to marvel at its loveliness long after the nightingale had grown quiet and still.

When the king drew back the curtain on the cage, he saw a lone almond-shaped seed lying on the floor beside the dead bird. To his eyes, the seed was dull, ordinary, though he was a bit curious about how it had gotten there. "Strange," he murmured, before casually flicking it away with his fingertip.

When I was nine, a wild dog started appearing at the edge of our backyard where the lawn gave way to rough patches of tall grass and weeds. He looked part German shepherd, part husky, part wolf. May was positive he'd come from one of our mother's stories, that she'd summoned him up late one night while she sewed by her bedroom window. He was skittish, full of bravado and fear as if he couldn't decide whether to cower on his belly and beg for food or to lunge for our throats. Many nights we listened to the eerie sound of his howls tearing at the darkness.

But in my mother's stories things were often not what they seemed. There were *The Three Little Pigs* and *Peter and the Wolf*. But there also was *Beauty and the Beast*. *The Firebird*. Besides, I didn't want to be one of the callous kings who didn't bother to appreciate a truly rare and precious gift. So I started leaving table scraps out by the garden and waiting at a safe distance to watch when the dog came by. I scarcely dared to breathe when he lowered his muzzle to eat. Once he was done, he'd raise his head and stare straight at me. Each time our eyes met, I knew we belonged together, that strange wild dog and I.

I wooed him with stolen leftovers, crusts of stale bread, and pails filled with water from the spigot. And I crept a little closer to my quarry each night. It took weeks, but finally he let me pet him while he ate. A good dog was just what we needed. *Lassie, Rin Tin Tin, Old Yeller.* And they were hard to come by. But no matter how many words I used to sway Mother over to my side, to get her to see how it could be, she wouldn't buy it. *He's dangerous. He always will be. If you want a dog, we'll get you a puppy. How about a nice yellow lab or a friendly little beagle? Something you can raise yourself and train right.* I couldn't believe the failure of her imagination. *No,* she insisted kindly but firmly, her reluctance to disappoint evident in the hesitancy of her speech and the pleading look that was her final answer. *He's a sometimes kind of dog. Sometimes he'll be good and sometimes he won't. He can't help it; that's just the way he is. It's in his nature.*

But I resisted this version of my mother's truth. I ate at her refusal with the same stubborn determination I used to consume peas and carrots, cooked cauliflower, and collard greens. I swallowed in silence and washed away the bitter aftertaste with cold glasses of milk. Eventually, I quit my constant cajoling, the endless wheedling clamor, and let the dejected slump of my shoulders and the beseeching message in my eyes do my talking for me. I was convinced that one day all would be dramatically revealed. My wild dog would turn hero. He'd drag us all from the burning house or kill a copperhead poised to strike my mother's ankle, or even better, rescue some neighbor's plump baby who had wandered off in the woods. It was only a matter of time before he would show his true colors and my mother would realize her mistake.

Weeks passed while I rode the roller-coaster waves of childish hope and despair. I ignored all my mother's bedtime stories about the terrible fates of those who foolishly chose to disregard good advice. I held on. I believed. I could see a small crack forming in her armor. Each day I became more confident in handling the dog, my dog. I scratched behind his ears. I patted his back. I talked to him while he lingered after his meal, both of us increasingly reluctant to be on our solitary way. We even played a game with dandelion puffs. I'd tickle his nose with their fuzzy tops until he bit them off with quick, muffled chomps of his teeth. It was exactly the kind of fun I had envisioned for so long. But one evening I was so excited I impulsively reached out to hug his neck before he could get away. My sudden move startled him. He snarled and snapped just as my face loomed close to his. And in just that second, the wolf was unleashed, his furious strength hot and moist as his teeth tore through my skin. It was in this way that I received my first real lesson in the consequences of choice and in the pain that so often accompanies that *sometimes* kind of love.

I had to have stitches, of course. My mother held my head still while the doctor sewed me up with sturdy black thread. I can remember the pressure of her fingers against my skull and the pinch of his needle as it pierced my upper lip. *What a steady hand you have, so nice and neat.* Several years passed and the scar faded with them, leaving me too old to believe in story magic, in werewolves and changelings and princes turned into frogs. Eventually I switched my affections to the garden. Plants flourished, or they withered and died, but they never bit back. So I chose to be the second son, the nightingale who buried his seed in the sand and waited for it to grow into happiness.

Long after my mother stopped telling us stories before bed, I still thought of them often, especially the nightingale's. As I got older, I was convinced I had it all figured out. Its meaning was obvious. It was all about being willing to take risks, to make choices in order to be happy. You couldn't just sit there with your seed. You had to do something with it. But perhaps accepting that you had to choose was relatively easy, while making the right choice was the hard part.

Choosing well and choosing wisely were the main themes in the stories the women in our family shared with each other when they were together. My mother, my grandmother, our aunts, great-aunts, and cousins all told stories of love lost and found, of female troubles and triumphs, of women who dared and those who didn't. These stories replaced the bedtime fairytales of my youth. They were told in kitchens and on porches in the lull of late afternoons while my mother sewed and their suppers simmered on the stove, before husbands came home or showed up to claim their wives' attention. When May and I were little, they'd shoo us away so they'd be free to talk. But as we passed through puberty we gradually gained entrance into the feminine enclave that surrounded us. It was as if they sought to offer consolation for the onset of menstruation, for falling victim to inexplicable mood swings and cramps and stained underwear, by allowing us the privilege of discovering the true stories of real women we knew.

At first, they made it seem as if we were getting to eavesdrop, that it was only because we were so quiet that they had *forgotten* we were there. But there was always an exchanged look in the beginning, an acknowledgment of consent between the teller of the tale and my mother before the story was relayed. These stories were not really so different from the magic tales on which we'd been raised. They, too, had the same strangely surreal quality that came with sudden trans-formations and seismic shifts in fortune. *You'd never know it to look at her now. She was pretty and smart, but bad luck followed her everywhere. Pulled the rug right out from under her. All those years and then finally she gets what she deserves, only it's too late.* They also stressed both recognition and interpretation of signs and warnings. Heeding good advice, no matter how obscure the delivery, was vital to determining the success or failure of the heroine's adventure. *That night she dreamt of a black dog. I say, if the shoe doesn't fit . . . She ought to have known not to marry a man who couldn't afford a ring.*

These stories belonged strictly to the women. They were never told in male company even if a man actually alluded to one of them. Take for instance, the tale of Miss Pruella Leech, a spinster schoolteacher who refused to give up gracefully when her suitor suffered a sudden change of heart. Many hours were spent mulling over the outrageous lengths to which Miss Pruella had gone to get him back. *Black magic.*

Traded her trousseau for a voodoo love potion. For three nights, the story went, Miss Pruella drank a concoction that tasted of salty blood and whispered over wax figures that she kept under her pillow. But to no avail. Her suitor, Floyd Eubanks, married his new love, Henrietta, and they settled down in a little white farmhouse on the outskirts of town. Still, Miss Pruella refused to be outdone. She cast aside the notion of a love spell and tried instead for a hex on the object of her lost love's affections. So when Henrietta's first child was stillborn, everybody wondered. In fact, from then on every time anything bad happened to Henrietta they all wondered if it wasn't due to Miss Pruella, who still wasn't satisfied with her revenge.

But if a man mentioned Miss Pruella's name and said something suggestive like, "That Miss Pruella, you just can't tell about a woman like that. Something about her is not right," Mother and her sisters, Grandmother, and Great-aunt Lil would all give a slight, disinterested shrug. *Goes to show what loneliness can do to a body. You sure can't find fault with those carrot cakes she makes for the church bazaar. I, for one, have never tasted better.* It was as if they all agreed with unspoken consent that a man would never believe their stories, that he couldn't be expected to accept that anything, no matter how fantastic, is possible when it comes to the dark, twisted workings of a female heart. Men needed to be protected from the truth while women needed to understand it.

Especially when it came to determining their fates, for one of the biggest preoccupations of these tales was the woman who ended up sad and alone. Her story was told in a way that expressed sympathy for her unfortunate plight, yet still implied it was at least partially her own fault. Miss Pruella could have ended up happy if she'd directed her attention toward someone else while there was still time. Rose Thornton could have eluded madness if she simply had agreed to adopt instead of insisting on carrying one dead baby to term right after the other. And Hilda Green could have kept her family together if she hadn't been too lazy to get supper on the table every night and to clean her house. *What could she expect? Who could blame him for wandering? She let herself go. And all those children were filthy, no wonder they turned to crime.*

When I got old enough to date, I realized that they began to tell stories about me too. My and my sister's romantic adventures became material for new tales. We treaded the same polished floorboards and faded carpets at home, walked the same worn paths between houses and gardens that they did. But we also found ourselves traveling as characters in an altogether different landscape woven from their words into a place, a destination that existed only within the circle of their voices. It was an odd sensation being divided into more than one self, a bit like looking at your own picture or staring into a mirror. I always found myself wondering, *is that really me? Am I really who they say I am?*

May and I were guided through our dating years with advice lifted straight from the stories we all knew. In high school, May was crushed when Scott Bell broke up with her right before the junior/senior prom. They patted her back, clucked sympathetically, offered tissues and cups of restorative tea all while Mother continued to pin May's dress. And when May said she didn't need the dress, she wasn't going, they all shook their heads. *Don't be a Pruella. Look what that got her.* May was pushed to accept another, less attractive offer from Donald Reese, who had severe acne and a donkey laugh. Still, she was praised, commended for making the best of a bad situation, for rising to the occasion. This was small consolation, May once told me, for having to suffer through one of the most humiliating nights of her life.

I, too, received large doses of the same medicine. Whenever I was the least bit haphazard with my appearance, they would pretend to mistake me for Hilda Green. *Ah, Hilda. I mean Regina, silly me. Of course, you two don't look a thing alike. I don't know what made me think of Hilda when I looked at you. It must have been something about the back of your head. Did you brush your hair this morning?*

Or if I dared to turn down a date, they would recall the infamous pickiness of Cousin Bebe. *Remember the time she refused to go out with a beau because she said he parted his hair on the wrong side? Wasn't he the one ended up a millionaire? Invented something or other. Made a fortune. Bet he never changed his part. Wonder if Bebe ever thought of him when she was an old lady living in her sister's spare bedroom since she never did manage to get a house of her own. Held out to marry that Rupert. Man was bald as a cue ball and a drifter to boot.*

When I met Michael, he charmed them all. They fell for him before I did. *What a storyteller and handsome too. Why it's like he stepped right off the pages of a storybook. Too bad Bebe is dead and gone, I'd have given anything to watch him make her head spin.* They acted as if my choice should have been obvious. *What are you waiting for?* I didn't dare mention my own doubts. They didn't leave them any room in the conversation. I knew if I confided in them and told them of the unsettling way Michael sometimes looked at other women or of my increasing suspicion that Michael actually believed some of the crazy stories he made up, they would dismiss my fears as paltry insecurities. *There are never any guarantees, especially when it comes to love. And after all what do you expect? He is a man.*

Night after night, I lay awake in bed and struggled to escape my mounting anxieties. My dreams were riddled with a spine-chilling, howling refrain. And I had a recurring nightmare of running through dense undergrowth, with vines and limbs grabbing at my hair and feet, the sound of heavy panting only a heartbeat away. But in the morning light, I reminded myself of the youngest nightingale, too afraid to choose, too scared to risk being saved.

I decided to share my seed like the third nightingale did with his love. I left my worries unspoken. I dressed them up instead in the long white gown my mother made me. I fed them wedding cake, chased them away with champagne bubbles and blushing smiles. I was going to be one of the lucky ones. My life was going to sing with happiness. I tossed my bouquet to sorrow, who stood by quietly watching in the corner, and promptly rode off into the sunset, waving farewell with a hand newly ringed in gold.

And I did make good on my promises. I kept house and planted a new garden. I made dinner and love with equal devotion. When Michael came home in a cloud of another woman's perfume, I brushed away the crumbles of fear with the same practiced efficiency I used to sweep the kitchen floor clean each night. When he unknowingly betrayed secret alliances with an all-too-familiar gesture bestowed upon another at a cocktail party or dinner, I smoothed over the dent it left just as I faithfully fluffed the sofa cushions each morning. And occasionally when his stories were so garbled I recognized them as fantastic acts of desperation, I sifted through the detritus and tossed out my gnawing fears along with the rancid trash.

But as time passed, these wounds would not heal. Their scars refused to fade, and I found it harder and harder to keep everything stitched up. The endless cycle of chores began to take their toll: the days, weeks, months, years when it was all I could do to stop myself from letting the food spoil in the refrigerator; from wearing my bathrobe all day long; from allowing myself simply to sink down past the thin layer of suds and let the gray dishwater close over my head and pull me into the dark watery absolution granted little bits and pieces of unused food.

Each time I've had to work up the courage to question my husband.

Where were you? Are you happy? Do you love me? And he has answered by bending and shaping an alternative reality with the same duplicitous ease a clown uses to twist balloon and air into recognizable fantasy. And every time he's handed me the story of our lives shaped into a grotesque form that threatens to pop with the slightest prick, I've felt myself splinter and fragment. Why do I feel it, if it's not there? How do I know it, if it's not true? He's turned my mirror into a kaleidoscope. *Devoted wife, loving mother, scorned spouse, betrayed lover.* I have been all these and none of them at the same time. Too many Reginas to count. It seems like I've spent my whole life drifting wordlessly, not knowing who or what or where I was, lost in other people's stories, other people's lies.

Only a few nights ago, Michael actually made it home for dinner on time. Our son, Mike, was outside shooting basketball when I heard Michael's car pull in the garage. I had fixed meatloaf, mashed potatoes, and string beans for dinner, one of their favorite meals. I could hear Michael's car door shut, the sound of his shoes stepping across the cement, their voices mixing as father and son began to play. And I couldn't help but be lulled by it, by the beauty of my own backyard framed in the window above my kitchen sink, by the simple pleasure of filling three glasses with freshly brewed tea.

When Michael came in a few minutes later, I asked if he wanted a drink before washing up and casually mentioned his secretary had called just a little while ago. I was watching him as I spoke because I was glad to see him for the first time in a really long time. I couldn't get over that, just how good he looked to me right then.

So of course I couldn't help but notice Michael's reaction when I spoke his secretary's name. *Cindy called.* Just those two words and the openness fell from his face with the same swift finality of a well-aimed shot. Mike was still outside playing. The patter of his sneakers and the bouncing ball filled the sudden emptiness in the room.

She did? His gaze flickered, and he jingled the loose change in his pocket. *What'd she say?* That was all it took, a handful of words coupled with body language I had grown to dread and despise. And I knew. I knew the whole story. I knew it all over again.

But I fell back on instinct. I smoothed. I fluffed. I tied up the wayward strands and tossed the rest away. It was a night like any other. I served my husband and son dinner, took my place at the table, and sat there while I tried to swallow back the acrid bile that rose to the top of my throat. Without saying a word, I waged war with the lumps of food that would not subside. I nodded and smiled and drank countless sips of cool tea in a feeble attempt to drown my enemy.

Later that night as I lay in bed staring at the shadows cast on the ceiling and listening to Michael's soft, even snore, I thought of all the times I had bitten back words of anger, expressions of outraged love. I pictured myself changed by a witch's spell into a tall garden urn, a frozen empty vessel that had filled over the slow spilling of time with collected drops of sorrow. My blood wasn't red; it was a light liquid blue. Within me was a cascading pool, fresh as rain, that eased down into the cracks and crevices of sun-baked earth to soak the dry papery skins of unused kernels. Then I felt a strange tickling inside, a feathery unfurling of new life, tender and green, rising up out of the damp darkness. And I was afraid to sleep, afraid of the new thing that had sprung up and taken hold.

In the days since, it has continued to grow. While I have eaten almost nothing, it feeds greedily on whatever is already there, doubling, sometimes tripling in size overnight. It's a massive coil of choking vine, a voracious parasite that promises to squeeze the life right out of me. It's constantly popping out new leaves, new shoots of waywardly wicked growth. I can hardly breathe, my chest and stomach are so full of lushly thriving vegetation. But I don't know how to uproot it. It's impossible. I can't even believe it's really there.

This afternoon after seeing Michael and Cindy together with my own eyes, after being forced to witness what they've done, I went for a long walk along the edge of the woods that surround the golf course. It's a path I've taken before. *Little Red Riding Hood, Sleeping Beauty, Briar Rose.* But this time, I had the feeling that something was following me. Something in the woods was creeping along and watching me from behind the trees. But no matter how hard I strained to catch the sound of a twig snapping or the crunch of old leaves that would give it away, all I could hear was the tumorous green tide that continued to surge along artery and vein, muscle and bone, with each knotted clutch of my hardening heart.

Now that the king has finally come home to his castle, I can scarcely move to greet him. My arms and legs are caught in a stiff, ropy web. *Peter Pan, Ali Baba, Rumpelstiltskin.* The gun in my hand is so heavy. He can't help it. It's in his nature. But the vine does all the work. It knows its own mind, how to twist and pull.

Pop, pop, pop goes the illusion. And my vision is cleared. I can see it all now from my tower window. *Arrowhead, Basket, Buttonhole, Chain.* It's a finely woven tapestry—all the flowers and trees, the cozy houses that dot the landscape, the people who are so small and slight. *Cross, Diamond, Feather, Fern.* I can't pick out Mike Jr. from the tiny figures busy scurrying to and fro. Can't manage to recognize my own child from so far away. *Sheaf, Split,* and *Star.* There is a bird perched beside me on the ledge. The nightingale. Poor little lost bird who let fear steal its voice and rob it of its one and only true pleasure. Though she did sing her final song, that memorable melody so full of what might have been. I wonder if that made any difference.

The metal tip of the gun grazes my temple as I lean my head against the stone arch of the window frame. Everything, so distant and lovely, like a dream. All at once, the bird is jolted. It leaps into the air and for one breathtakingly beautiful stitch in time it hovers there, a fluttering fold of pristine white, before it sails away as if suddenly succumbing to the irresistible pull of an unseen thread.

AT THE BEGINNING

One week later

Exactly one week after Regina Clayton died of a self-inflicted gunshot wound to the head, Dawn Renee Davenport briefly considered killing herself purely as a means of escaping the rest of her own wedding. *It would serve them all right*, she thought dully. *That's what they should get for making me so miserable*. But the thought was fleeting. After all, she wasn't crazy, just hysterical. As is every bride's right.

These kinds of thoughts and feelings were bound to occur when a girl realized that the love of her life was really just a stranger in disguise. This may not happen to every single bride, but it had happened to Dawn, who did not consider herself ordinary by any stretch of the imagination. It had, indeed, been Dawn's unfortunate lot for said realization to hit her *before* the ceremony. If only it had waited until *after*.

But there you go, not one thing had gone according to good fortune or even the carefully crafted plans of Dawn and her mother. Dawn, whose heart was supposed to be filled to overflowing with bridal bliss at the prospect of being united forever in sacred matrimony with her one true love, had never experienced such sheer, unadulterated terror before in her entire life. Forever is a long time. It might sound great as far as diamonds were concerned, but for a twenty-two-year-old straight out of college?

The enormity of it all was too much for Dawn to bear. Especially considering she was due to walk down that aisle any minute. Suddenly, all of her waiting had shrunk down to the size of a tiny little kernel of rice. Just one. Dawn was in no shape to deal with that, plus looking her absolute most radiantly beautiful ever, plus all the bickering and back-stabbing that was going on around her in the Sunday school room she and the bridesmaids were using to get dressed for the ceremony.

There were twelve of them—bridesmaids that is—including the maid of honor, Dawn's former favorite cousin, Ilene, who was too busy coping with a pesky pimple on her forehead to be any help whatsoever. One dozen slightly disgruntled young ladies who had all been granted the honor of coughing up a small personal fortune for the pastel blue chiffon dresses they were now struggling to get into. Slippery satin bows were to be tied with ribbons of a slightly darker shade of blue as straps at the top of each shoulder and as an accent around each princess-cut waistline. The dresses were long, relatively low cut, and flattered absolutely no one. Which helped matters not one whit.

This was only one of the many reasons Dawn was lying down in her slip with a cool damp washcloth over her eyes exactly one hour before she was scheduled to walk down the main aisle of the First United Methodist Church and pledge to honor and obey John Wesley for the rest of her days before God and everybody she had ever known as well as quite a few she didn't. Of course, *now* she would include the groom among those designated in the latter category—the strangers at her wedding.

It didn't matter one bit that she had dated him for the last four years. What it all boiled down to was that she didn't know him from Adam. Besides, he was from out of town, which she now understood meant that they might as well be from different countries, worlds even.

That was it. They might as well be from different *planets*. She might as well be marrying a little green man who had come to Earth in a flying saucer. More hot tears began leaking out the corners of her eyes.

This was another one of the reasons she was hiding behind the washcloth. Her mother had insisted. "Your eyes are going to be puffy slits if you don't get a hold of yourself," she had said. "The pictures will be ruined." This had only made Dawn cry harder. As if she had any control over her emotions. As if any of this was her fault!

The more Dawn thought about her mother's recent behavior, the more she was convinced that she didn't even know her own mother that well—and certainly not the bridesmaids. Strangers every one. And on top of it all—what she did know of them she didn't really like. Why had she asked them to be in her wedding? Why had she ever felt close to Melanie Price? The truth was, Melanie Price was a bitch. And Dawn's cousin Ilene was an unattractive loser. Why had she ever dreamt up this nightmare? Dawn couldn't stop a groan of frustrated despair as it oozed out from between her washcloth-covered lips. Moan, groan—she wasn't sure which it was and neither were the half-zipped bridesmaids. But it didn't matter. It was all the same.

Ilene didn't turn from the tall mirror she was hogging where it was propped up in the corner of the room. She was fed up with Dawn. In her opinion, Dawn had always been spoiled and self-centered. Yes, they had had a few fun summer vacations with their families all piled into a big cottage down at the beach—playing paper dolls on the screened porch during the heat of the day, reading each other strange stories from the National Enquirer, and using the Ouija Board to contact dead relatives and to ask about their future Mr. Rights. But that was then and this was now.

And in looking back, Ilene couldn't help but remember how all the biggest and best waves always happened to come along when it was Dawn's turn with the raft. Now, to top everything off, Dawn had met her Mr. Right and, so far, Ilene hadn't. Who really wants to be the *maid of honor*? Who cares about holding the bride's bouquet while the bride is busy exchanging rings and vows? Or being stuck making sure the damn train of her dress doesn't get in the bride's way as she makes her getaway on the arm of her new husband? They call that an honor? Dawn had always been the lucky one. In Ilene's humble opinion, even good luck was bound to catch up with you in the end. Poor, poor Dawn, boo-hoo-hooing over the difficulties of coping with her good fortune. Dawn would just have to deal with it. Ilene had been dealing with it for years, so it was more than time for Dawn to take a turn.

"You need a little help getting hooked in the back?" Melanie asked Ilene.

"Oh yeah, sure, that'd be great," Ilene answered with a quick nod over her shoulder.

"I can't believe Dawn is going to ruin her own wedding," Melanie whispered. "What is her problem?"

A slight, disinterested shrug was Ilene's reply.

No way was Melanie ever going to act so whacked out on her wedding day. Delicately, she picked up the edges of the fabric and eased the small hook and eye into place. Melanie was careful to avoid actually having to touch what could only be described as a nasty case of acne that had erupted all over Ilene's back. What with all those welts and boils, if Melanie didn't know better she'd swear Ilene had come down with the chicken pox. You did have to wonder a little about all the attention she was devoting to just the one on her forehead. "All set," Melanie said when she was finished.

Melanie was secretly hoping Ilene, the homely maid of honor, would move away from that mirror for just one second so Melanie could see how she looked. This was ridiculous, all these girls trying to get ready in a Sunday school classroom. It was obvious the church did not have the proper facilities. They would all end up looking like hell, but it was Dawn's wedding after all, what was it to Melanie? Still, Melanie's mother had impressed upon her the need to look her best in every situation. "Put your best face forward," her mother always urged. Maybe Ilene was acting on similar advice, which would explain why she was more concerned about her front than her back. Unfortunately this left Melanie stuck with having to make do with her compact mirror. Some people are so inconsiderate. At least Melanie didn't have as much to worry over as Ilene did.

She did have to admit *her* mother's advice had been right on target last night. Melanie Price was from Raleigh, the state capital, so it was perfectly understandable that she was less than thrilled about the prospect of spending the entire weekend in little ole po-dunk Riley, having to socialize with a bunch of hicks who thought they knew how to put on a party. Still, she had dressed up, fixed her hair and makeup the best way she knew how, and tried to put on her happy face. And boy was she glad she had when she got her first eye-full of Scott Preston at the rehearsal dinner last night, which had been held at their pitiful little country club. As far as Melanie was concerned, Scott had proven to be the highlight of the evening.

He was such a cutie! Too bad he was dating one of the other bridesmaids—Terry Anderson—one of Dawn's famous friends from high school. But after a few plastic cups of lukewarm beer, seemed Scott with the winning smile and the magic fingers had developed a bad memory. Terry who?

My, my, Melanie could not remember when she'd had such a good time. And the best thing was, after the wedding reception was over, she could pop in her convertible and speed on back to civilization and no one in Raleigh would ever be the wiser.

A bitch and a slut. Dawn could not believe she now had a bitch and a slut in her wedding party. Terry was miserable. She had hardly been able to ignore Scott sneaking off with Melanie last night when he had been her ride home. The whole thing had been humiliating. Now Terry was partly blaming Dawn for having such an unforgivably tacky friend, who was a bridesmaid no less. The pressure was coming from all sides. And John Wesley just didn't get it. He didn't get any of it, not even when his mother had shown up with a blue dress instead of a blush-colored one for the wedding. Dawn had tried to convey the proportions of this crisis to her fiancé. She had patiently gone over the detailed and clear instructions she had given his mother, who was to wear the other accent color—which was blush and not pink as everyone kept insisting—because *her* mother was wearing blue. "The mother of the bride gets to choose first," she had wailed. "We spent days and days looking for the perfect dress for my mother! The groom's mother isn't supposed to just go off and do whatever she wants. She said she'd wear blush." But John Wesley, the alien, had continued to smile his sweet little annoying smile and to insist that everything would work out all right.

Dawn, who had never even been tempted to smoke marijuana, now longed for one of those mother's-little-helpers pills the Rolling Stones sang about. One little pill about the size of the kernel of time she had left to get ready would fix her right up. Instead of the extra satin-covered buttons they attached in a plastic bag to the zipper of her dress, they ought to have given out emergency Valium. Safety pins could always be used in a pinch. Peace of mind was obviously much more valuable at a time like this.

Her nerves were shot, blasted to smithereens. She was about to tie the knot with an extraterrestrial while completely surrounded by people she could not stand. Never ever had she imagined these dire circumstances when she first began rehearsing her wedding day all those years ago. This was one of the things that Dawn found to be so incredibly cruel about finding herself in such dire circumstances. Not once had she taken this whole wedding business lightly. Not once. She had begun subscribing to *Bride Magazine* the minute she turned sixteen (her mother was the one who had insisted she wait that late). And she had played wedding religiously from the moment she was old enough to step into the toes of her mother's old high heels and toddle across the living room rug between two rows of dining room chairs.

Where was that thrill of excitement she always felt as she stepped her way across her mother's Oriental—an old filmy negligee pulled over her clothes, a cast-off lace tablecloth bobby-pinned to her hair, the wedding march humming across her lips? She felt closer to Mark Thomas and his little brother Bobbie, the two neighbor boys she bribed with her allowance to play groom and bridesmaid, than she ever would to any of the people who were around her today. Some said little Bobbie had grown up to be kind of funny. "A little *peculiar*" is what they said. But Dawn was not taking responsibility for that either. She wasn't to blame for having once suffered under the delusion that a bridesmaid was far more important than a minister.

What she wanted to know was: Where was the hope? The promise? Not one of those stupid magazine articles had ever so much as breathed a word about how it would really be. They had all been full of silly advice on picking out perfectly complimentary nail polish colors for you and your bridesmaids, sticking to a twelve-month-long diet and exercise regime tailored to help you achieve your ideal weight on the Big Day, and indulging in stress-reducing pleasures that included listening to classical music and taking long hot bubble baths. Stupid. So incredibly stupid. Dawn would be a shriveled-up prune by now. And what good would that do her?

Never had she come across any kind of real, helpful advice, much less an accurate description of a bride's frame of mind on the day of her wedding, how it felt just like standing on the edge of a very high rocky cliff and willing yourself to jump off into the weak, fragile arms of the stranger who waited in the tuxedo so far, far below. She thought she'd get sick every time she imagined John Wesley's voice calling thinly from so far away, "Don't worry—jump! I'll catch you!"

But before Dawn was able to allow herself to dwell too much on the gravity of her situation, before she drifted too, too far off the deep end, she was roused from her bridal reverie by a swift, pounding knock at the door. "Yoo-hoo . . . girls . . . ready for me? Just say cheese!" came the intrusive voice of the photographer.

"No! No, we're not!" warned Dawn. The man was a relentless idiot who was driving her insane. Her mother had picked him out from an exhibition of wedding photos posted in the Chapel Hill mall. He claimed to be a Chapel Hill photographer, but he really was from some crossroads at least thirty minutes from the nearest university. Dawn sat up and let the washcloth slide from her face. The rude interruption was just what she had needed to get her going. Sometimes getting pissed off was the only thing that put a stop to the stubbornly insistent trail of tears.

"Well, I *knowwwww* you don't want me to miss a minute," the photographer called through the door.

"I don't want pictures of me in my slip. So, hold on," Dawn snapped. Dawn's mother presented her the back of her unzipped dress. Her dress.

Her beautiful wedding dress. It was a simple satin gown—the same high-waisted princess cut as the bridesmaids', but with a more demure neckline and delicate cap sleeves. It fit Dawn like a dream. She didn't even want to think about all the time that had gone into picking it out. There were so many to choose from—puffy ball gowns and form-fitting sheaths, yards and yards of organdy, tulle, velvet and lace, seed pearls, sequins, embroidery. An endless array of choices that boggled the mind. Each dress presented an entirely different kind of image. You would be everybody's vision of traditional grace in one, or a daring sight in the latest fashion that no one could ever forget in another. So many options. But you had to choose one. Only one. That was it. Just like with the groom. From all those choices you had to select the one way you would see yourself for the rest of your life.

Dawn had finally opted for elegant simplicity. Nothing that would overpower her. No lace and sequins, just the softly flowing lines of shimmering satin. It was like being encased in liquid pearls. Luminescent. That was what she was going for. And after countless hours of searching, an all-out campaign to convince her father that no matter the cost she had to have that dress, and then the tortuous pin-pricking process of being fitted and fitted and fitted—she had finally achieved The Dress. Only to be caught trying it on for the final time two days before the wedding. Caught by John Wesley, the groom.

Everybody knew this was a disaster. He had stopped by the house to surprise her with some flowers. Just to say he loved her. The housekeeper hadn't known any better and had sent him on up to Dawn's room. And then the unthinkable occurred. He let out a small gasp of breath that sent chills down Dawn's spine before she turned to see him standing in the doorway, his lips slighted parted, the forgotten bunch of daisies hanging upside down in a loose one-handed grip by his side.

Her grandmother had warned her with a story about a girl whose train was ripped off her dress. The newly wedded husband and wife were stepping away from the minister to escape blissfully back up the aisle when it happened. As it turned out, this unfortunate incident was blamed on a bridesmaid. One version of the story said she was clumsy, but another admitted she was pea-green with envy. Dawn had listened patiently to her grandmother's repeated warnings and promised to be extra careful to make sure her own train didn't get caught on anything. But before she could even get to that point, John Wesley had gone and looked at her in her dress. Her grandmother hadn't told her thing one about that particular fix. No one had. She wondered if hers would become a story used in the future as an example of that kind of catastrophe.

So far, there were plenty others to choose from as well. Dawn was practically numb now from the avalanche of disasters that had happened in the past week. Ever since Mrs. Clayton killed herself and her husband last weekend, things had gone dramatically downhill. Dawn had known it was a sign but no one would listen. In all the wedding-gone-wrong stories everybody had taken such great delight in telling her, not a single one had involved a wedding that had to take place one week after a neighbor was driven to commit murder in a fit of jealous, heartbroken rage.

The Clayton thing had taken them all unawares. She guessed she had to admit that it had been too late to turn back even then. But still, she couldn't get over the feeling that they were helplessly compounding the one disaster with a whole series of their own. Dominoes. Ripples. Karma. When did it stop? When in the hell did it stop? She glanced down at her engagement ring. It was so top-heavy it kept sliding to the side of her finger. A girl's best friend, they say. A diamond is for freaking ever. And what else? What else lasts even longer than a lifetime?

"Ilene, honey, Dawn needs the mirror for a little bit," Dawn's mother said. "You look just fine anyway. Do you know where your gloves are? Don't want to forget those!" Her mother was using that perky, helpful voice that grated on her nerves. Ilene didn't seem to like it either. Dawn let her mother steer her toward the mirror. Hands patted and tucked, zipped, hooked, fluffed and smoothed. The whole time her mother was talking, talking on and on to Dawn in that perky, pep-me-up voice that Dawn despised. But she just let it wash over her, closed her eyes when her mother said close them, rubbed her lips together when her mother indicated she should by rubbing her own. Monkey see. Monkey do. She went ahead and let her mother treat her just like a big baby doll. It was easier that way.

Dawn's mother hadn't had a big wedding. Her mother had told her time and time again all about how they were too poor to afford anything fancy, just a minister in her grandmother's front parlor, her young mother dressed in her only Sunday dress holding a bunch of spring violets she had picked herself that morning. It had been years and years before her father had made lots of money and bought her mother a big diamond ring to make up for the one she'd never had. Now her mother's jewelry box was chock-full of all kinds of gems, but thinking that made up for everything would be to miss the point.

Dawn understood. She knew her mother was bent on having the wedding of both their lifetimes. That wasn't really what bothered her. What she couldn't forgive was the way her mother was railroading her through the whole thing. That's what it felt like anyway. Every second Dawn showed the least little sign of being a bit confused or overwhelmed or revealed even one ounce of uncontrolled emotion, Dawn's mother got this attitude. Her mother behaved as if she were driven to squelch any doubts Dawn might have by bullying her. "Didn't I tell you to make absolutely sure he was the one? Didn't I tell you that way back when?" It was like having Jekyll and Hyde for a mother. One minute she acted all proud and mushy, the next as if she were angry at Dawn, maybe even hated her. It was more than weird, but Dawn tried to block it all out while her mother deftly brushed a light tickle of loose powder all over her face.

"There now," her mother said. "You look positively radiant." There was an odd fanatical quality in the fixed look in her mother's eyes. Dawn tried to ignore any associations with those zombie women in *The Stepford Wives*. This was a time she was supposed to feel close to her mother, this was supposed to be one of the greatest moments ever in their entire history as mother and daughter. She offered her mother and the dimly lit mirror a forced smile.

"Yep. No dark smudges or any puffiness. No one would ever guess you'd been bawling your eyes out for the past hour," her mother added with satisfaction. "Now all we need is your veil and your gloves and you'll be all fixed."

Dawn considered her hair while her mother searched for the veil. At least Delma Matthews had not steered her wrong when it came to deciding how to do her hair for the wedding. "You want something easy," Delma had said. "Believe me, you'll have plenty of other things to worry about without wondering if your hair is falling down." After having to deal with making up her own mind about so many things—not just all the actual wedding plans but registering for gifts which had been an utter nightmare, having to pick out china and crystal patterns, silverware, pots and pans, sheets and towels, what color, what size, how many—Dawn was relieved to follow what sounded like good, solid reason. Together, they had settled on soft curls, leaving most of it down around her shoulders and pinning just the top part back at the crown of her head where the comb of her veil would sit. Little pieces of hair had been curled into loose corkscrews around the sides of her face. "For softening," Delma had explained.

Thank goodness Delma had known what she was doing. Dawn's hair was one of the only things to have survived intact so far. But that story Delma had told her this morning while she fixed her hair—Dawn could have done without that. Delma had gone on and on about what she called a *snake-in-the-grass* story, which Delma assured Dawn was entirely true.

"It happened right before my eyes," she swore. "I'll never forget it. It was the first time I was ever a bridesmaid and the first time my cousin Tina was a bride. There have been several other such occasions for both of us since then. Me, I've got a whole closet full of bridesmaid dresses and Tina, she's had more than her share of trips down the aisle, all of them in white and none in the same dress or with the same man. But you just don't remember them all like the first. That Tina, she was so head-over-heels in love. I have never seen anybody that bad off, not before or after.

"Well anyway, her brother was one of the groomsmen, you see. And they all went out after the rehearsal dinner to live it up a little before losing one of their number to the old ball-and-chain. One of them, not the bride's brother but maybe the best man, had ordered up a stripper as a surprise. Oh, they thought they were something. So this girl, this *woman*, pops up out of a cake and proceeds to twitch and shake all over the place. There was a recording of that stripping music and the guys were all cheering every time she flung a piece of clothing in their direction. They were hooting and hollering, having themselves just a good ole time. Of course, by the time the music stopped she was down to practically nothing. Alls she had on was a few spangles that did more to entice than they did to cover anything up, if you know what I mean.

"And what do you think the groom's reaction was to all this? Why he up and slept with the stripper on the very night before his own wedding. That's what. Just goes to show. What a scumbag. There was Tina all safe and sober at home, tucked in her girlhood bed, busy manicuring her nails and turning in for an early night's sleep, while he was off dilly-dallying with a stripper. I shudder to think what all diseases she might have been carrying. When Tina's brother let what had happened slip out right before the ceremony, all hell broke loose. It was exactly the kind of scene you would expect. Tears, yelling, name calling, the whole works. We had a time getting that girl ready to go down the aisle. And the groom ended up with a black eye that looked awful in all the pictures. I'm not even sure why we bothered. She was back home at her parents' before they could celebrate their first year's anniversary. But now aren't you glad John Wesley is not that type? Getting started out on the wrong foot can be a recipe for disaster. Before you'd know it, you might end up just like the Claytons. Which is no way to be, no way at all. Not in my book anyway."

"Ah ha, here it is," Dawn's mother said as she triumphantly pulled the veil from underneath a pile of cast-off clothing that was collecting wrinkles in a heap on a long table pushed against the far wall. Above the table hung a collection of pictures drawn by the Sunday school class and taped up for display. It was a crudely rendered series of portraits that illustrated the infamous Adam and Eve sampling forbidden fruit. What caught Dawn's attention was all the creative ways the children had found to avoid depicting any naughty body parts. That, plus the variety of expressions they had placed on Adam's and Eve's faces. In some, Adam looked doubtful and Eve, predictably sly. In others, Eve appeared anxious to please, a humble supplicant to Adam's overbearing self-satisfaction. One particularly eye-catching picture was a large rendering of the couple's head and shoulders. They stood side-by-side and looked straight out into the classroom. The snake was huge. It hung from a branch right between Adam's and Eve's heads, so all three—man, snake, and woman—confronted the viewer with the same direct gaze that issued a willful challenge. Adam held up a big red heart-shaped apple, one white ragged bite missing from each side. It was a bold picture—bright colors, thick confident brush strokes, and disturbing grins that spread widely across each face. It was as if they were all leering at Dawn, or taking delight in mocking her. "Try it. You'll like it," they seemed to say. Dawn wondered what kind of child would draw a picture like that. She wondered if the kid's mother had seen it yet and what she would think when she did.

"Hold still now," Dawn's mother directed as she reached up to slide the teeth of the comb in place.

"Owww, that hurts," Dawn said when she felt the pointed ends dig into her scalp.

"You'll get used to it," said her mother. "It's just for a little while anyway. Anybody can stand anything for just a little while. Before you know it, it'll be gone. Soooo pretty! And here are the gloves."

Dawn tried to get used to the strange new weight of the veil as she wiggled her fingers down into the ends of the elbow-length kid gloves. She became aware, again, of the bevy of activity that was going on around her. The bridesmaids were busy, busy, busy, a horde of bees, humming along, taking their own sweet time. For a moment, Dawn worried about John Wesley, what he was doing and thinking while he was getting ready. She felt a twinge of guilt when she did. As if she had something to feel guilty about. It wasn't like John Wesley was the one getting sacrificed or anything. He was probably not thinking anything anyway. At least that was what he always said whenever she asked what was on his mind.

"You're not mad at John Wesley, are you?" murmured her mother. She was helping Dawn with the second glove.

"No. Why would I be?"

"Well, I just didn't know if y'all had a fight or something at the rehearsal dinner," her mother said. "It's not like it would be a big deal, if you had. Stuff like that happens all the time at weddings. It wouldn't have to mean anything. Just a tiff. Pressure. Nerves."

"We just wanted a minute alone," Dawn said, "just one minute. And people were everywhere, bothering us nonstop. I thought weddings were supposed to bring a couple together, not tear them apart. So we agreed to meet each other outside on the patio by the swimming pool for just two seconds. That was all. Just to say hello and catch our breaths. And be together for one cotton-picking second on the night before our wedding.

Nobody was mad, not until those jerks came out there and picked up John Wesley and threw him in the pool. That did have a way of kind of spoiling the moment."

"Well I'm glad," her mother said as she stepped back to take an overall look at Dawn, her child, her one and only baby girl all grown up.

"Glad?" Dawn asked.

"Of course," her mother said. "I wouldn't want you two love birds upset with each other when you are here, at the beginning of everything. You both are going to be so happy. And just look how pretty you are, I'm so proud to be your mother." Dawn's shoulders got a quick, awkward squeeze before her mother called out, "Let the photographer in, girls. We're ready for some pictures!"

Dawn's mother clearly felt the matter was settled, that there was no need even to mention John Wesley's foiled attempt later last night to serenade Dawn from beneath her bedroom window. Dawn had been downstairs in the dark sneaking a drink from the brandy decanter in her father's library. Ilene was passed out snoring in the middle of Dawn's double bed upstairs. Ilene had shyly suggested that it would be more fun if she slept in Dawn's room rather than in the guest room down the hall. "It'll be like old times," Ilene said. "We can stay up all night, if you want." But she had already fallen asleep before Dawn managed to finish brushing her teeth. So much for the comforting camaraderie of female companionship. Ilene had been a real, all-around downer as maid of honor. And there wasn't a whole lot of time left for her to redeem herself. Dawn could already see that if she had to do it all over . . . But that was beside the point.

Exhausted, but too keyed up and nervous to sleep, Dawn was contemplating drinking herself into oblivion on the library sofa when she heard rustling out in the azaleas behind the house. Shrubbery branches breaking and a few mild curses. And then, what was unmistakably John

Wesley's good-natured baritone belting out the words to "Close to You."
He had claimed it as their song, but had kept his crooning private in the
past. Shouted, the tune lost its romantic melody. The Carpenters would
not be asking him to join their group, that was for sure. But Dawn had
to admit it was sweet, even if it did sound horrible.

He was her Romeo. Dawn started smiling in the dark. They did belong
together. They were meant to be and this was a sign. Dawn raised the
library window to call out to John Wesley before he woke the whole house.
She found him standing in a patch of moonlight right beneath her bedroom window. Her bedroom was in an upper corner of the house, so from
her position in the library she could make out only his shadowy profile. He
was leaning back unsteadily on his heels, his hands gripping an unlucky
azalea for balance and support. His head was rocked back on his shoulders.
Apparently, his eyes were closed tight in an effort to concentrate.

So earnest, she had to give him that. She almost started laughing
when she noticed the tail of his shirt was hanging out the back. But then
she glanced up at her window only to see Ilene leaning out. Not just
looking, but hanging all the way out the window as if she thought she
was Rapunzel and might offer him a braid up! Was she crazy? Didn't she
know he was singing to Dawn? Why would he want to serenade her ugly
cousin? Before she could set matters straight, male laughter erupted
from around the far side of the house and a rowdy group appeared and
grabbed up John Wesley and bore him off into the night. People! They
just couldn't see fit to let them alone!

Dawn tossed back the rest of her drink. And what did Ilene think she
was doing, mooning over Dawn's fiancé there on the edge of Dawn's win-
dowsill? Dawn's precious sliver of happiness dissolved into a torrent of
tears that left her headachy and cross when she woke up the next morning on that lumpy old couch.

Her mood hadn't improved much as the day progressed. Even though

Dawn smiled and smiled while the photographer cracked obnoxious jokes and arranged them in absurdly stiff poses, she really couldn't say if she would ever be able to get over all this. Too much water under the bridge. That is what they say. Dawn had never believed in it before, but now she was starting to see the world in a whole new light. No wonder they called you a matron after you got married. Even if you didn't show it from the outside, your mind was bound to put on weight, grow thick and sturdy from all you had been put through. Presto-change-o and poof! Forget the ruby red slippers. Your high-heeled strappy sandals were magically replaced with worn old-lady shoes that laced up and were extra-wide to accommodate swollen, broken-down feet.

Dawn's headache was returning. Instead of a gossamer veil, she could swear it was the wooly heft of a scratchy wet blanket that had been anchored to the top of her head. She had never felt the unfairness of life so completely before.

Finally, the pictures were over, for the time being, and the photographer was ushered out. Dawn's mother followed behind him, to do who knows what, leaving Dawn feeling slightly bereft by her mother's sudden absence. "Dawn, you look like you just lost your best friend," said Jane, a cute blonde who had been one of Dawn's favorite sorority sisters in college. "But never fear! I've got just the thing to cheer you up." She pulled out a pint bottle of peppermint schnapps. "Not only will this lift your spirits, it'll give you fresh breath at the same time." Several of the bridesmaids giggled while Jane twisted the cap to break the seal and handed the bottle to Dawn for the first sip. Dawn didn't hesitate but belted a healthy toot right down. Girlish cheers went up and the schnapps was promptly handed around the Sunday school room.

Immediately everyone's spirits were improved. This was fun. This was how weddings were supposed to be. Dawn decided she loved Jane. She was always going to keep in touch with her no matter how far apart they settled. Dawn and Jane would end up as old ladies together, lifelong friends who had shared the ups and downs of raising their families. They would get together for vacations, ballgames. It would all be great.

Terry decided Melanie had really done her a favor. She had actually never been able to trust Scott and now she knew why. Instead of dreading the ceremony, now Terry relished it. She hoped Scott spent the whole time realizing how badly he had screwed up, that Terry would never take him back. He could just eat his heart out. This would be the only time he got within ten feet of her at a wedding ceremony. Though maybe it wasn't such a bad idea to invite him to her wedding when she did find the right guy. Then he could really get a good look at all that he was missing.

Ilene was suddenly flooded with the fond feelings of nostalgia. Dawn was like a sister to her. She was so grateful Dawn had given her such a prestigious place in her wedding. This really did mean a lot. It was something they would remember all their lives—Ilene, the maid of honor at Dawn's wedding. Yes, Dawn was getting married first. But the wedding had already been so screwed up, and Ilene was sure hers, when her time came, would be so much better. It was as if Dawn had done her a favor by being the first to go so Ilene could benefit from all her mistakes.

Melanie glanced around at all the girls' faces and thought that maybe it wasn't such a terrible-looking group after all. And it was always nice to know you were easily one of the prettiest in the crowd. Besides, wasn't she having a good time?

"I've got a story," piped up Crystal Banks after carefully blotting the corners of her mouth with the back of her hand. Crystal was another Riley girl. The way she nonchalantly reclined in one of the undersized wooden chairs emphasized the nature of her belonging. She had, in fact, sat in these same chairs side by side with Dawn as they colored their own Sunday school pictures while their teacher told them Bible stories. Years ago, yes, but Dawn still remembered that Crystal always shared SweeTarts she snuck in to help pass the time. The intensity of their flavors heated by Crystal's sweaty palm had provided delicious but unsanctioned relief.

"It happened to some college friends of mine on their honeymoon," Crystal continued when she saw that she had everyone's attention. Crystal, who was smarter than she was pretty, had been president of Beta Club in high school and had gone on to attend a big university on scholarship. She had always known things—Dawn didn't know how, but she did. "They got through the wedding and all just fine. But they had to spend the first night of their honeymoon in town because their flight wasn't until the next day. I think they were going to Puerto Rico or somewhere like that. So they spend the night in this beautiful five-star hotel and it was all pretty amazing—you know, *hot*," said Crystal. "It was their honeymoon and everything. So there they are lying in bed the next morning and, 'Surprise!' out jump some friends of theirs who had been hiding in the closet all night. Talk about embarrassing!" Crystal chortled and slapped her leg.

"Oh my gosh, you mean they had heard everything?" Terry asked.

"Oh, yeah," Crystal said. "Everything."

The bridesmaids laughed and exclaimed, all of them attempting to make light of the horror that swamped each girl's unwed heart. When the bottle of schnapps passed through Dawn's hand again, she took two fortifying swigs instead of one. She could check the closet, under the bed, and behind the shower curtain. She'd make sure she did. They weren't spending the night in town anyway. There weren't any hotels in Riley, not reputable ones. Surely no one would bother to follow them out of town? They had to let them go sometime. All this harassment couldn't go on forever. Could it? She bet their car would be wrecked. It was too small a town to find a decent hiding place. Who knew what kind of nasty tricks those guys would think were funny. They were bound to go beyond a couple of tin cans and some shaving cream. And then there was the honeymoon. Dawn had no idea where John Wesley was taking her.

"Speaking of honeymoon surprises, I hear Dawn's going to have one," announced Jane, who was emboldened by her schnapps success.

"Ooooo, *Dawn*," someone teased.

"Tell us, Jane. What is it?"

"Yeah, we want to know."

"Tell, you have to tell."

Dawn felt herself flush bright red. "Don't ruin John Wesley's surprise, Jane," she pleaded.

"Oh, I hear he's got more than one surprise," Jane laughed.

"What do you mean?" said Dawn. "The only thing I don't know about is where we're going on our honeymoon. And it's supposed to stay that way until John Wesley tells me. No one else is supposed to know."

"That's not what I'm talking about," said Jane, who was clearly enjoying herself.

"Then what?" asked Dawn.

"It's about last night, sort of," Jane said. "You've probably already heard and just don't want any of us to know."

"What?" Dawn demanded. She was half-laughing and half-panic-stricken.

"The way I heard it, he got shanghaied," Jane said.

"I know about that," Dawn said. "I saw a bunch of them grab him from my backyard."

"Yeah, but it's what they did to him after," said Jane, who was beginning to realize she had made a big mistake bringing all this up. But it was too late to get out of telling it now. Everybody was watching. Besides, it was funny. Jane didn't know what had happened to Dawn's sense of humor. When Jane got married, first and foremost, she wanted to have a good time. "They painted him with iodine."

"Iodine? But I didn't see anything at the brunch this morning," Dawn said.

"It wasn't his face they painted, silly girl. It was his *tallywacker*." The room broke out in shrill giggles that quickly escalated into uncontrollable cackling and unladylike guffaws. Someone snorted and that sent everyone further out of control.

"Oh, my side," someone cried.

"My mascara is going to be ruined," another girl complained.

"But it's too, too funny," Ilene insisted while she wiped at her eyes. "That stuff takes forever to come off."

Lost in abandoned laughter, the bridesmaids were caught off guard when the door popped partially open and revealed the head and shoulders of Dawn's father. "What's going on in here? Everybody decent?" he asked while his eyes did a fatherly scan of the room. "Anybody want to let me in on the joke?"

"No, Mr. Davenport. It's nothing really," Crystal said.

"You girls are just having too much fun. I hate to be the one to break this up, but I've been informed that it's time for you all to go on and get lined up in the vestibule for the procession. Dawn and I will be right behind you."

Somewhat sobered by Mr. Davenport's announcement, the girls quickly pulled themselves together and fell into assigned order as they filed out of the room. Only Jane looked back at Dawn on the way out to give her a little smile.

Traitors, that's what they all were, thought Dawn as she stood mutely swaying on her satin-slippered feet. Nothing in this world was sacred. Not one damn thing. Dawn attempted to dry her sweaty hands by smoothing them across her skirt. She refused to cry at this point. Absolutely refused. She would have to save up the rest of her tears for after the ceremony. She had the rest of her life to cry about all this. Damn it. She was not going to cry now. Her mother would never forgive her, and she would probably never forgive herself, either.

"Looks like it's just you and me, kid," Dawn's father said, "at least for a few more minutes anyway."

Dawn tried to get comfort from his presence. She did love him. He had been a good father, as far as that went. He looked distinguished in his tux; even the soft thickening around his jawline only added to his look of solid, prosperous dependability. Dawn wondered how he had looked at his own wedding, how her mother had seen him that day.

"You know, sport, it's still not too late to call the whole thing off," he said. "Forget all this hoopla. It's not too late to back out. Do you hear me?"

"Yes, Daddy," she said. She could feel the threatening prickle of a fresh onslaught of tears. He better cut out this sentimental stuff or there was no way she could keep it all together. She knew he meant well, but kindness was the last thing she needed.

"I'm serious. It's not too late," he repeated, this time without the smile. "Your mother would get over it. Hell, if I know her, she probably wouldn't mind doing all this rigmarole all over again."

"It's time," called a voice from the other side of the door.

"I guess we better go." Dawn took a deep breath and then reached for the train of her dress and folded it over her arm. She was ready. Or was she? There was her father right there telling her it wasn't too late to back out. Maybe *this* was a sign! Maybe that's what all this had been about. Maybe God, or her guardian angel, had been trying to contact her this whole time to warn her that this was not to be. That despite all of John Wesley's wonderful attributes, he and she were not meant to be together.

Dawn and her father made their way down the hall and out the side door of the Sunday school wing. He took her arm as they started down the sidewalk that led to the front steps of the church. It was hot. This wasn't the softened, burnished warmth of Indian summer, but the searing heat of mid-season. All the while Dawn carefully navigated the steep stone steps, her mind boiled in the afternoon sun. She could turn to her father and say, "Okay, Daddy, I've changed my mind." She could turn and run away and never look back. She could give back the ring, all the gifts. She could move to Raleigh, or Charlotte, or maybe even another state. It was even possible to live outside of the South. Other people did. It wasn't too late. Here she had been thinking of needing a sign *not to* marry John Wesley. Now she needed a sign if she was, indeed, *supposed to* go through with it all. God, please, she needed a sign. Something.

Just as they reached the top step, just as her father's hand closed over the heavy metal door pull, a convertible rounded the corner. The top was down and the two girls riding in the front seats yelled and waved when they spotted Dawn and her father.

Charlene Macrae considered herself lucky to be out riding around with Candace Blanchard. Riding in a convertible made Charlene feel wild and carefree. She loved the wind in her hair and the way everybody looked with longing when they rode past. Candace honked the horn. And then without thinking, the two girls yelled in unison, *"Don't do it!"* before Candace's foot hit the accelerator and they sped off down Main Street in a bright red flash.

Dawn couldn't believe her ears. She asked for a sign and she was given one. *"Dawn, do it!"* They couldn't have been any clearer. Her prayers had finally been answered.

Her father had paused and was waiting. "Well?" he prompted.

"Okay," she said with a nod. "I'm ready."

"Ready to do your old man proud?"

"That's right. Lead the way," she answered in a voice braced by her newfound conviction. Floating way up on cloud nine, Dawn failed to wonder why her father's movements were so startled as he turned, once again, to open the door.

The wedding director sprung to life the minute they showed up in the vestibule. Full of happy-happy smiles, she handed off Dawn's bouquet, flipped the top part of the veil over Dawn's face and swept the train into its proper place. Dawn's confusion and dread had disappeared. She was dizzy from the heady scent of the flowers in her hand and with eager anticipation

by the time the staggered organ chords announced her grand entrance—
"Here Comes the Bride." In accordance with tradition, the entire congregation paid homage by rising dramatically to its feet. The moment they all
had been waiting for had finally arrived.

As Dawn and her father made their way down the aisle, it was just like
in her dreams—the candles, the music, the heads all turned to watch and
admire. Seeing it through the veil only heightened her sense that this
was really it—her dream—and she was inside it, living it for always.
From underneath her canopy of fine white netting, everything looked
beautiful and fitting. She had reached her peak, surrounded by the tender hope and love of everyone who had ever meant anything to her. And
there was John Wesley waiting at the end, just for her. She had been chosen. Indeed, she had been blessed.

Whitney Elliot silently cursed Dawn's veil as she craned her neck trying
to get a glimpse of Dawn's face. She was DYING to see if Dawn had been
able to replicate her meticulous makeup instructions. Whitney offered to
come over and do Dawn's face, but Mrs. Davenport said she was sure
they could handle it. YEAH, RIGHT, was what Whitney had to say about
that. She guessed she'd just have to wait to get a good look at the reception. Then Dawn's face would tell the whole story.

It would be a shame if they botched the job, because Dawn wasn't a
bad-looking girl. She was quietly pretty, while Whitney's beauty was BIG.
Dawn was a single pink rose. Whitney, a full dozen luscious RED, hot-
house, long-stemmed AMERICAN BEAUTIES. Next time Whitney got
married it would not be one of those rush jobs. She'd opt for a big to-
do like Dawn, something more in keeping with what she deserved. She
could still wear white—no one was going to STOP her. After all she was

still YOUNG. It's not like she was a dried-up OLD WOMAN with wrinkles and all. Now, that would be ridiculous.

Ovaline Simpson, who had already reached past her prime when she babysat for Dawn years and years ago, could scarcely remember who it was she had come to see married. It didn't help that her eyes weren't what they used to be. Besides, Ovaline was troubled. Her deep concern, the fear and worry that preoccupied almost every second of her days and sleepless nights, was that her dear cousin Louise would die before Ovaline's new teeth were ready.

On Ovaline's right sat Ernestine Lambert. She had generously offered to give Ovaline a ride to the church. Ernestine barely bothered to notice the flowers. She had been terribly distracted ever since Randy Fox's outrageous confession in church last Sunday. Completely discombobulated. Ernestine hoped the trauma hadn't sent her into senility. She knew she had invited someone to tomorrow's Sunday dinner, but she didn't know who. She kept looking around hoping that someone's face would jog her memory. More than anything, Ernestine hated to be caught unprepared.

Randy's wife, Debra, was sitting toward the back of the church trying to be inconspicuous. She hadn't wanted to come, but her mother begged and pleaded, said it would be good for Debra to get out. Debra knew that was just an excuse. Her mother, who was already dabbing at her eyes with a lacy handkerchief, loved weddings. But if anybody ever asked Debra, she would say they were nothing but trouble.

Debra had to concede that her mother had warned her about Randy. "Think long and hard before you make your bed with that one," she said. "He's one of the most slippery fish there ever was." But Debra had been bound and determined. Though she should have known—the way Randy wouldn't make eye contact the whole time they were exchanging vows and their honeymoon spent in a crummy fishing shack.

Debra seemed oblivious to the sympathetic looks Lucy Macrae kept casting her way. Lucy was trying not to picture her ex-husband's recent wedding to a local beautician as she watched Dawn. Lucy doubted she, herself, would ever find someone else. She hated that now whenever she looked back at her own wedding, she was filled with sadness over the brevity of their happiness. Lucy felt a light touch at her shoulder and looked over at her son, Bucky. He had put his arm around her back just like his father used to do. He looked so grown up in his tie and jacket. Lucy had bought him a clip-on to wear to the Claytons' funeral. It made things easier since she didn't know how to tie a tie. Bucky had been through so much. Oh how she loved her children! Someday she could look forward to Bucky's marriage and to Charlene's. Her babies' weddings—that gave her something to smile about.

Reverend Cooper's warm voice rumbled through the ceremony. Promises were made, rings exchanged, and a couple united in holy matrimony. Soon it was time to mark the completion of the ceremony with a kiss. The minister granted the customary permission. John Wesley lifted Dawn's veil and bent to press his lips against hers, as the first triumphant notes of *Trumpet Voluntary* broke from the horn of the lead player in Riley High's marching band. In this same instant, two birds flew from an opened cage that sat on the floor in the choir loft between two benches. This had been another of John Wesley's valiant attempts at romance.

Ideally, they would have been a pair of white lovebirds, but John Wesley had only been able to get his hands on a couple of doves—pale gray and a little plump. It was a lovely sentiment. And for a few seconds, everyone was overcome by the sweetness of this gesture. But the birds, terrified by their brief captivity, were desperate to make good their escape. They turned on the crowd, swooping down around their unprotected heads. Appreciative sighs quickly turned into screams of outrage. The torture was furthered by the unsteadiness of the attack. The birds rose and fell with the same unpredictability of a couple of bumble bees. Only instead of gathering nectar and pollen, they began distributing squirts of excrement on the good clothes of Riley's friends and neighbors. One of the birds actually landed on Lorna Everette's carefully coiffed up-do. Her shrieks reached a fevered pitch before her husband Richard was able to shoo it off. But it was too late. Her hair was left looking like a broken nest.

Casey Hart scrunched down in her seat and tried to take it all in. She had been responsible for writing up the wedding announcement for *The Matthews County News*. The next issue had already gone to bed with the write-up, since it was usually a matter of just filling in the blanks. Now, the article wouldn't say what really happened. Casey figured it didn't have to. Everybody would find out about it anyway. And years from now when

Dawn turned to the clipping in her wedding scrapbook all of it would come back to her just the same. It was bound to. Somehow the catastrophic nature of this event cheered Casey up. She found herself marveling at the way life does go on. No matter what.

Drawn instinctively by the light spilling from the stained glass window that hung in the apex behind the pulpit and above the choir loft, the birds switched the direction of their frantic attentions and began flinging themselves, two ashy angels, at the feet of Christ at the crucifixion. It was a bizarre and unsettling tableau—the birds repeatedly slamming their bodies against Jesus' stained glass feet right above the heads of the minister and the bride and groom. The entire congregation was united by their suffering as they unwillingly bore witness to the struggle and their collective doom.

Pigeons. That's what Dawn kept thinking. Pigeons. They weren't doves. They were pigeons. Outdone by a couple of overfed pigeons. Those nasty birds marked the end and the beginning. This was it. Really it. Now that her veil was lifted, it was all so clear. She had allowed herself to be fooled by all the pretty clothes, the flowers, the romantic glow of candlelight, and the piles and piles of presents wrapped in shiny pastels.

This wasn't a celebration so much as it was a sentencing in disguise. She and John Wesley had walked right into a beautiful trap and sealed the bargain with a kiss. It was way too late now. Nothing could save them from the same tragic fate of those pathetic birds. They would spend the rest of their days compelled by the strange and mysterious bonds of love. They would fling themselves against its promising glimmer, never knowing when it might shatter the fragile, feather-covered bones of their short lives.

Dawn was struck dumb by the harsh delivery of this revelation granted to her as she stood on the threshold of her new life and stared into the eyes of her beloved, who would henceforth and forever be her partner in crime. Despite her best efforts, unbidden tears ran in twin trails of liquid mascara down the gently curved slopes of her powdered cheeks. What a mess, an awful mess. A fiasco. But Dawn was smiling too. For her heart now knew the terrible, wrenching joy of unbidden flight.

She couldn't believe that no one had ever breathed a word of this to her. In all their asinine advice, why hadn't anyone even so much as hinted at the agonizing transcendence of true love? Deep down in what was left of her heart, which had inevitably broken into a pile of bits and pieces the size and consistency of a handful of uncooked rice, Dawn knew. She knew they'd all have something to say.

And that, they did. From the youngest to the oldest, the poorest to the richest, every last one of those people in Riley, North Carolina, could sing a song that fit that tune. Some would sing it for fun and others only if they had to. But, Lord yes, it was in each and every one of them to do it, just the same.

ACKNOWLEDGMENTS

Over the lengthy course of this novel's creation, I have benefited from the kind interest and encouragement of too many people to name. From my teachers at North Carolina State University—Angela Davis-Gardner, William Henderson, John Kessel, Lucinda MacKethan, and Lee Smith—to helpful readers and valued confidants such as Mildred Boyd, Millie Dysart, Dan Karslake, and Grace Simpson, I have been fortunate to have had so much support from so many.

Of course, the book that you are now holding in your hands would not exist without editor Ami McConnell and Thomas Nelson. I am deeply indebted to Darnell Arnoult for putting this manuscript in Ami's capable hands. Darnell is among my most trusted readers as are: Pamela Duncan and Lynn York, whose friendship and camaraderie have sustained my writing for many years and helped me over more than one rough patch; my sister Betsy Gilmour, who always "gets it" and feels duty-bound to tell me what she really thinks; and friend and mentor Lee Smith, whose work inspired me from the very beginning and whose encouragement and wise counsel I would be lost without.

I am also extremely lucky to have been given two parents, Sally Thompson and Cecil Cooke, who remain united in their seemingly unshakable conviction in my capabilities—what a miraculous gift.

Lastly and most importantly, I want to thank my husband, Alan, for daring to make that cataclysmic leap with me. It was his protracted willingness to suspend disbelief that ultimately provided the wind for this novel's wings and not only allowed my fictional dreams to soar, but to become reality.

INTERVIEW WITH VIRGINIA BOYD

Q: *One Fell Swoop* has a unique format in that it is told in the voices of various members of the community through vignettes. Tell us a little about how that developed.

Well, I began with the concept of linked stories, with the idea of exploring the ripple effect of tragedy in a small town. I knew from the beginning that I was interested in capturing the different perspectives of the same event, different "takes" on the same story. Ever since I read William Faulkner's *The Sound and the Fury* in high school and then Lee Smith's *Oral History*, I have been fascinated by this phenomenon and how fiction can capture one of the most elusive aspects of our reality.

Q: Writing in first person can be a controversial choice these days; a lot of people push third person as being more "literary." But to me, there's no better way to capture a first-person account, now is there? Besides, "voice" can be such a powerful tool in developing character and in shaping the story. It seems a shame not to use it.

For me, story is steeped in an oral tradition. I "listen" for it. I listen to hear what my characters are going to say and for the narrator's voice, for the tone, the inflection, the word choice, the rhythm of the language. I read aloud the entire time I'm working, the first time I type in the words and then again and again as I go back over it. Maybe this is because I'm Southern. All I know is that I was raised in a family of talkers, stories, anecdotes, you name it, these people never shut up! It's impossible to read the newspaper with my mother's side of the family because they're too busy talking to you about what's in the section you haven't gotten to yet. And I'm embarrassed to admit, I find myself doing the same thing to my husband.

In fact, the members of my family were all such big talkers—some of them quite long-winded and verbose—that I didn't say a whole lot when I was kid. It was hard to get a word in edgewise. But I listened. Every night at the dinner table, my father led Socratic lessons in history and philosophy. His stories almost always have a lesson or a moral to be learned. My sister, on the other hand, turned her everyday life of going to elementary school into high adventure with lengthy tales of startling conflict and resolution. She still is able to recant entire conversations—verbatim. I do not recommend getting in an argument with her. While my father and sister tend to tell stories where they're acting as the central—or at least one of the main—characters, my mother collects other people's stories. She enjoys reporting on the "goings on" of friends, family, acquaintances, and— quite often—complete strangers. She is the one who is most likely to drop in some tidbit about somebody else's life during the conversation. Regularly, she sends me newspaper clippings. Things she couldn't point out to me at the time, I guess. Unusual obituaries and wedding announcements are her favorites. They just arrive in the mail, all smudged and folded; no note or anything. Just someone's story, saved and presented for me to appreciate.

The town where I grew up was an entire community of talkers. Believe me, everybody had a story to tell. It was a small town, so maybe it was because there wasn't a whole lot else to do. Or maybe it was because everybody actually knew their neighbors and cared about their lives. But telling stories—gossiping, whatever you want to call it—figured prominently in the social fabric of the town. People interacted by swapping tales. Stories were a sort of social currency. They had a real value and were constantly being exchanged. At the grocery store. Around the dinner table. Over a few drinks. Across the counter at the corner drugstore. On the church's front steps. You never knew when you might run into one, delivered orally, right there on the spot. And there I was listening the whole time.

Q: **The murder/suicide referenced early in the book is never described or viewed directly. Why is that?**

The significant question for me was not "what" but "why." I was inspired by a terribly sad event that did happen in my hometown when I was a child. It has haunted me ever since and has become a seminal event in what I see now as my own—as well as the town's—coming-of-age. I wasn't interested though in going back and doing research on what really happened. I didn't want to write a factual account. I wanted to write fiction, which is a story that grows out of real life, memory, and imagination. I wanted to be free to follow my own impulses and not feel obligated to record any type of "official" truth.

One reason I believe this story has had such a hold on me is because of its universal nature. As an adult, I read and hear about things like this happening in the news all the time. The mother who kills all her children. The husband who kills his pregnant wife. The son who kills his parents. And every single time, I have to wonder why. How is it that seemingly normal people end up doing some of the things they do? And how do the rest of us make sense of what has happened? Where is the meaning in all of these sad stories that have actually happened to real people who live right up the street and right around the corner from us?

Q: **What do you hope your readers will discover through this story?**

I don't think of my fiction as being didactic in any way. I'm not writing with a particular answer in mind, only questions. I really do see fiction as a mirror that offers a reflection of the world—it's a way of seeing ourselves and our lives. But like any good postmodernist, I believe that what you see is largely influenced by who you are at that time. I expect each reader of *One Fell Swoop* will have his or her own interpretation of this story—just as all the characters glean something different from the Claytons' story in the novel.

Q: **Was there a particular character that you most closely identified with? Who was it and why? Whose voice was the most fun to write in? Why?**

There is a part of me in all of the characters. I've given them some of my memories, feelings, opinions . . . Like Casey Hart, I was a long distance runner in high school. And like Suzanne

Hunt, I was a very superstitious little kid and I do remember hearing gun shots from a house up the street while I was looking for fool's gold in our gravel driveway. However, sometimes I end up identifying with characters in ways I hadn't planned or imagined.

I took a couple of theater/acting classes in college and find that I apply some of the same thinking when creating one of my characters. In order to write from a particular person's perspective, you really do have to crawl into his or her skin. How does he walk? How does he talk? What is he really thinking? But you can never get away from yourself entirely. A part of yourself always bleeds through, whether you're conscious of it at the time or not.

It was very draining to go to the places I did with Cindy Worthington and Michael and Regina Clayton—to become those people, to live those lives, even if it was just on paper. I felt great sympathy for them all, but probably Regina Clayton the most. I really enjoyed writing Troy Matthews' story. He and I are very different from each other—which always makes it more interesting. And Delma's snake fixation allowed me to have a little fun with my own. I also have a real soft spot for Bucky Macrae and hated it when I realized he was going to end up at the wrong house for supper—that was so embarrassing!

Q: This story is steeped in Southern culture. How important was place to the telling of the story? Could it have taken place in a rural area of a Western state just as easily?

I've already mentioned the universality of the basic story line, which I believe is timeless as well. To a great extent, it would be the same story if it were set in any small community—on the West Coast, on the prairie, or even in a neighborhood in New York City. However, some people argue the devil is in the details which would be drastically altered by each location.

It's tricky to try to decide how much of a story's meaning is influenced by the social and cultural filters that are applied to it. Of course, I can speak only for myself, but I believe that as a native Southerner, I write from within the psychological shadow of my region's history. Who I am is inextricably tied to where I'm from—and to the notions that the rest of the world holds about what that means.

I'm the daughter of a debutante and a marine. I was raised *to know better*; to say "yes ma'am" and "no, sir"; to recognize an insult even when it comes with a smile; and to sing the marine corps' hymn. I was well disciplined in the fine arts of sucking it up and toughing it out and in saying what I mean without seeming to say anything at all. It doesn't matter that I didn't live during the War Between the States—I've inherited that legacy along with pieces of the family silver, a stack of handmade quilts, and my Grandmother Cooke's pound-cake recipe. If you've grown up in the South you don't really need to read Joseph Conrad's *The Heart of Darkness* or travel to equatorial Africa to know good people can get caught up in bad situations. That things are always more complex than they may seem. That the darkness you fear in others lives in you as well. That within each and every human heart lies a vast and mysterious landscape. And that no matter how hard you try you can not escape your past—or anyone else's.

Q: This is your debut novel. How has becoming a published author changed you?

It's given me license to write. Thank goodness. And just in the nick of time. It took a number of years for me to find a publisher for this novel. Bolstered by supportive friends and family, I wrote another novel in the interim, but I don't think I could have gone on just writing one manuscript after the other and never getting any of them published. I was holding on to writing as if it were the slippery edge of a very steep and rocky cliff and I was dangling by my sweaty fingers from it. At times like these, you are almost obliged to start to doubt your own judgment, to question your sanity. It's such a relief to be saved before I lost my grip completely.

I'm also incredibly excited that *One Fell Swoop* is going to "live" after all—in other people's minds and imaginations. A book comes to life only when someone else reads it. I gave this novel everything I had at the time and it broke my heart when no one would give it a chance. So I think getting published has changed my luck. The dark cloud that was looming over me has blown away. I'm not stuck on that cliff anymore; I'm headed off down the road in an entirely new direction.

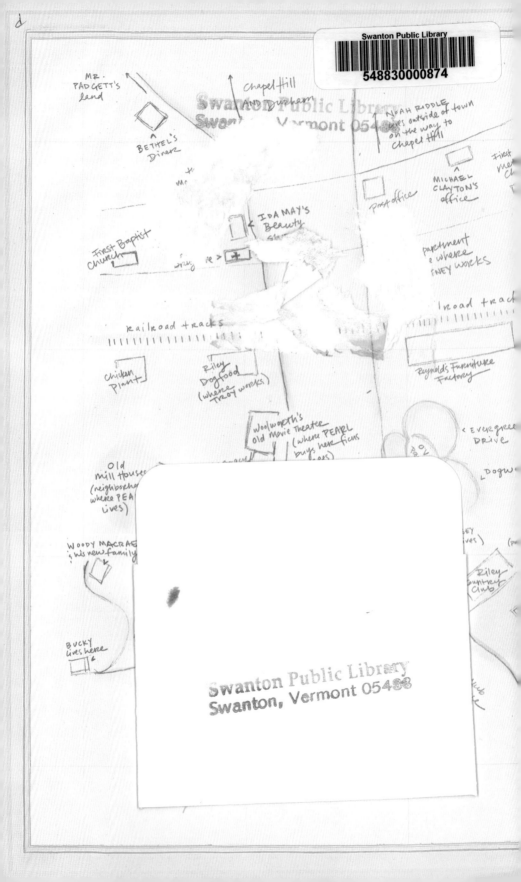